MARBLEHEAD:

A Novel of H. P. LOVECRAFT

Selected Works by Richard A. Lupoff

Edgar Rice Burroughs: Master of Adventure (1965)
The Case of the Doctor Who Had No Business, or *The Adventure of the Second* Anonymous *Narrator* (1966)
One Million Centuries (1967)
Sacred Locomotive Flies (1971)
Into the Aether (1974)
Edgar Rice Burroughs and the Martian Vision (1976)
The Triune Man (1976)
Sandworld (1976)
Lisa Kane (1976)
The Crack in the Sky (1976)
Sword of the Demon (1977)
The Return of Skull-Face (with Robert E. Howard) (1977)
Space War *Blues* (1978)
Nebogipfel at the End of Time (1979)
The Ova Hamlet Papers (19?9)
Stroka Prospekt (1982)
Circumpolar! (1984)
Sun's End (1984)
The Digital Wristwatch of Philip K. Dick (1985)
Lovecraft's Book (1985)
Countersolar! (1986)
Galaxy's End (1988)
The Forever City (1988)
The Black Tower (1988)
The Final Battle (1990)
The Great American Paperback:
An Illustrated Tribute to Legends of the Book (1990)
The Adventures of Professor Thintwhistle
and His Incredible Aether Flyer (1991)
Night of the Living Gator (1992)
Hyperprism (1994)
Before 12:01 ... and After (1996)
Claremont Tales (2000)
Claremont Tales II (2001)
Terrors (2005)

THE HOBART LINDSEY/MARVIA PLUM MYSTERY SERIES

The Comic Book Killer (1988)
The Classic Car Killer (1992)
The Bessie Blue Killer (1994)
The Sepia Siren Killer (1994)
The Cover Girl Killer (1995)
The Silver Chariot Killer (1996)
One Murder at a Time (2001)

MARBLEHEAD:

A Novel of H. P. LOVECRAFT

by

RICHARD A. LUPOFF

With an Introduction by

Fender Tucker

RAMBLE HOUSE

First Edition

ISBN 978-0-9774527-3-6

Published: 2006 by Ramble House
Cover Art: Gavin L. O'Keefe
Preparation: Fender Tucker

TABLE OF CONTENTS

MARBLEHEAD: The Director's Cut	9
Introduction by Fender Tucker	
A Quiet Celebration on Barnes Street	15
A Visit to the Metropolis	26
A Martooni and a Boilermaker	38
The Quiet Hours of the Night	53
Nigger-Man and Yaller Girl	65
Over His Head in the Seekonk	77
"Barbarossa Will Rise, Mister Lovecraft!"	89
"Volstead Gives Each Sip a Little Extra Savor"	101
A Visit to Parkside	113
The Rum Trade in Action	128
The Ghosts of Angell Street	143
What's in it for Hiram Evans?	155
"I am Related to the Salem Phillipses"	166
Lovecraft Plans a Book	178
The Theological Term for the Quality	188
Nothing More Demeaning to a Gentleman	199
Two Lost Frenchmen	211
"They Produced Messages"	222
Driving Collectors to Distraction	234
Fungi from Yuggoth	252
Lovecraft Meets a Printer	264
His Name on the Contents Page	282
Once the Kikes Infiltrate	293
The Old Ghostly Carriage	307
Its Whiplike Anteridia	326
Quahog, Correctly Pronounced Quog	341
Lovecraft Dons a Copper Helmet	356
The Steaming and Rancid Stew of Races	370
An Explosion in Brooklyn	385
A Case for Dr. Doyle	396
Lovecraft Quotes Ecclesiastes	407
A Single Snowflake	420
A Weird and Incomprehensible Species	434
Christmas in the Cathedral	446
Marblehead. End of the line	458

Marblehead — The Director's Cut

Fender Tucker

For the title of this introduction I couldn't resist using one the most popular Hollywood catchphrases for "the version that wasn't ruined by the studio heads". But this huge novel of what may have happened in 1927 is not strictly a "director's cut". Richard Lupoff wrote it completely and had complete authorial control at all times. It's just that this version of the novel was never published —until now.

The germ of the idea of the book infected Dick Lupoff in 1975 when he read Joe Gores' *Hammett.* And what a germ! A fictional mainstream book with lots of action and adventure with a real, beloved author as the hero. Lupoff even had dinner with Gores to see if he'd mind if he wrote a vaguely similar book about his favorite horror writer, H.P. Lovecraft. Joe gave his blessing.

So, in 1976 Lupoff spent several weeks visiting Lovecraft sites in the Providence, Boston and Salem areas, including Marblehead. He interviewed everyone he could find who knew or remembered Lovecraft: Julius Schwartz (his onetime agent), Donald Wollheim (onetime editor/publisher), Kenneth Sterling (onetime collaborator/revision client), Charles Hornig (onetime editor and friend), E. Hoffmann Price (friend and sometime collaborator) and especially Frank Belknap Long (HPL's protégé and probably his closest and longest-enduring friend).

In September of 1976 Lupoff began writing and one year and 556 pages later he delivered a major mainstream novel to his publisher at the time, Putnam. They said it's too long and needed to be cut in half. My, how times have changed. So Dick, after a few fitful attempts to emasculate the text, gave up and rewrote the novel from scratch. And in 1980, after Putnam said they wanted it to be more of a genre novel, an adventure novel with car chases and gunfights, the long-suffering author took it to Arkham House, where editor Jim Turner welcomed it—with a few revisions—and *Lovecraft's Book* was published to substantial fanfare, with excellent reviews and sales. It was published in the UK, Spain and Portugal, too.

But what about the original 160,000 word manuscript that was almost spayed? Where was it? Lupoff didn't have a copy and assumed it was lost forever but then in 2000 a friend, Charles Brown, reminded him that back in 1976 Dick had loaned Charles a carbon copy of the text to show his father in Florida, who was dying. The copy was still in Brown's basement! Dick was ecstatic and envisioned the eventual publication of the mainstream novel he had worked on for more than a year.

But what publisher would be crazy enough to publish it?

Flashforward to 2006 when print-on-demand technology makes limited edition works eminently feasible and Lupoff's and my meeting in Petaluma CA at the house of mystery writer Bill Pronzini changed everything. "We can do this thing," I said. "We have the technology."

Brushing off my puerile dependency on bad TV clichés, Dick Lupoff saw that his dream of telling the complete, original story of Lovecraft's 1927 odyssey was indeed feasible. All he had to do was send me the 556 pages to scan and OCR, and the original manuscript—which always had his favorite title of MARBLEHEAD—would then be in digital format, ready for publication. He sent me the poorly photocopied pile of papers, and the result of our partnership is in your hands. A mainstream novel of 1927, sort of in the mold of John Dos Passos' *USA,* full of action, ideas, manners and personalities.

Car chases were rare in 1927 but read on and you'll find that solo airplane trips across the Atlantic, personal submarine excursions in Cape Cod Bay, underwater hijinks by Houdini's brother and cement overshoes worn by Mafiosa henchmen fill the excitement bill. Not to mention sordid antics by Ku Klux Klansmen, proto-Nazis, rumrunners and even wild west cowboys totin' shootin' arns. And come to think of it, there *is* a sort of car chase from Providence to Salem in a classic 320-horsepower SJ Duesenberg at the nerve-wracking speed of 35 mph!

But the biggest treat for modern booklovers is not the action, but the incredibly vivid panoply of ideas that energized the pre-depression world. Hitler had barely revealed his plans for the future and with the help of the amazing character, George Sylvester Viereck, Americans were dealing with seductive philosophies that to us now are no-brainers—our current vice-president's notwithstanding. But not so in 1927.

The cast of characters in MARBLEHEAD is immense and colorful and the descriptions of the eastern seaboard from New York City to Portsmouth are as vivid as if they had been written in 1927. Take a look at Gavin O'Keefe's beautiful mapback of the area and imagine you're in a time machine because this book is the next best thing to one. And the food! How can a novel that claims to portray a slice of time and space *not* tell us what each character eats at every meal at those fantastic old restaurants that are sadly gone forever. Even though I share H. P. Lovecraft's distaste for seafood, I couldn't help salivating every time the literary characters interrupted their philosophizing and motoring to get something grand to eat. No McDonald's or Taco Bells in 1927 Marblehead!

If you're asking yourself whether having read LOVECRAFT'S BOOK will spoil MARBLEHEAD, take it from one who has read both, one after the other: LOVECRAFT'S BOOK is like a succulent appetizer at Lock-Ober's; MARBLEHEAD is having the appetizer, an entrée and finishing it all off with homemade vanilla ice cream smothered with a tureen of hot fudge—with Viereck, Vince Starrett and Sonia Lovecraft as table companions.

Bon appétit!

MARBLEHEAD:

A Novel of H. P. LOVECRAFT

CHAPTER ONE:

A QUIET CELEBRATION ON BARNES STREET

ALTHOUGH HOWARD had put aside his reading and not yet lifted pen for his evening's correspondence, he still wore the squarish, rimless glasses that he used for close work. He sat slumped in his old high-backed leather chair, the dark wool of his suit blending with the color of the chair.

He sat alone in the room, fingers steepled beneath his prominent chin, gazing out the tall wooden-framed window into the chill Providence evening. The sky was completely black, what stars might have been shining covered by the thick clouds that had loomed through the afternoon. Now a wet snow was falling, the large flakes illuminated by the streetlamps of Barnes Street before turning to chilly puddles when they hit the pavement beneath the lamps and the surface of Barnes Street itself.

Howard glanced at the stack of papers near at hand—incoming letters awaiting reply, amateur journals, portions of his own manuscripts and those of revision clients. He raised the glasses carefully and rubbed his eyes with forefinger and thumb, then settled them once more, adjusting the metal arms in the short dark hair above his ears.

Surely the most intriguing item in the stack was the letter that had arrived from New York City, neatly typed on the letterhead of the Jackson Press. This, Howard would discuss with a trusted friend; all the more reason to anticipate the arrival of young Belknapius and his parents. Not that he mistrusted his two aunts, Annie Gamwell and Lillian Clark, both of them puttering about the apartment while considerately avoiding his immediate vicinity.

But neither aunt was of a literary predilection, while Belknapius, for all his tender years—little more than a child of twenty-three as compared with Grandfather Theobald, Howard's, ancient thirty-six—was a promising youngster indeed and a published author already. Just this year Paul Cook had issued a slim volume of the young man's verse: *The Man from Genoa and Other Poems* by Frank Belknap Long, Jr., Athol, Massachusetts, 1926. 1926—a mere matter of hours and the year would be sped, '27 upon the unready world, and what would the new year bring?

Howard leaned forward and peered into the darkness of Barnes Street, trying to pierce the snowy gloom to the westward and down College Hill toward the corner of Congdon Drive where Barnes curved away into Jenkes Street, and up which the elder Frank Long would guide the perky new Essex of which Belknapius had written with enthusiasm.

Perhaps Howard would join young Long in the ranks of the booked. The Jackson Press letter had arrived as a total surprise, provoking thoughts—indeed, in retrospect, outrageous fantasies—of an offer to collect Howard's stories and issue them to the public in suitably dignified form. After all, there was surely sufficient material by now, nearly twenty had appeared in Henneberger's magazine under the tutelage of Baird or Wright. And that wasn't counting the Houdini ghost-work or any of his other revision work. He could select his very best efforts for the book, undoing such mischief as the atrocious change of title that had been inflicted on poor "Arthur Jermyn," omitting the Herbert West series he'd unwisely undertaken for *Home Brew*.

That was one pitfall that he must avoid in future, writing to order. Aesthetic considerations must govern; when mere commerce, the requirements of editors, were superposed upon the shoulders of the muse she invariably fled, holding herself aloof thereafter until the pure flame of artistic passion had burned away the dross of material greed.

But the Jackson Press letter had not dealt with those carefully wrought stories that Howard labored so carefully over before affixing his chaste and dignified by-line, H. P. Lovecraft. The letter had delved into other matters altogether, and the signature appended to the businesslike message was one that gave Howard such doubts and difficulties as must needs be discussed with another mind of like inclination to his own. At one time he might even have discussed the matter with Sonia, but that phase of his life was a closed volume. The final dissolution of their marriage was a subject difficult and painful to contemplate, marking as it would not only the failure of an enterprise so hopefully undertaken a mere few years ago, but also an unseemly proceeding for a gentleman. Yet, even though the marriage endured as a legal obligation there was little remnant of the brief intimacy that Howard and Sonia had enjoyed during their time together in New York.

Howard sighed, set his reading glasses to one side and rose from the chair. He stood at the tall window for a moment and watched several automobiles make their careful way up Barnes Street, climbing College Hill toward the Moses Brown School for Boys. No sign as yet of the elder Long's little matchbox-shaped car, but down the hill and toward downtown Providence the lights glimmered feebly through the steady, damp snow, setting a mood for the onset of the new year that was a subtle amalgam of the festive and the melancholy, a mood that reflected Howard's own feelings about himself, his life and his career.

From the kitchen Howard's pretty, spirited Aunt Annie bustled into the parlor, a steaming coffee-pot in her hand. She asked Howard if he would like a cup and he followed her back to the kitchen, accepted a freshly-filled cup, added three spoons of sugar. He lifted the steaming, syrupy concoction and sampled its flavor, then added another spoonful of sugar and nodded his satisfaction.

"Thank you, niece," he intoned solemnly. "How great a comfort to old Grandfather Theobaldus that his descendants care for him in his declining years."

Annie laughed, dodged around Howard's tall, somber form and rejoined her elder sister Lillian, setting out sweetcakes and *hors d'oeuvres* for the Longs and themselves. A quiet evening at home was the pleasantest and most economical way to welcome 1927.

Bestowing a grandfatherly smile on his two aunts, Howard carried his coffee back to the parlor and stood once more at the window overlooking Barnes Street. At last a car that he recognized from advertising pictures as a new Essex swung from Jenkes into Barnes. The driver swung the car over to the curb beneath the leafless boughs of a tall elm. Through the closed window and the soft, muffling snow the sound of the auto's engine died, then the glow of the headlights, also softened by the whirling flakes, disappeared.

Howard stood, looking down into Barnes Street, waiting for the arrival of his guests.

~ ~ ~ ~ ~

In the rear seat of the Essex, Frank Belknap Long, Junior, waited for his father to climb out of the car, into the damp, frigid Providence air. Frank Belknap Long, Senior, opened the passenger door and helped his wife to alight from the car, then Belknap—everyone called him that to distinguish him from his father—folded the seat forward and climbed from the car also.

After the stuffy air of the car and the long ride from the Longs' home at 100th Street and West End Avenue, the air here was rhapsodically refreshing.

Frank Long reached back into the Essex and drew out a few brightly-wrapped belated gifts for the Lovecraft aunts, Mrs. Gamwell and Mrs. Clark. Belknap held his own gift for his friend Howard under one overcoated arm. It was a copy of *The Ghost Pirates* by William Hope Hodgson that Belknap had ferreted out in one of his prowls of the old book stalls along Fourth Avenue. Howard would enjoy the book, of course, for its *outré* theme and dark atmosphere, but even more, Belknap hoped, it would remind his friend of the many enjoyable hours they had spent together prowling just such book stalls during Howard's stay in the metropolis.

They made their way up the wooden steps to the front door of 10 Barnes, then waited until the door was answered by Howard Lovecraft's Aunt Annie.

"Doctor Long, Mrs. Long—May—and Belknap. We're so happy to see you. Please, come along inside!"

The glass-paneled door shut with a thump and Belknap followed the others into the Lovecraft parlor. Howard set down a steaming cup and advanced to shake hands formally with the visitors.

"Doctor. Mrs. Long. Belknapius."

Howard's second aunt, Lillian Clark, emerged from the kitchen wiping her eyeglasses and the ceremony of greetings was repeated. After the visitors' wraps were hung and refreshments served the party separated into two groups, the senior Longs and Howard's aunts remaining in the front parlor overlooking Barnes Street while the two younger men withdrew to Howard's study where they could discuss matters of interest to literary persons, *fantaisistes* like themselves, undisturbed by mundane conversation.

Howard thanked Belknap for the Hodgson and presented him with a Poe collection in return, then asked if Belknap had as yet seen the January *Weird Tales.* "Aha, I thought not," he responded to Belknap's negative. "Old Farnie sent me a couple of copies, you're welcome to have one. The magazine should be on the stands next week, I suppose."

Belknap Long watched Howard delve into a stack of papers beside the ancient Postal typewriter that stood on Howard's wooden desk. "I'll never understand how you get saleable manuscripts out of that antediluvian machine," he commented, "it must be older than I am."

"The truth of the matter is that I despise typewriting." Howard continued to rummage through the stacks. "But at the rates Joe Henneberger pays, I could hardly pay to have a professional secretary. Using that noble old damned machine makes the strain of typewriting just a bit more bearable. Ah! Here it is!"

He turned toward Belknap, holding a familiarly red-bordered magazine. Long took the magazine, examined its crudely painted cover illustration and clucked over it before turning to the table of contents. "I never did get over the return to the smaller size. You know, I enjoyed the old oversized *Weird Tales* far more."

"Commerce, Belknapius, commerce."

"Well, let's see what we have here. I'm happy to see that interminable Leahy serial ending at last. Ah, 'The Horror at Red Hook.' Well, congratulations, Howard. A fine story, I greatly enjoyed reading it when you sent me the manuscript. Glad to see that friend Farnsworth made no objection to it."

"Wright is an odd one, all right." Howard chuckled at his accidental pun. "But he went for 'Red Hook' so I have no complaint on that score. At least my residence in your city yielded a couple of passable yarns if nothing more."

"Yes, I liked 'He' as much as the new story. But surely you enjoyed living in New York to some degree or you wouldn't have stayed as long as you did, Howard."

Lovecraft took a few paces, head down, hands locked behind his back. "I suppose I did. Certainly the book shops are treasure troves yet, and there were other attractions. The surviving architecture of colonial days is interesting. But the mongrels, Belknap! The Asiatic hordes and mongrel multitudes that throng the streets of that city! I fear that the United States has simply lost New York to those swarthy foreigners! May the hills of His Majesty's Colony of Rhode-Island and Providence Plantations never suffer the sullying tread of such!"

Belknap made a noncommittal sound hoping to placate his friend. Howard's Anglophilia and antiquarianism were traits of long standing, widely known among his friends. In a sense they were admirable traits; certainly Howard defended his positions with logic and eloquence. But on occasion they tended to become a trifle out-of-proportion to the topic at hand.

"Is there anything else of interest in the issue?" Even as he asked, Belknap's eye was scanning the contents page. He read aloud the blurb that accompanied the listing of his friend's contribution. " 'The cults of darkness are rooted in blasphemies deeper than the well of Democritus.' Hah! What has the well of Democritus to do with your yarn?"

Howard shrugged dark-clad shoulders. "Your guess is as good as mine, O Belknapius. Who can fathom the whims of editors? Yes," he went on, answering Long's previous question, "there are a couple of interesting pieces in the issue. Do you see a little story called 'The Lost Race' by someone named Robert E. Howard? A new man for *Weird Tales,* I think, and quite promising. He shows a real feeling for the ancient world of the northern barbarians. I recommend the story very highly. I may even send a note to Wright about the man."

Belknap was still studying the pulp magazine. " 'Ye Goode Olde Ghoste Storie,' " he read. "By someone called William A. P. White. They'll never get anywhere running silly stuff like that. Well, let's have a look at the letter page." He slid onto an old wooden chair and turned the pages of the magazine. Finally he stopped, held the magazine open with one hand and unconsciously brushed his small, neatly-trimmed young man's moustache with the other. "Why, look here, Howard. Did you read this letter from a fellow named Ramsauer in Brooklyn?"

Howard Lovecraft had read the letter and so indicated, but he didn't discourage Belknapius from reading it aloud.

" 'Such writers as Frank Owen, H. P. Lovecraft, Arthur J. Burks and Bassett Morgan are genuine finds of the century.' Very nice, I would say." Long looked up and smiled, his own rimless eyeglasses, similar to the reading glasses Howard Lovecraft had set aside in the parlor, caught the color of a shaded electric lamp. "I'd be very happy to see the fans writing that kind of thing about me."

"Yes, surely." Howard drew a long breath, then added "Whoever this fellow is, he puts together a somewhat odd bag of writers. Owen is certainly an artist in whose company I am happy to find myself. The others—I am not so certain. Still, kind words make pleasant hearing."

Belknap was still flipping the pages of *Weird Tales.* He stopped when he came to his friend's story and studied the accompanying illustration.

Lovecraft chuckled. "Not too impressive, is it?"

"I'm glad you are the one to say so, Howard. Kind of a vague scrawl of monsters, eh? Not quite what the story puts me in mind of, I'm afraid. Where does Farnsworth Wright find these illustrators of his? You'd think there should be some competent delineators in Chicago!"

He closed the magazine and handed it back to Howard, who restored it, somehow, to its place in the stack of materials from which he had extracted it. "I suppose, Belknapius, that Wright hires the best men he can get for the pittances that Joe Henneberger pays. You know *Weird Tales'* pay rates as well as I, and they are anything but generous! Not that Henneberger is being tight, I suppose. You know the magazine has been near collapse almost from the day of its birth. The wonder is that Henny keeps it going at all."

"Still, Howard, I cannot help wondering what might have followed if you'd only gone out there to take it over when Ed Baird left. Henneberger so clearly wanted to hire you!"

"And live in Chicago?" Howard Lovecraft made a face that showed his disdain for the very idea. "New York was enough of an affront to my nature. I am too much a product of this old New England atmosphere, nephew, ever to leave it again for any lengthy periods. I don't mind traveling to visit friends and to see such survivals of colonial times as offer themselves, but to sever my permanent attachment to old Providence and make a home in the crude, noisy middle west is totally beyond the pale. Never again will I give up living where I can see my precious College Hill, Federal Hill, Swan Point. The Seekonk. And Boston, Salem, Marblehead." He held his hands out as if to encompass the geography. "This is my home."

"Still," Long countered, "as you said, Howard, there is commerce. One must make a living."

Lovecraft nodded solemnly. "That is the other matter I wished to discuss with you, Belknapius. I have had a letter. I would let you read it yourself—you may see it in a few minutes—but the signature will be a surprise to you."

Long nodded agreement and Lovecraft began to read the letter on the Jackson Press letterhead. " 'My Dear Mr. Lovecraft,' he opens, 'You will forgive, I hope, my writing to you. Your name has been suggested to me by mutual acquaintances, one of whom, Mr. Reinhardt Kleiner, is a loyal subscriber to a number of periodicals edited by myself. The other is Mr. Abraham Merritt, an employee of Mr. William Randolph Hearst, for whom I have done much work as a journalist and editor. Mr. Merritt tells me that he is acquainted with yourself and with your work, and that you might be interested in a proposition which I wish to make to you.'

"What do you think of that?" Lovecraft asked Belknapius, looking up from the letter.

"A. Merritt. I remember the occasion clearly, he called at our apartment in New York to invite you to lunch at his club. And I was too busy to come along! I've regretted it ever since."

"Well. To continue. There is not much more to the letter. 'I have been engaged in a good deal of editing and writing on matters of current and historical interest, but have found, regrettably, that in many quarters my by-line is held in suspicion. I seek nothing but honest reporting and the rectification of historic injustices, and I would wish to enlist your aid in bringing about this rectification.

" 'Financial aspects of such work would be subject to discussion, but I believe that the pay would be most attractive to yourself.' And he goes off," Lovecraft added, "asking me to contact him at my earliest convenience. And that is all that there is to the letter."

Belknap Long stroked his round, boyish chin with the handsome cleft. "All too mysterious for my little mind, Howard. What did he mean by his by-line being held in suspicion? And just what is it that he wants from you? Is he just some revision client?"

"Hardly! I don't mind polishing up other writers' prose for a fee. That's honorable enough work. But that is not what this fellow wants. But wait till you hear his name. Or—better yet—He folded and turned the letter so the younger man could read the typewritten signature beneath the ink-scrawled flourish at the bottom of the page.

"George Sylvester Viereck!"

"The very!" Howard Lovecraft chuckled loudly. Long joined in weakly.

"I'm glad that you can laugh at Viereck now, Howard. Time was when the very mention of his name and you would virtually froth at the mouth."

"That was long ago."

"True enough. But—have you changed your views that much? I remember things you wrote about Viereck in the United Amateur Press Association that were blood-curdling!"

"Well. You recall the events of the day, Belknap. Viereck was making the Kaiser's case in the public press during the Great War. You recall the scandal of 1915, the German embassy money, the G-men capturing the Heinrich Albert documents and implicating Viereck in the whole ugly propaganda operation of the Hun."

"I was hardly more than an infant in 1915," Belknap Long smiled.

"You were participating in the United."

"Yes." Long and Lovecraft were both silent for several moments during which the conversation from the parlor drifted through to Howard's study. Then Long said, "Yes, I remember those events. I remember that uproar in the United over it, also."

"That buffoon Goodwin," Howard mumbled. "And you remember the outcome, Belknapius?"

"I remember you wrote a poem about it, about Goodwin's coming to Viereck's defense. But I'm afraid I don't remember the lines."

"I've got it here somewhere." Again Howard bent to the stacks of miscellaneous documents that comprised his filing system.

Before he emerged there was a timid knock at the door of the study and the voice of an aunt inviting Howard and Belknap to the parlor for ice cream and candy. "It's nearing midnight. We'll welcome 1927 with a little feast."

"Just a few minutes, Niece Lillian." Howard straightened, a small, neatly printed amateur journal in his hand. "Here, Belknapius, *The Conservative*, October 1915. The thunderbolt had struck in August, when the European struggle was just a year old. Then young Goodwin made his asinine remarks and I responded in verse."

"I remember now. He'd said something about 'No kidding.'"

"And I responded, here," Lovecraft read:

"No kidding, Goodwin, you with wisdom say
That England likes not George Sylvester's way:
The honest truth poor Viereck ne'er could speak,
And Britons hate a liar and a sneak!"

"You were rather hard on the fellow, Howard." Belknap tugged at the crease in his woolen, trousers. "Did Viereck ever receive *The Conservative?*"

Lovecraft shook his head. "I doubt it. Of course, if he is a friend of Kleiner's, Reinhardt might have shown him a copy."

Belknap rubbed his chin. "'The honest truth poor Viereck ne'er could speak,'" he quoted. "And now he wants—what was the phrase?"

Howard read the line from Viereck's Jackson Press letter. "'Honest reporting and the rectification of historic injustices.' To Kaiser Bill, presumably. Remember what I called *him?*"

"Bill Hohenzollern," Belknap supplied, and Howard Lovecraft joined him so they completed the phrase in unison, "head of Berlin Butchers' Local Number 1914."

He slipped the slim magazine back into its place and started toward the door.

"Have you answered Viereck's letter?" Long asked.

Lovecraft shook his head. "I need to give it some thought. The man is a legitimate *fantaisiste,* you know, Belknapius. Have you seen his book *House of the Vampire?* It dates from before his involvement with politics. Not really a bad effort. Perhaps I ought to talk with the man, at least. Certainly if he's recommended by A. Merritt there must be some—"

He stopped and they both laughed at the obvious play that must follow, then rejoined Howard's two aunts and Belknap's parents for ice cream and coffee and the welcoming in of 1927.

CHAPTER TWO:

A VISIT TO THE METROPOLIS

THE FIRST DAY of 1927 was cold and damp, with a light rain still falling early in the afternoon when Howard rose. After the departure of the guests the previous night his two aunts had retired, leaving Howard the lone possessor of the Lovecraft-Gamwell-Clark household. This was his preference. He was long accustomed to nocturnal habits, preferring the quiet and privacy of the late night hours to the bustle and distractions of the day. More often than not it was his practice to sit up through the night reading, working, or simply sitting and dreaming the waking dreams that he had indulged in since boyhood and that, along with true dream-experiences—all too often nightmares—provided the basis for so many of his fantastic short stories.

The Longs were already present, their new Essex drawn once more to the curbside in Barnes Street, when Howard emerged from his bedroom. He greeted them and his aunts, then withdrew to the kitchen to devour a breakfast of sweet black syrupy coffee and scrambled eggs prepared by his aunt Lillian, accompanied only by the younger Long.

Belknap pulled a small briar pipe from the pocket of his suit coat and fingered it as he watched Howard add a few more spoonfuls of sugar to his cup, then Belknapius slipped the pipe back into his pocket and in its place accepted a cup of coffee. They spoke again of their literary enterprises, their amateur activities and their work for Joe Henneberger's *Weird Tales* magazine. Howard mentioned that he was looking forward shortly to receiving proofs of his lengthy study for the forthcoming journal *The Recluse* to be issued by W. Paul Cook, the wizard of Athol, Mass.

"I was very pleased with the job he did on *The Man from Genoa*," Long volunteered. "His new periodical should be a worthy showcase for your work, Howard."

"Sometimes I despair of achieving the coverage I have sought in my work. Did I tell you the title I finally settled upon for the study? *Supernatural Horror in Literature.* Simple and accurate, I hope."

"Suitably dignified as well."

"I wonder if I ought to add my newer discoveries, though. As written the piece omits a number of worthy authors. I've only just discovered this Englishman, William Hope Hodgson.

"The volume you gave me looks very promising. I read a few pages before retiring. He certainly starts off with a bang. That opening sea chantey has an authentic feel to it, and then Jessop's story of signing aboard the *Mortzestus* in San Francisco."

Howard walked to the stove and returned with the pot of coffee, refilling Belknapius' cup as well as his own, talking as he moved about the room. "I know almost nothing about the author, but I believe he did have some sort of nautical background. A promising writer, I think he was killed in the Great War. One more crime for which Bill the Butcher should be made to account."

He replaced the porcelain-gray pot and returned to his seat opposite Long. "For millennia man has associated the sea with weird and sinister themes. Some of Poe's greatest works have nautical themes."

"Well, and your own, Howard. 'Dagon' for one."

"Yes," Howard Lovecraft admitted. "Don't omit your own tale of the Jormungandar. I wish you'd finish that thing and get it into print somewhere. It's one of your better pieces."

Long chuckled softly and grinned, not speaking.

"Methinks, Belknapius, that thou has a secret hidden beneath thy cap this day!"

"I sent the yarn off to Farnie weeks and weeks ago. Would have sent it sooner but I couldn't think of a name for the peculiar thing. Finally called it 'The Man with a Thousand Legs.' "

"A trifle lurid, perhaps. But, more's the point, what said Brother Pharnabus when he saw the manuscript? Did he fiddle the way he usually does, or did he give you a sensible answer?"

"He's taken it. I have his letter at home. It's to run some time next summer. And to celebrate, you're invited to join me at the Albee Theatre tonight. They're putting on a gala new year's show. I don't know that the film will be of exceptional merit but they're co-featuring an appearance by Nicola the Conjurer."

"Capital, my good fellow!"

They joined the others in the parlor. The senior Long was nattering on about the events of the day, whether Coolidge would seek an additional term in the presidency, Secretary Mellon's plan to improve Prohibition enforcement by spiking all industrial alcohols with irremovable poisons (the Providence *Journal* reported that Mr. Franklin L. Dickson of the Rhode Island Office of Food and Drugs disagreed with Secretary Mellon's idea, calling the tactic excessive), the un-attributed rumor that the United States planned to extend diplomatic recognition to the Bolshevik regime in Russia, the seizure of United States oil holdings in Mexico, the statement by Commerce Secretary Hoover that one and three quarter million radios had been sold during 1926 bringing the total number in the US to five million, the prediction by Professor Tchijovsky of the University of Moscow that war would break out in 1929 inevitably.

Professor Tchijovsky based his prediction upon the study of sunspots.

The two aunts retired to prepare a light evening meal while Howard, Belknap, Frank Long, Senior, and May Doty Long sat in the parlor. The short New England winter afternoon had fled. The all-day rain had thinned to a gray mist that hung over Providence like soft gauze. May Long, wearing a long necklace of dark beads, ran the strands up and down in her hands until Annie Gamwell popped her head back into the parlor and announced that dinner was about to be served. Then May dropped her beads and crossed to the kitchen to help bring out the food. She was from old Newburgh money.

Afterwards Frank Long, Senior announced that he and his family would return home early the following day. That would be Sunday. He was a highly successful dentist and oral surgeon and his practice demanded that he be present, rested and steady of hand, Monday morning.

Howard bundled himself into sweater, suit coat and overcoat, muffler, hat and gloves, and accompanied Belknap and his parents to the Essex. He had a severe problem with cold weather—not merely a dislike of it, but an actual physical peculiarity that made him acutely uncomfortable, lethargic, and drove him almost into a coma if he ventured out into it without precautions.

Long Senior managed the Essex back down College Hill without great difficulty. Despite the moist snow of the previous day and today's rain, the streets had not frozen over and driving was relatively safe and easy. He pulled up before the Albee Theatre and got out of the car so Belknap and Howard could tilt the folding seat and extricate themselves without disturbing May Doty Long.

Howard shook hands with Frank and with May and promised to visit them in New York shortly, then he and Belknap made their way into the somewhat sparse crowd in the shelter of the Albee's marquee. The evening of January 1 was not a very festive one. Shop windows and restaurants still featured Christmas decorations that would be removed in the morning. Men in overcoats and fedoras, women in fur wraps, long coats and hats passed, their faces pale in the artificial light, their breath merging into the misty air.

Belknapius purchased general admission seats and they made their way through the gilt-and-plush lobby into the auditorium where May Busch and Pat O'Malley were gesturing their way through the last reel of *The Perch of the Devil,* a tiresome photoplay with none of the glamour or fantastic theme promised by its title. A pit orchestra provided little relief from the banality of the performance.

During the intermission Belknap indicated that he was eager to witness the performance of the famed Nicola. "I suppose any illusionist or escape artist will be old hat to you, Howard, after your association with the late Houdini."

"Houdini always credited his colleagues fully for their skill. He bitterly resented what he regarded as imitators who tried to exploit his own fame. That was one reason for his encouraging his brother Hardeen to tour opposite himself. He told me that if others were to capture the overflow of his own audience, it might as well be one of his family."

"Hah! Sad, very sad, his death last Halloween. I regret that I never met Houdini."

Lovecraft suggested that they leave their coats on their seats and stroll in the lobby as the intermission proceeded. "I don't know that you would have liked him entirely, Belknapius. He was a strange man, a paradox. Incredibly dynamic. Enthusiastic with a contagious charm. But arrogant, abrasive. He seemed, somehow, to epitomize the Jewish *arriviste.* I could get along with him all right, but could never fully warm to him. It was a matter of blood, I suppose."

"That story you ghost-wrote for him. . . ?"

" 'Imprisoned with the Pharaohs.' I suppose there will never be another issue of *Weird Tales* like that one."

"It was certainly your issue, Howard. The Houdini story with accompanying cover illustration. Your own 'Hypnos' and 'The Loved Dead' that you revised for Carlton Eddy. I wish I'd had a yarn in that edition, but Wright moves in mysterious ways. But you've never told me the extent of your relationship with Houdini."

Howard Lovecraft drew a deep breath and held it for a few moments while he paced, hands folded behind his back. "Farnie Wright set the thing up, of course. Houdini sent me a note with the barest sketch of an idea. He claimed to have spent a night in a pyramid while touring some years ago. I have no idea whether he'd ever *been* to Egypt. But I wove a tale from the slim thread he provided, and to give the man credit, he expressed great pleasure with the result.

"I only met with him a few times. Once to discuss the manuscript, once or twice when he invited me to the theatre to witness his show. No question, grandson, he was a magnificent showman. And I will credit him for using his Ryan Special knowledge to combat fakirs and mediums when he could easily have used their very trickery to his own benefit."

Howard paused as the soft chime sounded, announcing the end of intermission. As he moved back to his seat with Belknap Long he added one more reminiscence.

"He loved the grand gesture, of course, and could be lavish in his generosity. I recall one afternoon in 1924, receiving a telephone call from him."

"That was when you were living in Brooklyn with Mrs. Lovecraft."

Howard flushed slightly. "Yes. Houdini was in New York between tours and he called to invite me to the theatre. That is, Sonia and myself. We joined him and Mrs. Houdini and did have a gala evening."

"What production did you attend."

" 'Outward Bound.' You recall the drama?"

Belknap nodded his enthusiasm. "Of course. The supernatural drama by Sutton Vane. I hope that all of you enjoyed it!"

"It was Houdini's choice. He was very affected by it. You recall—all the passengers on an ocean cruise, gradually coming to the realization that they are the souls of the dead, bound for the hereafter. I believe that Houdini selected that play very carefully. He hadn't got over the death of his mother. He never did, of course. So you see, Vane's theme was right down Houdini's alley."

He shook his head. He dropped his voice almost to a whisper as the houselights dimmed. "But I found the play distasteful. Excessively sentimental. I despise the maudlin. Utterly despise sentimentality.

"But I liked Mrs. Houdini immensely."

Nicola gave a bravura performance. He lived up to his billing mixing magic, humor, and escape tricks. He performed Uncanny Sorcery, demonstrated Chinese Mysteries, showed off the Secrets of India. (Nicola was really a world traveler and had performed in South America, Africa, Australia, China and India, bringing back with him local costumes, color and traditions from each country he visited.)

He made one his assistants into the Elastic Lady and for his grand finale he escaped from the Torture Chamber.

"That last is my only complaint," Howard Lovecraft commented as he and Belknap Long left the auditorium. "Copied directly from Houdini. Houdini would have bounded onto the stage and denounced Nicola as a thief."

They made their way to the Rathskeller beside Providence's City Hall at Dorrance and Fulton for an after-theatre snack. Belknap picked up the tab for them both. He had a roll and juice; Howard, a bowl of spaghetti, a large slab of hot apple pie with two scoops of ice cream, one vanilla and one chocolate, and several cups of sugar-filled syrupy coffee. Belknap left the change from his dollar bill as a tip for the waitress.

Outside they shook hands and Belknap joined his parents at their hotel. Howard made his way by streetcar back to College Hill, found at Barnes Street that his two aunts had retired for the night, and took a small snack from the kitchen before retreating to his study. He wrote letters for several hours, including one to Farnsworth Wright praising the new author of 'The Lost Race,' then changed from his woolen suit to his nightshirt and climbed into his old bed, pleased with the first day .of the new year.

He spent the following weeks living out his comfortable routine: much correspondence, polishing efforts on *Supernatural Horror in Literature* for Cook's magazine (Cook wrote, mentioning the possibility of issuing Howard's story "The Shunned House" as a slim volume uniform with the book of Belknap's poems he had put out in '26), continuing revisions for such clients as Zealia Reed, Eddy, Adolphe de Castro, Wilfred Talman, Hazel Heald. It occasionally struck him as odd that so many of his revision clients were women.

He worked less on tales of his own, although he struggled with some new tales and resurrected a few from old amateur journals, painstakingly tapping out new typescripts on his antique Postal machine and sending them off to Wright. Farnie accepted "The White Ship" and "Pickman's Model" for use later in the year. But he turned down "In the Vault" and "The Call of Cthulhu," the latter one of Howard's own favorites. There was no understanding the maddening Wright. Sometimes he would reject a story and then buy it on resubmission, giving no explanation for the change of attitude!

The Dream-Quest of Unknown Kadath was completed, a strangely surrealistic tale of almost novel-length, based largely on Howard's recurrent dreams of incomprehensible black rubbery creatures carrying him away to unknown lands, gibbering and caressing him as they flew through starry (or sometimes starless) night skies.

He didn't, himself, know what to make of the story. He shoved the pages of tiny, spidery manuscript writing into a bottom drawer of his desk and left them there.

He had always been interested in astronomy and the mysteries that lay not in the skies but beyond them. Some of his earliest published works, other than his own amateur productions, had been a series of astronomical pieces for the *Pawtuxet Valley Gleaner* some twenty years before. Now his imagination soared heavenward again and returned with an idea of a malign *something* dropping to earth. He didn't have a full grasp of what he wanted to do in the story. Something he'd read in the Providence *Journal* or *Bulletin* about the work of the Polish-born Frenchwoman, Marja Skoldowska Curie, had got mixed up with the notion of a strange meteorite.

The ideas whirled about, merged, surfaced in a yarn called "The Colour Out of Space." He laid the narration against his beloved New England countryside, in an inland valley to the west of Salem, Massachusetts (which he called "Arkham" in his regional tales of terror). He built into the story all of the fears of creeping degeneracy, madness, and helplessness that hovered in the back of his mind, part of his family heritage. He thought the story was a good one, but not quite the kind of thing that *Weird Tales* featured. The theme was too modern and scientific, not gothic enough for Wright's taste even though Farnie did run a fair number of "weird-scientific" stories in his magazine.

Howard put "The Color Out of Space" in a desk drawer, also, although he vowed to take it back out one day and find a proper market to which to submit it.

He had another letter from George Sylvester Viereck on the stationery of the Jackson Publishing Company. This time instead of expressing a generalized interest in meeting with Lovecraft, Viereck invited Howard to come to New York and see him at his office. He suggested a date early in February, adding that if Howard found this inconvenient and preferred another, he need only offer an alternative date and Viereck would make himself available if he was in town.

Howard examined the level of his bank account (low as ever, with Henneberger paying little and late, and the small income he had inherited from both the Lovecraft and the Phillips sides of his family growing perpetually less adequate in this era of rising prices). He sent a letter back to Viereck expressing his dedicated Anglophilia but reviving an ancient theme that Briton and Teuton were at least first cousins if not brothers, and admitting the possibility of a reconciliation.

Howard Lovecraft's letter to Wright concerning the author of "The Lost Race" had brought no response, but another *Weird Tales* veteran, the Chicago newsman and poet Vincent Starrett, wrote to Lovecraft at Providence and mentioned that he expected to spend several months on the East Coast early in 1927. He was tired and discouraged with life in Chicago and planned to find lodging near New York and work on a fantasy novel involving the Fountain of Youth.

Howard wrote back to Starrett and suggested Belknap Long's home as a contact point through which he could be reached. Starrett had done a handful of stories for *Weird Tales* under its original editor, Edwin Baird. When Baird split with publisher Joe Henneberger, Starrett had followed Baird over to the detective story field while Lovecraft remained with *Weird Tales* and its new editor. Even so they had maintained their friendship via correspondence.

Sunday, February 13, was a better day than most for the time of year. Howard bundled himself into warm traveling clothes, bade his aunts good-bye and hauled his battered, heavy suitcase via streetcar to the downtown Providence Union Station. He spent the railroad journey to New York looking through the day's *Providence Journal,* letting even the comic section occupy his attention briefly. The only worthwhile feature was Henderson's "Roger Williams Visits his Old Home Town," but the anachronisms in the feature were annoying and he set it aside.

World events were moving in chaotic fashion toward some sort of crisis that Howard endeavored to fathom. The German cabinet crisis seemed to have ended for the moment, with President von Hindenberg persuading Chancellor Marx to form still another government. A civil war was raging in China but daily dispatches did more to confuse the issue than to clarify it. Certainly there was Russian interference in the situation, something that went back to the pre-Bolshevik days but that had grown intolerable since the rise of Lenin, Trotzky and Stalin. And there weren't even two contending sides. More like five or six factions, at least half of them led by generals or marshals named Chang or Chiang. It was chaos.

Only orderly imperial Japan seemed to be handling itself in civilized fashion. The death of the old emperor, Yoshihito, had brought forth funereal pomp and tradition unmatched in the occidental world. The newspapers had reported the monarch's cortege, the catafalque drawn through the demon-haunted night by a team of four sacred black-and-white oxen. The new emperor, the young Hirohito, one hundred twenty-fourth ruler of his line, had followed his father's body past a million silent, prostrate mourners as the procession made its way lit only by paper lanterns to the traditional resting place of the emperors at Asakawa. Howard wished that he could have witnessed the obsequies—had he done so, he knew, he would have been the only foreigner present.

He had to admire that action by the Japanese. Here was a race, yellow though they were, who knew enough to hold themselves in purity and separation from the other strains of mankind. Unlike the foolish United States with its odious commingling of white and yellow, Briton and Teuton and bestial Slav.

He sighed.

The office of the Jackson Publishing Company was at 202 East 42nd Street. Howard made his way downtown from the Long demesne by elevated railroad, paying the five cent fare out of carefully budgeted funds. He had forced himself to rise before noon despite his longtime practice of sleeping until well past the middle of the day and remaining awake most of the following night. At 42nd Street he made his way across Manhattan on foot, observing the theatres and bookshops as he strode. The rewards of the metropolis—the small cafes, the remnants of architecture surviving from an earlier day (although hardly in this section, to be sure!), and most of all the numerous antiquarian bookstalls—were sadly offset by the bustling, crude throngs with their accents and foreign tongues, their dark skins and their barbaric ways.

He made his way to the Jackson office and was greeted by an efficient receptionist who asked him to step into Mr. Viereck's office.

Viereck rose as Howard Lovecraft approached his desk. The office was a combination of businesslike clutter and luxury; the man was of a height with Howard, just under six feet tall, and wore a suit of astonishingly casual tweed material, more suitable, Lovecraft thought, for a country gentleman than a metropolitan businessman. Viereck's tie was of a voluptuously patterned silk, a carnation sprang from his lapel, a handkerchief from his breast pocket. The man himself wore longish, brown hair that curled over his ears. Deepset dark eyes peered through modern tortoise-shell spectacles.

He extended a hand in greeting. "Mr. Lovecraft. I am so pleased that you were able to join me." He offered Howard a seat of luxurious leather upholstery.

"I am familiar with a number of your books, particularly *The House of the Vampire.* I was particularly taken by your notion of the psychic vampire Reginald Clarke. He is quite unlike any other rendition of the vampiric theme I have come across."

Viereck, seated once more behind the polished wood of his desk, smiled. "That was a very long time ago. I'm afraid that fiction is something for which very little time remains to me." His English was precise, flavored with only the slightest suggestion of his German birth. "The affairs of the contemporary world contain more of inter-est."

"A pity. One might almost wish, sir, that you had con-tinued in the vein of your early works. Your poetry, I thought, was quite admirable."

"But obsolescent. The romantic school was doomed."

"And your essay into the weird was most promising."

"That was two decades ago, Mr. Lovecraft."

"Still—" Howard's eyes roved the row of volumes be-hind Viereck's chair "—I recently looked through the pages of your novel once again. I was most taken by a particular passage. I wonder if you have a copy here."

Viereck rose and walked to the bookshelf. "I permit myself the indulgence," and he reached for a gold-stamped green volume, "of keeping my works at hand." He stood, studying the book fondly, then handed it over to Howard.

"The dream of Ethel in which, ah," and here Howard, turning the pages of the book, quoted, " 'She saw Clarke as she had seen him in days gone by, grotesquely trans-formed into a slimy sea-thing, whose hungry mouths shut sucking upon her and whose tentacles encircled her form.' "

He shut the book and returned it to Viereck. "I was dis-cussing with young Belknapius Long, a fantasy author of whom you may have heard, the common connection between themes of the sea and feelings of terror. Your own mention in the novel is a striking example."

Viereck shook his head, his loosely curled hair dancing with the movement. Once more he laughed. "Such matters are ancient history, Mr. Lovecraft. Flattered though I am by your enthusiasm, I wish to discuss the world of 1927, not that of 1907. So much has changed, so many errors have been made, and yet such promise is present, the world may rise to Olympian heights or plunge into chaos and tyranny in the next decade."

"I quite agree. For much of the time I attempt to hold myself aloof from the vulgar squabbles and petty disputes of the political world, but matters of global import find their way through even to His Majesty's Colony of Rhode-Island and Providence Plantations. The situation in Europe, that in China, the *Bolshevist* threat. The world is in sorry straits, Mr. Viereck. But what service could an old gentleman who spends his declining days scratching away at little moody tales contribute to the salvation of mankind? I fear that the world is plunging into chaos, even extinction. But in the scale of the cosmos, such is the inevitable fate of all worlds, anyway."

"Sir, I cannot accept your pessimistic view."

"Sir, you are not required to accept it."

There was a moment of tense silence, then Viereck leaned forward, wrists on his desk-top, hands upraised placatingly. "Let us not quarrel. I really have in mind a more constructive scheme than that." He stopped and sat upright again, pulling a gold watch from the pocket of his tweed vest. "Will you join me for luncheon? I've made a reservation at the Waldorf. We can talk further."

CHAPTER THREE:

A MARTOONI AND A BOILERMAKER

VIERECK HAILED a taxi in front of his office building and they sped back to Fifth Avenue, then downtown to 34th Street. "You are familiar with New York?" Viereck asked Howard.

"I lived in Brooklyn at one time, but am a born and bred Rhode Islander. I find much of interest here, but have never considered New York my home."

Viereck nodded. "I am European-born myself. But I have lived in the United States since 1895. Since I was eleven years of age. I consider America my home, almost my bride, while the country of my birth will forever remain my fatherland. I tell you this, Mr. Lovecraft, because many seem to find it hard to understand."

"Your activities during the Great War are very well known, Mr. Viereck."

Viereck raised a hand as if to gesture in reply but the driver pulled to the curb and a uniformed doorman opened the door of the cab. Viereck paid off the fare and he and Howard climbed from the taxi. They stood for a moment gazing across the street at the splendid shopping facade, then entered the Waldorf and, Viereck in the lead, made their way to the Turkish Salon where their reservation was held.

They sat in plush Turkish-style easy chairs set on rich Persian carpets. Before their waiter approached a Turk in old-style pantaloons and vest appeared, bowed, signaled forward an olive-skinned boy who poured cups of thick coffee from a long-necked pitcher of hammered brass.

Viereck lifted his miniature decorated cup and toasted, "To better understanding, Mr. Lovecraft."

Howard considered a moment and raised his own cup, sipped the muddy mixture.

"Mr. Lovecraft, as I mentioned, I believe that the world stands at the brink of a new era. Whether it will be an era of justice and good feelings or one of villainy and bitterness is yet to be determined. And it is my strong conviction that the unliquidated heritage of the Great War is the most serious threat to international harmony and progress.

"You asked what a person like yourself could contribute to the rectification of these wrongs."

"Indeed. I had my day of railing at the mighty. They move on their plane and I on mine. Perhaps it is difficult for a man like yourself to understand the position in which I find myself. My family is one of the elder and more distinguished in the city of Providence. It would hardly be seemly for me to take part in petty squabbles."

Viereck looked surprised. "Petty squabbles? Mr. Lovecraft, we are discussing the fate of nations!"

Howard did not reply.

"And as for family, Mr. Lovecraft." Howard looked up at this, waited for Viereck to continue. "It is not widely known, but there exists a link of blood between the royal House of Hohenzollern and the Viereck family."

"I was unaware of that, sir. Nor would I be quick to announce it were I in your position. The late butchery is remembered in many quarters."

"The injustices of the settlement, the treacherous manner in which the war itself was ended, must be redressed. I have no shame in my relationship to the Kaiser. I take pride in it. You are aware, perhaps, that I was the first journalist to whom His Majesty granted an interview following the war."

"And are you a restorationist? Would you set Wilhelm back on his throne?"

Viereck paused before replying. The coffee-boy approached and freshened the cups of both men. When he had moved on to serve others Viereck said, "The German people must decide for themselves between empire and republic, between the old colors and the new. I can tell you this, sir. I have nothing but reverence for President von Hindenberg but the man is over seventy-nine years of age. His constitution is strong and his will is iron but no man escapes death forever. Once the President is gone from the scene, I do not expect the republic long to survive.

"What new form of governance replaces this republic, we shall see." His carefully manicured hands moved gracefully through the air, punctuating each point, his mobile face changed expression with each change of phrase.

Howard Lovecraft, stone-faced, replied, "I read your piece about that portrait-painter, the so-called National Socialist who wound up in jail afterwards. How does he fit in with restorationism?" Before Viereck could answer, Lovecraft added, "I have read many of your pieces. You have associated with a fascinating range of personages. Aleister Crowley, Herbert George Wells, Ramsay MacDonald, those degenerates Freud and Ellis. How could you associate with such men?"

"Such men as Freud and Havelock Ellis? Why, they have given us the keys to human understanding. Their insights are among the most profound in the history of thought! Associate with them? I admire them as I do few others on the face of the earth!"

"And yet," Lovecraft persisted, "you knew others with whom you broke."

"Whom do you mean, sir?"

"Mr. Roosevelt. Mr. Wilson. Although," and Howard permitted himself a slight smile, "I thought your characterization of the late Woodrow was apt."

"That he wished to be remembered as the greatest Englishman of his generation? I fear that the President did not take kindly to that comment. But actually, all that I sought in my exchanges with Mr. Wilson and Mr. Roosevelt was an even-handed policy by America toward the European powers. How much to our nation's credit that we alone rejected the shameful Treaty of Versailles!

"Did you know how Germany was tricked at the end of the Great War? She was never beaten! While diplomats and propagandists spoke glibly of peace with honor, peace without victory, they were plotting all the while to betray Germany and seize her rightful belongings. Why, with the Tsar overthrown and the Russian Empire out of the war, Germany could have fought on indefinitely, could have made her way to final triumph. But she was tricked into the false armistice, and when she had voluntarily laid down her arms her traitorous foes leaped upon her defenseless body and ravaged the innocent nation.

"But I can tell you this, Mr. Lovecraft. I can assure you of this. Sooner or later Barbarossa will arise. He may come crowned as an Emperor, he may come as a Dictator risen out of the ranks, or he may be the elected Representative of the People. But sooner or later he will heed the call of his race. All countries speaking the German language will be united under the German flag, just as all people who speak French are united under the tri-colored banner of France!

"I do not believe that the Kaiser will sit contentedly in Doorn watching the flow of the world about him. Do you know what Mussolini said to me about the Kaiser? A man once schooled to rule could never be satisfied with a lesser post, and the Emperor at Doorn is no different from Napoleon at St. Helena! There speaks a wise man, of another fine and noble man whose only error was to believe in the nobility of men of lesser breed. Like the late Mr. Wilson." There was a silence, then Viereck added, "By the way, the *bon mot* concerning President Wilson which you kindly attributed to me, was in fact spoken first by His Majesty, Wilhelm II, when I met with him and the Empress Hermine."

"I think that I understand where we stand, sir. I think that you do as well." Howard put down his cup with a clatter. "I thank you for the invitation to luncheon but I do not truly see much point in continuing this conversation. If you will excuse me."

Before he could rise Viereck had reached forward and grasped him by the arm. "Please, Mr. Lovecraft."

"What more can be achieved, sir? A dozen years ago I wrote that you were a liar and a sneak."

"I was called worse than that. I am concerned with the present and the correction of the errors of the past, not with raking up ancient slights."

"You know that I am loyal to the United States."

"As am I, sir."

"And to the Anglo-Saxon race and the Crown at Windsor;"

"Did you not also write that Briton and Teuton are brothers?"

"At one time, perhaps." Grudgingly, he slid back into the soft cushion of his armchair.

Viereck signaled a waiter. "If I may, Mr. Lovecraft." The waiter disappeared, to return with plates of dolma, skewers of roast lamb and tomatoes and peppers, thick disks of soft, warm bread. Howard watched Viereck for clues as to how to eat the alien food, followed Viereck's lead and commented appreciatively.

"All of this aside," Howard finally said, "I do not quite understand why you wished to meet me. Frankly, Mr. Viereck, it was my hope at first that the Jackson Press was interested in bringing out a volume of my stories. I have held discussions with such houses as Putnam's and Simon & Schuster, but nothing has materialized. It was in hope of gathering such a collection for your company that I first responded to your contact."

"Ah, fantasy, fantasy. No, that isn't quite my intention, I am afraid."

"You have totally abandoned your interest in fiction, then?"

"Not quite," Viereck said. "In fact I've been working on a little book for some time now along with a friend. Perhaps you've heard of Paul Eldridge? No? Well, a good fellow; we've done a slim little thing on the theme of long life. It's in the final stages now and we should have it in our publisher's hands shortly."

He leaned back, patted his rather vivid lips with a linen napkin. "But I do not publish any fantasy, or any fiction at all. At least, not to date. But should other matters work out to mutual satisfaction—" he leaned forward, tapped a tile-inlaid table-top with one fingertip "—I think we might reconsider that policy."

He arched an eyebrow inquisitively at Howard Lovecraft.

Howard slumped in his seat, steepled his fingers beneath his long jaw, closed his eyes to give consideration to Viereck's suggestion. Presumably Viereck wished to hire Howard for some sort of ghosting or revision work— or for an outright assignment—in the field of politics. Could he write pro-German propaganda? Certainly he had despised the Kaiser during the war, but actually his feelings toward the deposed ruler were not as strong as he had implied in his quarrel with Viereck.

In fact, there were strong forces moving in the German republic. And Viereck was not unalterably wedded to the idea of imperial restoration. Could Howard square such work with his own loyalties to the English crown? And what, precisely, was it that Viereck wanted of him?

Somehow, through all the thicket of argument and history, that element had never fully emerged.

Howard opened his eyes and found Viereck gazing patiently at him. "Exactly what is it that you wish of me?" Howard asked.

Before he replied Viereck reached inside his tweed jacket and drew out a silver cigar case. He reached forward and offered a cigar to Howard, who gestured his refusal. Viereck extracted a black cigar, replaced the case, drew a tip-cutter from another pocket and used it, then found a silver flint- and-alcohol cigar lighter in his clothing and lit the cigar. He drew deeply on it, leaned back and exhaled blue smoke toward the velvet plush ceiling of the Turkish Salon.

"I seek merely an honest observer, to meet with a group of important and distinguished personages and to write honestly of those meetings."

Howard Lovecraft shook his head unbelievingly. Viereck was one of the most successful of all journalists in the country. "Why don't you do it yourself? You have the reputation, the outlets and the associations. Besides, I fear that I am growing a trifle too old for such active pursuits as journalism. It's about time for this old gentleman to retire to a warm spot beside a cheering log, a rug upon my lap and a cat beside the hearth." He attempted a smile as he spoke, to suggest that the words were not entirely serious, yet even to his own ears they carried more conviction than he intended them to, or at any rate than he consciously intended.

"But how did you come to select me, Mr. Viereck, in all seriousness."

Now Viereck smiled. "As for your advanced years, I suspect that I am of a more senior vintage than you and it doesn't stop me from pursuing an active career. I think you place yourself in the chimney corner prematurely. Would you try an experiment with me? Let us write our birth-dates on slips of paper and exchange them."

Howard agreed and reached inside his dark woolen suit jacket for the trusty black Waterman he always carried, and for the small spiral pad that he used to keep stray notions for stories until he could reach home and transfer the notes to his commonplace book. He carefully wrote

August 20, 1890, on a corner of the top sheet, creased and tore it off and folded it.

Simultaneously Viereck drew a silver-filigreed Schaeffer and monogrammed alligator notebook from inside his tweed jacket. Howard caught a glimpse of Viereck's motion as he made his own. Viereck jotted a few figures and they exchanged slips. Howard read the numbers *31-12-84,* frowned for a moment in puzzlement, then said, "Ah, the European fashion. For a moment I wondered what the thirty-first month was called." They both laughed. "Yes, you are correct, of course. By nearly six years. But that does not explain your selection of my humble self for this prospective assignment."

Viereck tapped the ash from his cigar, placed it carefully on the edge of a standing ash-tray provided by the management of the Salon. He leaned forward, gazing with utmost seriousness through his tortoiseshell spectacles, a single curl of his luxuriant hair fallen carelessly on his brow.

"Let me be utterly frank about this, Mr. Lovecraft. For most of my adult life I have devoted the greater part of my energies to the task of explaining the cause and the nature of the German nation to the American. I have been accused of the most vile crimes and dishonorable actions. During the Great War, when I and my family were residing at my wife's ancestral home in Mount Vernon, I was forced by hostile mobs to leave that city and return to live in Manhattan, and was able for some months to see my wife and sons only by sneaking back to Mount Vernon under cover of darkness and sneaking away again before dawn the following morning.

"I have been vilified, harassed and threatened. For all that I am widely published and widely read, my words are greeted in too many quarters with suspicion. My objectivity in the matter of America's position and Europe's future is highly suspect.

"What I need is a man of high intellect and elegance of expression—I do not flatter you but merely state the truth to say that you are that man—whose heritage is Old American and whose ancestry is Anglo-Saxon. I am European-born and of German ancestry, you see, and my credentials are thus shadowed. Yours, sir, are impeccable. Does that answer your question adequately?"

"And your intention? Just what future do you propose for the European nations?"

Viereck waved one hand airily, with the other retrieving his smoldering cigar. Before he answered he puffed its gray tip back to a reddish glow. "The Versailles agreements must be revised. The question of German reparations must be settled once and forever. Lost territories must be restored. The threat of *Bolshevist* expansion must be met. I visited Soviet Russia, you know, and attempted to secure an audience with Lenin, who was then still living, or with Trotzky, or at least with Premier Rykoff. I, who have exchanged letters and who have visited the crowned heads and sash-decorated Presidents of nations, was fobbed off onto some petty officials."

He leaned back expansively. "Within the United States there must also be reform, but domestic improvements go hand-in-hand with correctives to the world order. There are several groups working for reform within this country and in the world order. There is no formal alliance among them, but progressive-minded Americans of many classes and movements maintain an informal alliance. I would like you to attend a small social gathering of a few such persons. You will be under no obligation, of course. Will you attend? Perhaps an informal gathering at my home one evening soon."

It surely seemed a harmless investigation. Howard agreed; he shook hands with Viereck as they left the Waldorf, then turned his steps downtown as he embarked on a tour of book-scouting at the shops and stalls of lower Fourth Avenue.

~ ~ ~ ~ ~

Back at the Longs' for dinner Howard received a message from Vincent Starrett. Starrett had telephoned during the afternoon and left the number of a friend through whom Howard could reach him.

Howard lifted the earpiece of the telephone and gave Central the number; when the call was answered he identified himself and asked if the other party was indeed Vincent Starrett.

"No, this is Alex Laing, Vincent's host. I'll call him to the phone."

Starrett replaced Laing, his voice flatter, drier, with a Midwesterner's steadiness that contrasted with Laing's New York stridency and Howard Lovecraft's own mild New England tone and his carefully cultivated Briticisms. Starrett was staying with Laing for a few days before moving on to Beechhurst and his writing project. He'd taken a leave of absence from newspapering in Chicago and didn't know when (if ever) he'd go back to it, but his past record of occupational ventures into the writing of poetry, fiction and criticism, into editing and publishing, had always led back to the city room and, he expected, would do so again.

Laing's place was an apartment in the Studio Building on West 10th Street. Howard agreed to join Starrett and Laing for the evening.

Hesitantly he interrupted young Belknapius's concentration on a poem he was worrying into shape (it was called "The White People" and would appear in *Weird Tales* the following November). Would the child care to join his grandpa on the ride downtown and the visit with Starrett and Laing? Belknapius admitted to being sorely tempted but insisted that "The White People" had to be finely tuned to pass Pharnabus's scrutiny, and work deferred merely piled up until it overwhelmed the striver. Thus: Howard was to express Belknap Long's regrets to the others.

He took a leisurely ride downtown, shivering slightly even in the interior of the streetcar, disembarked at 10th Street and looked for the number he'd been given.

The Studio Building was more modern than Howard really cared for, its brick exterior tending slightly to Spartan simplicity, yet it was designed with a certain grace and dignity that spoke well of its makers. Howard rang the apartment buzzer and was greeted at the foyer door by Alex Laing and Vincent Starrett.

The former was a short, dynamic man whose movements were as vigorous, almost to the point of abruptness, as his speech. He was a native New Yorker, tough and bright.

Starrett was tall, broad-shouldered, with a classic profile and a great pompadour of dark hair that glistened beneath the ceiling light. His handclasp was hearty; he gave the impression of a northern bear.

The three men were nearly of an age.

Howard opened the conversation. "You and I have a great deal to discuss, Vincentius. I want to hear all about Bairdy and Pharnabus and Joe Henneberger, what's happening in Chicago and what your plans are for this *magnum opus* you're undertaking. But first, Mr. Laing, I wonder if I might prevail upon you to detail some of the history of this remarkable building. It is one of the more interesting structures I've seen of late."

"Ah, Alex," Starrett interjected, "Howard is a great student of antiquities and he positively dotes on architecture. I've had letters from him thousands of words in length detailing the fanlight design and gambrel roofs of colonial survivors in Pennsylvania and Maryland."

Lovecraft gestured deprecatingly. "I'm hardly the student that Vincent makes me out. But I do have an interest in the design of buildings. I trust you know something of this one's history."

"A bit."

"I should place its construction at the late 1850s. Am I correct? That's really after my period, I much prefer the eighteenth century to the nineteenth."

Laing's laugh resembled the bark of a husky. "I'm not much on that kind of stuff but the landlord gives out brochures with your lease. Let me see if I can dig one up."

He rummaged through a tall chiffonier, emerged with a tattered pamphlet printed on heavy, yellowish stock. "Here you go."

Howard caught the pamphlet in midair, frowned at the almost roughhouse behavior of Laing. He concentrated on the slim pages, shook off an offer of refreshment without speaking. After a few moments he looked up, sparkling-eyed. "Ah-*hah!* Listen to this! Vincent, do you know anything about this building? No? Then, it was designed by Richard Morris Hunt, best known for the Vanderbilt mansions in the East 50s. Ah, vulgar and gingerbready, those. This building has far more to recommend it. The Studio Building has been a headquarters for the arts and literature since its construction. John LaFarge and Winslow Homer both lived in this building.

"I congratulate you on your place of residence, Mr. Laing."

Richard A. Lupoff

"You want that thing?" Laing indicated the landlord's brochure still held by Howard. "Keep it. I don't need the thing!"

Howard thanked him and slipped the brochure into a pocket.

"Listen, if nobody wants any refreshments here, let's get out and see a few sights before they roll up the sidewalk. Okay, Charley? Lovecraft?"

They strolled from the Studio Building to Seventh Avenue, then turned down until they came to an Italian restaurant just off Sheridan Square. Outside the restaurant a battered black alley cat approached to beg for food. Howard knelt on the sidewalk and offered the cat a sniff of his hand. "Sorry, pussy, I have nothing for you. Wait around, though, I'll bring you a snack afterwards."

The cat meowed and brushed Howard's knee, then retreated into the shadows.

Inside the restaurant they were approached by a tuxedoed *maitre d'*. Alex, in the lead, reached into his pocket, then shook hands with the captain. "This way, Mr. Laing." They trooped past couples and groups at red-checkered tables, through a curtained arch and into a second dining room virtually identical to the first.

When the waiter approached Laing drew him down to the table and told him something in a low voice, then they all ordered dinner. Over antipasto Howard asked Starrett for a report on the Chicago crowd.

"You're the only man I know who could ask that and not expect to hear about Scarface Al Capone, Torrio, Dion O'Banion and the rest of that crew!"

"You're speaking of the rum-runners and other criminal types. I realize that your professional associations require familiarity with such but I would much prefer to see them shipped back to Sicily or County Cork. Of course I was seeking information on the *Weird Tales* circle."

Starrett reached for a celery stalk, studied it abstractedly for a moment, then crunched off the last inch or so and spoke around it .

"You know, Howard, I've always been in sympathy with that magazine, but I just don't believe there's enough of a following for that kind of material to support it. At least, not more than just barely. Joe Henneberger takes a lot of harsh commentary but the miracle is not in his paying lit-

48

tle and late—it's in his meeting his bills at all! He and Wright make sacrifices to keep that magazine alive."

"I have mixed feelings about Brother Pharnabus, Vincent. I am somewhat of a conservative old codger myself, of course."

"One had noticed," Starrett smiled.

"But that fellow will not run a story that has the least tincture of innovation in it. He seems terrified of using anything not thoroughly familiar to his readers."

"Makes innovation seem impossible, eh?"

"Ah, but it is not! A few of us in the circle have found a way to fool Brother Pharnabus!"

"Are you sure you want to mention this in the presence of Alex?"

Howard turned toward Laing. "Don't worry, pal," Laing snapped. Before Lovecraft could resume, Laing signaled to a waiter and in a moment the remnants of the antipasto were cleared away and a steaming tureen of minestrone was placed on the table. "I'll be the daddy," Laing said, ladling the soup into bowls for them.

Howard said, "I just wouldn't want this to get back to Pharnabus. The trick is simple. You just take your returned manuscript and wait for six months, then send it back to Farnie with a note saying you've made the changes he recommended and you agree with him that they add greatly to the story's merit."

"What changes?" Starrett asked.

"No changes! But now that he's seeing the story a second time Farnie doesn't have to contend with something he's never encountered before and he can judge it on its merits!"

Starrett and Laing burst into laughter. "Have you actually done that to him?" Laing demanded.

"Oh yes. He took 'The Cats of Ulthar' that way, and 'The Outsider,' and 'The Music of Erich Zann.' I was heartbroken when he returned 'Erich Zann' the first time. When I sent it back he bought it."

"Good for you, Lovecraft!" Laing slapped him on the shoulder. "I'll have to watch for that trick where I work!"

Lovecraft's face clouded. "I should have asked, sir. I did not realize that you were a literary man yourself."

Starrett said, "I should have mentioned that, Howard. Alex works for a publisher down on Broadway."

"Experimenter Publishing," Laing amplified. "You know them? Nice line of magazines, *Science and Invention, French Humor. . . .*"

"What's that?" Starrett's eyes twinkled.

"Risqué stuff like 'Heavens! Some port wine on my dress! How can I take it off?' 'Right there. . .on the side. . .those little hooks.'"

Starrett and Laing burst into laughter. When they had subsided, Howard Lovecraft asked if that was all the company produced.

"Oh, no," Laing paused to break a chunk of bread off a hard-crusted loaf, "we do other stuff. A lot of radio stuff, the old Dutchman who runs the outfit loves science. And some magic books. And he has something that he calls *Amazing Stories.* Got a thousand year old man to edit it for him. I don't have much to do with it but I was looking at some copy the other day, we got in a script from your Chicago buddy Ed Burroughs that you wouldn't believe, Charley! Green men and egg-laying women and a weird doctor cutting off people's skulls and swapping their brains around!"

"Hah! Good old Ed. You know, he doesn't live in Chicago any longer. Moved to the west coast years ago. Nice enough fellow, I was sorry to see him leave. But he said his family couldn't take the winters. Say, maybe that would be an alternate market for you, Howard. You really shouldn't be so dependent on *Weird Tales,* you know. One disaster and you'd have nowhere left so send your yarns."

"Sure, Lovecraft. Send over anything you got. I don't buy for the science book but I'll see that your stuff goes right."

Howard agreed to consider the matter.

Their *entrees* arrived, Howard's a mound of spaghetti drenched in tomato sauce and topped with a single gigantic meatball. He watched the waiter deftly place other dishes in front of Alex Laing and Charles Vincent Starrett, then produce a wicker-covered bottle, uncork it, and present a tiny portion for Laing to sample.

"Is that—" Howard half-asked as the waiter, having poured three glasses of dark-red fluid, disappeared.

"Chianti. Right offa the boat."

"But—what about the law?"

Starrett and Laing laughed.

"To printer's ink and vintner's brew, two nobler fluids ne'er joined their flow." Starrett touched his glass to Howard's and Laing's. He and Laing sipped, commented favorably and began to dine.

Howard Lovecraft, still holding his glass suspiciously before him, sniffed once at the dark wine, took a tiny sip and put the glass down. He sampled his spaghetti—it was excellent—and took a second, slightly larger, sip of the Chianti.

Three bottles later they had finished their *entrees.* For dessert Howard had two portions of canoli with his black, sweet espresso. On the way out he took a sliver of meatball, carefully wrapped in a napkin, for his battered friend of the sidewalk.

Laing led the way, Howard swaying slightly, eastward on Eighth Street. Vincent Starrett diverted their progress down the steps of a cellar bookshop whose light still burned and he and Howard had a good browse—the only purchase was a clean *Mystery of the Yellow Room* that Vincent picked up for twenty cents. "Ben Abramson offered me this Leroux for 85 cents," Starrett triumphed. "I told him it wasn't worth it and he said I'd never do better! I'll have to write to the old coot about this! It's the first and as nice a copy as I've seen. Of course, they don't make books the way they used to."

"I don't understand you first edition collectors," Howard commented. Somehow, he found his speech a trifle slurred and his tongue a bit clumsy but his thoughts were as sharp as ever. "I should think that a last edition would be more significant than a first. The author's final word, as it were."

"Interesting thought," Starrett replied. "But no one understands a collector except another collector anyhow. Isn't that right, Alex?"

Laing said, "Come on, let's find a speak."

In the next block Laing stopped and knocked on a residential door. It opened a crack, then shut and opened again, completely. He led the way into a grimy corridor, then through another door that led into a brightly lighted room where a small orchestra played and *chic* couples, the women in bobbed hair and short skirts, flung themselves around a dance floor.

At one side of the room stood a polished bar of dark wood, a brass rail a few inches off the floor in front of it, a mirrored wall behind it. A hearty fellow in a brass-buttoned red jacket presided.

Howard Lovecraft felt himself overcome by an impulse and commanded, "Coachman, whip up the team and let us go!"

The man grinned and approached the three newcomers. Vincent Starrett said "Let me have a martini. Don't bruise the gin." Laing asked for something called a boilermaker.

After a lengthy silence Howard realized that the bartender was looking at him expectantly. He turned to Starrett, then to Laing, then said, "Ah, the same for me."

"The same what?" the bartender asked.

"The same as my companions," Howard explained.

The bartender shrugged and turned away.

"You gonna drink a martooni *and* a boilermaker?" Alex Laing asked Howard.

"I've never tried either. I thought it would be a good way to discover which I prefer."

Alex Laing glanced past Howard at Charles Vincent Starrett who was studiously examining his image in the mirror. "O-h-h," Laing nodded.

Later Howard had vague recollections of being lifted by Starrett on one side and Laing on the other, of being placed in the back seat of *a* taxi, and of being helped into the Longs' apartment at 100th Street. The next morning he blinked once and shut his eyes again for the next six hours. When he did get up he couldn't find his hat, his good gray fedora that he'd owned for years, and he was heartbroken at the loss.

CHAPTER FOUR:

THE QUIET HOURS OF THE NIGHT

BEFORE HOWARD returned to Providence he told his friend Belknapius about his extended interview with Viereck, the brief session at the Jackson Press office on 42nd Street and the longer dialogue at the Waldorf. Long sat listening attentively, chewing on the stem of a cold pipe, grinning at Howard's narrative.

"You didn't spring across the table and throttle the fellow with your bare hands, at least. Back during the Great War you might have, you know. I remember times when even the mention of Irish separatism, no less the Kaiser, could bring you to a rage."

"Viereck seemed actually to be a fairly decent person, grandson. I still cannot go along with his ideas of Pan-Germanism, of course. And as for the Kaiser, and that painter fellow with his so-called National Socialism—"

"I'm aware that socialism is anathema to you," Long interjected.

"That's one thing for which we can thank Mr. Viereck. He is the only man I know who has succeeded in getting a definition of National Socialism out of Herr Hitler. Did I ever mention it to you, or did you chance to see his article about the interview he did with Adolf in Munich a few years ago? No? A very odd thing. He says that he uses the term to mean the science dealing with the common weal. It has nothing to do with Marxism—in his view, of course. What he winds up with is something like Mussolini's fascism. Hitler also has some interesting racial theories. I think he's rather a crude fellow, it seems unlikely that a people like the Germans would ever place such a man in power. But he has some worthwhile ideas."

"But what, specifically, does Viereck want you to do, Howard?" Long glanced at Howard expectantly. "And—do you know what he meant by that remark about his connection with the Hohenzollerns?"

"To reply to your questions in inverse sequence—I do not know what his remark meant. I have a sneaking suspicion that he may have been referring to some sort of left-handed blood-tie, if you take my meaning, sonny.

"Regarding what he wants me to do, it would apparently be some sort of journalistic task. He seems impressed by my Old American credentials. Nice to encounter someone who appreciates the value of deep-sunk roots and lengthy blood-lines. Sometimes I find myself wondering if everyone in America did not just limp down the gangplank from a steerage hold except for thee and me, Belknapius. And occasionally I have my doubts about thee!"

They had a good laugh at that.

"At any rate, we left it rather inconclusive. I am invited to a gathering, date indeterminate as yet, to meet the people Viereck admires. Beyond that, we shall simply have to see.

"And so, with grateful thanks for your solicitous hospitality, I shall hie myself to 125th Street and board the next homeward-bound iron horse. Providence calleth. As does my desk and my work!"

He was home in time for a late repast with his two aunts. Afterwards he read his accumulated mail and examined his copy of the February *Weird Tales,* the first sign of which had been its appearance in the Providence station on his way home. Strange is the way of publishing!

The cover illustration was a truly distressing work featuring a lurid female figure, and the only story of particular interest was "The Man Who Cast No Shadow," one of those Jules de Grandin concoctions of Seabury Quinn's. It was really amazing, they were foolish little stories, clumsily crafted, shallowly characterized, dealing with the most hackneyed themes of vampirism, lycanthropy, walking mummies and the like—yet they did possess an undeniable naïve charm all their own.

Howard pored through the rest of the issue, finally examining the letters from readers featured in the Eyrie. He was delighted at the suggestion of one Sophie Wenzel Ellis of Little Rock, Arkansas. "Why do you not select a group of your best stories and issue them in book form?" asked Reader Ellis. "I should like to see you publish more stories of the sort which is exquisitely fanciful, such as 'The Woman of the Wood' by Merritt, 'The Moon Bog' and 'The Outsider' by Lovecraft, and 'The Dreamer of Atlanaat' by Price."

Now there was company in which he would take pleasure! He had admired Merritt for years, ever since encountering his short story "Through the Dragon Glass" in the *All-Story Weekly* a decade before, and his fine novel *The Moon Pool* (a well read but tenderly preserved first edition of which still graced Howard's shelf) two years later. As for Ed Price—why, there was as tough and vinegary a youngster as Howard had encountered in his life. And a good craftsman, too, still learning his trade, improving with each passing year.

Howard was so elated by the Ellis letter that he couldn't contain himself. His aunts had retired for the night so there was no one about the Barnes Street apartment he could talk with, consequently he fortified himself with a pot of fresh coffee, bundled into his warmest clothing and essayed out into the February night for a walking tour.

Even though the air was cold he felt secure, at home in his own city. He'd wrapped a scarf around his head to replace the lost fedora, and he was able to stay reasonably warm, free of the numbing lethargy that overcame him when the temperature dropped too far. He did miss the fedora, though. If ever there was a strong argument for the enforcement of prohibition, Howard's unhappy experience in New York provided it. How could a gentleman maintain any semblance of decorum when his tongue was clumsy, his vision fuzzy, his equilibrium destroyed by alcohol!

He drew the scarf, an old gray woolen veteran, closer over his ears, shoved his hands deep into overcoat pockets and made his way down Barnes Street to Prospect, then turned left and headed through the still New England night, a solitary traveler through the heart of his most loved hours. At Angell Street he turned again, walking slowly by moon and starlight. There were no houses still illuminated at this hour, the sparsely distributed streetlamps did not burn so late either, and no automobile headlamps moved through the quiet section at this nocturnal hour.

The only sounds were the occasional barkings of dogs, yowls of alley-cats; Howard strained his ears in hopes of detecting the purl of the Seekonk but it was as yet too far distant.

Angell Street sloped upward as far as the highest point of College Hill, then fell away again toward the Seekonk and East Providence beyond.

Howard stopped at the sight of two blazing orbs, spoke softly and was rewarded by their wary approach. He crouched on the sidewalk and called softly until the cat, deciding that he was at least provisionally trustworthy, advanced to within arm's reach. It was a big black tom, veteran of many an alley scuffle, and like most felines of its ilk, almost pathetically affectionate when greeted by a truly sympathetic human being. Howard stroked the cat, earning a low purr as his reward.

Oh, how this fellow reminded him of Nigger-man, the dear companion of his boyhood! Nigger-man had been a truer friend to Howard than any contemporary, or for that matter, than any member even of his family with the possible exception of his Grandfather Phillips. He'd had his playmates about the streets of College Hill, but he'd always been a shy child, and in at best irregular health. But he'd known every tom and tabby for blocks around, and been friend of them all.

He gave the black tom a parting scratch behind the ears and continued along Angell, savoring the stillness of the Providence night. Finally he halted before a tall wooden house, studying the angles of the pitched roof, the brick chimney, the rising lawn and covered porch and bay windows. He stood, one hand on the wooden picket fence that surrounded the lawn and trees and house; Howard gazed upward, unmoving.

It was the house where he had spent the days of his childhood, the first home that he could remember. Here he had his only recollections of his father, Winfield Scott Lovecraft, dressed in dark outfit and gleaming buttons, looking so splendid that even now, nearly thirty years after his death, Howard could visualize his father as he sat in his favorite chair.

But his father had suffered from intermittent paralysis, from growing madness, perhaps—Howard shuddered at the thought, but could not put it from his mind for all his efforts to do so—from syphilis. Winfield had been hospitalized and had died. And some twenty years later Howard's mother had followed her husband, to the same asylum and finally to the same fate.

He shuddered.

It had been his grandfather who had been the light and the inspiration of his boyhood, his grandfather who had helped him to overcome his fear of darkness (to the point where he lived, as a matter of choice, mostly by night), who had inspired his love of the fantastic, the exotic, the bizarre.

Whipple Phillips had filled the Angell Street house with wondrous books, the works of Anne Radcliffe, Monk Lewis, Charles Maturin; he provided young Howard with endless hours of deliciously terrifying ghost stories and had encouraged his childhood reading of Arabian Nights, of the tales of the brothers Grimm and of Nathaniel Hawthorn.

How the family fortunes had fallen, to the point where Howard and his surviving aunts had to make do with a rented apartment instead of the splendid house before which he now stood, living on their tiny legacy and his own small literary earnings!

His musings were interrupted by a soft but persistent brushing against his leg. He looked down and again those eyes blazed up at him. The tom had followed him and was demanding further homage.

"Ah, Nigger-man," Howard whispered, "if only I had you back. Here is our home and all." He lifted the cat and held it close to his face, petting and cooing to it in a display of tenderness he would never have made before human witnesses. "Nigger-man, are you really back from that land where go all who depart the mortal plane? Have you come back to haunt your old house and your old friend?

"You'll not find me here at Angell Street very often, and pets are unwelcome at Barnes. It's a cruel world to which you've returned, dear Nigger-man."

Regretfully ho placed the cat on the cement and turned back. He had thought to continue along Angell Street to Blackstone Park, to stand at the edge of Narragansett Boat Club and gaze into the black waters of the Seekonk, but the chill of the February night was penetrating his garments and Howard instead returned to his home and the warmth of his bed.

His last thought before falling asleep was that he would set out tomorrow to find a replacement for his lost fedora; from that thought his mind wandered into the half-asleep world of fantastic shapes and images he had known since childhood, and thence into deeper slumber and even wilder dreams from which he wakened hours later, unrested.

He awakened to the sight of his aunt Lillian hovering over him, concerned. "You were out very late, Howard. I heard you return to the house. Was there anything wrong?"

He shook his head, explained that it was merely a nocturnal stroll. He mentioned meeting the reincarnated Nigger-man and their visit to Angell Street.

Aunt Lillian said that she would prepare some breakfast while Howard shaved and dressed.

After eating, Howard examined the day's mail. Greatest interest lay in letters from W. Paul Cook, Clark Ashton Smith (or Klarkash-ton, as he signed his letters), and from Howard's wife Sonia.

Cook's missive contained cheering and exciting news. The wizard of Athol had decided definitely to publish a book of Howard Lovecraft's authorship! He wished to use "The Shunned House," and hoped to obtain for the volume an introduction by Howard's friend and protégé Belknap Long. Howard found the idea of an introduction for "The Shunned House" almost ludicrous. It was only a short story! Yet, in that case making it a book was a similarly foolish project, and Cook was willing to do it. An introduction would help it to bulk up. Well, everything balanced out sooner or later.

Howard determined to send Cook an immediate reply, more in demonstration of his enthusiasm for the project than in acceptance of Cook's willingness to do the book. That, Cook had received from Howard long ago. But Cook also sought information on Howard's completion of his final revisions to the proofs of "Supernatural Horror in Literature." *The Recluse* was well along, Cook was eager to receive Howard's final corrections so he could assemble the issue, and time was fleeting. Howard vowed to finish up the task as quickly as he could.

He even toyed with the idea of adding sections on several contemporary writers, Smith, his own protégé Belknapius, perhaps even George Sylvester Viereck, the last if only for the sake of *The House of the Vampire*. It was a vexing problem and the novel was a vexing book. Its excellence was unquestioned, but there hung over it an indefinable air of decadence, just as there did over Viereck himself.

And here was Howard back once more pondering the problem of Viereck's approach to him. Cook's determination to issue Lovecraft's book made Howard feel more independent in his potential dealing with Viereck. The eventual Jackson Press collection of his stories no longer appeared a lone hope of being "booked." But Howard did not wish to abandon the possibility, either. Well, he would not pursue the matter with Viereck, but if Viereck contacted him again he would go along as far as the suggested meeting.

Meanwhile he turned to the letter from Klarkash-ton. Smith was still distressed by the suicide of his mentor George Sterling despite Howard's having suggested that a man might know when life had reached a point of burdensomeness and redundancy. It was all well and good to rationalize over such matters, Smith said, but when a dear friend, sponsor, teacher departs with such sudden and premature decisiveness it is hard to accept.

Smith went on about a mutual friend, the young writer Wandrei, waxing joyous over Wandrei's prose. This was an enthusiasm that Howard could share, and had expressed to Wright in hopes of gaining an outlet for Wandrei's own stories. The youngster was still learning, of course, but he was dedicated and talented and had the potential to become a worthwhile writer, not a mere hack like all too many of the *Weird Tales* authors.

Howard took paper and pen and began to compose a reply to Smith, the latter perched far away atop his mountain in northern California, a strange hermit-like being. Howard mentioned his own work on "Supernatural Horror" and the stories he had recently attempted, encouraged Smith to produce more of his own admirable efforts, and signed his missive in the fashion of his childhood alter-ego and occasionally-summoned fictional creation, ABDUL ALHAZRED.

Finally he unsealed the envelope that bore the return indicia of his wife, Sonia Greene Lovecraft. She had returned from her own unsuccessful sojourn in the Midwest, and was ensconced once again in Brooklyn, the location of their joint domicile of past years.

Howard poured himself a fresh cup of coffee and adjusted his rimless glasses before reading the letter. He gazed out the window of his study, assured himself that he was undisturbed in the room, then slumped down into his chair and began to read.

"My Dear Howard," the letter began, "I must write to tell you of a chance meeting the other day as I was coming out of Wanamaker's on Fourteenth Street. Whom should I meet but our almost-neighbor Theo Weiss. He was as dapper and dashing as ever, having been in Wanamaker's to check out the latest fashions, and he recognized me at once from the occasion upon which we were introduced by his late brother Ehrich.

"Theo is very busy and prosperous, having taken over much of the paraphernalia and the booming that Ehrich had always done so well. He is still not fully recovered from the tragic loss of his dear brother, but is carrying on well, and is doing his all to sustain poor Bess in addition to maintaining his own obligations.

"Our talk turned naturally to you, dear Howard, and to the work you had done for Ehrich. Theo reminded me that Ehrich had been so pleased with your work, and wished you to continue to serve as his amanuensis and 'ghost.' Theo said that Bess told him, one of the letters that Ehrich wrote from his very death-bed in Detroit was an invitation to you to join him for part of his tour (which he, of course, did not realize even then was to be his farewell tour!), and to assist him in preparing a series of articles exposing spiritualistic fakes. Ehrich knew that you had as low regard for the ghoulish practitioners who prey upon the bereaved and the innocent, as he himself possessed.

"The world suffered a great loss last Halloween!

"But of immediate concern, Howard darling, is that Theo expressed his strong desire to see you the next time you should be in New York, and I will add to his invitation my own wishes to see you again. As you know, my situation in Providence was an untenable one. I do not blame your two aunts for the unfortunate outcome, but you must also understand my own circumstances. Your aunts, reared in the aristocratic tradition, may consider 'trade' beneath their standing, and the thought of a daughter-in-law (or niece-in-law) operating a millinery business from their very house must have been unacceptable to them.

"But I am of humbler stock, as you know, Howard dear, and I must make my way in the world as I can. Thus, the impasse which developed with Mrs. Gamwell and Mrs. Clark. I have never blamed your aunts for being different from myself, but I must say that I think they always blamed me for being different from them.

"But if I cannot live in Providence, Howard, you can still live in New York any time you choose to do so. Or if you prefer to maintain your home in Providence, at the very least, please pay me a call when you visit New York. My home is, as ever, yours, as I am still, my darling Howard, your wife!

"I think you would enjoy seeing and hearing the new radiola-panatrope I have had installed in my living room. It is a fully customized system with a Mohawk chassis, Kellogg tubes, a lovely Liberty speaker and Balkite power unit. The machine is electrified, and picks up broadcasts from all over the country. The other night I was listening to WJAR broadcasting from Providence, and could not help feeling closer to you, Howard, and yet missing you terribly.

"Howard, please do not keep yourself from me all the time. Remember that I am still your wife!"

Howard read the familiar signature, folded the letter and placed it in a drawer, sighing. If he intended to replace the missing fedora today there would be no time for work or for correspondence before his expedition. Well, such activities were best performed during the quiet hours of the night anyway. He bundled into warm clothing, wrapped a woolen scarf once more around his head, and took the streetcar down College Hill to the center of Providence.

He entered the Outlet Company, found the gentlemen's hats department, and asked a salesman to show him a fedora, size 7, in dark gray, not too expensive. By the store's closing time he had narrowed the choice to three hats. When the chimes sounded and the salesman pointed out to him that the store was about to shut, Howard rejected one of the hats on the basis of a too-narrow brim, one as being too light in shade, and settled on the remaining one.

Before boarding the car to return to Barnes Street he stopped at the Old Corner bookstore and examined their stock of gothic and fantastic volumes. Sadly he patted the spines of a few old friends—books from his personal library which he had reluctantly parted with at the time of his mother's death six years earlier. If ever the family fortune revived, he would retrieve as many of his old books as could still be located, and make a start at recreating the family library with its thousands of volumes, that had departed along with the Angell Street house.

After dinner he wrote letters for several hours, looked at "Supernatural Horror in Literature" and marked a few minor changes, then pocketed some scraps of beef and went for his nocturnal stroll, following the familiar Barnes-Prospect-Angell route. His feline co-conspirator, the reincarnated Nigger-man, joined him as he turned from Prospect onto Angell and accompanied him to the old house. There Howard unwrapped the bits of food he had brought along and spread them carefully on a scrap of *Providence Bulletin*. Nigger-man set to with an enthusiastic word (or what must have been a word in the language of the felidae), purred as he dined and fastidiously washed paws and whiskers at the completion of his midnight feast.

Soon the nocturnal walks, the meetings with Nigger-man and the midnight repasts at Angell Street became a fixed pattern in Howard's life, broken only when the weather was unusually cold, or when a fresh snow or freezing winter rain was falling. Then Howard would remain beside the heat register in his den at Barnes Street, worrying about his friend but unable to offer succor.

Sometimes he would turn back after the rendezvous with Nigger-man, others he would continue on to the Boat Club, to Narragansett Park, or on a particularly pleasant night, to the Swan Point Cemetery where lay Phillipses and Lovecrafts in the ancient soil above the banks of the ice-choked Seekonk.

At times, as he passed Angell Street on his way home the spirits of the past would rise and accompany him. He could see himself riding in a polished carriage with his mother, the beautiful Susie, and his grandfather Phillips,

Grandfather spinning endless tales of glittering wonders while a liveried Negro coachman whipped up the team. The coach would pull in at the grand gate as Howard stood, hands plunged in pockets against the night's chill. A footman would dismount and help Miss Susie, young Howard with his shining curls, and hearty Grandfather to dismount. Then, laughing and joking the while, they would make their way into the big house while the coachman and the footman tended to the needs of the horses and the cleaning of the carriage against their next use of it.

On such a night the Howard Lovecraft of 1927 would bid farewell to the ghostly Howard of thirty years ago. He would return to his work at Barnes Street, leaving behind Nigger-man to tend to his own catly occupations for another twenty-four hours. Then, at Barnes Street, at his desk, Howard would work on whatever project happened to be in hand; just now it was an ambitious undertaking, nothing less than a novel, albeit a somewhat short one, called *The Case of Charles Dexter Ward.*

Howard was of two minds with regard to the past. In one context he was a passionate antiquarian, feeling that he had been born after his time. He affected eighteenth century styles of spelling and prose, maintaining now that civilization had reached its highest point in the days of the Georges, its downward course beginning with the mindless blunders of the third George and the resulting, ill-considered rebellion of the American colonies. Then again he would revise that opinion and maintain that the peak had been reached two centuries earlier, during the reign of the great Elizabeth; or yet again, that the supreme moments of human experience had been those of the classic Grecian era with their cool rationality, their appreciation of the intellect and the importance of the arts.

Then his mind would span the cosmic eons of time and the overwhelming horrors of primal chaos would come crashing down to eradicate any illusion of the possibility that order, rationality, dignity could endure as other than ephemeral happenstances in the blind turning of the universe. Then the mind would recoil, shuddering in despair.

Such was the theme of *Charles Dexter Ward,* a tale in which the malevolent forces of antiquity reached down through the rolling centuries to seize control of the present from those hopeless mortals inhabiting the earth. This was a theme that Howard used over and over, the cosmic horror of a malign entity or a blind force reaching through time and space to crush before it helpless man. Such was the theme of "The Colour Out of Space," and such was the theme of still another tale that he'd toyed with but not yet undertaken, a sequel to the great Poe's *Narrative of A. Gordon Pym,* or if not exactly a sequel then a tale of some associational nature, that would go beyond the staggering but tantalizing climax of Poe's work, that would explain the region beyond that where shrouded giants and snowy-plumed birds guarded the cryptic cataract of mist.

But for now he concentrated on *Charles Dexter Ward,* kept up his correspondence as best he could, maintained his contacts with amateur journalism—the proofs of "Supernatural Horror in Literature" were at last, *mirabile dictu,* corrected and returned to Cook—kept up his reading, and awaited new developments from the New York situation, where neither Starrett nor Alex Laing nor George Sylvester Viereck had bothered, of late, to make contact with him.

CHAPTER FIVE:

NIGGER-MAN AND YALLER GAL

THE MARCH *Weird Tales* featured another in its series of lurid covers by the oddly named C. C. Senf. As usual there was a strange, deformed male figure—in this case, a grotesque, macrocephalic dwarf—and as usual he was menacing a largely unclad female, in this case a lovely creature most of whose clothes had been torn away by brambles. Howard had seen a photograph of Senf posed with editor Farnsworth Wright and could understand the basis of Senf's strange portraits. He was an odd-looking, dwarf-like man himself; posed beside the towering Wright he had looked ludicrous. He might do Howard's own fictional painter, the tragic Richard Upton Pickman, one better. He not only painted his grotesques from life, he made them self-portraits!

And Farnie Wright had already accepted "Pickman's Model" for use in *Weird Tales!* Howard shook his head at the prospect, hoping that Senf would not be distressed by the yarn.

Meanwhile, the current issue contained Howard's "The White Ship," one of his older, Dunsanian efforts, but still a respectable piece, he believed. There was no artwork with it—more likely a blessing than a curse, that!—and Wright's blurb was for once not in lurid bad taste. "He sailed into the boundless sea," Howard read of his own story, "beyond the boundaries of fabled Cathuria, and strange was his voyage."

But the pleasure of the issue lay in the Eyrie where readers' missives continued to praise Howard's contributions. This time a Helmuth Stiller of Milwaukee had written, " 'The Horror at Red Hook' by H. P. Lovecraft is in my opinion the best in the January issue. . .You can never give me too many of Lovecraft's yarns."

There was a satisfaction in that, indeed.

The first break in Howard's increasingly comfortable routine came early in March. Winter had not relinquished its grip on the Hew England coast, but occasional breezes from the south carried a hint of warmth to follow; Howard's friend Nigger-man had been joined by a lovely green-eyed, orange-coated female whom Howard dubbed Yaller Gal. Yaller Gal would wait patiently when Howard distributed the evening's scraps on the sheet of newspaper he brought them in; Nigger-man would advance, seize the largest morsel in oversized yellowish fangs, then Yaller Gal would sniff daintily at the rest of the night's offering and choose whatever tasty bit pleased her fancy.

The phantom carriage rolled most nights, and on occasion Howard encountered the spirits of seventeenth and eighteenth-century Rhode Islanders when he reached the Swan Point Cemetery at the eastern extreme of Angell Street.

He kept abreast of world affairs through the pages of the Providence papers, an occasional copy of a daily imported from Boston or New York, or the new weekly review *Time*.

The tenth of March was an unusually warm day, the afternoon hours (the first that Howard observed) were sunny and the air was filled with the odors of new life pushing up from the earth, green buds springing from the limbs of the elms, oaks and maples that lined the streets on College Hill.

The postman's whistle signaled the afternoon delivery and Howard stepped out into Barnes Street to retrieve the delivery. There were letters from both Starrett (the postmark indicated that Vincentius had indeed moved into his rented quarters in Beechhurst) and, on the dignified Jackson Publishing Company stationery, George Sylvester Viereck.

Starrett's letter was little more than a social note. He mentioned that his fountain-of-youth novel was coming along fairly well. He had a contract for the book from George B. Doran, a gentleman and a fine publisher, but rumors were circulating up and down publisher's row that Doran had been engaged in merger talks and Starrett was somewhat worried. What if Doran should be taken over by some house with a lesser tolerance for fancy? Vincent's book—as yet unnamed—contained not only the notion of the famous fountain but (he sketched in his plan briefly for Howard) a series of postscripts to the careers of various fictional figures down through the years. Cyrano would duel again in Vincent's novel, Sancho Panza and his woeful master would again bestride their mounts, Long John Silver and d'Artagnon would draw swords. . .unless George Doran came under the sway of too conservative a house.

Meanwhile, Vincent was getting back to Manhattan for an occasional sabbatical from his sabbatical, and hoped that Howard would do the same. If so, Alex Laing's digs seemed a suitable drop-point for messages.

Howard would reply to Starrett, offering consolation and encouragement with his novel. Should the book be turned out of its home, certainly there would be another for it somewhere. And yes, he would be delighted to spend some further time, perhaps a full-scale book-scouting expedition, with Vincentius.

He had certain reservations about Vincent's friend Alex Laing, but these he kept to himself.

Viereck's letter was a more serious matter than Starrett's. It was not the expected invitation to that gathering of personages in New York that Viereck had mentioned at the Waldorf. Instead, Viereck said that William Randolph Hearst had personally asked him to do a story on the two notorious anarchists and murderers currently languishing in Dedham Prison near Boston. The vital part of the case was not merely that the two men were killers, but that they were foreign radicals who had come to America to spread revolution and anarchy here, and were now, as the date of their execution approached, being made the darlings of every socialist, Communist, anarchist and non-specific lunatic fringer in the country.

Viereck was to gather interviews with Massachusetts Governor Alvin Fuller, Judge Webster Thayer who had presided over the original trial of the two back in 1921, and Warden William A. Hendry of Dedham Prison. Viereck might also meet with the two criminals themselves, dis-tasteful as such a confrontation would doubtlessly prove, for the sake of journalistic completeness.

Perhaps, if it was not inconvenient, he might call upon the Lovecraft establishment in Providence, while he was in the region. Or, better yet, if Howard could spare the time, he would meet Viereck for dinner in Boston.

In any case, Viereck was eagerly awaiting Howard's response.

Howard lowered the letter to his desk and rose to his feet. He paced around the room, then picked up the letter again to see if Viereck had mentioned the date of his projected trip. Yes, he would be in Boston on the 21st of March, would meet with Governor Fuller that afternoon, visit Dedham the next day and return to Boston, then travel back to New York on Wednesday, March 23.

Howard drew his Waterman from his pocket and wrote out a reply, accepting Viereck's invitation to meet at his hotel in Boston for dinner the evening of March 22.

On Sunday, March 20, Howard accompanied his aunts to the Providence Elks Hall. They purchased tickets to the debate between Clarence Darrow and Reverend Gray, on the question, "Is Man a Machine?" Darrow took the affirmative side.

Howard discussed the case and the advocates with Annie and Lillian as they rode the streetcar to the Elks Hall, Howard lecturing his "granddaughters" mainly on his feelings regarding Darrow; regarding the subject of the debate, there was little question in Howard's mind. It was, essentially, just another way of coming at the question of evolution, or religion versus science, or rationality versus blind faith. But regarding Darrow, Howard had very mixed feelings.

At the time of the Leopold-Loeb case three years ago, Howard had been horrified to see the defense that Darrow had put up for the two cold-blooded murderers, quoting Freud in the courtroom, citing some so-called "college mentality" as an excuse for the inexcusable crime of the two killers. There were suggestions of sexual inversion on the part of Leopold and Loeb, sadistic impulses, contempt for their victim and for society.

When Darrow succeeded in getting the two youths off—that is, in securing for them life sentences at the Joliet Penitentiary instead of the quick and unhesitating execution which their actions clearly merited, Howard had indignantly researched Darrow's past and discovered that the man was a radical, a dangerous anarchist and probable Bolshevik who should have been removed from the public eye for the sake of the common good.

But then Darrow had gone almost directly from his million-dollar defense of Leopold and Loeb to a defense without fee, that of the heroic schoolteacher John T. Scopes in Dayton, Tennessee. Howard had followed that trial in each day's dispatches from Judge Raulston's impromptu outdoor courtroom, partly distressed but also somehow reveling in the circus atmosphere that carried over the hundreds of miles. He had silently cheered when young Howard Morgan testified that, yes, Mr. Scopes did teach that man was descended from the beasts rather than created whole by the Almighty. He had cheered again at the transcript of Darrow's examination of William Jennings Bryan, the champion of Fundamentalist doctrine.

And now, in 1927, he was coming to cheer Darrow in yet another confrontation, and to watch the forces of narrow-mindedness being humiliated beneath the withering attack of modern thought.

The debate was no disappointment. Although the crowd was largely against him, Darrow demolished his opponent with all the power of logic and scorn, and sent Howard home happy. He stopped for a snack, then wrote a lengthy letter describing the debate before departing on his nightly walk, meeting Nigger-man and Yaller Gal at the usual place and continuing on to Swan Point Cemetery for a pleasant hour.

Tuesday afternoon he boarded a train at Union Station and rode to Boston, paging through a copy of *Literary Digest* and a copy of *Time* on the way. The world was continuing its merry dance down the road to disaster. The English politician Winston Churchill had condemned the United States for its late entry into the Great War, claiming that the war had been prolonged by America's delayed involvement; in Italy the Vatican had issued a statement by Pope Pius XI condemning Premier Mussolini's theory that placed the state in a position superior to that of man; the Jew Aaron Sapiro, suing Henry Ford over material that had appeared in Ford's *Dearborn Independent* had subpoenaed Ford to appear as a witness against himself; Alexander Kerensky, the deposed Russian revolutionary, was calling for another revolution in Russia to depose Stalin and Trotzky; the Chinese situation was a confused as ever, and the American ship *Preble* had been fired upon by Chinese gunners at Wuhu on the Yangtze in Anwei

Province; Harry F. Sinclair the oil magnate had been found guilty of contempt of the U.S. Senate for refusing to tell about his dealings with the Harding administration; and the little town of Coffeyville in southeastern Kansas had erupted into something approaching a full-scale race war over the thwarted attempt to lynch a Negro malefactor.

Howard abandoned the magazines on the train. Let some other traveler read them if he could!

~ ~ ~ ~ ~

George Sylvester Viereck slipped his gold-cased Ingersoll watch from his vest pocket, checked the hour and replaced the watch. He had returned to the Copley Hotel earlier than intended, somewhat frustrated by the day's events, and was impatient for Lovecraft's arrival. It wasn't the man's fault, Sylvester told himself, but it would be a blessing if he should happen to arrive early.

He drew a last bit of smoke from his cigar and stubbed it out in an ashtray, then paced about the lobby of the hotel, trying to occupy himself by admiring the cut-glass chandeliers, the huge paintings that were hung on the walls, the chic women and well turned-out men who circulated through the lobby.

If he could get Lovecraft to write the things he wanted written about his associates, about Hiram Evans, about Count Vonsiatsky, about Reverend Curran and his associates, about Heinz Spanknoebel and the rest of that crew coming out of the Midwest, and—here was the surest way to get around Lovecraft's anti-Germanism and his suspicious New England nature—about Leonora Schuyler. . . then the spotlight of ill-favored publicity might well wink out, or better yet turn to a rosy glow of warmth and good feeling.

America might be made over by peaceful, internal means. If she could not, then there was still the inevitable military confrontation that must arise in Europe for the rectification of the Versailles injustices. The Pan-German Reich would in time be dominant in the western world, and if America chose not be a partner she would be a vassal.

But a front man was needed. Everyone who had tried to speak for the movement had become embroiled in controversy. Even the congressmen and senators who managed to retain their own regional popularity were denounced in Washington and by the national dailies and weeklies. Viereck himself had never escaped the taint of his controversial writings during the Great War. If only that cursed Secret Service man and those counterespionage agents Bielaski and Lester had not done their dirty work, everything might have been different.

But as it was, his name had been dragged through the mud along with those of the whole operation, from the Ambassador, Count von Bernstorff, and his military attaché Captain von Papen, down to Dr. Albert, the banker Schmidt, the chemist Schweitzer and all the rest.

Sylvester had escaped his past, in part, by using pseudonyms on many of his writings—he was Eugen Vroom, George P. Conners, James Burr Hamilton, Donald Purtherman Wicketts and Dr. Claudius Murchison. But none of these would stand up to too-close scrutiny; he needed a man who was an authentically talented writer, with an impeccable Old American pedigree and no trace of a sympathetic relationship to the German cause.

A happy coincidence had brought him to this Howard Phillips Lovecraft. Viereck's fellow-editor and Hearst associate Abraham Merritt had recommended Lovecraft. Then out of the blue a faithful subscriber to Viereck's German-American publications, Reinhart Kleiner, had sent a letter-to-the-editor recommending Lovecraft to Viereck. Kleiner had also included some old quotations from Lovecraft's writings during the Great War and they certainly showed no danger of Lovecraft's being accused of pro-German sentiments. On the other hand, they showed that Lovecraft might be a hard man to win over.

Still, he was an eager man, and ambitious in his own eccentric way. Not greedy for money but obviously in need of it, which was a card that Viereck could play at any time. And even more, eager for literary recognition, for the publication of his works in some form more dignified and less ephemeral than the trashy pulp-paper journals where they usually appeared.

That was another card in Viereck's hand—his ace, in fact.

And there was still another, a card which he thought of as his joker. That one he would prefer not to have to play, but if necessity dictated, man must respond.

He stopped his pacing, examined his pocket-watch again, then looked up to see Howard Lovecraft, his tall figure clothed in his familiar dark overcoat and dark gray fedora, striding through the glass-and-polished-brass main doors of the Copley.

~ ~ ~ ~ ~

They shook hands and Viereck invited Lovecraft join him for dinner at Locke-Ober's if he had not as yet dined. Lovecraft accepted.

They proceeded on foot, Viereck mentioning his admiration of the Boston skyline and architecture, more of a human scale and softer texture than that of thrusting, dynamic flew York. He touched a rich vein with the comment. Howard Lovecraft went into a dissertation on the beauties of Georgian architecture, the purity of line exhibited in the churches and dwellings of colonial New England and the tragedy that more of them did not survive than was the case.

Once at Locke-Ober's on Winter Place they checked their coats and hats and Sylvester suggested to Lovecraft a cocktail before dinner. "I am more and more amazed, Mr. Viereck, at how little attention anyone pays to the Volstead law nowadays."

"An unnatural imposition upon freedom of choice, Mr. Lovecraft."

"Perhaps. I have been an ardent teetotaler from childhood."

"As you are naturally entitled to be."

"But I shall accompany you for sociability."

Viereck smiled and asked the captain to show them to the bar before entering the dining room. They were shortly seated on comfortable tall seats leaning against the mahogany. Viereck ordered a Gibson and Howard Lovecraft, to Viereck's uplifted eyebrow, followed suit.

"I trust that your researches have been successful," Lovecraft volunteered.

Viereck frowned. "Only in part. I did see Governor Fuller yesterday, as planned. His concern with the case is, it seems to me, a narrow one. You are familiar with the background?"

Howard sipped at his clear drink, made a sour frown at its strange and unpleasant taste, stared at the tiny onion floating in his glass. "I know who the criminals Sacco and Vanzetti are, of course. One would have had to be living on the planet Uranus at least, these past years, not to have heard of them."

"Yes. There is a great deal of uproar over their politics, of which I need only say that they are Red anarchists."

"I should think you would be very fond of them, Mr. Viereck." Lovecraft took another sip of his Gibson.

Viereck asked why he should like the two.

"They were draft evaders during the Great War, you know. I should think that you would approve of that very highly. They would have fought against Germany had they served."

Viereck said nothing.

"I volunteered for service myself," Lovecraft resumed. He sipped once more at his Gibson and Viereck saw a faraway look in Lovecraft's eyes. "Yes," he went on, "I went down to recruiting headquarters and signed up to go and fight Butcher Bill." He took another sip. "Filled out my papers, passed my medical examination. Do you think I'd have made a good soldier, Mr. Viereck?"

"That was long ago, Mr. Lovecraft."

Lovecraft emptied his glass and placed it back on the dark surface of the bar with care. "No need to call me Mr. Lovecraft. You might call me simply Howard."

"Thank you, Howard," Viereck said. He finished his own Gibson and signaled to the bartender for a second round. "I shall be honored if you call me Sylvester, then."

"Sylvester," Howard Lovecraft said carefully. "Not George?"

"I prefer Sylvester."

"Well, oh, another of those. The onion was very good. I came home from recruiting headquarters. Home was on Angell Street then. A wonderful house. My grandfather Phillips's house. I go there every night almost, and visit my old cat Nigger-man and Yaller Gal, and sometimes I can see Grandfather Phillips and pretty Susie and little Howard riding out in Grandfather's coach. We have a Negro coachman and footman and a beautiful team of fine horses. Ah, George, I mean Sylvester, it's lovely to take those rides at night. I put my head on Susie's lap."

Viereck gently took Howard's glass from him.

"I wasn't quite finished with that."

"I think we'd better have our dinner. Come now." Viereck guided Lovecraft from the bar room back to the main dining room and secured a table for them near a small orchestra. "Locke-Ober's is the best restaurant in Boston, in my opinion. There is no cuisine like a New England sea food dinner. Exquisite!"

"But they wouldn't let me go. I wanted to go lick the Kaiser all myself, and you know what they did? Those aunts. They called in *their* doctor. *Their* doctor. And he examined me and said 'Oh, little Howard, poor Howard is such a sickly child.' Sickly child. I was twenty-seven years of age. Such a sickly child. And *he* went back to the recruiting place and they cancelled the whole thing and I had to stay home. Ah, poor Howard. Poor Howie. Ah."

Viereck shook his head. "You are indeed a teetotaler, Howard. Some food will be a great help." He signaled to the waiter and they were supplied with menus.

Watching Howard peer at his menu blearily, Viereck said, "I recommend the seafood most highly. Either the *coquille St. Jacques* or possibly a plate of oysters for an appetizer. There is an excellent anchovy salad here. Or perhaps you would like to begin with a bisque. The lobster bisque. . ."

A look of horror spread over Howard Lovecraft's face, making Viereck fear that the liquor had overcome Howard's stomach and that he'd best be got out of the dining room before it was too late.

But instead Howard said, "I have a total aversion to sea food of any sort. A single taste, even the odor of fish in any form, provokes a deathly illness. I suffer from a severe allergy, you see, which was unsuspected at the time of my boyhood. The first time I was given sea food it provoked the most violent of reactions, nearly fatal in severity, and I have sedulously avoided all products of the sea ever since."

Viereck began to speak, to offer to order no fish as part of his own meal, but Howard anticipated the offer. "Please feel free to choose any item of your own liking, Sylvester.

I shall simply avoid those dishes which I know would prove harmful to my constitution."

Sylvester signaled the waiter and they ordered.

As soon as the waiter had left Howard said, "Yes, I perceive a comic irony. I would have served in the war but was prevented, the Sicilians were called to serve but refused. You see, if we could have traded places, all would have been satisfied. Instead, all were thwarted."

He lifted a celery-stalk from the relish dish and bit off its tip.

"I did not get to see the Sicilians," Viereck resumed his summary. "I telephoned Warden Hendry and he told me that the prisoners were unavailable today, they were to be closeted with their lawyer Thompson. But they would be available another day. I pressed him. Tomorrow? And he agreed. So my appointment is set for tomorrow. Perhaps you will join me?"

Howard shook his head. "Absolutely not. I have no interest in setting foot inside Dedham Prison, and less in meeting those two criminals. They are scum of the lowermost sort. I fear that my nostrils would rebel at the experience."

Viereck indicated that he could understand Howard's reluctance. Their conversation grew more general in nature, dealing chiefly with world events and the political situation in the United States and abroad. Viereck claimed little better understanding of the Chinese confusion than Howard Lovecraft possessed. "I expect that the *Bolshevist* hand is behind much of the misfortune in China. Are you familiar with the name Mikhail Borodin?"

Howard was not.

"He is a strange man. The Soviet Russian government disclaims responsibility for him, yet he acts for the furtherance of Bolshevism in China. He hands out large amounts of money drawn from an unnamed source. And time after time, from violent events a thread seems to lead back to him."

"He is in China?" Howard asked.

Viereck nodded, added "Acts of hostility toward the western powers can only lead to confrontation between China and the states of Europe and America. China will be driven into Russia's arms. And all of this, Mister Borodin orchestrates." He laughed at his own quip, joined nervously by Howard.

Taking a morsel of food, Viereck placed his fork carefully on the edge of his dish, chewed meditatively. The small orchestra played a quiet, tasteful selection, a restful contrast to the raucous jazz music of the day. "I fear that I tend to revert to theme, Howard, but it seems to me that the situation in China is still another part of the heritage of Versailles."

Howard Lovecraft looked up from his plate. Sylvester Viereck was relieved to see Lovecraft's eyes clearing from the glazed appearance the earlier liquor had produced. "Versailles? What does that have to do with China?"

Viereck smiled. "You did not follow the news reports too closely, then. All too few did. The German concession in Shantung Province was seized by Japanese forces at the end of the Great War. At Versailles the Chinese representatives demanded the return or Shantung to Chinese control. The Japanese agreed to withdraw at some unspecified date, but refused to concede that their withdrawal be made part of the Versailles agreements. They would deal directly with the Chinese.

"Do you know what the Japanese representative said? I was at Versailles, Howard, as a journalist. I could hardly believe the things I saw and heard. Japan was represented by Baron Hakino. He claimed that it would be a slur on the good name of Japan to make Shantung part of the Versailles agreements. A slur! Good heavens, what about the Chinese? And what of the German influence that had brought wealth and advancement to China?

"Germany was thrown out of China. Japan rushed in from the east, Russia from the west. That is why China is torn today, and why westerners are in fear of their lives anywhere in the Middle Kingdom! Versailles, Howard! There is the reason!"

CHAPTER SIX:

OVER HIS HEAD IN THE SEEKONK

THURSDAY AFTERNOON Howard rose and examined the Providence *Journal*. His attention was taken by a report from China. The nationalist army (now which one was that, he tried vainly to recall) had taken Nanking and Chinkiang. The arriving army had been met with a general strike by the workers of the cities. The tactic used to discourage the strike and motivate the resumption of work was direct: strike leaders were beheaded in the public square. Following the show the workers of the rest of the cities had returned to their stations. Closer to home, the Rhode Island Senate had passed a measure designed to permit the remarriage of divorced persons. Howard sniffed at the latter report. Why would anyone wish to marry again after a divorce?

Friday's mail was awaiting when Howard rose, but once more he examined the newspaper before opening his letters. With order being restored in Nanking it was learned that 155 westerners were missing. Assassinated by the strikers? Kidnapped by the nationalists? No one knew. Meanwhile, American and British warships stood off the city and bombarded it with their heavy guns. Well, that would teach the Chinese a lesson.

The only important letter was one from Viereck's Jackson Publishing Company. The long-promised meeting had been scheduled for the following Friday, and Viereck enclosed a list of the key persons whom he wished Howard to meet and eventually to write about. Howard looked at the list, raised his eyebrow several times as he studied the names and credentials cited by Viereck, then set the sheet of Jackson letterhead carefully aside for study before the meeting.

For now, he took pen and paper and wrote to Viereck at the 42nd Street office, accepting the invitation for the following week. He wrote also to his wife, still living in Brooklyn where they had lived together (or, more accurately, living there once again, having moved to Providence, briefly, before separating from Howard and then having taken up residence temporarily in the Middle West).

"My Dear Sonia," Howard opened this letter. "I am most appreciative of your thoughtfulness in describing your encounter with Theo Weiss. Without knowing the younger Weiss as closely as I did his deceased elder brother, I can state that my superficial impression, at least, was a more favorable one than that which I held of Ehrich 'Houdini.' The younger Weiss manages to present more the appearance of a gentleman, although one a bit more modern and flamboyant than is to my personal delectation, and to comport himself without the egotistical aggressiveness of his brother.

"As for your kind offer of accommodations when my interests bring me to New York City as they do from time to time. I am certain that you fully grasp my feelings about New York with its teeming mongrel crowds and clamorous modernity, but the metropolis does contain a number of attractions, as well as both social and business acquaintances whom I visit from time to time. I will therefore be most pleased and grateful to accept your kind offer of lodgings, especially in view of my frequent impositions upon the young Long, whose tolerant and hospitable parents must nonetheless find my presence more a nuisance than a pleasure when I turn up continually upon their doormat.

"It is vital, however, that you understand that my presence in your domicile implies no greater relationship or intimacy than that to expected between guest and hostess; that is to say, that *our relationship shall be entirely platonic* and that there be no attempt to restore any other basis than that!"

He appended the information that he would arrive in New York the following Thursday evening for a stay of unspecified but not great duration, and would be pleased to see Sonia at that time. He then wrote several letters to friends in New York, advising them of his pending visit, and mailed all of the outgoing missives after consuming his dinner.

This night he altered the usual path of his nocturnal tour, swinging northward on Butler Avenue where it crossed Angell Street, thereby missing the Narragansett Boat Club, and swung eastward on Irving Avenue to reach the River Road. At this point the Seekonk was wider than at the Narragansett Club, and Howard peered through the midnight darkness toward Walker's Point in East Providence, enjoying the solitude and darkness of the hour. He was firmly convinced that death spelt the total dissolution of the personality and the utter end of awareness, yet he felt somehow that if any awareness persisted beyond the tomb it must be like this moment: still, cool, dim, with the very movement of time itself slowed to a standstill or nearly so. There were no intrusions, no obligations, only a peaceful sense of relief.

A shrill noise shattered Howard's meditation. For a moment his perception was so confused that he could not decide whether the scream was that of a ship's whistle somewhere on the Seekonk or farther up along the Pawtucket River, or a distant locomotive shrieking as it charged along silvery rails running north and south through the city.

But the scream persisted and with a shock Howard realized that the screaming was that of a human. He ran in the direction from which the sound had come, in the direction of the Seekonk.

He saw a car pulled to the edge of the River Road, a large, closed car. There was a sound of voices, curses, grunts, blows being struck. A final inarticulate shriek and a loud splash from the river. Howard ran forward as he saw dark figures running back from the edge of the water, across the narrow strip of green that separated the River Road from the bank of the Seekonk.

The figures scrambled into the car without taking note of Howard's approach. He heard the powerful engine of the machine roar into life, saw its electric headlights blaze with sudden brilliance. The automobile's tires spun for a moment on the surface of the River Road, then it sped away, the steady rising growl of its engine broken by the shifting of gears.

Howard ran to the river's edge and peered into the dark water. Near the shore the Seekonk was fairly shallow and a bright moon threw enough light to penetrate a few feet beneath the surface. Howard strained his eyes and saw three white blobs submerged only a couple of feet beneath the rippled top of the river. He bent nearer to the water and saw that the two upper blobs were a pair of hands. One of them broke the surface, clutching frantically toward Howard. Then the other followed. The central blob of the three was a face, dead white in the moonlight, the mouth open in a scream that emerged only as a stream of air bubbles.

Howard tugged his topcoat off, tossed it and his suit jacket onto the grass. He kicked off his shoes and leaped into the water. He was, himself, at best an indifferent swimmer, limiting his rare essays into the shallows off the beaches of Cape Cod during summer holiday with Belknapius and other friends, dog-paddling sedately a few yards away from the shore, then cautiously returning to the supporting sand.

Now he was over his head in the Seekonk late at night on the 25th of March. The temperature was sixty degrees or less. But a man was drowning.

Howard seized the two struggling hands in his own and tried to tug the man toward the bank. He could not move him. He tried raising him toward the surface of the river but the man didn't rise an inch; it was as if his feet were anchored to the bottom of the river some seven or eight feet below.

The man shifted his grip from Howard's hands to his biceps, then to his torso. He struggled desperately to climb up Howard and get his face out of the water. All that happened was that Howard was pulled down into the water, his own face dragged beneath the surface. He clamped his mouth shut and strained against the water rising into his nostrils.

He tugged away from the man, striking at the man's hands until he broke their grip on his body and tried to stroke his way through the Seekonk but the man secured a fresh grip on the cuffs of Howard's trousers. For what seemed hours they remained stationary, Howard paddling to keep his head above the surface, slowly regaining his lost breath, his legs held by the other's hands' grasp on his trouser cuffs.

Finally Howard realized that the other man must be dead. He turned and leaned forward as best he could, straining against the dead man's fingers, trying to loosen their frantic dying grip on his trouser cuffs. He was unable to get the fingers open. At last he turned away again and tried to find a way out of his dilemma. He was growing colder and colder, and the old lethargy that struck him when he was exposed to low temperatures was beginning to make itself felt.

He twisted and thrashed, ducked himself beneath the cold waters of the river, managed to push his face back into the air and stabilize his posture. There was only one course left to him. With numbing fingers he struggled to unclasp his belt and tug his sodden trousers down, over his shoes, leaving them floating in the grip of the corpse.

He paddled to the river's edge and pulled himself up onto the bank, sat panting for a moment, then located his discarded suit jacket and topcoat and struggled back into them. He started back along the path he had taken to the river, crossed the River Road—there was no traffic whatever at this hour—and past darkened houses. He should run to the nearest house and pound on the door, he knew that, but somehow the prospect of standing in an opened doorway, sopping wet and trouserless in suit jacket and topcoat was more than he could cope with.

Instead he set out for home, at first walking determinedly, then faster and faster until he found himself running, gasping for breath, pursued by the image of a pale face screaming up at him, illuminated by white moonbeams, through the dark waters of the Seekonk. Only when he was out of breath did he slow to a dogged stride, arriving home at Barnes Street on the ragged edge of exhaustion.

He fumbled for his door-key, realized that it was in the pocket of his trousers floating in the dead man's grip in the river. He pounded on the front door of number ten until a light appeared inside the foyer and he saw the pale face of his aunt Annie Gamwell peering through an opening in the curtains. Howard stood with trembling hands. His aunt ran to the door and admitted him.

Within minutes he was out of his drenched shoes and socks and shirt, wrapped in thick towels and sitting with his feet in a tub of hot water while both his aunts twittered and fussed around him. Annie stroked and petted him while his aunt Lillian brewed a cup of strong tea and brought it from the kitchen, standing by while Howard downed it and then hurrying back to the kitchen to fill it again and return to his side. This time he simply held the cup, warming his hands against its china sides.

He told his aunts what had happened at the river.

Now Lillian stayed beside him while Annie pattered to the telephone and placed a call to Providence police headquarters. She chattered into the telephone, seemed to engage in a brief quarrel with the police, then held the earpiece toward Howard and said that the police insisted on talking with him. He pulled his feet from the tub of water, patted them dry with a chenille towel, tied the braided cord of his old gray woolen bathrobe about his waist and went to the telephone.

At the prodding of the policeman he told his story of the car at River Road and the events that followed his hearing the scream. The policeman told him to stay where he was, took the address from him (for what was surely the sixth or seventh time) and told him to be ready for a visit.

Howard took a few sips at his second cup of tea, then told his aunts that the police were on their way and retired to dress in his warmest winter suit. The police had not told him that he would have to return with them to the Seekonk, but he surmised that he would have to do that.

Within minutes the police were at the door of the Barnes Street house. Annie admitted them and Howard rose to his feet in the parlor. There were three—a beefy sergeant in tunic and visored policeman's cap, a patrolman in similar uniform, and a detective in civilian clothes.

They sat down in the parlor and made Howard go over his narrative still again. Midway through the story the sergeant, acting at the detective's directions, used the telephone briefly, returned to the circle with a comment that the wagon would meet them at the River Road site.

The detective asked Howard to come with them. Annie and Lillian fluttered around the group of men, worriedly asking Howard if he would be all right, pleading with the detective and the uniformed sergeant not to arrest their nephew. Finally the detective turned to the women and told them that Howard was not under arrest but was needed to provide information.

Howard tied a woolen muffler around his throat and pulled on his warmest winter overcoat. He went downstairs with the police, climbed into the back seat of their prominently marked automobile and watched as the patrolman brought the automobile's engine to life. They set off for the Seekonk, Howard directing them along the route he had taken on his walk earlier in the evening.

They parked the patrol car and Howard led the police to the bank of the river and pointed to the spot where the victim had been thrown in. His trousers were still floating in the corpse's grip. In a moment there was a siren's wail and Howard turned to see a white-painted police ambulance pull to a halt beside the patrol car. White-uniformed attendants climbed from the ambulance and joined the police at the edge of the water.

The uniformed police patrolman borrowed a stretcher pole from an ambulance attendant and tried to pull Howard's abandoned trousers from the grasp of the corpse, without success.

Finally, to the dismay of the ambulance crew and the uniformed policeman, the detective commanded them to climb into the river and drag the corpse from its waters. Howard was given back his soaking trousers and transferred the keys, small change and wallet—even though the latter was cold and wet—to his pockets. He watched, morbidly fascinated, as the corpse was dragged across the river bank to the ambulance and loaded through the rear of the vehicle. He could see why the victim had been unable to swim to the surface of the river, and why it had taken the full ambulance crew plus the uniformed policeman to drag him from the river. His feet were encased in a large bucket of cement. Howard had heard of this form of gangland killing but never before had he come to terms with the reality of it.

When the body was safely stowed in the rear of the ambulance the uniformed patrolman climbed in along with the crew and the white vehicle drove away.

The detective and police sergeant turned back to Howard. He followed them to the patrol car and climbed into the back seat, asking if they would drive him home. "You'll have to come down to Elbow Street, sir," the lieutenant told him. "We'll have to take your statement—"

"What, again?" Howard interrupted.

"I'm sorry, sir. You'll have to give your statement once more to a stenographer and then certify it. I suppose you could do it in the morning, if you absolutely must, but we'd much prefer if you'd just come with us and give it now."

Howard pondered for a moment. Well, as long as he was dry again and relatively warm, he might as well go on and get it over with. Better than having to vary his routine by rising early in the morning and making his way to police headquarters.

He assented and the patrol car, driven now by the beefy uniformed sergeant, climbed down the western slope of College Hill and made its way through the deserted late-hour streets of Providence to the police building on Elbow Street. Howard walked up the steps of the old brick-and-concrete structure with the detective at his side. He still had his cold, wet trousers in his hands. As they entered the building the detective took the trousers from Howard and handed them over to a desk officer. "They'll need a pressing, of course," the lieutenant told Howard, "but at least he'll dry 'em for you."

They settled in a dingy office and a male stenographer, his collar open and tie hanging down, drew up a chair and poised his pencil above a green-tinted pad. Once more Howard recited the events of the night, from the time he'd first heard the scream to the moment he called the police from Barnes Street, or rather to the moment that his aunt had called the police for him. The lieutenant stopped him and asked for details from time to time, pressing him for a description of the murder car—in the darkness it was hard to identify except that it was a closed car—a large one. The lieutenant pressed him to identify the brand but Howard could only guess. A Reo, perhaps, or a Marmon or even a foreign machine, a Hispano-Suiza. He had seen only the dark bulk of the car until its headlights had blazed up, and then he'd seen only the two brilliant disks and not the car itself.

The lieutenant pressed him for the number and appearance of the men but here Howard was able to tell little more than he had about the car. Dark figures. Several dark figures. Low voices, he couldn't make out what they'd said. Men's voices, though, no women. Two or three at least, maybe as many as five. Two at least, the detective wanted to know, or three at least? Howard rubbed his jaw, struggled to remember. Three at least. All right.

And the face in the water. Had the man said anything that Howard had made out? Only screams before he hit the water. Once Howard saw the face, only a look of terror, of desperation.

Had the man grabbed Howard? How could that be? No, Howard had gone to him voluntarily to try and pull him from the Seekonk. The man had clutched Howard in his panic. That was all. Had Howard fought with the man? He explained his efforts to get free, his final abandonment of his trousers. And why hadn't he gone to the nearest house, or to one of the yacht clubs nearby? Howard explained as best he could.

Finally the detective seemed satisfied and the stenographer went off to typewrite his notes. The detective said that Howard would have to wait and sign the typewritten statement. Meanwhile he drank coffee with sugar. He asked the detective if he knew who the murdered man was. "I've been with you, sir. How could I?" He thought about it briefly, then left the office.

When he came back he had a different look on his face. He invited Howard to take a little walk with him in the corridor.

Outside the dingy office, in a green-on-green painted hallway lighted by dim electric bulbs the lieutenant walked along beside Howard. Howard waited for the detective to speak.

"You ever hear the name Morelli?" the detective finally asked.

Howard pondered briefly. "Never."

"You ever get over to Federal Hill, Mr. Lovecraft?"

Howard shook his head. "Not if I can help it. That was once as fine a neighborhood as this city possessed but it has in recent years become overrun by the mongrel hordes of noxious aliens. I have no desire to visit those environs. The sight of the old architecture overrun by yellow mongrels would probably turn my stomach."

The detective cleared his throat a couple of times. "Well, sir, be that as it may." He halted and Howard did likewise. "My point, Mr. Lovecraft, is that there is a notorious gang operating out of Federal Hill, known as the Morelli Gang. You're certain you've never heard of them? Perhaps it will ring a bell.

"We know that they're into every form of crime from muggings and holdups to vice and racketeering. They bootleg rum from ships standing offshore beyond the three-mile limit, they supply half of the speakeasies in Rhode Island and they're out to get the rest of them. They run prostitutes, gambling, dope."

Howard shook his head incredulously. "Why don't you round them up, then?"

The lieutenant laughed, a short, harsh sound. "First of all, it isn't such a simple matter to round them up. We go after them and they run to earth, Mr. Lovecraft. When we do find some of the Morelli's, we have a terrible time pinning anything on them. *We* know what they're up to, but you can't just conjure proof out of thin air.

"They have some smart legal help, and they have a code that keeps the rest of the underworld from giving us any help against them. Even their own victims, strange as that may sound to you, sir. They settle their own differences."

"Then you mean, officer, that not a single member of this Morelli Gang is behind bars?"

The detective's face showed a look of grim satisfaction. "Not quite none of them. Our colleagues across the line in Massachusetts had better luck than we. They got a Morelli—the gang is named for its leader, you understand; it's largely a family affair but the Morelli Gang isn't all made of people with the Morelli family name. They got a Morelli by the name of Madeiros. Got him good, on a murder rap. He's in Dedham Prison now, awaiting his date with the electric chair.

"In fact," he went on, "Madeiros would have been fried years ago, but he pulled a clever trick." He clenched his jaw and struck one fist into the palm of the other hand. "He went to the D.A. and told him that the Slater and Morrill payroll job was a Morelli operation. Said that he was part of the gang and one of the killers. You know, Parmenter and Berardelli, the paymaster and the uniformed guard, were both gunned down. Madeiros says he and the Morellis did it, sir!"

"And because this Madeiros person confessed to murder, the State of Massachusetts will *not* execute him?" Howard Lovecraft was horrified.

"Roughly speaking, sir, that's exactly the case." The detective clapped his arm around Howard Lovecraft's shoulders and they resumed their stroll along the green-painted corridor. "You see, Massachusetts has those two wop *Bolshevists* Sacco and Vanzetti awaiting execution for the Braintree killings. They've been appealing their conviction for seven years, sir. And when Madeiros confessed that he and the Morelli's were responsible, why, Judge Thayer had to order a stay for him—Madeiros' own conviction has nothing to do with Braintree—until all appeals are exhausted by those other two dagoes!"

Howard shook his head. "That's appalling. But I must ask, lieutenant, what the situation of the three dagoes in Braintree—"

"They're in Dedham now, sir, excuse me, it was the payroll job that took place in Braintree, or more properly South Braintree, Mass, sir."

"Thank you. What has the Massachusetts situation to do with the crime that transpired tonight in Providence? What had that poor devil in the Seekonk to do with *Bolshevists* in another state?"

"Ah, you see, sir. The Morelli gang operates out of Providence, out of Federal Hill to be precise. And it was Celestine Madeiros who implicated the Morelli's in the South Braintree crime." He halted, withdrew his arm from Howard's shoulders and stood facing Howard. "The victim tonight, we've good identification from the coroner's office, he took fingerprints from the *corpus delicti,* sir, and they match a set in our files that belong to Celestine Madeiros' brother, sir. I think that the killing tonight was intended as a warning to Celestine against spilling too much dope on the Morelli's. He's a doomed man anyway, Madeiros is, but the Morelli's aren't above eliminating his family, one by one, should Celestine blabber too much over there in Dedham. I imagine that tonight's work will quiet him down a bit."

In silence they made their way back toward the front of headquarters. The officer at the desk returned Howard's bedraggled trousers. The detective thanked Howard for his cooperation and said they'd be in contact with him later on, as the case developed, if it developed. A uniformed officer chauffeured Howard home in a police automobile.

CHAPTER SEVEN:

"BARBAROSSA WILL RISE,
MISTER LOVECRAFT!"

AFTER A MERE few hours sleep Howard had to rise and make his way to the Union Station in order to reach New York for the meeting at George Sylvester Viereck's apartment. He looked at the day's mail before leaving Barnes Street and found the April *Weird Tales* with a single reference to himself. A Reverend George I. Foster, rector of the Church of the Good Shepherd in Cleveland, wrote to the Eyrie that "Among your own writers that I most admire are Lovecraft and Quinn (tied for first place), with Burks, Hamilton and Morgan a close second."

Such notices warmed Howard's insides, not merely because they gratified his ego but because they must, in some degree, reflect the feelings of Farnsworth Wright when he selected them for inclusion in the magazine. There were all too few markets for the kind of story he produced (this train of thought reminded him to pursue the matter of "The Colour Out of Space" with Vincent Starrett's brash friend Laing), and it was most important to stay on favorable terms with editor Wright and publisher Joe Henneberger out in Chicago.

He filed away the magazine with a final annoyed glance at its lurid cover, another Senf design, this time showing a shaggy giant clutching an uprooted tree and about to smash it upon a grecian-looking maiden. What could that mean, Howard wondered briefly before putting it from his mind.

On the train he idly flipped the pages of H. L. Mencken and George Jean Nathan's green-covered *American Mercury,* smiling appreciatively at the *bon mots* it contained, nodding agreement with a third of the attitudes expressed (he loved Mencken's iconoclasm) and raging silently at the other two-thirds.

As the train pulled out of Boston to continue its trip southward he tossed the magazine onto an unoccupied seat and took Viereck's letter from the inner pocket of his jacket. He turned to the paragraph concerning the evening's meeting.

"I do not mean to imply a meeting in any formal sense," Viereck had written. "The gathering will actually be more of a social affair. You will find Mrs. Viereck and myself at home at the address given, which is located at 103rd Street and Riverside Drive. There will be a number of persons present whom I wish you to meet, and whose company I am certain you will find pleasant as well as instructive.

"If you have the same difficulty in coping with large numbers of new acquaintances as I, you will surely be pleased to receive a little advance information, a playbill as it were, regarding some of the more influential persons whom you are to meet. I will be most pleased to bring about an introduction of yourself to the following persons, all good friends of mine:

"Mr. Heinz Spanknoebel, Mrs. Elizabeth Dilling, Dr. Hiram Evans, Reverend Edward Lodge Curran, Dr. Maude DeLand, and Count Anastase Andreivitch Vonsiatskoy-Vonsiatsky. These individuals are all engaged in patriotic work of various sorts. They represent a number of organizations which are independent of one another but which will all contribute, ultimately, to the betterment of America and the emergence of a sensible world order. I am confident that you will find them fascinating and inspiring personages, and that they will be most pleased to become acquainted with such a man as yourself.

"With your indulgence, I will attach a few lines of information about each of the distinguished guests named above. There may be a few others at the gathering, all of them persons of a *simpatico* outlook of course, and all of whom, I am sure, you will be pleased to meet and exchange views with."

Howard looked at the brief information provided by Viereck about each of the persons he was supposed to meet.

Heinz Spanknoebel—if ever there was a poor name to place at the head of the list, in view of Howard's residual anti-German bias, Viereck's alleged purpose, it could only have been Wilhelm Hohenzollern himself—was, according to Viereck, traveling from Detroit to attend the meeting. He was a chemist, an associate of the great Henry Ford.

Mrs. Elizabeth Dilling, of Kenilworth, Illinois, was the founder and head of the Patriotic Research Bureau. That sounded innocent enough, Howard thought. Also, Viereck wrote, she was an authoress, busily researching the intertwined tentacles of atheistic Bolshevism and international Judaism. Howard had never heard of the woman's project and wondered if it bore any resemblance to his friend Donald Wandrei's story "The Red Brain." Plagiarism was out of the question—Donald's story, which Howard Lovecraft had recommended in a letter to Pharnabus, had been accepted but had not yet appeared in *Weird Tales.*

Dr. Evans—Howard noted that he was a dentist—looked like a fascinating character and one whom Howard would be most intrigued to meet. Viereck mentioned that Evans was traveling by train all the way from Atlanta, Georgia. He was the Imperial Wizard of the Invisible Empire, Knights of the Ku Klux Klan. Howard's thoughts whirled back to his own investigation, years earlier, of the Klan. He had read the Reverend Thomas Dixon's factual novel *The Clansman,* and had written in his own amateur journal *The Conservative* that he had made "a close historical study of the K-K-K, finding nothing but honour, chivalry, and patriotism." Howard had found the Klan to be a "noble but much- maligned band of Southerners who saved half of our country from destruction at the close of the Civil War."

But Howard had written those words a dozen years earlier, and he had been referring not to the modern Klan founded in 1915, the year of his writing, by William Joseph Simmons. He had written of the *old* KKK that traced its roots to Pulaski, Tennessee and its founding in 1866, the Klan that had been headed by Brigadier General Nathan Bedford Forrest and that had been disbanded at General Forrest's own behest when it had outlived its usefulness.

What the Emperor Evans of the *new* Klan would have to say, Howard would be eager to hear.

The Reverend Edward Lodge Curran was listed by Viereck as President of the International Catholic Truth Society. Viereck had little else to say about Curran, but Howard's curiosity and suspicion were both piqued even by the brief entry. His curiosity rose to ask how Father Curran and Dr. Evans would deal with each other. The Klan, while most prominently dedicated to keeping the southern Negro in his place—certainly a worthwhile objective—was also known to oppose Catholics, Jews, and foreign-born elements. Viereck himself fell under the last heading, and at least there seemed to be no Jews on Viereck's guest-list. But how would Curran, a Catholic, react to the presence of the Klan Emperor Evans—and *vice versa?* As for Howard's suspicion, he found the name Curran somewhat disquieting. Irish nationalism, anti-Briticism, and pro-Germanism were old by-words that had risen to new heights during the Great War and never fully subsided. This Irish priest in league with the German-born Viereck might also represent a dangerous alliance.

Maude S. DeLand was another person about whom Viereck had supplied only the skimpiest information. She too was a doctor; unlike Hiram Evans who had abandoned dentistry for Klan politics, Maude DeLand was a medical doctor, a psychiatrist at that. Ahah! Howard's eyes gleamed as he fit together these parts of the jigsaw puzzle. Viereck was himself a student of psychology, a great admirer—according to his writings—of the Viennese Sigmund Freud. Viereck's interest in Freud must have led him to DeLand. As for her presence in a meeting which seemed to be principally political. . . Howard read the short lines Viereck had provided. . . Dr. DeLand was the American representative of the Englishman Sir Oswald Mosley. Well, well—it would be fascinating to watch Dr. DeLand and Father Curran exchanging small talk over tea and *petit* sandwiches!

And Viereck's list concluded with the glamorous name of Count Anastase Andreivitch Vonsiatskoy-Vonsiatsky, formerly of Imperial Russia and presently of Thompson, Connecticut. According to Viereck, Vonsiatsky was the chairman of the All-Russian National Socialist Labor Party. Howard did not like the term *socialist,* or that of *labor party,* but he was willing to see what ideas the Count espoused. George Sylvester Viereck, he remembered, was an ardent admirer of the leader of the NSDAP, the National Socialist Deutscher Arbeiters Partei. And that party, despite its name, was neither a socialist nor a labor party in any usual sense of the words.

It looked like a dazzling gathering of people. At the very least, Howard was assured of one of the more fascinating evenings of his life. And if anything came of it, some ghost-writing or revision work, or even a book of his own, that would be so much the better!

He folded Viereck's letter and slipped it into his pocket long before the train reached Manhattan. Once it did, Howard debarked at 125th Street and took a crosstown car to West End Avenue, then transferred to a downtown car to drop off his effects at the Longs' and rest before walking to Riverside Drive and seeking the Viereck apartment.

The Longs' Negro maid admitted him to the apartment and Howard made his own way to Belknapius' study where the young man sat hunched over his typewriter, puffing furiously as his pipe, the much-marked rough draft of a short story beside him and a revised version on the platen. For a lengthy moment Howard stood in the doorway to the room, silently observing his protégé at his labors.

Then Belknapius swiveled around and looked up at Howard, a wide grin spreading over his face. He took the pipe from his mouth and placed it carefully in an ash-tray that stood in the clutter of his desk. "Howard," he exclaimed.

"Grandfather Theobaldus meant not to intrude upon thy courtship of the muse," Howard intoned.

"Hah! The muse is being a very difficult lady today. I've had this story finished for months, sent it off to Pharnabus, got it back with a note from the esteemed editor saying that he liked it pretty well but it wasn't *quite* balanced enough for his tender little taste buds. So I've been working over the thing until I could tear my hair out and I can't get it right. Some muse! A tease of the worst sort! I'd trade her for a modern flapper in a minute."

Howard had a good long laugh at that. "Well, what's the story, dear child, is it something I've seen before?"

" 'The Space-Eaters.' Of course you've seen it. Does anything make its way from West End Avenue to East Ohio Street without a preliminary detour by way of Providence-Plantations?"

"Oh-ho! 'The Space-Eaters,' is it? Farnie didn't quite go for the *magnum opus,* eh? Mind if I take a look at what

93

you've been doing with the poor helpless husk, grand-son?"

Belknap stood aside so Howard could see the marked-up draft and the fragmentary revision on his desk.

"Do you really consider it my *magnum opus,* Howard?" Belknap asked from behind Lovecraft. The other did not reply at once, but stood shuffling sheets of manuscript, pausing to read a paragraph here or there, to study one of Belknap's hand-written revisions and make a know-ledgeable, approving sound over it, then to move on to the next and grunt negatively when he preferred the ex-isting version to the revision.

Finally he turned away from the manuscript and said, "As far as I am concerned, the story was just fine all along. But I must concede this much to Brother Pharn-abus and his fussiness, the new version is decidedly supe-rior to the old. Press on, noble Belknap, and you shall surely produce one of the best tapestries that e'er M'sieu Wright hung in Joe Henneberger's garden.

"As for me, of course I am delighted with the story. Never before have I found myself the subject of another's narrative, and you toast me up so deliciously at the end, I'm sure that when the time comes for my actual demise I shall lie somewhere abed wishing for that cozy little ter-mination you provide.

"And such charming last words you permit me to speak. 'Crawling—ugh! Crawling—ugh! Oh, have pity! Cold and clee-ar. Crawling—ugh! God in heaven.' I love it, Belknap, every bit!" And he all but collapsed in laughter.

"I did have one other thought for the yarn, Howard. I'd thought of opening it with some quotation from one of the lost books, the Necronomicon itself if you don't object. What would you think of some little paragraph to set the tone, perhaps a reference to the madness of those who investigate that which is sealed to the eyes of man?"

Howard rubbed his lantern jaw, then slipped into Belknap's wooden-backed typing chair. "May I?" he asked, reaching toward the stack of pristine manuscript bond. Almost before Belknap could nod assent, Howard had his Waterman in hand and poised over the sheet. He closed his eyes in concentration for a few seconds, then inscribed a few careful lines in his compact, spidery hand.

When he handed the paper to Belknap the latter read it aloud: *The Cross is not a passive agent. It protects the pure of heart, and it has often appeared in the air above our sabbats, confusing and dispersing the powers of Darkness.* Belknap looked from the blue ink to the author of the lines. "I always thought of you as a rather militant atheist, Howard."

"You dislike the paragraph?" Howard reached for the sheet.

Belknap pulled it away. "No, no. It's just fine. Merely— surprising to find you writing about the power of the Cross."

"Ah, but *I* did not create the sentiment, I merely pro- vided you with the quotation, grandchild. You should take up your inquiry with the author of the words, not their humble transcriber."

"I have not seen Abdul Alhazred the mad Arab around 100th street very often. Not lately, anyway."

"Ho, I fear that Abdul gibbered away the last of his in- sanity some time ago. Perhaps you'd best attribute the new paragraph to some later figure through whose hands the dreaded book passed."

"Yes, I shall do that. Well," Belknap paused while he placed the sheet of paper carefully with his growing manuscript, "for how long may we expect the pleasure of your company this time, Howard?"

Howard examined his wrist-watch. "In fact, I'd best be on my way to Viereck's digs right now. I shall return after the evening's festivities, then stay the night. Tomorrow I shall proceed to Brooklyn, where Mrs. Lovecraft has asked me to be her guest."

~ ~ ~ ~ ~

Howard walked the short distance to Riverside Drive, then northward to 103rd street and the apartment building where George Sylvester Viereck made his home. It was a modern building, well constructed, with imitation Moorish pillars flanking the main entrance and a splendidly tiled and furnished lobby. A doorman guided Howard to the elevator and he rode with the gray-uniformed and re- spectful operator to Viereck's floor. The elevator operator stepped from his car and directed Howard to Viereck's doorway.

A uniformed maid took Howard's hat and topcoat inside the apartment foyer, and Howard spotted Sylvester, attired in proper dark suit and wing-collar this time (Howard was relieved that the former tweeds had not been evidence of an even more bohemian style in the Viereck *ménage*). Viereck crossed the plushly-carpeted floor and grasped Howard's hand in a warm gesture.

"Very pleased you could attend, Howard. Almost everyone is here and people are most eager to meet you."

Howard flushed. "You are too kind."

Viereck took Howard Lovecraft's elbow and guided him into a large living room. They had to take several steps down as they entered the room; a large tapestry covered most of one wall, showing medieval hunting scenes against a bucolic setting. The opposite wall held several large paintings in ornate frames of gilt scrollery.

A dozen or no persons were scattered through the room, standing in twos and threes or seated in comfortable furniture arranged in conversational clusters.

Sylvester guided Howard around the room, making introductions. All of the persons on the list Sylvester had mailed to Howard were present, as were A. W. Dilling, the husband of Mrs. Elizabeth Dilling, Countess Vonsiatsky (the former Marion Ream Stephens), and of course Viereck's own wife Gretchen. There were a few others present, to whom Viereck also introduced Howard.

One was George Pagnanelli, a young man whose clothing clearly indicated a lack of funds, yet who managed to maintain at least a neat semblance of propriety. Pagnanelli explained that he was the editor of a publication called the *Christian Defender* and handed Howard a copy. It was a sloppily produced piece of semi-literacy, inferior in all ways to most of the amateur journals Howard was familiar with. He folded the small pamphlet and placed it inside his jacket, excusing the act on the grounds that he wished to peruse the publication in solitude and at his leisure, so he could give it his full attention.

Pagnanelli's Italian name caused Howard to suspect that he was somehow involved with the two *Bolshevists*, Sacco and Vanzetti, whom Viereck had assayed to interview at the Dedham Prison in Massachusetts. All of that brought to Howard's mind his harrowing experience in the Seekonk's cold waters and his strange interview at the police headquarters in Providence. But Pagnanelli's features and his accent indicated a more easterly origin than the Italian: Greek, Howard surmised, or perhaps Armenian. He would have to watch the swarthy Pagnanelli, and the Count and Countess Vonsiatsky, to see how they dealt with each other. This should offer a clue regarding Pagnanelli's true ancestry. In any case, something did not quite ring true about the man, and Howard was more relieved than annoyed when Pagnanelli excused himself to leave the room briefly.

Sylvester Viereck strode up and propelled Howard toward another pair of men engaged in deep discussion. They paused and looked up at the approach of Howard and Sylvester. One of them, Howard recognized as soon as he heard the name. He was Heinz Spanknoebel, a heavy-set, middle-aged man in a plain business suit. He had the hands and the manner of a worker, but an air of intelligence and seriousness.

The other man was more elaborately turned out, wearing a row of miniature military decorations on the breast of his jacket and a monocle in his eye. Viereck introduced him as Dr. Otto Kiep, a ranking member of the consular service. Kiep clicked his heels and made a quarter-bow as he shook hands.

"Did you hear what happened in Detroit?" Spanknoebel asked Howard as he joined the group. "They tried to get Mr. Ford. Almost got him, too, but he was too smart for them."

"I fear that I don't know what incident you refer to," Howard apologized.

"Oh, it happened yesterday. I'll bet that Jew Sapiro was behind it. Probably imported some mobsters from Chicago, half of them are Jews too, Hymie Weiss, Mickey Cohen, Diamond, Siegel. They can't stand the truth!"

"Yes," Dr. Kiep nodded, almost bowing again, "absolutely so. They have no loyalty to anyone but themselves. Their countries mean nothing to them. Nothing means anything to them but themselves."

The conversation slowed for a moment as a maid in black uniform frock and white lace apron offered a tray of miniature sandwiches on toothpicks to the group. Howard took a tiny bologna and cheese sandwich and drenched it in searing mustard from a cobalt-blue dish on the same tray.

"Mr. Ford was driving his coupe through Freshet Heights. Do you know the Detroit area, Dr. Kiep, Mr. Lovecraft? Well, it's a good district, the river runs right through it. This car pulled alongside Mr. Ford's car and tried to force him off the road, right into the river. He almost went into the river. If he had he probably would have drowned. But Mr. Ford managed to ram a tree instead. Lucky thing he wasn't going too fast or that might have been as bad.

"They got word to the plant as fast as the police got their report of the accident. Me and some others got right out to Freshet Heights to see if Mr. Ford was okay. You know Kuhn, Dr. Kiep? Me and my pal Fritz, we got out there to Freshet Heights and there was police cars and ambulances and Mr. Ford standing there kind of bruised up but he didn't want no stretcher or anything. He saw us and he come over to us and says 'Look what the Jews done now, boys! They must of thought they had me! Not that it would do them any good, Cameron'd carry on the work anyhow, but we must really have 'em on the run!'

"You know that Jew Sapiro is suing Mr. Ford over the stuff in the Dearborn *Independent?* He must know he's gonna lose so he had some of his gangster friends try and get to Mr. Ford personally. But it didn't work! He's okay and he'll be back at work on Monday if you ask me."

Dr. Kiep said, "I congratulate Mr. Ford on his quick action and his narrow escape! I would happily drink a toast to him. Ahah!" He turned and reached out an immaculate hand.

A waiter in cutaway was approaching with a tray of long-stemmed, shallow-bowled glasses filled with pale yellowish liquid. Dr. Kiep took a glass, as did Heinz Spanknoebel. When the waiter extended the tray to Howard he felt constrained to accept one also.

"To Mr. Henry Ford, his noble struggle and his miraculous escape from the threat upon his life," Dr. Kiep pronounced ceremoniously.

The three of them lifted their glasses. Howard saw that Kiep took a small sip from his while Spanknoebel downed the contents of his glass at a gulp. Howard looked into the bowl of his glass, saw that the yellowish liquid was filled with tiny bubbles that rose and burst by the hundred. He could even feel the tiny droplets of moisture against his face.

He took a small, gingerly sip of the stuff, found it not unpleasant although perhaps in need of some sweetening, took another sip and lowered his glass.

"Great stuff," Spanknoebel rumbled.

"Very nice champagne," Kiep commented. "Not as good as pre-war, of course, but then what is?" He laughed gently at his own witticism. "But seriously, Mr. Spanknoebel, how is your organization coming along? You know, we are prepared to offer reasonable support."

"Mr. Viereck has told me so." He turned to Howard. "You are aware that some stuff we talk about here, shouldn't be talked about anyplace else. Of course, any pal of Sylvester's must be okay."

Howard smiled wanly.

"The older groups," Dr. Kiep continued, "the Steuben Society, the various Deutscher-Amerikaner cultural societies that Mr. Viereck himself worked for so faithfully, have rather seen their day. We need something more directly— if not as yet more openly—political in its orientation."

"Yeah. What we had in mind, we want to call it something like—you speak any Dutch, Lovecraft? German, I mean. It's—what do you think of this, Dr. Kiep, *Freunde des Neuen Deutschlands?*"

Dr. Kiep smiled broadly. "Friends of the New Germany. Very nice, Mr. Spanknoebel. And what do you think of this, Mr. Lovecraft?" He turned inquiring eyes upon Howard, looking up from his own short stature at Howard's taller form.

"What new Germany do you mean, Dr. Kiep? The republic? Or something to follow? Is it your opinion that the Kaiser is to be restored? Or will this fellow Hitler come to power?"

"Barbarossa will rise, Mr. Lovecraft."

"Yes," Howard nodded, "I have heard that phrase before."

"Thing are gonna change," Spanknoebel put in. "And not just in Europe, either. Things are gonna change all over the world, including right here. A lot of people are going to be sorry they didn't get into line when there was time to get. Do you follow?"

"I'm quite certain that I understand you, Mr. Spanknoebel. If you will excuse me, please."

"What for, you belch or something?" Spanknoebel burst into tearful laughter. Lovecraft inclined his head in a gesture somewhere between a nod and a bow. The move was mirrored by Dr. Kiep and Howard left the group, champagne glass still in hand.

CHAPTER EIGHT:

"VOLSTEAD GIVES EACH SIP
A LITTLE EXTRA SAVOR"

WITHOUT A clear goal in mind, Howard started across the room. Through a window facing eastward he could see all of Manhattan stretched beneath him, the lights of 125th Street blinking on the north, the avenues stretching up and downtown, and farther to the east the dark rectangle of Central Park with only the glittering illumination of the Central Park Casino, and the snakelike progression of automobiles through the dark, their headlamps moving pairs of night-gleaming cat's eyes.

A feminine hand caught at his sleeve and drew him into a group, the group comprised entirely of persons he had been introduced to earlier in the evening. Before anyone spoke there was another arrival of a server with *hors d'oeuvres* and Howard took a small napkin-load of dainties, placing his champagne glass on a handy coaster.

The hand had belonged to Marion, the Countess Vonsiatsky, a woman in her fifties, to Howard's eye, overfed, overdressed in a frock of beige rayon bias-cut in the latest style: She was smoking a pastel-colored Russian cigarette in a long holder. "You are Mr. Lovecraft, aren't you? One meets so many people nowadays. Mr. Viereck told me that you were a literary man, I think it's so important to use the power of the printing press to win public sentiment to one's cause, don't you, Mr. Lovecraft? And it's so wonderful—so wonderful—to have people get together informally and see to it that their work all tends in the same direction, don't you agree?

"You have met—you must meet my husband, Count Vonsiatsky." A much younger man, Howard Lovecraft put him little beyond thirty, if that. The Count wore dinner jacket with pointed lapels and a small lapel insignia of the old Tsarist eagle. He bowed formally.

Howard somewhat uncomfortably returned the gesture.

"And here, of course," turning to indicate a heavy-set, round-faced man wearing a black suit and clerical collar, circular horn-rimmed spectacles and closely cropped hair, "is the Reverent Curran." Howard shook hands with the priest following a momentary pause while the latter transferred an *hors d'oeuvre* from his left hand to his mouth and a tall champagne glass (half full) from his right hand to his left.

"And dear Dr. Evans," the Countess burbled on. Evans was a smallish, dynamic man with sand-colored hair and a rumpled tan business suit. He stuck his hand out and mumbled something that Howard didn't understand, a word that might have been *Ayak*. Wasn't that some kind of Eskimo canoe, Howard wondered.

Rather than ask Evans to repeat his greeting, Howard mumbled a *pro forma* How-do-you-do and shook Evans' hand. The latter looked momentarily disappointed, then in a drawl that smacked more of the arid Southwest than the deep South where he made his headquarters, Evans said, "You a friend of Sylvester's, you're welcome to any party I visit, Mr. Lovecraft."

"You came in on New Haven Rail Road?" Count Vonsiatsky asked Howard. To the latter's affirmative, the young Count said, "I am locomotive man, you see." He held up his hands showing slim, aristocratic fingers whose tips, like the palms of his hands, were blunted with calluses. "Your train was pulled by Baldwin locomotive, Mr. Lovecraft. I am expert in technology of railroads. When *Bolshevist*s and overthrown and tsar returns to Russia, then imperial railroads will run on time. Just like Mussolini's! Hah!"

"Are you a railroader?" Howard asked politely.

"No," the Count shook his head. "I work, did work, in Baldwin locomotive works. In every department!" he grinned. "But unfortunately political work takes too much of time. I was required to give up career in manufacturing."

The Countess laid a fleshy arm on her husband's formal sleeve. "My Anastase is really very democratic, don't you think? Working like any ordinary wage-earner, when we really have all the money one could want. But when the new government take power in Russia he wants to give his country the best transportation system in the world.

Isn't that a grand undertaking, Mr. Lovecraft, Father Curran, Dr. Evans? Don't you think that's just wonderful? You do know about the new government that's going to take over in Russia, don't you, Mr. Lovecraft?"

"I think Mr. Viereck mentioned it." A waiter passed by and they all exchanged empty glasses for full.

"Gretchen does entertain so beautifully," the Countess gushed, "of course she's from Westchester stock and I've always thought that if you have to live in New York at all, Westchester is quite the nicest part of the state, although I don't see why she and Sylvester couldn't simply move to Connecticut where the quality of persons is higher, but then—did you say where you hail from, Mr. Lovecraft? Did I detect just the slightest hint of a New England twang? Or possibly even old England." She restrained a giggle. "You really ought to chat with Dr. DeLand about England, she is *such* an Anglophobe!"

"Pardon me, don't you mean Anglophile?"

"Of course! I'm so silly. Dear Anastase has all the brains in this family! I'm just so lucky to be a woman, am I not, so I don't really need to be too clever. Although of course there are so many clever women nowadays, it's almost hard to tell people's gender any more, without meeting them I mean. Ha-ha! But what with bobbed hair and the new bandeau headpieces and the flapper styles you sometimes can't tell even then!"

The Count pressed heavily on his wife's hand to silence her. "You have heard, Mr. Lovecraft, of All-Russian National Socialist Labor Party?"

"Just barely, I'm afraid. But I assume that your objective is the removal of the *Bolshevists* and restoration of the empire. I must say that I am fully in sympathy with any such objective."

"Indeed. Very well."

"You know, the *Bolshevists* are mostly atheistic Jews," the Reverend Curran put in. "Trotzky, Zinoniev, Litvinov. Now this fellow Stalin—they all use false names, you know—he's quite an interesting case. I understand that he used to be a seminarian under the name of Djugash-vili. Odd that he should become a Red. But the counter-revolution will make the Russian Empire a Christian land once again. And that's just one of the benefits to be gained."

"Amen to that!" Hiram Evans interjected. "And not Papist, either!"

"Ah, well the Russian church did separate from Rome. But better to be Christians, even schismatics, than atheists."

"You must pardon my obtuseness," Howard said, "but I do not quite see how you can conduct a revolution in Russia when you are in the United States."

"Ahah! Very good!"

"But everybody seems to be trying it. That fellow Kerensky just the other day."

A black expression crossed the Count's features. "On one point I agree even with Bolsheviki—Bolshevists. Kerensky is bourgeois fool. Ideals of liberal democracy cannot survive. Kerensky was leader of original revolution to overthrow tsar, Lenin and Trotzky used him as, what, fine English expression. Horse's paw? No, as stalking cat. Yes, Bolsheviki used Kerensky and democrat socialists as stalking cats to overthrow tsar, then Bolsheviki threw out Kerensky. Really very funny!"

"And your plans, sir? How can you overthrow the Reds?" Howard reached toward a passing server and snagged a dainty spiral of pink bologna and white cheese.

The Count made a vigorous hacking gesture with his hands. "In United States alone are 300,000 Russians loyal to throne. Think! Only need is for funds to equip army and ships to return to Russia. One month to overthrow Bolsheviki. Six months to establish firm control. Mr. Lovecraft, do you know anyone who has visited Red Russia? You do, yes, whether knowing or not. Mr. Viereck was there, met *Bolshevist* bureaucrats. He gives advice, as does my good friend, unfortunately not present tonight but is close co-worker of Herr Spanknoebel," he gestured toward the chemist, standing some yards away engrossed in conversation with Elizabeth Dilling and the swarthy Pagnanelli, "Herr, Mr. Fritz Kuhn."

A white linen towel, the neck of a green champagne bottle protruding from it, appeared between Howard and Count Vonsiatsky. Howard held his glass automatically for a refill, was surprised to see that the pourer was not the formally-clad waiter but George Sylvester Viereck himself, grinning broadly as he tipped the champagne into his guests' glasses.

"Just in from St. Pierre de Miquelon. The choice is not quite as broad in the United States as in Europe, but somehow Volstead gives each sip a little extra savor, don't you agree?"

Father Curran held out his glass for a refill, then turned back the lapel of his clergy suit. "You're under arrest, Sylvester. You might not have recognized me in my Christian disguise but I'm really Izzy Einstein the famous prohibition agent!"

"That's where you are wrong," Viereck replied. "I knew you by your beak. *You* are under arrest. I'm really Moe Smith!"

They both burst into laughter, joined loudly by the Countess Vonsiatsky, then less certainly by Howard and Dr. Evans. The Count looked nonplussed by the whole joke. His wife, as soon as she recovered her breath, drew him aside and began explaining it to him.

After everyone had recovered, Viereck placed the newly empty bottle on a table and said, "Howard, you seem to have charmed the Countess."

"Oh, but Mr. Lovecraft is a most charming man, Sylvester." The Countess leaned forward, her bulk threatening to tilt over and knock Howard and Sylvester sprawling. "Mr. Lovecraft was about to tell us about his home, weren't you, Mr. Lovecraft?"

Howard flushed. "I was born and raised in His Majesty's loyal colony of Rhode-Island and Providence Plantations."

Countess Vonsiatsky giggled again. "How wonderful, how wonderful! Well, perhaps we shall all live under the reign of crowned heads again someday."

"But you see, Howard," Viereck recaptured the conversation from the Countess, "tonight's gathering represents a sort of informal coordinating committee of many groups. Count Vonsiatsky's All-Russian Party, Dr. Kiep, whom you met earlier, representing the German equivalent group, Dr. Evans of the Ku Klux Klan, Father Curran of the International Truth Society, Dr. DeLand speaking for the Imperial Fascist League, Mrs. Billing's Patriotic Research Bureau, and of course Herr Spanknoebel's Friends of New Germany."

Viereck's face grew serious, he brushed a lock of rich, curling hair away from his forehead. "There are those who think that the present age of wild excesses will continue indefinitely, but they are wrong. Some sort of collapse, some drastic change, is inevitable. And when it comes— what will be the result?

"I ask you, are you prepared to see Europe and America go the way of Soviet Russia? We must make ourselves ready. Western civilization is like a green fruit tree, with the nations hanging from its limbs, ready to fall or be plucked. Russia has already fallen, and see who picked it up! Germany is swaying. General von Hindenberg is seventy-nine years of age, my friends! I have corresponded with him, I have met him. He is a fine old soldier, but what comes after? This politician Marx cannot hold Germany together. A new Reich awaits its chance to flower.

"And here in America—why, only the heroic Palmer raids of a few years ago saved us from an outburst of riot and revolution. But this do-nothing Coolidge will let everything go. And after Coolidge, why, who is to follow? Governor Smith?"

"We'll never see the Pope in the White House! They'll be blood in the streets first!" Hiram Evans shook a rough fist before him, then, "Pardon, Reverend."

Father Curran coughed nervously. "Well, it does present a problem to all, that I'll admit. But we should be able to work out a non-denominational approach, don't you think? A sort of—what a good colleague of mine in Michigan calls a Christian Front. Catholics and Protestants in unity to stop the forces of atheism and the international bankers."

"Say," Evans put in jocularly, "you know what happens if you turn a nigger inside out? You get a kike!" He collapsed in laughter at his own joke.

"Now," Viereck said, "if you'll excuse us for a little while, I must chat quietly with Howard." He took Lovecraft's elbow and steered him through the gathering, up the stairs from the sunken living room. The walked along a narrow hallway and entered Viereck's study. The room was lined with books and furnished in overstuffed maroon leather studded with brass.

Viereck showed Howard to a comfortable wing-chair, sat himself in an armchair facing Howard. He reached and pressed a small button on the wall near his chair, then picked up a mahogany humidor and offered it to Howard.

"I do not smoke, thank you."

Viereck extracted a long cigar from the humidor, closed the casket-like box and fished his cigar-cutter from his pocket. By the time he had lit the cigar a servant had entered the study. "Howard, what will you have to drink?" Viereck asked.

"Could I have a cup of coffee, please?"

Viereck raised an eyebrow but nodded to the servant. "A glass of *schnapps* for me, and bring the bottle along, as well." The servant departed.

"Now, Howard, what do you think of the people you've met this evening?"

Lovecraft reached forward and dragged a leather ottoman in front of his wing chair. "I'm afraid that Dr. Evans struck me as somewhat uncouth, Sylvester. As for the others, a most interesting group, although weighted a bit more to the Germanic side than the Britannic."

Viereck nodded pensively. "You're absolutely correct. On both counts. I'm afraid that Dr. Evans. . ." He gestured airily and heaved a sigh. "Yes, he is a bit of a diamond in the rough. But if you found him less than polished, you ought to have known his predecessor, Colonel Simmons.

"But do you see what is evolving, Howard? There is going to be a world order. I think that we may be living in the dawn of a new world-empire comparable to Rome at its greatest extent and its greatest advancement. But the new world-empire will be a greater one than Rome. We have today means of transportation and communication that would have made the greatest of the Caesars pale with envy. Think of Roman legions fitted with tanks and with wireless telephones, think of Roman aerial observers carried aloft in aeroplanes and balloons, and not only observers but gunners and bombardiers! Think of the Roman fleet equipped with ironclad battleships and U-boats!

"The empire would never have fallen, and the thousand-year night of the middle ages would never have descended upon Europe! Howard, you have studied history. It is only about four hundred years since Europe began to awake from her long slumber. Think of the progress that these years have seen, and of what another thousand years may bring to the world! That is what we lost with the fall of Rome, and that is what the new world-empire will bring to the planet. A thousand years of stability, discipline and progress! We will sweep away the *Bolshevist*s with the back of one hand, the bourgeois democracies with the other. And then we shall march!

"This is what I ask you to join, the movement which you can assist. Count Vonsiatsky will lead the new world-empire in Russia, Mosley in Great Britain, the Currans and the Evanses and their fellows in America. You—"

He halted in mid-phrase, responding to a discreet knock at the door; at Viereck's word the door opened and the servant entered again, bearing a tray with the liquor and coffee Viereck and Howard Lovecraft had requested. The tray was deposited and the servant exited at Viereck's direction.

"Now," Sylvester resumed, pouring steaming coffee from a Gorham silver pot into Howard's bone-china cup, "we need to document this new world-empire, we need a historian, we need a man who can present the case for the future to the people of America. We need a man with a broad view and a long vision, who can see not merely the Ku Klux Klan, the Friends of the New Germany, the Imperial Fascist League or any other member-body, but who can see the whole of what we are doing. And he must be a man of native stock, best of all of English an-cestry, to dispel any possible cloud that might hover over our movement."

Howard considered Viereck's words, stirring spoon upon spoon of sugar into his coffee. Finally he sipped at the mixture and set the spoon down, satisfied. "What about this fellow Pagnanelli? Isn't he a journalist of some sort?"

Viereck made a disdainful sound. "Some sort of ruffian. Have you seen the sheet he gets out?"

Howard reached inside his jacket and extracted the copy of the *Christian Defender* that Pagnanelli had given him. He spread it on a table-top between himself and Viereck. He scanned a few paragraphs of the prose. "Pretty crude, I have to concede that."

Viereck nodded. "That, plus the problem of Pagnanelli's ancestry. I should hardly call him an Old American. Of course, being European-born myself, I hardly cast scorn upon him for his foreign birth. But for this particular need, we must have someone whose credentials as an American are impeccable."

Howard put down his cup. "In that case you should know that I am not exactly an American super-patriot. I happen to think that the American Revolution was one of history's tragedies, provoked by a blundering monarch and led by men who would have hung as traitors had a few crucial military engagements evolved in slightly different fashion. There remains an anti-English strain in American politics to this day. I ask you, sir, have you followed the current mayoral campaign in Chicago?"

Viereck admitted that he had, to some extent.

"The Republican Thompson who was thoroughly discredited and routed from office four years ago has been running a scurrilous campaign backed by racketeer fortunes, playing for the votes of ignorant and violent Irishmen, rum-sodden louts and hoodlums. And what is his campaign slogan? *Kick George III in the pants!*

"I've seen actual quotations from Thompson's campaigns. Some of my closest friends and business associates either live in Chicago or come from there. He was elected mayor the first time by promising that he would punch King George in the snoot if he ever set foot in Chicago. I suppose he meant George V, not III. He once said that he would never sing 'God Save the King.' Not that anyone asked him to! But I have done it, and would again! He pressed the legislature in the state of Illinois to declare the legal language of the state to be American, not English! Perhaps that is what he speaks!

"And all of this—" Howard was warming to his subject "—all of this is quite obvious pandering to the Irish. And, you must pardon my saying this, Sylvester, but I must be honest with you—and the Germans! Thompson's constituency is largely Irish and German, and the man panders to them, to the O'Banions and the Guilfoyles and the O'Donnells, and sells them out to the Colosimos and the Gennas and the Torrios and the Capones!"

Viereck shook his head slowly from side to side, a patient smile on his lips. "This is petty, Howard."

"The poor fool Dever doesn't stand a chance," Howard resumed, not giving Viereck an opportunity to say anything more. "And you will see in Chicago a combine of Sicilians with their bootleg rum and beer, and ignorant Irish and German immigrants that will utterly ruin that city and spread, spread inexorably."

Sylvester tried to lay his hand on one of Howard's to calm him. Howard drew his own hand back as if Viereck had prodded it with a red-hot poker, but Lovecraft subsided. There was a momentary silence, then he said, "I suppose something might be worked out. I would never favor the Kaiser over Albion, but if Wilhelm or General von Hindenberg would try to reach an accommodation, some arrangement might be possible."

Viereck had pushed himself to his feet and paced to and fro. A small fire was burning in a stone fireplace at one side of the room and he stood with his back to it, holding his *schnapps* glass and speaking to Howard.

"I ask you to consider this possible future," he said. His voice was warm, the image that he presented was clearly one of which he was fond. "You are aware of the dynastic interrelationships of the European monarchies. Three families of immediate concern are closely united by bond of blood. In England, the Windsors—more properly, the House of Hanover."

Howard Lovecraft nodded.

Viereck said, "In Germany—presently exiled in the Netherlands, at Doorn, the Hohenzollerns. I know that Wilhelm II is prepared to return to Germany whenever the summons comes. Should it arrive too late for him—" a solemn look appeared on Sylvester Viereck's face "— Kronprinz Friedrich Wilhelm Victor August Ernst will surely shoulder the burden in his turn."

He whirled and looked deep into the dancing flames of the wood-fire that burned at the side of the room. There was a silence punctuated only by the snap of a knot in the firewood. "And in Russia, if the Romanoff Tsar survives, I know that a restoration will be accomplished."

He sipped at his *schnapps*, strode across the thick carpet and stood before Howard. "I do not believe that the Tsar does survive. As you are aware, rumor and hint are all that emerge from Soviet Russia, with regard to the fate of the royal family. But if the Romanoffs are extinct, then a collateral line of Hohenzollern or Hanover descent could be summoned to the palace."

Howard rose to his feet. "You seem very well versed in the intricacies of European royalty, Sylvester. Didn't you once mention that you had a personal relationship with the Kaiser? Isn't your interest in European politics a personal one?"

Viereck took off his tortoise-rimmed spectacles and placed them carefully on his desk-top. He drained off the last of the *schnapps* in his glass and placed it carefully on the silver tray beside the tinted-glass bottle. "I do indeed have a personal interest in all of this, yes. Howard, I will trust you not to spread indiscriminately the information which I will give you. Have I your word that this will be neither written down, nor published or transmitted in any way, nor repeated to any person without my express, prior approval?"

Howard shook his head, his expression an amalgam of puzzlement and dissent. "I cannot make such a pledge regarding information whose nature I do not know. Surely you would understand that."

Viereck nodded, pondered. "If I assure you that the information is of a purely personal—and highly sensitive—nature. Could you give your word?"

Howard frowned. "In that case, I could."

"Very well. Howard—" He refilled his glass from the bottle, tested the exterior of the silver coffee pot with his fingertips, refilled Howard's cup. "Is that still hot enough? I can summon a servant."

Howard tested the coffee, found it satisfactory, began spooning sugar from the pot-bellied bowl beside the pot.

"I was born in Hamburg, Germany, on the last day of the year 1884, Howard. My mother was a respectable but quite ordinary German woman of middle-class background. But my father was of a background which I can only describe to you as somewhat lurid."

Again he sighed, drank off half of his *schnapps*, poured more from bottle to glass. "My paternal grandmother was Edwina Viereck. I do not know that the name would be at all familiar to you. In her day she was a famed beauty, the leading romantic and dramatic actress of the Berlin stage. She was a woman of hot blood and high spirits, the toast of the demimonde, but she had other admirers of a more elevated identity.

"Among her lovers was my grandfather. He could not, for reasons of state, acknowledge paternity, but royal funds provided for the upbringing of the child, who kept the last name of his mother. His name was Louis Viereck.

His father was no less a personage than the Kronprinz of Prussia, later King and still later Kaiser Wilhelm I. Yes, I carry a heritage of shame and glory. My blood is royal but my stripe is sinister. In the coming world-empire, I would hope to gain recognition. The present Kaiser has recognized me, at least to the extent of greeting me as *vetter*—cousin."

He drained the last of his *schnapps,* whirled, flung the empty glass into the blazing fireplace where it shattered. Howard did not comment on the melodramatic gesture. Instead, he said, "I don't know whether you and all of those men and women out there," and gestured toward the doorway that led back to the larger room, "are a group of eccentrics pursuing some kind of bizarre dream —or whether there is anything real to all of this."

"I assure you, Howard, this is entirely real." Viereck peered deeply into Lovecraft's eyes. "After von Hindenberg goes—perhaps even before—the silly German experiment will end. There will be a National Socialist regime coupled with a restored monarchy. The same pattern will develop in England. The crown will survive, the government will perish. Mosley will come to power. It has happened already in Italy. It is coming in Spain. Vonsiatsky will bring it to Russia. And something like it will come to America. There may never be an emperor in the White House—although I would not rule that out too easily—but National Socialism or something very like it lies ahead for this nation. Believe me, Howard. This is your great opportunity. Believe me."

CHAPTER NINE:

A VISIT TO PARKSIDE

BELKNAP LONG was up hours before Howard Lovecraft; Howard had arrived well after Belknap retired for the night, and as usual he slept well into the next day. By the time Howard rose and declared himself ready to face the day, Belknap suggested that they head out for a meal: a somewhat late lunch for himself, breakfast for Howard.

They took a downtown car, climbed off and strolled eastward on 42nd Street. At Fifth Avenue they halted before the Public Library and let the crowd jostle past them on the busy sidewalk. "Did you know, Belknapius, that this site once held a superb example of Egyptian architecture?" Howard pointed at the imposing facade of the library and clucked his tongue disapprovingly.

"Egyptian? That's a new one on me. I know there are pyramids in Mexico; I've even toyed with the notion of laying a story against the setting of Quintana Roo in Mexico. All sorts of occult and exotic possibilities there, Egyptians, Atlanteans, whatever you please. But I never dreamed of Egyptians in New York City!"

"Not actual Egyptians, I'm afraid, although that's a charming notion. No, the old reservoir that stood here for some threescore years. A pity you don't know your own city better, grandchild. New York has a marvelous architectural heritage. Or it had, anyway, until more recent administrations set about to demolish everything of beauty and historical merit and replace it all with edifices of cold modernity—or worse, such as the neoclassical— no, one ought to rather to say *pseudoclassical* monstrosity we behold."

Belknap blew out his breath. "I thought it a rather handsome structure, actually. Don't you care for the library?"

"I suppose it's rather all right in its own way. But there formerly stood on this spot a reservoir designed by one James Renwick. Magnificent structure, I only wish I'd been brought here as a child to behold it. The structure stood until the turn of the century.

"The style was Egyptian, with tapering towers at each corner and in the center of each long wall to aid the eye in comprehending the scale and form of the building. The walls were forty-five feet high, built of solid hewn granite, and wide enough to accommodate strollers day and night. Imagine the magnificent view of the city provided by that walk!

"Well—gone now, simply gone. Come along, child." He turned and drew up at the corner, waiting for the signal-man in the traffic tower to change the signal, then led the way to an Oriental restaurant above a bookstore.

After they had eaten, Howard shook Belknapius by the hand and thanked him for his hospitality. "I'm off now to remote and demon-haunted Brooklyn, grandson. If the werewolves don't devour me and Syrian thugs fail in their never-ending schemes of abduction, I shall communicate shortly. Otherwise, tell Brother Pharnabus that 'The Space-Eater' has my blessing and that he'd better treat my favorite grandchild well or I shall return from the dark beyond to haunt his evil heart."

Long disappeared into the throngs out for a Saturday's shopping, and Howard made his way to a subway kiosk, fished in his pockets for a nickel to pay the fare, and boarded a wicker-seated car bound for Brooklyn.

He climbed from the train, walked the short distance to the address of his wife's apartment house, checked his wristwatch before entering the building. It was a very different apartment structure from the home of either the Longs or the Vierecks—or, for that matter, Vincent Starrett's bachelor friend Alexander Laing. This was a functional building of red brick and cement construction, its age somewhere between twenty and forty years. Quite nondescript; anonymous, in fact, like ten thousand similar tenements in the boroughs of the city.

Howard's contemplation of the architectural cipher was broken by the sound of his name being called in the familiar voice of his wife. He turned and saw Sonia striding along the sidewalk, a broad-brimmed hat framing her still-attractive face (she had not surrendered to the bob-or-shingle style dictated by the helmet-like cloche hats of recent years), her fox-collared cloth coat buttoned for its full length, a bag of groceries cradled in one arm and a folded tabloid clutched under the other along with her purse.

"Howard!" she cried again and increased her speed along the pavement. She thrust the brown paper sack into his arms, drew him to her with an arm around his shoulders and planted a warm kiss on his cheek. "Oh, Howard dear, I'm so glad to see you again!" She dropped her arm from around his shoulders and slipped her hand beneath his elbow, laying her head affectionately on his shoulder for a brief moment, then released him and fumbled through her purse until she found the key to the front door of the building.

She unlocked the heavy door and shouldered it open, holding it and chattering at Howard as he climbed over the low threshold into the dank flagstoned lobby. Howard tried to remonstrate with her for the public exuberance and affection of her greeting, but she gushed an unbroken string of inconsequentialities all the time that their footsteps were echoing up the stone staircase to Sonia's apartment.

Inside Sonia disposed of her coat and hat, took the bundle of groceries from Howard and set it on a kitchen counter, then returned to the living room where he waited.

"You look just wonderful, Howard. Here, put your feet up, come, this is your home, don't be stiff." She plumped up a cushion behind him, shoved a hassock in front of his chair. "I have so much to tell you, there's so much I want to hear from you, I don't know where to start. You know I'm working in the city again. The opportunity out west turned out to be a big disappointment so I had to come back. But I'm just as happy. You know, there's no place like New York, is there?"

Howard started to respond but Sonia resumed her talk first.

"I hope you're doing well, Howard. You're such a talented man, I hate to see you wasting yourself. Are you still in amateur journalism?" She was in the kitchen now, bustling; Howard could hear the opening and closing of the refrigerator door, the clatter of kitchen implements and dishes. "I'm just fixing a little snack, Howard, and then we can have dinner later, the evenings are getting longer now but I'll be happy when daylight saving comes in again, I think that was one of the best things they invented in years, even though it was for the war, it's an ill wind, as they say.

"Did you have any trouble getting out here? I know it's been so long." There was a final clatter and she emerged once again, drew up a chair near Howard's and sank into it with a great sigh.

He watched her move: even though she was in her middle forties, some seven years older than Howard's own thirty-seven, she remained a handsome woman, even a beautiful one. Her hair was long and lustrous, still the rich, dark shade it had been when they first met at an amateur journalism convention in Massachusetts. "The Brooklyn and Manhattan Transit Corporation performed in its usual stellar fashion."

Sonia laughed and reached for Howard's hand. "I have missed you, Howard. I wish that things had worked out differently for us, but it is so good to see you. I try to keep up with your activities, you know. I'm afraid that I just haven't the time any longer for amateur journalism but I buy every issue of Henneberger's magazine just to see if you're in it, or little Belknap or any of our other friends. I'd even like to try another story myself, some time, but you know I don't have any real talent for literature. When we did those two little stories together, why, you know how much more of your talent was responsible for their acceptance than my own."

Howard demurred.

"Now, 'The Invisible Monster'—horrid title that was stuck upon a fair story—was really your own, Sonia. As was 'Four O'clock.' I merely touched up the prose a little."

"You sell yourself short, Howard! You must not do that! Let's be honest about this. I contributed little more than the bare notions for those stories. I should never really have taken the by-lines for them, the least we should have done was share them."

"Well. . ." Howard pulled his hand away from Sonia's, but did so in a gentle manner. He stroked his chin thoughtfully. "I fear that my talent is a minor one. I have a certain facility for dealing with the prose expression of fantastic sights and notions, but as a talent I fear that I will achieve little recognition and deserve no more."

Sonia grew vehement. "That isn't so! There are a dozen authors or more who owe their success and much of their income to you. You call yourself a revisionist and charge them a tiny fraction, as if all you did was correct commas and spelling. Where would any of them be without you? What chance would Zealia Bishop have had, or Carl Eddy, or Adolphe de Castro? None! What would ever have happened to poor Ehrich Weiss's stories? You did so much fine work for him, why just the other day Theo was asking after you, Howard, you know they were both so fond of you, and Bess too. It seems like yesterday that Ehrich was alive. You know, he thought the world of you, Howard. He was one of your greatest fans. His death was such a tragedy!"

Howard shifted uncomfortably in his chair. "In fact, Sonia, we'd been corresponding. Houdini wanted me to do some work for him, some ghost-writing of a series of pieces on spiritualism."

Sonia burst into laughter, to Howard's puzzlement. She saw the uncomprehending look on his face, said, "Howard, what a funny play on words. You were ghost-writing about spiritualism!"

Howard smiled wryly. "Unintentional, I assure you."

"But anyway, you really should speak to Theo. He's taken over all of Ehrich's work, you know. They even look alike. Theo is bigger than Ehrich was. But he does almost all the same acts, and he writes also. I know he'd be so happy to see you, Howard."

"Perhaps. I expect I'll be doing some other work shortly. I don't know how much time I'll have for revision work or for ghost-writing."

"Oh, how wonderful! I always thought you should do things of your own, not work on other people's material. Oh, Howard, you know you have so much to offer the world, and you spend all your time on correspondence and revisions." Her face grew clouded, then brightened once again as she leaped to her feet. She disappeared from the room for a few seconds, reappeared carrying the folded tabloid she had brought home.

"Here, Howard. You look at this for a few minutes. I'll go and start dinner cooking and we can have a nice cozy evening at home, just like old times, Howard. Here, you look at the listing of radio programs and see what you can get on the set while I do a few little things in the kitchen. Here." She held the paper to him.

He took it gingerly and opened to the front page. "The *Graphic*. Ah, Sonia." He shook his head. "There are several decent papers in this city. Why can't you read something sensible, like the *Post*. A good, dignified newspaper. Or one of the others. The *Herald-Tribune* isn't so bad, and the *Times* is usually reliable even though it's a Jewish sheet."

He clucked and began leafing through the paper with its slangy headlines and sensational composographs. Before he had reached the radio program listings Sonia was back beside him, her hand pressing the newspaper out of the way. Her face was flushed and her eyes glistened with unshed tears. "Howard! Please don't act that way. How can you despise the Jews so? You know that I am a Jewess! Yet you married me. You have always said that you admired me, that you thought I was an intelligent and virtuous person. I try to live up to your expectations. How can you so despise my race?"

"I was not referring to *you*, Sonia."

"But how can you make that distinction? You despise the Jews but not me? What about your friend Loveman? You've said over and over that he is one of the men you most admire in the world, and he is a Jew. You did the work for Harry Houdini, you know that his name was Ehrich Weiss. You know that his brother Hardeen is Theo Weiss. You know they are the sons of a rabbi. How then can you speak of the Jews as you just did?"

"My dear, I made reference to the race, not to individuals. There are exceptions to every rule. Just as the finest and most advanced of races, the great Anglo-Teutonic breed, produced the aberration of Kaiser Wilhelm, so a debased people may produced any number of admirable individuals—as individuals." He shook his head.

"We shall speak of this again, Howard." Sonia took her hand away from the newspaper and Howard opened it once again. He found the radio program listing, checked his wristwatch and decided to search for *Roxy's Gang,* couldn't locate it, but turned up station WEAF and *The Eveready Hour.* They were presenting a comic dialogue by Moran and Mack and he sat back in his chair to enjoy the broadcast.

Delicious odors wafted from the kitchen. Howard closed his eyes, slipped down in his chair, feet still raised on the hassock, let the *Graphic* fall to the floor, and lapsed into a half-sleep.

He was awakened by Sonia's kiss on his cheek.: He opened his eyes and sat upright. She had set a table for them, turning one end of the living room into a dining space. There was a white cloth on the table, and a candle burning at its center, between the place settings.

"Come, Howard dear, I'm sorry I was so cross. Do you want to freshen up? Dinner is almost ready. I thought we could have our meal here, then go out for dessert. There's a wonderful new place that opened in the neighborhood, I know you'll love it. Come."

He washed and returned, found that Sonia had placed the first course on the table. "Aha, my dear Mrs. Lovecraft, mushrooms *au gratin*. A delight to the olfactory, optic, and gustatory systems." He sliced one of the stuffed mushrooms, tasted it, smiled at Sonia. "Delicious."

"Oh, Howard, you don't know how much it means to me to hear you say that."

"That the mushrooms are delicious? But of course they are."

"That wasn't what I meant. I mean, to hear you call me Mrs. Lovecraft once again. Howard, you don't know what that means to me."

The Eveready Hour was ending on WEAF, the closing sequence a fast series of jokes by Eddie Cantor. The news followed, the lead item being a statement by Secretary of Commerce Hoover regarding the dangerous situations in Mexico (where the Huerta government had seized United States oil interests) and China (where the contending forces in the civil war posed a continuing threat to foreigners and their activities).

"Business is the underlying force that gives civilization its whole basis. Without business there would be no government, no culture, no commerce. Let irresponsible persons in every country take warning that the United States of America, and other civilized nations, will take measures to protect their citizens and the affairs of their citizens, if the countries involved cannot meet their obligations."

Sonia rose and switched the controls to play records through the same chassis and speaker that had carried the radio broadcasts. She placed a Bach piece on the panatrope, cleared her own and Howard's empty dishes from the table and carried them to the kitchen. She returned with a salad of hearts of lettuce and watercress, tossing the greens in a huge wooden bowl before serving them to Howard and herself.

"I don't understand what the Secretary of Commerce is doing," Sonia commented. "He seems to be threatening foreign powers. Isn't that the task of the Secretary of State? Or is his job to conciliate foreign powers while the War and Navy departments make the threats?"

"Oh, Kellogg is too busy with the armaments conference to bother with little problems like China and Mexico. Besides, I suppose that Mr. Hoover is thinking about making a try for the Presidency next year, if his chief decides to retire."

"Do you think he will?"

Howard shrugged. "I've been involved with some political activities that are a good deal more dramatic than the first steps in the Presidential dance, of late. Tell me, Sonia, what do you understand of the political situation in your own country?"

Sonia stopped a forkful of salad greens halfway to her mouth. She reddened. "What do you mean, my own country? America is my country, Howard. I have lived here since childhood. I am an American citizen. My daughter is an American citizen."

Howard gestured placatingly. "Of course, of course. I referred to the country of your birth. To Russia. What are your feelings about the Romanoffs, Kerensky, Lenin, Rykoff, all that crew?"

Sonia snorted. "Tyranny or tyranny, that is all the choice the poor Russian people have. Did I ever tell you why my mother fled Ukrania? She and my father, old Shifirkin, were Jewish storekeepers in Itchno. Things were so bad for the Jews, old Shifirkin just ran away, poor man. Poor man! I should say! What about his poor wife? Ah, so Mother bundled me up and off we went, first to England, then to the golden land of opportunity, America. Jews had nothing to be very happy about under the old regime."

"I think your memory may be shadowed by your race, Sonia."

Eyes flashing, Sonia pointed her finger. "Did you ever hear your friend Harry Houdini's comment when he came out of Russia from touring? When was that, do you remember? I do! He was there in 1903, and he got Lebedoeff the old secret police boss to let him try an escape from a prison wagon, and he did! But when he came out of Russia he said it was like coming out of a prison.

"As for the new government—well, at least they do not persecute Jews. They only oppress everybody, a very egalitarian attitude. Very admirable!"

The music on the panatrope had ended and Sonia rose to remove the shellac disk and dispose of the used needle. In the silence of the moment a weird skirling sound floated through the air, a shrill piping of an unknown melody, in some jarring minor key. Howard sipped at a glass of water, set it in place and wiped his mouth.

"I see that our old neighbor the Syrian is still in residence."

"A harmless old man."

"I expect not. He's probably conjuring up some malign creature from the hellish regions beyond the dimensions of space with those piercing sounds of his. Or at any rate he's conjuring up a headache for me!"

Sonia laughed and switched back to a broadcast station that carried in melodies by the George Hall orchestra playing at the Hotel Taft. "That sounds like Dolly Dawn singing. Listen to that, a cabin in the pines. Hah! What does she know? A solid building in the city, with electric lights and steam heat and plenty of water when you need it, that's the life!"

Howard snorted. "Mere romantic imagery." He laughed.

Sonia cleared away the salad dishes and served broiled veal birds with brown roasted potatoes and spring asparagus under hollandaise.

"What I mean to ask," Howard resumed, "deals with the present situation in Russia, and with events yet to come. In your opinion, would the Russians respond to a new revolution? Would they throw out Rykoff and Stalin and that whole crew, and call back the Romanoffs?"

Sonia dropped her knife and fork with a clatter. "The revolution is devouring its children, Howard. You know what pattern is being followed. They'll kill each other off yet." She paused. "But the people will never call back the

Tsar. Even if he's still alive, which I have my doubts! I hope they can go ahead from this terror, but they can never go back. Never."

Howard stroked his chin contemplatively. "Have you ever heard of a Count Anastase Andreivitch Vonsiatsky?"

Sonia burst into laughter. "Anastase! Every Russian in America knows who he is! A petty nobleman, and Howard, you cannot comprehend how petty the nobility had got under the old empire. He arrived in America without a ko-pek to his name and found some rich climber twice his age to marry. Now everybody's happy, he has a big house and a Duesenberg and all the money he needs and she gets to call herself a countess. Hah!"

"Have you ever heard of the All-Russian National Socialist Labor Party?"

"Oh, of course. Vonsiatsky's little phantom army. He's going to sail back to Russia and overthrow the Reds, find some flea-bitten Romanoff hiding in a stable somewhere and put him in as front man, and make himself the Mussolini of Russia. All he's worthy of is a good horse-laugh!"

She speared another veal-bird and transferred it to Howard's plate. "Good, dear, I'm glad you still like my cooking." From the loudspeaker standing on an end-table by the sofa, the lilting voices of Dolly Dawn and her Dawn Patrol crooned on about some shine whose hair was curly and whose teeth were pearly.

~ ~ ~ ~ ~

They ordered their dessert and coffee at Jahn's ice cream parlor a few blocks from the Parkside apartment. Sonia called for a dish of vanilla. Howard ordered a concoction called a kitchen sink and plunged into the mound of multi-colored scoops of ice cream, syrups, maraschino cherries, crushed pineapple, preserved strawberries, ground nuts, sprinkles, marshmallow and whipped cream.

"Ah, now," he almost gasped between spoonfuls, "I will concede that New York has ice cream parlors that Providence cannot touch. There may be one or two at Cape Cod that compare favorably to these, but New York is still the champion."

Sonia reached to the next table and picked up an abandoned copy of tomorrow morning's *Sunday Journal*.

She looked at it, laid it on the marble-topped table beside her coffee cup and asked, "Did you know that my daughter is in Paris now?"

"Really! I thought she was so busy being a flapper she had time for nothing else."

"Yes. In fact, I suppose that's why she was so eager to go. There's a whole colony of *émigré* Americans living there, artists and poets and novelists. Florence said she just couldn't live in America any more. I think she was driven out by Prohibition."

"I'd hardly call that a powerful force. Seems to me that you can get a drink any time you want one."

Sonia gave him an arch look. "You were always a dry, Howard. I used to take a sip of wine now and then and I remember how you would frown. Aren't you T.T. any more?"

Howard's face grew flushed and he spooned a blob of almond-rocca ice cream with cherry syrup into his mouth before replying. "I must confess that I've had a few drinks. But only in the interest of education or of social conformity, for all that I despise the latter." He pressed a hand against his forehead, determined to direct the conversation back onto its former path.

"If Florence wasn't satisfied with jazz music and hip flasks in America, what is she doing in France?"

"Well, I suppose I can't condemn her for wanting to try a different country, considering that I've lived in a few of them. But I'm pleased that she isn't just loafing with the bohemian set drinking French liquors and condemning America. She has a good job. She's working as a correspondent for the Hearst interests, reporting on the American community. I always look for her work in the *American* and the *Journal* and the *Mirror.*"

"All right. Good for her." Howard returned to his kitchen sink.

Sonia set the *Journal* aside. "I don't see anything of Florence's in the paper. Do you want to take it with you, Howard? You might enjoy looking through the *American Weekly.* I know you do admire Mr. Merritt, the editor."

Howard said, "I suppose so," and slid the newspaper back toward his place. "I'd be happier if he would write more fiction but I suppose the salary he receives makes him keep his attention focused on his editing."

Sonia reached across the table and put her hand on Howard's. "Maybe you should offer him some of your work. I imagine that Mr. Hearst pays better rates than Mr. Henneberger."

"I am sure that he does. But look at his publication! Howard slid his hand from beneath Sonia's and slipped the *American Weekly* section out of the thick newspaper. "I do not think it would be appropriate to place my works and my name in such a periodical. Merritt must have made his own peace with his own conscience and I will not be the one to condemn him, but I cannot place myself on that level."

~ ~ ~ ~ ~

Back at 259 Parkside, Howard asked Sonia to provide him with bedding to be placed on the sofa. She told him that she had hoped he would join her. He pointed out that his letter had been absolutely unequivocal on the subject, and if she would not provide him with separate quarters he would return to Manhattan and stay at West End Avenue.

Sonia heaved a sigh and fetched linens for him. He accepted a chaste good-night kiss as well. As Sonia disappeared into the bedroom she said, "My door will not be locked, Howard."

He called, "Good night." In the darkened living room a few stray patches of light made their way up from the street-lamps. Howard lay on his back, hands clasped behind his head, watching the ceiling. Every time a car passed, its headlights were somehow reflected upward and traced a weird pattern of shadow and light across the ceiling, from Howard's feet toward his head or from his head toward his feet. He tried to unravel the mechanism of the light's travel from the street to this upstairs apartment, realized that the hilly streets of Brooklyn would make such patterns unavoidable. It was like watching the ripples of moonlight on water, restful and relaxing. Howard's eyelids drooped.

The moonlight rippled on the surface of the cold water and he shivered with the penetrating frigidity. He had trouble getting air and opened his mouth to draw in a breath. He realized that he was under water and tried to rise to the surface but his feet were anchored to the bottom. They were encased in a bucket of concrete.

Why had they done this to him? He had nothing against the Morelli's. He had nothing to do with the men at Dedham. He tried to reach the surface and his hands broke through into the night air, into the moonlit Providence night, but his face was deep beneath the water of the Seekonk and he couldn't breath. He tried again to pull himself up but could not. He opened his mouth and tried to scream for help, to scream for help, to scream, to scream, to scream.

He sat bolt upright, the sound of his own voice ringing in his ears. He looked around, totally disoriented. This wasn't the bottom of the Seekonk. He was dry. But where was he? Was this Providence? He didn't recognize his Barnes Street room, or was he back at Angell? No! He must be in New York. There was a weird skirling music. Was he at Belknapius' home? But the piping!

Suddenly Sonia was there, bustling out of her bedroom in a flannel dressing gown, calling to him in concern. "Howard, Howard, what happened?"

She ran to the sofa and sat beside him, put her arms around him. He laid his face against the softness of her.

"Sonia!"

"It's all right, Howard. You must have had a dream. You know you always had trouble with dreams. But it's all right now."

He only shook.

"It's all right, Howard. Just hold on to me." He felt her arms around him, her hands holding his back, pressing him to her. "Come, dear, don't be afraid."

The Syrian music was still going on. Howard managed a feeble laugh. "You're right, Sonia. It was a dream. I am very sorry to have wakened you. It must be that damned Oriental with his weird music. He must never sleep. Or maybe there are two of them and they work in shifts. *Hoooooo!"* He shuddered once more, but the warmth of Sonia was working on him, making him feel more secure and unmenaced. "I'm all right now, thank you."

She showed no sign of leaving him alone again.

"Maybe you could tell me about the dream, Howard. You know that Dr. Freud says that dreams are very important, and we have to write them down or tell someone right away or they simply fade out and we lose them."

"Freud—another Hebrew."

"No matter. What did you dream."

Howard drew a deep breath, let it out, rubbed his face with his two hands, trying to set his thoughts in order. Finally he managed to reconstruct the nightmare and describe it to Sonia.

She nodded, barely visible in the late-night darkness of the room. "Do you know what that could mean? The water, the drowning, the trapped part?"

Howard said he knew exactly what the dream meant. It had no deep revelation to provide. It was a re-enactment of the drowning of Celestino Madeiros' brother by the Morelli Gang. Howard told Sonia of the incident and its sequel at the Providence police headquarters.

"Well, at least the mystery of the nightmare is solved, dear Howard. I should think that experience would give you bad dreams. It was like your story about the cheapskate undertaker."

" 'In the Vault,' yes. Life imitates art, eh? In fact, I suppose that the river is an added element of horror. It would take some doing to work that added theme into the story, but there is surely some way to do it."

"Would you like a warm cup of cocoa, Howard? Something before you go back to sleep?"

He shook his head. "No, thank you."

"Then come." Sonia stood up, drawing Howard with her by his hand. He was clad in an old-fashioned night-shirt, of the sort he had worn all his life and saw no reason to exchange for the flashy modern pyjamas. "Come, dear," and Sonia drew him with her across the room, through the doorway.

She drew him onto the bed with her. He lay rigidly, the Syrian music whining faintly but penetratingly in his ears.

"Howard, dear."

Sonia put her arms around him, drew his head once more onto her chest. She stroked his neck and his shoulders. Slowly he was able to relax, and finally, beneath a warm quilted comforter, to sleep.

~ ~ ~ ~ ~

He awoke to the odor of bacon frying and coffee brewing, looked out the window into full daylight, a day well advanced. He couldn't find his wristwatch, padded into the living room still in nightshirt and found his watch beside the sofa. It was already after noon.

Howard looked through the newspaper more fully (the most interesting item being the announcement by the Victor Talking Machine Company of the development of an Automatic Orthophonic Victrola that could change its own records, playing as many as twelve selections once set up properly), shaved and dressed, and joined Sonia in the kitchen for breakfast. Afterwards he placed a telephone call to Alex Laing's apartment in the Studio Building, hoping to find that Vincent Starrett was in town. He was, and Howard arranged a meeting at Laing's.

He spent the afternoon with Sonia, strolling through Brooklyn observing old architecture, and toward sundown asked if she would like to join him for the evening. "I'd love to, Howard," Sonia said, "but I know what a night-owl you can be, and I must rise early and go to work. You know, the spring hats are selling briskly. I think the cloche and toque are both on their way out, and we shall see broad brims and longer hair for women." She paused and grinned. "A lot you care about millinery trends! Well, I don't blame you. But one must survive on this earth. I think I should spend a quiet evening and retire early. You take a key and return whenever you're good and ready."

Howard tried to persuade her, but Sonia was adamant. "I know you, Howard. You're far too courtly to admit it, but you'll be very upset if I have to go home while you're still involved with book talk with your friends, or off on one of your famous walking tours or looking for a late-night feast. You go ahead."

They returned to Parkside together. Sonia brewed a pot of tea and after drinking a cup Howard took his leave.

CHAPTER TEN:

THE RUM TRADE IN ACTION

AT ALEX LAING'S apartment on West 10th Street, Laing was bustling around the living room sorting manuscripts and worksheets while Vincent Starrett, leonine shock swept up from his high brow, smoked a pipe and read. At Howard Lovecraft's ring of the doorbell Laing had admitted the visitor and returned at once to his work.

"Just a bunch of stuff from the office," he tossed over his shoulder. "One thing about Gernsback, he doesn't like idlers around the place. Everybody gets enough to take home and stay out of trouble! Be right with you."

Starrett held his book out toward Howard. "Ever see anything like this before? I came across it over on Fourth Avenue yesterday afternoon. *Gaston de Blondeville* by Mrs. Radcliffe. One hundred one years old this year! Isn't it lovely?"

Howard accepted the book, admired its spine and front matter. "Lovely condition, Vincentius. First edition, too, Colburn, London. An interesting work. Odd that it should lie unpublished for nearly a quarter century after its author's death. I congratulate you."

He handed back the book, watching a self-delighted grin spread across the Chicagoan's face.

"By the way," Howard went on, "do you have the rest of it here or is that put away?"

"Rest of it?" Starrett asked, puzzled.

"Of course. Didn't you get the other volumes? Didn't you know that *Blondeville* was a four-decker?"

"A four-decker? Oh, my God!" Starrett smote his forehead with the heel of one hand, clutching the book in the other. He opened it, turned to the front matter, then to the end of the book. "Oh, my God," he moaned again, "no wonder I got such a good value. And I call myself a bookman! This makes me want to tear my hair out. In fact I think I will!"

"Well, if you really feel the need to read all four volumes, I can lend you the other three some time. I think I still have the whole set up in Providence. Not that I consider myself a serious collector."

Laing had finished his work and bounded up to stand beside Howard. "Poor old Starrett! Too bad, Vinny. Listen, anybody want a quick snort of rotgut? Want to drown your woes, Vin?"

Starrett shook his head sadly, the grand shock of hair bobbing with each move. "I'm afraid it would take more than a glass of bathtub gin to make up for this *faux pas.* I don't know whether to feel sorry for myself or angry with myself or just embarrassed for acting such a fool." He laid the book aside.

"Anyway, let's clear out of here. I need some fresh air. Maybe we'll run into somebody who can take my mind off my woes."

They clapped their hats on their heads and headed out into West 10th Street, wandering down Sixth Avenue to prowl the little cafes and bookshops, open at all odd hours and days to accommodate the bohemian residents of Greenwich Village. Passing a half-subterranean bookshop on West 4th Laing stopped Howard and Vincent with a hand on the elbow of each. "There's a fellow I know! Howard, I think you ought to meet him if you're serious about dealing with my outfit." He indicated a young man —almost a boy—standing among the dusty stacks in the store, poring through old volumes in classic bookman's pose.

Howard asked, "Why, who is he?"

"Nice youngster. A literary agent in a small way."

Howard said he'd never used an agent, nor felt the need to surrender ten percent of his already sufficiently meager earnings for the dubious privilege of having his manuscripts pass through an extra pair of hands on their way to market and his checks do the same on their way back to him.

Laing grinned wryly. "I don't know if I should say this, Lovecraft, it might be talking out of school. But we're a little bit slow, down at Experimenter Publishing. In fact, if you have an agent who doesn't mind making a little bit of a pest out of himself, you have a lot better chance of getting your money and you're certain to get it faster. Unless you think you want to come up and hang around the office yourself."

"This is a bit premature, isn't it? I haven't sent anything to your company."

Laing laughed, a quick, harsh sound. "Right. But you mentioned a story that sounded pretty good to me. I think old Dr. Sloane'd go for it, but we're a little bit slow and unsteady about sending out checks. Mr. Gernsback tries to keep on top of stuff but he's all involved with his broadcast projects. You ever listen to our radio station, WRNY? Gernsback's puttering around in his lab, trying to work out a way to send pictures just like sound."

"Television, of course."

"Yeah. Mr. Gernsback invented it, did you know that?"

Vincent Starrett, who had been studying the books in the nickel bin, put in an astonished "Oh, come on Alex! He didn't invent television, did he?"

"The word, the word, Vince. Cripes, everybody and his brother has little flicker tubes in their lab. Mr. Gernsback invented the *word* television."

Starrett laughed gently. He'd picked two or three somewhat battered volumes from the bin. "Well, I think I'll go inside and stand and deliver my shekels to the proprietor. I see your young mogul is still engaged. Do you want to remain out here and we'll go on, or shall I invite the boy to join our company?"

Laing headed down the steps. "Come on, Howie, I'll introduce you to the kid."

At Laing's introduction Howard Lovecraft shook hands with the youngster, a dark-haired, bespectacled, serious-meined individual. "Yes, I do a little agenting," the boy admitted. And at mention of Howard's name, the youngster's face brightened. "Of course I know who you are. I've read a lot of your stories. I'd like to do an interview with you some time for my amateur magazine. Have I ever sent you a copy?"

Howard said that the boy hadn't, and pulled pen and notepad from his pocket to give the boy his address. In exchange he got a slip with the youngster's mailing address. The boy bought a thick fantasy novel and joined Laing, Starrett and Howard Lovecraft as they left the shop. A few minutes later they had settled around a table in a dimly-lit coffee house a few doors farther west.

Howard asked Starrett what progress he'd made on his novel.

"It's going along pretty well," Vincent admitted. "You know, I just took a vial of water from the Fountain of Youth and I'm following it through a few hundred years of history as it passes from hand to hand. Of course," and he paused for a dramatic beat, "I have it pass through some interesting hands."

"You'd mentioned that," Howard said.

"Oh."

"Not to me," the youngster said. "Of course I've read your stories, too, Mr. Starrett. But I didn't know about your novel."

"Please, just Vincent, not Mister, all right? I think I'm going to call the book *Seaports in the Moon*, do you think that's any good as a title? I'm just a trifle worried that it sounds like one of those space adventures that your employer publishes, Alexander, but I'm inclined to try it anyway and see what George Doran has to say about it."

In one dingy corner of the cafe a group of Negro musicians in tuxedos were setting up music stands and assembling instruments. A waitress appeared and took orders from the foursome at the table; Howard ordered a slice of hot apple and cinnamon pie *a la mode* and a cup of coffee.

Starrett changed the subject. "How did you make out with your friend Viereck, Howard? Anything going to develop from that?"

Howard spread his hands as if trying to set the whole experience with Viereck on the table between them. "I don't really know," he confessed. "He is a strange man, and he has some much stranger friends. Some of them from out your way, in fact. Did you ever cross paths with a Mrs. Dilling from Kenilworth, Illinois?"

Starrett nodded. "You cross paths and rub shoulders and a few other things with all sorts of people when you're in the news game, Howard. You ought to try it some time. You mix with the swells of society one day and with the dregs that night. Or vice versa. Sometimes it's hard to tell them apart. Yes, Mr. and Mrs. Dilling are well known citizens. Very respectable. They do tend to get involved with some funny political groups, but that's about all that's noteworthy about them. I think they never quite for over the Palmer raids and the big red scare a few years back. Mrs. Dilling sees a Bolshie behind every tree and a Wobbly under every bed, I think. I covered a speech of hers once where she accused the Civil Liberties Union, the council of churches, and the YMCA of being Red covers! Hah!"

He paused while the waitress served the food and drinks they had ordered; during the lull the band started to play some rough, syncopated tune and a burly, sweating Negro began to sing about his troubles with his woman home in Rolling Fork, Mississippi.

Howard made a low remark about savages and their tribal rites, then yielded to Starrett who had more to say about Illinois and its politics.

"The interesting thing is, of course, that the most respectable people and the racketeers hobnob as a matter of course. You must have seen photos of some of the gangster funerals in the tabloids. Solid silver coffins, whole fields of flowers, aldermen and state officials acting as honorary pallbearers when the bootlegger barons give each other their send-offs. Pah!

"Listen, I just had a letter this week from an old pal who works for the *Trib,* Colonel McCormick's sheet."

While Starrett fished in his pockets for the letter, Howard said, "That's a relief of sorts. For a while I thought Hearst had everybody working for him."

"Here it is." Starrett laid the envelope on the table, pulled a couple of sheets of folded newsprint out. "Lingle predicts," he intoned. "Newspaperman for fifteen years. Independently wealthy, too, so nobody can bribe him. He says, 'If you think the past four years were fun, wait till Wednesday. Poor Dever doesn't stand a chance.'

"You know," Starrett looked up from the letter, "the mayoral election is Tuesday. In Chicago, I mean. New York is already amply covered by its own press. But Chicago politics is much more fun. We got rid of Thompson back in '23. Put in Judge Dever. At least he makes a feeble effort to control the mobs, not that it does much good. The last really sweet assignment I had in Chi was those nickel murders last year, you remember them? But Jake says, 'They don't even want Dever. Thompson is going to come back in by a landslide. Just to be on the safe side, the whole Republican-Thompson-Crowe bunch have got this nincompoop Robertson to run as an independent and drain a few extra votes away from Dever. So it's back to Big Bill the Builder and Scarface Al can abandon his Cicero digs and move right into City Hall.

"Isn't that lovely?" Starrett folded the letter and stuffed it back into his pocket.

"That's the rum trade in action," Howard asserted. "If Prohibition were properly enforced these mobsters would all be where they belong, behind bars, and this corruption could be cleaned up. But the people don't want reform, they want to wallow."

Starrett shook his head with its great shock of dark hair. "You're only half right, Howard. It isn't Prohibition laxity that promotes crime. It's Prohibition itself. You know what Capone says about himself? I've met the man, he's absolutely amazing. 'I'm an honest businessman supplying a need.' That's his rationale, and I think he really believes it. And you know something?" He put his hand on Howard's wrist for emphasis. "I halfway believe it myself!"

The trumpeter of the Negro band ran through a sequence of particularly raucous notes, overcoming conversation for a few moments. Howard concentrated on his pie until the solo ended and a gravel-throated singer began to moan about a jellyroll. "Silly nonsense," Howard commented.

Then, turning back to the table, "No, Vincentius, I cannot agree. Wild and licentious behavior would be the certain result of a loosening of restraints. Given the opportunity, the great mass of humanity seeks its lowest common denominator, and it is the duty of those in power to raise the level of the masses, not pander to the grossness of their impulses."

Starrett laughed. "All I can say to that is what Henry Mencken says to his critics. You may be right."

"I thought that was Branch Cabell said that," Alex Laing chimed in. "You sure it's Mencken?"

Starrett said, "No."

Before they parted, Howard agreed to send "The Colour Out of Space" to the young literary agent, who would get it to the Experimenter Publishing Company and make sure that Howard was paid with reasonable promptness. Alex Laing said he'd keep his eye out for the story and guide it through the superannuated handling of editor Sloane. Then Starrett and Laing walked back toward the Studio Building while Howard and the youngster shared a subway ride back to Brooklyn.

Howard checked his wristwatch as he entered the apartment at Parkside Avenue. It was only a little after two o'clock, so he read for a while, then made himself comfortable on the couch and managed a night's sleep without nightmares. He found a note from Sonia in the morning, saying that she had had to leave for work.

~ ~ ~ ~ ~

Howard felt that he had accomplished a fair amount on his visit. The arrangement for "The Colour Out of Space" looked promising, and if it succeeded he would be happy to have expanded his markets, no longer having to rely exclusively on *Weird Tales* for a professional outlet.

He worked over a set of notes for a time, then went to the telephone, lifted the earpiece from its cradle and gave the number of the Jackson Publishing Company.

George Sylvester Viereck was at his desk, and a secretary put Howard's call through to him. Yes, Viereck was pleased to hear from Howard and, yes, he was free for luncheon today. Oh, just one moment. He checked his calendar. He was planning to meet Father Curran for lunch, but he was sure the Father wouldn't mind. Would Howard care to meet them? Certainly, Viereck's office on 42nd Street would be fine if Howard cared to come up; they were going to meet Father Curran at the restaurant.

Howard shaved, left a note thanking Sonia for her hospitality, and rode the BMT subway into Manhattan. He was early for his appointment, as he knew he would be, and spent nearly an hour walking around, enjoying the city.

When he reached Viereck's office, the publisher rose and shook his hand vigorously. "I'm very glad that you came up here first," Viereck said. "I meant to ask what you thought of our little gathering the other night. In confidence, of course. And—whether you think you will be able to join us in our enterprise."

He opened a humidor, extended it toward Howard. Howard shook his head. Viereck extracted a cigar before closing the humidor and turned his attention to the business of clipping its end and getting it alight.

Howard told him that he'd found the people fascinating in their variety and eccentricities.

Viereck nodded, rocking slightly in his leather swivel chair. Viereck blew a smoke ring toward the ceiling and watched it slowly swirl upward. "No questions regarding their eccentricities," he conceded. "But most of the geniuses and most of the leaders of mankind have always been eccentric in one way or another. The Caesars, Napoleon, Katherine of Russia." He drew again on his cigar. "You are surely familiar with Sigmund Freud, the Viennese genius?"

Howard muttered noncommittally.

"But to business," Viereck resumed. He leaned forward across the glass plate that covered the top of his desk. "We need a documenter, an historian, we need—if you please—a 'party theoretician.' I believe that you are the man for the job. I hope you will join us."

Howard pulled his notes from his pocket, looked at them and returned them before speaking.

"I think there is something I can do for you. We will of course have to reach an understanding with regard to schedule, payment, and the like. But I believe that a volume might emerge from my conversations with the representatives of the allied movements."

Viereck nodded, a lock of graying, curly hair tumbling onto his forehead.

"You spoke, at your home, of a coming world-empire. The more that I observe of America away from my own home and my own beloved colonial survivals, the more I become convinced that a new leadership and a new social order are needed, I believe that I could put down in a volume the blueprint for a new social order, both for this nation and for the world community."

"Excellent, excellent." Viereck leaned back once more. "And have you gone any further into development of the book?" At Howard's hesitation he added, "Of course, I realize you have had only a very few days. I hardly expect to see anything from you as yet. but if you have had some thoughts. . ."

"I have had a few. The title I am mulling over is *New America and the Coming World-Empire.* I think it has rather an impressive sound to it. In it I would hope to set forth a synthesized plan involving the Mosley group in Great Britain, your restorationist movement involving the Hohenzollerns—if you can provide me with assurances that the family is truly purged of the errors of 1914—the overthrow of the Reds in Moscow. And of course, a reordering of our domestic society to assure the control of this country by Old American and other northern types. The Negro, the Slav, the Oriental must all be put in their place if they are to remain in this country at all!"

Viereck nodded. "Very, very satisfactory. Of course I will do all necessary to place you in contact with sources of information and assistance from within the groups involved."

He placed his cigar on the lip of a brown-glass ashtray and slid open the center drawer of his heavy desk. He took a yellow pad from the drawer, set it on the desk and reached to a marble-based penholder for a writing instrument. They discussed schedule and contract terms while Viereck jotted notes. Finally he called his secretary from the outer office and instructed her to prepare a Jackson Press contract for *New America and the Coming World Order* by H. P. Lovecraft.

He rose from his swivel chair, circled the desk and shook Viereck's hand. "Come along, then," he said heartily, checking the watch that he pulled from his vest pocket, "we're keeping Father Curran waiting."

"Do you know Canfield's?" Viereck asked as they reached the lobby. Howard said he didn't. "Very nice little place." They walked to the corner of Fifth Avenue, then turned uptown. "I hope you don't mind a little walk," Viereck commented. "I've been at my desk all morning and I need some fresh air before I eat."

Howard said that was all right.

As they strolled along they passed a newsboy hawking early editions of the *Evening Sun*. The boy was shouting something about a submarine and a drawbridge and Viereck paused to buy a paper, letting the newsboy keep the full nickel that he tossed him.

"I hope it's all right with you. I want to see what this story is about. Submarine craft make a kind of hobby with me and I couldn't resist the headline." Viereck halted and folded the paper to expose the story. "Incredible. The submarine *S-17* rammed a drawbridge in the town of Vallejo, California. I never heard of such a town. It must be on the Pacific Ocean, I suppose."

"No, Sylvester. A friend of mine lives in Auburn, another town in California. He's mentioned Vallejo in letters, it's quite far inland. I believe there is a network of inland waterways leading into San Francisco Bay, and that Vallejo is located on one of the waterways."

Viereck nodded in understanding. He read through the story, commented, "Thank God, it was a minor mishap. I had thought of the *S-51*, the tragedy of that craft. You recall, it was. . . just a year and a half ago. Thirty-four men lost off the coast of Massachusetts." He shook his head, creases marking his brow. "Well, but this happening at Vallejo is a mere embarrassment."

He tossed the newspaper into a trash container as they turned right again at 44th Street and turned in under a canvas canopy at number 5. They entered a richly paneled hallway with converted gas fixtures providing illumination and a dark, wooden ceiling.

Howard stopped in his tracks. "I hope you don't mind if I spend a moment examining the woodwork here. This is a very fine example of mullioned barrel vaulting; such ceilings are seldom seen any longer. I would guess that this was put in some seventy-five years ago." He walked a short distance, eyes fixed on the woodwork overhead.

He returned to Viereck's side, said "Lovely. In general my preference is for the work of the eighteenth century, even some of the seventeenth. But there were craftsmen even into the late eighteen-hundreds. What did you say was the name of this place?"

They delivered their topcoats and hats to a coatroom attendant; Viereck handed over a gold-topped mahogany walking stick as well. "It's called Canfield's Gambling House, although open gaming is no longer permitted. Founded by a gentleman named Richard Canfield, and I believe you are quite correct about the date of the structure, although Canfield didn't take it over until near the end of the century.

"They serve a fine table here, and one sees a number of noteworthies. But—ah, I see that Father Curran has arrived before us."

Viereck said a few words to the *maitre d'* and they were ushered to a white-linened table where Father Curran, Roman collar in place and beaming smile at the ready, was sipping a tall, gracefully shaped glass. The glass appeared to contain water with an olive in it.

The priest lowered his glass and rose at the approach of the others. They shook hands all around, Viereck renewing his introduction of Howard Lovecraft and Father Curran. As soon as they were seated a waiter approached and asked if they wished a beverage before ordering. Viereck pointed to Father Curran's glass and indicated that he would have the same. Howard merely nodded to the waiter.

"You have to order water here?" he asked as soon as the waiter was gone.

"This isn't water with an olive floating in it," the priest laughed. "Have you never heard of a martini, Mr. Lovecraft?"

Howard shook his head. "I keep forgetting how little attention anyone pays to the Volstead Act any more. The congressman must be spinning in his seat."

Sylvester Viereck briefly explained Howard's relationship to the political groups and mentioned his plan for *New America and the Coming World-Empire.*

Curran grinned and said that he would do all that he could to assist in the preparation of the book. "We don't feel that we have to organize any rabble, you understand. We will do our homework, of course. We need grassroots support and it may be necessary at times to exert direct pressure. There are any number of ways to do this. Dr. Evans' organization seems to do extremely well at that. Sometimes," he leaned forward confidentially and lowered his voice, "I have to suppress a little giggle at some of Klan paraphernalia and mumbo-jumbo. They do seem to appeal to a rather juvenile streak in their adherents.

"But they also seem to reach a very deep level of motivation. The trappings, the robes, the secret liturgical language. Of course this is no new discovery. But they're quite good at it, with their kleagles and klexters and kludds. They don't even have to keep a straight face inside their hoods. Who's to know?

"Do you know their identification ritual? Truly remarkable. And Dr. DeLand gave me the most amusing parody

of it the other night up at your place, Mr. Viereck. She—
oh, the waiter. Shall we have another round?"

Sylvester Viereck indicated that he had a busy schedule for the afternoon and begged to be excused from the
second cocktail. Father Curran and Howard agreed and
they ordered their luncheon (Howard selected a broiled
lamb chop with whipped potatoes and baby sweet peas
along with a salad of fresh fruit and gelatin), then Curran
resumed his peroration.

"When Klansmen meet, you know, they are supposed
to exchange a whole series of arcana. Not being a Klansman myself—"

"I should hardly think you eligible," Howard interrupted.

"You're quite right, of course. And not being a member
of the organization, I am not supposed to know their ritual. but somehow I've managed to pick up a bit of it. It
goes like this. 'Ayak.' 'Akia.' 'Cygnar.' And so on. Have
you any idea what that means?"

He looked from Howard to Sylvester and back, dark
eyes dancing behind his round spectacles.

Sylvester shook his head from side to side. Howard
said, "I don't know the meaning, but in fact Dr. Evans did
greet me with some oddity the other evening and I was
rather puzzled over it. I believe that it was part of your
'Ayak,' 'Cygnar,' phrases."

"Actually the secret Klan ritual—you won't mention this
to Dr. Evans, will you, Sylvester? He doesn't know that I
know and he might be upset. The Klan ritual is a group of
words formed from the first letters of other words. I believe the technical term, Mr. Lovecraft, you would know
far better than I, is acronyms.

"So 'Ayak' simply means, *Are you a Klansman*. 'Akia'
stands for *A Klansman I am*. And so on. 'Cygnar,' I think I
mentioned, means *Can you give number and realm?*
Rather like one priest asking another the location of his
parish and the order in which he was ordained."

Sylvester Viereck conveyed a bit of chopped sirloin to
his mouth, put down his fork and chewed contemplatively. He took a sip of water. "I don't see what that has
to do with Dr. DeLand."

"Ahah! Of course not. Well, as you know, Dr. DeLand
has close ties with the Imperial Fascist League in London.

She likes to keep up with the British press, and she was telling me about a cartoon feature in the *Daily Mirror*—"

"Hot Hearst's tabloid?"

"Not at all. The *London Daily Mirror.*"

"Ah. And—?"

"And she came across a cartoon feature, some silly thing about a penguin, a rabbit and a dog. They speak in some sort of silly monosyllabic gibberish. It's for children, of course. But Dr. DeLand tells me that to build circulation they've started a kind of club for children who read the strip in the *Mirror.* They have ranks like Gugnunc, Grand Gugnunc and the like, badges like those silly *Potok-Kotop* things the KKK members wear, and a secret liturgy just like the Klan's 'Ayak' 'Akia' script. I found it so amusing, I made a little note of it."

He reached inside his black woolen suit jacket and extracted a black-and-gold notebook. "Ah, here. *The* first Gugnunc says to the second Gugnunc, 'Gug?' The proper reply is, naturally, 'Nunc!' This leads to 'Ick ick pah boo?' 'Goo goo pah nunc!' And so on! I think it's delicious! No one but a dada poet could have conceived the Gugnuncs. Or the Klan, I'm afraid."

"In all seriousness," Howard said, "I have meant to ask you about the, may I say, odd juxtaposition of ideological and, ah, philosophical groups that seem to be coming together. The Klan, for instance, to the limit of my information, is quite dedicated to upholding the supremacy of white, native-born, Protestant Americans."

Curran and Viereck both nodded.

"How, then, can you work in association with them? Is the Klan not anti-Catholic? And similarly," with which he turned toward Sylvester Viereck, "in another context—"

"Well, let's handle one problem at a time," Viereck interrupted.

Howard said all right.

"Well, you see," Gather Curran explained, "the Catholic Truth Society, despite the International in its name, operates primarily here in the Northeast. We have chapters from New Jersey through Massachusetts. As you might guess, we have great strength in Boston, and a lesser amount in Providence and other nearby cities."

"I would guess that, yes."

"We have allies. One of my closest friends is a fellow-priest who works out of Michigan. Perhaps you've heard some of his radio sermons for children. Charlie Coughlin is his name, very lovely man, full of love for the little ones. And for all the downtrodden of the earth.

"We've not done much together as yet, but Charlie has some very progressive ideas about social justice, and we've toyed with a scheme for combining my own efforts here in the East with his in the Middle West. If we can, we'd like to get some Protestants of similar sentiment working along with us, too. We're not quite as narrow-minded as we Catholics are sometimes made to look, you know.

"I don't know quite what the movement will be called or exactly how it would work, but it's beginning to come into shape. Charlie has played with some names, I think his best effort is the Christian Front."

Howard shook his head. "I still don't see how you can make your efforts fit neatly with those of the Ku Klux Klan."

"Well, you see, Mr. Lovecraft, the Klan's greatest strength is of course in the South, extending somewhat into the Northeast and as far west as Illinois and Indiana."

Howard nodded.

"My own efforts have been largely confined to New York and surrounding states, while Father Coughlin is in Michigan. So the area in which we overlap is not nearly as great as that in which we supplement each other. And in the areas where we *do* overlap, I must say that Dr. Evans and the Klan have shown admirable flexibility of. . . well, of emphasis, if not of philosophy."

Howard said, "I still don't follow."

"Well, to put a fine point to it, Mr. Lovecraft—in its own region, in the South, the Klan is opposed to Negroes, Jews and Catholics. In *our* region, where our efforts conjoin, Dr. Evans is using his Imperial Wizardhood to influence his followers in the direction of opposing Negroes and Jews."

"Only," Howard put in, half a question.

"Only," Father Curran confirmed.

The dialogue was interrupted by a ripple of comments and applause that swept through the room. Howard and the others turned to see the object of attention. A dapper, finely-made, almost tiny man had entered the room. He wore a flashily cut suit of the latest style, a silk necktie with jeweled stickpin. On his arm was a flamboyant woman of early middle age, hair done in an extreme bob, ropes of beads hanging from her bodice, the hem of her silk skirt rising above her knees.

The *maître d'* was bowing and ushing the couple to a choice table not very far from that which held Viereck and Curran and Howard Lovecraft.

When the couple were seated the man signaled to the captain and said a few words to him. Shortly waiters radiated to the tables in the room. The waiter standing over Howard's shoulder said, "A round of drinks, anything you'd like. Compliments of the Mayor and Miss Guinan." He inclined his head a few degrees toward the newly occupied table.

"Well, we were just about finished, I'm afraid," Father Curran apologized, half to the waiter, half to Howard and Sylvester. "Perhaps we could get a bit of liqueur with our coffee and cigars."

CHAPTER ELEVEN:

THE GHOSTS OF ANGELL STREET

HOWARD STAYED over one more night, bunking in at Belknap Long's home. The following day, Tuesday, he caught an afternoon train back to Providence, mulling over the results of his visit to New York. He was fairly well determined to write *New America and the Coming World-Empire* even though writing to meet the requirements of others rather than to satisfy the strivings of his own artistic impulse was, to him, a repulsive practice.

The fact was that he did feel distress at the direction of American society. The license, the corruption, the rampant racketeering and bootlegging of the time was certain evidence of a doomed civilization. The Madeiros drowning that Howard had witnessed and in which he had played an involuntary part continued to haunt him, and his nocturnal strolls along Angell Street no longer carried him as far as Swan Point or any other Seekonk locale. He tended nowadays to stay closer to College Hill, keeping his midnight *rendezvoux* with Nigger-man and Yaller Gal, indulging in his visions and fantasies of the ghosts of Angell Street past, then returning to 10 Barnes to spend the rest of each night reading or writing.

He got up "The Colour Out of Space" into proper form, grumbling at the necessity to pound out typewritten copy when he would have preferred a gentlemanly manuscript. When the story was finished he looked up the address of the young literary agent he had met through Alex Laing and sent him the story with instructions to place it with *Amazing Stories* and forward the magazine's payment less commission to Providence.

To prepare himself for *New America* he set upon a triple course of research. He would write to Mrs. Elizabeth Dilling in Illinois to get information on various domestic and foreign groups. He would meet again with Hiram Evans, Heinz Spanknoebel, Dr. Maude DeLand, Father Curran, Count Vonsiatsky and as many other leaders of the coming world empire as he could reach. Of course Sylvester Viereck himself should prove a valuable source, both through personal testimony and through the periodicals and books for which he was responsible. He'd given Howard some fliers at the 42nd Street office and Howard leafed through them idly: *The Re-Conquest of America*, "a remarkable picture of the all-pervading system of British intrigue in this country." *Our Debt to France*, "a mine of information for those who want the truth about our debt to France and what Germany has done for us in the past. . . President Wilson refuted." *Roosevelt*, by George Sylvester Viereck, "an astonishing exposure of British propaganda; Dr. Dernberg's secret visit to Oyster Bay; Roosevelt and the Kaiser." *The Poison in America's Cup*, by Philip Francis, the man who puts the Americanism into the New York *American*, "how British propaganda has debauched the United States. . . should be in the hands of every American who desires to save his country from the Octopus of British Capitalism and British intrigue." *The Memoirs of Von Tirpitz*, "secret history of submarine warfare, glimpses behind the scenes of empire, the growth, glory and decline of Germany's navy."

Howard unscrewed the cap of his Waterman and made a few notations of the fliers. Some of the publications were inexpensive pamphlets; others, costly books. He'd have to pen a note to Viereck asking if complementary copies were available; surely, if Howard was himself to become a Jackson Press author, copies of Viereck's older publications should be made available to him at discounted rates if not altogether without fee. The titles and descriptions indicated a heavy anti-British, pro-German bias.

New America and the Coming World-Empire would show no such bias, and Viereck had best understand that fact and accept it at the earliest possible moment. Howard would never prostitute his talent to the production of propaganda in behalf of a cause which he did not sincerely support, and he was a dedicated Anglophile. But he was prepared to abandon his longtime enmity of the Kaiser and the Reich if Viereck's new empire had any chance of realization. Then there would be a grand alliance of the northern races, the Anglo-Saxons, the Teutons, the Scandinavians. The inferior southerly types, Slavs, Mediterraneans, Semites, would be reduced to a level where they could no longer threaten the neo-classical civilization which must surely rise under the new world empire.

For the third source of information, he would use his own connections to cross-check the information coming from Mrs. Dilling's Patriotic Research Bureau and from his own investigations into the allied neo-imperial groups. Vincent Starrett was an invaluable conduit. He himself was highly knowledgeable concerning conditions in Chicago and all of the Midwest, a region in which there was much political activity. What Starrett could not provide, he could obtain for Howard from his friend Lingle of the Chicago *Tribune.*

Howard's wife Sonia also had useful sources of information. She knew numerous Russian *émigrés,* had been able to provide Howard with a second view of Count Vonsiatsky without hesitation. She could, at Howard's request, write to her daughter Florence in Paris and gain on-the-spot information regarding conditions there. And there was also Theo Weiss, the magician and escape artist billed as Hardeen and younger brother of Howard's former client Harry Houdini. Theo had toured Europe repeatedly, was still a prominent stage artist, and might well act as a direct source of information or as a conduit of data from European sources.

Finally there was George Pagnanelli. Here was an enigma. Howard had hardly spoken with Pagnanelli at the Viereck *soiree,* but even the few minutes he had spent with the journalist had intrigued him. Pagnanelli's journal, the *Christian Defender,* had been crudely produced and upon reading had proved to be even more crudely composed. It was a typical subliterate hate-sheet, something almost beneath Howard's notice.

But Pagnanelli himself had seemed far more intelligent, far more sensitive and alert, than the material he was handing around. Further, while his swarthy, Mediterranean appearance was in keeping with his name, the way he spoke English was not. Howard tried to compare Pagnanelli's accent with any he had heard before. Whatever the speech-pattern was, it was *not* Italian. If anything, Pagnanelli's speech resembled—slightly—that of Howard's wife Sonia. And Sonia was Russian-born; her English, learned in Liverpool during her family's temporary residence there after leaving Russia, was tempered more by Sonia's Slavic origin than by her British education.

Why did Pagnanelli, who passed himself off as an uncouth, native-horn American of Italian descent—speak like an educated man, but with a Slavic accent?

Sitting slumped in his favorite wing-backed chair, the hour late, both Annie and Lillian long since retired, Howard sat with only the ticking of a clock and the ghostly recollection of his dead cat Nigger-man to keep him company. By an electric lamp he restudied the *Christian Defender*, trying to puzzle out Pagnanelli's game. For the moment it defeated him and he refolded the hate-sheet and filed it away for re-examination another time.

Lying on his desk in the litter of unanswered correspondence was a letter from his fellow *Weird Tales* contributor Robert E. Howard. Having got into correspondence with the man, Howard Lovecraft first learned that the other was a Texan, a resident of the tiny, dust-swept community of Cross Plains.

The Texan revealed himself to be an amazingly prolific storyteller; Lovecraft took the hint of his letters and tracked down an array of stories by his correspondent, stories that had appeared under various by-lines in every sort of pulp magazine. Stories seemed to pour from the fellow's typewriter, not just borderline fantasies such as those which he sent to Pharnabus for *Weird Tales* but boxing stories, tales of piracy, historicals, Oriental stories. The Texan mentioned that he was an admirer of Vincent Starrett's Chicago pal Ed Burroughs (Lovecraft wondered at the way threads stretched from man to man, forming a web of amazing complexity and symmetry), and was toying with an interplanetary somewhat like Burroughs' long-running serial. And he was an even greater fan of the Englishman Arthur Sarsfield Ward and his titanic yellow peril series that ran under the by-line Sax Rohmer. Robert Howard wrote that he was playing around with the notion of doing a serial in the general mode of Ward's stories.

Lovecraft shook his head at the ability of the Texan to turn out the volume and variety of material that he did, most of all, at the man's endless stream of humorous and serious westerns. Following his usual practice, Lovecraft christened the Texan with a personal nickname, "Two-gun Bob." Robert Howard took to the name, and in return began using several of Howard Lovecraft's correspondence-names: Theobaldus and Ec'h-Pi-El.

Now Howard Lovecraft took the opportunity to write and ask the Texan if he knew anything about the background of Hiram Evans and his revived Ku Klux Klan. Howard Lovecraft took the opportunity to combine errands, riding a trolley down College Hill to downtown Providence one afternoon. He purchased a supply of stamps at the central post office, posted the letter he had written to Cross Plains, then made his way to police headquarters.

He located the detective lieutenant who had investigated the Madeiros drowning; the incident still bore heavily on Howard's mind and the silence of the Providence police force in its regard nagged at some corner of his consciousness at odd moments of the day and night.

The lieutenant came to the front desk when the duty officer informed him of Howard's presence. They walked to the lieutenant's office and sat at opposite sides of the battered wooden desk. The lieutenant kept a hot-plate on top of a low cabinet, a pot of ancient coffee steeping at the hot-plate's lowest setting. The lieutenant poured a cup for Howard and one for himself, then settled back in his wooden swivel chair and asked Howard what the visit was about.

Howard indicated only that the Madeiros killing still bothered him, wondered if there had been any developments. "At the time, you indicated that you knew both the identity and the motive of the killers," Howard reminded the officer.

The detective's heavy eyebrows flew upward. "Did I?" He seemed genuinely amazed. "We've got the incident marked down to persons unknown. Do you have information that might assist us in our investigation, sir?"

Howard sputtered. "You said it was the Morelli Gang. That the killing was a warning to Madeiros' brother in Massachusetts not to say any more about the South Braintree hold-up."

The detective leaned forward. "South Braintree?"

"The Sacco and Vanzetti case! Why am I explaining this to you?" Howard was livid. "You explained this all to me, weeks ago! Have you been stricken with amnesia?"

The lieutenant picked up his heavy mug of coffee and leaned back in his chair, sipping the stale coffee, gazing at Howard Lovecraft over the rim of the mug.

"We'll certainly be in touch with you if there's any need for your further help, Mr. Lovecraft. For the moment, though, I regret to tell you that our investigation of this crime is entirely stymied. Would you like a ride home? I'll have a plainclothesman give you a ride home. That was up on College Hill as I recall, out toward the Seekonk, is that correct?"

His fingers feeling icy despite the hot mug they held, Howard rose and walked before the lieutenant back to the front desk. The lieutenant escorted him to a side exit and guided him into an unmarked police vehicle. The driver wore civilian garb. The lieutenant leaned in the driver's window and spoke to him for a moment, then straightened, thanked Howard once again for his interest and assistance and disappeared back into the police headquarters.

The driver pulled onto Elbow Street, made his way through a few circuitous turns, then began to climb Cranston Street as it rose to the southwest, away from the Providence River.

"This is the wrong way," Howard called to the driver. "We're to go to College Hill, this will take us to Federal Hill."

The driver looked over his shoulder at Howard. "I'm sorry, sir, we have to make a little detour. I'll have you home right afterwards, sir. If you'd like, we can stop and you could telephone your family that you'll be a little late."

A momentary fantasy whirled through Howard's brain, of the driver kidnapping him, carrying him off into some sort of secret imprisonment—or worse—at the behest of a secret cabal of crooked police and racketeers. But if that were the case, the driver would hardly offer to stop and let him telephone his aunts. So, this had to be some innocent—but thoughtless—act on the part of the lieutenant at headquarters and the driver.

"That's all right," Howard told the driver. "My aunts are quite accustomed to my shifting for myself, and we don't all keep identical hours anyway. Drive on at will."

The driver said, "Yes, sir," and Howard ignored him, devoting his attention to the architectural features of Federal Hill. This was a section of the city which he had of late slighted in his rambles. Many of the older structures still standing were of great age and interest. Some of the tall white church steeples survived from colonial times, and Howard occasionally peered across the intervening depression from College Hill, admiring the spires and planning, some time, to visit the buildings themselves.

The car swung left on Huntington Avenue and cruised through the Mashapaug Pond district. The driver swung left again on Plymouth Street and pulled up before a modest private home.

"Right in here, sir," the driver spoke respectfully. He climbed down from his seat and opened the rear door for Howard. The driver escorted Howard to the front door of the house, pounded an ornamental knocker. A maid answered the door and took Howard's and the driver's hats, then ushered them into a cozy parlor fitted with comfortable furniture of twenty or thirty years before, a horsehair sofa, embroidered footstools before the easy chairs, antimacassars on the backs of the chairs and sofa. The walls held framed prints of pastoral scenes and hand-tinted photo-portraits of men and women garbed in turn-of-the-century fashions.

A concealed panatrope played classical music.

One corner of the room held a small Catholic religious shrine.

A man rose from the sofa and approached Howard. He was of middle years, hair graying heavily, his clothing of good quality and a conservative cut. The police driver introduced the two.

"Mr. Howard Lovecraft, Mr. Joseph Morelli."

Despite the older man's obvious Mediterranean origins Howard was favorably impressed with his dignified bearing, his conservative style and courtly manners. He extended his right hand and felt it gripped in a warm, strong grasp by Morelli.

Morelli placed his other hand warmly on Howard's shoulder, guided him to a comfortable seat. "I've heard about you, Mr. Lovecraft. I am very happy to make your acquaintance." He spoke with a trace of an Italian accent.

"Can I offer you a cocktail, or perhaps a glass of wine before dinner?"

Howard turned to the police driver, said, "You may go now. Stop in the kitchen for something before you go."

Then, to Howard once more, "Mrs. Morelli and I will be pleased if you could stay for dinner with us. We're both great admirers of literature and seldom meet a distinguished man like yourself."

Howard was delighted, dumbfounded, astonished by Morelli. He agreed to stay, accepted a glass of red wine in order not to offend his host. Morelli personally changed the recording every time the music ended; except for a tendency to select composers of a more southerly persuasion than Howard might have preferred, his taste was elegant and unimpeachable.

They spoke of culture; Howard was delighted. Morelli's area of expertise fitted neatly into the lacunae of Howard's own informal and largely self-conducted education. Morelli spoke of baroque composers, mostly Italian of course, illustrating his points with recorded samples of each as he described his compositions, humming bits of the few whose works he had no recordings of. He spoke of Albinoni, of Corelli and played for Howard a selection of the Christmas Concerto, he rhapsodized over Ricciotti ("Grossly underrated, Mr. Lovecraft, a master of stature approaching Vivaldi's), he played a recording of the Flute Concerto by Pergolesi.

He concluded with a paean to Luigi Cherubini, placing on the panatrope (he had one of the new automatic orthophonic machines) a series of disks with the D Minor Mass, accompanying the recorded voices in a clear tenor during the *Quonium tu solus sanctus*, then resuming to the sofa and weeping openly as the chorus joined in with their *Cum Sancto Spiritu*.

As the recording drew to a close Morelli crossed the room and shut off the panatrope. "Did you know, Mr. Lovecraft, that the great Beethoven was influenced by Cherubini? Yes, they were both in Vienna in the year 1805 and probably met, although no one knows. *Fidelio* is clearly inspired by Cherubini's *Les Deux Journées*. Cherubini even commented on Beethoven's work. He had reservations about Beethoven's use of voice, considering him brusque. Of course he was correct. Beethoven returned to orchestral music."

Responding to some signal undetectable by Howard, Morelli indicated that dinner was ready and led the way into the dining room, where a table was set with sparkling crystal and bone china laid against the background of a lace tablecloth cream-colored with age.

They were joined at the table by Morelli's wife and daughter. Both of the women had worked in the kitchen preparing the meal, but sat with Morelli and Howard while it was served by a uniformed maid. Conversation with the maid was entirely in Italian.

Mrs. Morelli was a heavy-set woman, dark of hair and complexion, whose English was much more heavily accented than her husband's. She spoke little during the meal.

Miss Morelli was slim, with long, glossy black hair and flashing eyes. Howard estimated her age at twenty, and was pleased when she mentioned that she traveled by streetcar each day, all the way to Pembroke Women's College near Howard's home.

"I had planned at one time to attend Brown University," Howard told her. "Unfortunately, poor health precluded my doing so. I nonetheless take advantage of their excellent library facilities, where the staff are most gracious about permitting me access to the stacks." He went on to describe his researches for "Supernatural Horror in Literature."

Miss Morelli was herself majoring in English Literature and they exchanged opinions of a score of authors, all to Howard's utter delight. "But," Howard wondered, "do you feel totally safe traveling entirely across the city each day by streetcar?"

"She's a real American girl," Joseph Morelli put in. "I'd send her in a car but she won't go in one. A real American girl."

"I'm really quite safe," Miss Morelli insisted with a smile.

Howard had three servings of pasta and two of veal, and an Italian pastry he'd never tried before for dessert. Only the calamari upset him, and he managed to avoid it without making a major display of his revulsion for sea food.

At the end of the meal Mrs. Morelli and Miss Morelli disappeared once more and Joseph served Howard sherry and walnuts in the parlor once more. Then he pulled an ancient engraved gold watch on the end of a decorated fob from his vest pocket. "I'm so sorry, Mr. Lovecraft, but we're a very quiet family. We retire early here. Please do not consider me inhospitable, and please come to visit us again."

Morelli guided him to the door. Howard's hat reappeared and he shook hands with Morelli, stepped onto the front stoop of the little house. The unmarked police cruiser was waiting at the curb, its engine running, the plainclothes driver standing with the door open for Howard.

They drove a few blocks, then the driver stopped the car and turned to Howard. "Mr. Morelli is a reputable citizen, his family are lovely people, don't you agree?"

Nonplussed, Howard grunted assent.

"Don't bother them, Mr. Lovecraft. Don't hang around headquarters too much either. And leave the Madeiros case to the police. It's being investigated fully. We'll contact you if we need you. You understand this, sir?"

Howard nodded numbly.

The driver turned away again, stepped on the self-starter switch, and chauffeured Howard home to Barnes Street.

Howard passed up his solitary ramble for the night, spent the following hours reading material from Viereck and examining the day's newspapers for material relevant to *New America and the Coming World-Empire.* He had pretty well decided to open a journal, inscribing in it items of interest from the day's press. In addition to his voluminous correspondence, he already maintained a commonplace book with brief notations for use in works of fiction. The new journal would be a companion piece which he would consult later when it came time to prepare his manuscript for the Jackson Press.

He didn't know *which* items would be useful, of course . . .but he felt that somehow everything would fall into place, in time, just as the many people and organizations he was moving among seemed somehow connected on a grand scale. Vincent Starrett's friend Jake Lingle was right, of course, about the Chicago mayoral election.

Thompson, who had retired in 1923 after two terms as mayor and let the hapless Arthur Lueder take his beating for him, had cannily un-retired and beaten William Dever, the man who'd outpolled Lueder. Thompson was vehemently pro-German and pro-Irish, conversely anti-British —but how much of that was real conviction, and how much of it a clever pandering to an electorate heavily characterized by German and Irish immigrants and their children? And Thompson was tied in with the rum-runners, alky-cookers, bootleggers and speakeasy operators, the racketeers and gangsters who made Chicago notorious. Were the Colosimos, Espositos, Zutas, Torrios, and Capones of Chicago connected with the Morelli Gang in Rhode Island? If so, that made a connection, also, to the anarchists awaiting execution in Dedham Prison.

Somehow it all had to fit together. Howard tried to make an outline of the relationships as if he were going to write a story shout them, but somehow the techniques that produced his short stories failed to expose the pattern when he applied them to these real persons.

There was more trouble in China. Chang Tso-lin's army raided the Soviet Russian embassy in Peking. The warlord's hand-picked Premiere was a fellow with the unlikely name of Wellington Koo, and he surely had his hands full. The Five Powers—the United States, Britain, France, Italy and Japan—were demanding safeguards of their citizens and their interests and threatening intervention in China on a scale unmatched since the Boxer Rebellion of 1900.

But still the situation came back to the influence of the Soviet Russians. If and when Vonsiatsky succeeded in overthrowing the *Bolshevists*, Russia and China might make peace. Or was there a place for China in Viereck's projected world empire? Yet another item in the news bore upon the Chinese situation. Senator Borah of Idaho was suggesting that the United States recognize the Red government in Russia and make an alliance of war against China. Borah saw the situation as a racial conflict of white against yellow, transcending completely the differing political systems of the nations involved.

In Italy a young man named Tito Zaniboni was convicted of plotting to assassinate Benito Mussolini and instigate a revolt against the fascist state, while in Massachusetts Governor Fuller had set the execution date for

Sacco and Vanzetti as June 10; Celestino (or Celestine, the newspapers rendered the spelling differently) Madeiros would be kept alive as long as Sacco and Vanzeti's case persisted, on the chance that he might be needed to give testimony regarding the involvement of the Morelli Gang in the South Braintree killings.

Closer to home, Secretary of Commerce Hoover inaugurated television broadcasting by appearing in a presentation carried by telephone lines from his office in Washington to the Bell Laboratory in New York. Radio station 3XN of Whippany, New York, transmitted the actual broadcast, in which Hoover predicted a popularity for television as great as that already being realized by radio. Lovecraft made a note of his suspicion that Hoover was building himself up for a try at the Republican nomination for president, should the taciturn Calvin Coolidge decide against seeking another term.

Among the Democrats, the Catholic governor of New York was clearly striving for nomination. In anticipation of objections to him on religious grounds he'd sent a letter to the *Atlantic Monthly* denying the power of the church over the state, while an Episcopalian lawyer named Charles Marshall challenged Smith's assertion, citing John Joseph McVey's *Manual of Christian Doctrine* and its assertion of the supremacy of church over temporal authority.

Right in Providence an uproar arose over the sensational novel *Elmer Gantry*. The book was already banned in Boston, and in Providence Mayor Dunne was being pressured to follow suit. But President Faunce of Brown University denounced the Boston move and urged Dunne to stand fast against narrow-mindedness and book-burners. Howard applauded silently. The Providence police department took the matter under advisement pending an investigation of the book's effect on public morals.

In the Atlantic Ocean off Cape May, Mew Jersey, Captain G. F. Steele of the steamer *Osceola* reported seeing a mystery plane plunge into the sea. The army, navy and coast guard all denied ownership of the plane or knowledge of the incident.

Howard closed up his journal and turned to his correspondence.

CHAPTER TWELVE:

WHAT'S IN IT FOR HIRAM EVANS?

IN CROSS PLAINS, Texas, a beefy, rather odd young man named Robert Ervin Howard received a letter addressed to him in the familiar, spidery hand that he recognized at once as belonging to his fellow author Howard Phillips Lovecraft, the eccentric antiquarian of Providence, Rhode Island. Bob carried the incoming mail to his solitary bedroom, stopping first in the kitchen to accept a morsel of the chili his mother was cooking. His father, the only doctor in Cross Plains, was out visiting patients.

He set aside the Lovecraft letter, knowing that it would be written in tiny script that would take long deciphering, and opened the other two envelopes instead. The one from Chicago bore the return indicia of *Weird Tales* magazine, and inside was a letter of acceptance for his story "The Dream Snake." Well and good—too bad that *Weird Tales* was so slow about paying. But at least the magazine represented a fairly steady market, for all the crotchets of its editor. The other letter was also from a magazine publisher; this one, *Ghost Stories*. Bob had sent them one of his John Taverel manuscripts, "The Spirit of Tom Molyneaux," and—*hosanna!*—the envelope contained a check! Every sale was a boost to his author's tender ego, and the *Ghost Stories* money would help him keep up his interest in the yarn he was working on now, a boxing piece called "Waterfront Fists" that he hoped would go in *Fight Stories*.

He slit open the letter from Howard Lovecraft and carefully unfolded and densely inscribed sheets of paper. As usual there was a mock-ceremonial greeting and a jocular tone to the letter, but once Howard Lovecraft got around to saying what he wanted to say. . .ah, there was indeed a message.

Bob scanned the letter carefully. Okay, Lovecraft wanted some information on a transplanted Texan named Hiram Evans, D.D.S. A dentist? Bob read more. Evans was indeed a onetime dentist, but had gone into politics and organizational work and was now calling himself Imperial Wizard, Knights of the Ku Klux Klan, operating out of headquarters in Atlanta, Georgia. Lovecraft had met him at a gathering in New York City. Bob scratched his head. The Klan was a familiar presence in Cross Plains; he was not himself a member, being constitutionally inclined to avoid personal involvement in boisterous social groups. About the most social that Bob ever got was his membership in a sort of round-robin correspondence group called the Junto.

But—for a friend. . . .

He pulled open the top drawer of his desk, lifted out the heavy old six-shooter that he kept there, made sure that it was loaded, and shut the drawer. He took a look at "Waterfront Fists," decided that it could wait a few hours, and shoved the gun in his trouser pocket. He started for the door, then went back to his desk, and grabbed his *Ghost Stories* check. Might as well kill two birds with one stone.

On his way out of the house he stopped in the kitchen again. His mother was still there. Bob snuck up behind her, put his arms around her and gave her a bear-hug. She reached up and patted his cheek. When he finally released her, popped a bit of hamburger meat into his mouth and told him to be home in time for dinner.

Outside the Howard house, Bob's dun-colored Chevrolet stood ready to go. He pulled a bandana from his pocket, swirled it across the windshield a couple of times to clear the reddish dust away, checked under the car and beneath the hood to make sure that his enemies hadn't laid any traps for him and got into the car.

A few minutes later he was in town. He cashed his check, stopped in at the saloon for a glass of whiskey, then strolled across the town's only street to the Cross Plains *Review*. He shoved open the door and whipped his revolver out of his trousers pocket, pointed it at the only occupant of the front office and roared, "Reach! Ah'm goin' ta blow yew ta hell, yew yaller-bellied snake-eatin' buzzard yew!"

The sharp-featured, leather-skinned man bent over a stack of galleys leaped into the air, whirled to face Bob, and let out a breath like a hiss of escaping steam. "God damn you, Bob, will you ever grow up and stop playing outlaw! You almost give me a heart attack!"

"Aw, come on, Lindsey, don't be such an old stick in the mud. You know I was just kidding. I got to talk to you."

"Well, God damn it, put that cannon away first and *then* we can talk. You know I don't like firearms. What do you think this is, some kind of wild west show?"

Bob shoved the gun back in his pocket. "You've got no sense of sport, Lindsey. Anyway, I need some information."

The newsman's eyes narrowed. "What kind of information? Why don't you go to the library?"

Bob lowered his voice. "I don't want to say this too loud."

"Ah, come on. You're playing games again. Can't you see I'm working? If you want to hang around here, why don't you write some more stuff for the *Review?* I don't know why they ever stuck a good brain like yours into a body that belongs on an autumn grizzly, no wonder it made you strange. Well, what do you want?"

"Maybe I'd write for you if the *Review* paid a little better. Do you know what the magazines are giving, nowadays?"

"No, and don't tell me."

Lindsey came over to Bob and slapped him on the biceps. "Don't see how somebody as flabby as you can be so strong. If you were just a little bit mean you could have been a great football player up at Payne College, Bob. Underneath all that craziness of yours you're just too nice a fellow, that's your trouble."

Bob smiled, the grin turning his soft face into a parody of a happy baby's. "Well, come on, Lindsey. Can we go someplace private and have a little talk?"

"You're serious, aren't you? Okay, just hold on a minute."

Lindsey closed up the *Review* office, put a *back-in-fifteen-minutes* sign on the door and took Bob Howard by the elbow.

"How do you know it'll be fifteen minutes? What if you're gone for an hour?"

"I'll be back in fifteen minutes from some time, Bob. Don't let it worry you."

They crossed the street, got into Bob's Chevy and Bob got the engine roaring, threw the sedan into gear and lurched away from the wooden sidewalk. He drove out a ways into the post oak country toward Brownwood. When they were a mile or so out of town, Bob pulled the car off the road and climbed out. He pulled his gun, crouched down beside the sedan and slowly circled the car, peering into the distance to see that no one lay in ambush.

"I swear, Bob, you get yourself so mixed up with those wild stories that you write, you don't know where fantasy stops and the real world takes over."

Bob looked narrowly at the smaller man. "Never mind that. I have enemies and if I don't keep an eagle eye out they're going to bushwhack me one day. I'm just looking out for myself, Lindsey, and don't you worry about it."

Lindsey shook his head.

"Well, will you tell me now what you want to know, or did you just come by to waste my afternoon and make the paper late again?"

Bob said, "I just got a letter from a friend of mine. He needs some information about Wizard Evans."

Lindsey looked serious for the first time. "Hiram Evans?"

Bob nodded his head.

"Listen here, Bob, now you're a nice young fellow and most folks like you pretty well, but you aren't a member of the Klan, and you know it isn't such a good idea to get too inquisitive about an organization you don't belong to."

"I don't want any secret stuff, Lindsey. But you're a member and since Doc Evans is kind of a legend around here. . ."

"Klan's a kind of secret society, boy. You don't see any *kotop-potok* buttons on my blouse, do you?"

"Come on, Lindsey, everybody knows you're the kligrapp for the county."

"I never said so, son. Listen, if you want to learn about the Klan, why don't you just join up?"

Bob grinned. "Thought you didn't know anything."

"Son, I didn't say that. I didn't say I'm not in the Klan and I didn't say I am. But if you want, I'll try and see to it that the kleagle comes around to your house and has a chat with you. That's how you get information about the Klan. Talk to the recruiting officer."

Bob Howard raised his six-shooter to eye level and pointed it at the newsman's chest. In a low, deadly voice he said, "If you don't want hot lead goin' in small and comin' out big, Lindsey, you'll tell me what I want to know."

Lindsey laughed. "Now you're playing baby games again, Bob."

"By the count of five."

"Cut it out, Bob, or I'll tell your daddy and he'll take that toy away from you!"

Bob started to count.

"Now stop it!" Lindsey's voice cracked in the middle of the sentence.

Bob reached up with a massive thumb and notched back the hammer on his gun. He kept counting.

"Bob—!" Lindsey was sweating. "Okay, I'll tell you about Hiram Evans. Good God, man, I told you, you don't know what's real and what's make-believe! You could have killed me with that thing."

Bob didn't say anything.

"Say, *do* you have any bullets in that gun?"

Bob pointed the six-shooter at a flat rock and squeezed off a shot. He blew the smoke away from the muzzle of his gun, then stuck it back in his pocket.

Lindsey made his way back to the Chevy on unsteady legs. He sat down on the driver's-side running board. Bob Howard strode over and sat beside him.

"God damn it, Bobby! Okay, you want to know about Hiram Evans. What can I tell you, I hardly know the man. He hasn't been in Cross Plains but a couple of times in his life, once back when he was kleagle himself, just out selling memberships, and then he went up so fast, he wound up as king kleagle for the whole state of Texas and next thing anybody knew he was Grand Dragon of the Realm Of Texas, that is."

"That's like, chief of the Klan for the state, right?"

"That's right."

"But he isn't that any more?"

Lindsey shook his head. "There's no holding Hiram down. He made it to the Imperial Palace. That's Klan headquarters. national headquarters. In Atlanta. Hiram hasn't been in Cross Plains since back during the great war, you were just a tyke, Bobby. I remember your dad taking you around with him on his rounds, you and that funny dog of yours, Patch."

"Never mind Patch! He's dead! What about Evans?"

"Well, Bobby, you act like there was something dramatic going on. You know, he just rose in the organization, that's all, from Kleagle to King Kleagle. Grand Dragon of the Realm of Texas. On up to Grand Goblin for the Southwest, and then Imperial Kligrapp."

"Yeah, that's like secretary, right?"

Lindsey was sweating. He clenched his mouth.

Bob reached into his pocket and fingered his revolver.

"Son, you are crazy. Yes, he was national secretary. He didn't think old Reverend Simmons, the old Imperial Wizard, was doing right. I don't know everything that went on in Atlanta, and I don't want to know. All I know is, there was some kind of falling out, and Simmons got booted upstairs to a fancy title and no power, and Hiram became Imperial Wizard. Then after a while Simmons left the Klan altogether.

"Now, is that what you want to know?"

Bob scratched his head. "I guess it is. Except, what's in it for Hiram Evans? Why does he do all the work?"

"He's an idealist, Bob. He's interested in keeping America a decent, honorable country. Our country is menaced by all sorts of foes. Foreigners, Popists, kikes, niggers, wets, adulterers, why, the list just goes on and on. The Klan works tirelessly to keep America free of allegiances to causes, governments, peoples, sects, and rulers that are foreign. The Klan supports the Christian religion. The Klan esteems the United States of America and its institutions above all other governments, civil, political, and ecclesiastical, in the whole world. The Klan faithfully strives for the eternal maintenance of white supremacy.

"That's what it's all about, Bob."

Bob Howard took his right hand out of his pocket, pulling his six-shooter with it. He used the front blade-sight of the gun to scratch his head. He looked suspiciously at the newsman.

Lindsey grinned sickly. "Well, and the Imperial Wizard does pull down a nice little salary. I don't really know exactly how much, but when Evans kicked Simmons upstairs he gave Simmons a pension of a thousand a month. Uh, and the Wizard does control the Searchlight Publishing Company that puts out newspapers and magazines and books for the Klan. Uh, and the Gate City Manufacturing Company. They make Klan regalia and the like. And the Clark Realty Company for land and buildings."

Bob nodded several times. He stuck his gun back in his pocket. "I guess I can answer my friend's letter now. You want a ride back to town, Lindsey? I was kind of thinking of heading over to Brownwood for a hamburger before I get home. I'll buy."

"That'll be fine, Bob, just fine. I can always get a ride home from Brownwood easy enough."

"Grand, that's just grand. We'll chow down a bit at the ole chuck-wagon, maybe, uh, mebbe whet our whistles a wee drap, too. Let's go, pardner. Giddyap, yuh ole Chevro-let!"

Lindsey shook his head in despair.

"Say, pardner," Two-gun Bob addressed him, "yew got an ahr-glass thar? Ah wouldn't want muh ole maw to worry 'bout her favorite cowpoke arrivin' late fur chow at thuh ole corral!"

~ ~ ~ ~ ~

Ec'h-Pi-El read Two-gun Bob's letter concerning Hiram Evans, the dentist Imperial Wizard of the Invisible Empire, with a growing feeling of confirmed discouragement. Sonia's opinion of Count Vonsiatsky had been bad enough—and Howard's own exposure to the exiled Count had been largely in concert with Sonia's judgment. But now that he was hearing—or rather reading—Two-gun Bob Howard's letter, Howard Lovecraft began to see things moving in a shadowed direction.

Evans had been unimpressive in person; an uncultured lout would have been Howard Lovecraft's judgment of the man. Now Robert Howard wrote with the news that Evans was nothing but a small-time opportunist who'd somehow made good as the head-man of a crowd of nobody's playing somebody by putting on exotic robes and carrying out bizarre ceremonials. The opinion that Father Curran had expressed over luncheon with Sylvester Viereck supported this judgment, and of course Curran was merely forwarding word from Maude DeLand, at that!

The whole alliance of organizations that Viereck saw as the nucleus of his world empire, looked more to Howard Lovecraft like a congeries of charlatans and buffoons!

And yet—and yet Viereck himself was clearly a man of substance as well as intelligence. Was he being taken in by these people, or did he see some virtue in them that Howard missed? Or, yet again, did he have some further, hidden motivation? Viereck was definitely the man who held his cards close to his vest; his record during the Great War proved that. Perhaps he was playing some kind of double or triple game now. If so—what was Howard Lovecraft's proper move?

He took pen and paper and began a letter to Viereck. He expressed his misgivings about the partners in the embryonic movement. Dr. DeLand and Mrs. Dilling seemed authentic, or at least Howard had no reason to think otherwise. But Heinz Spanknoebel gave the appearance of little more than a ruffian, a thug. Count Vonsiatsky might have real political ambitions but he seemed more interested in comfort and wealth. Hiram Evans was probably a petty crook.

This did not mean that any of them were totally impotent. Any, in fact, might accrue a sufficient number of followers that (if they were effectively organized and directed) they might make real trouble. But did Viereck really understand what he was dealing with?

As for Father Curran and his absent mentor, Father Coughlin, now there was a tougher nut to crack. For one thing (and Howard had to approach Viereck very delicately in this regard, in view of Viereck's own sentiments) there was a distinct odor of *Irishness* to both the present and the absent priest. Viereck's proposed world empire might include Germany as an equal partner with England and the others, and Howard could even stretch his imagination to see England participating as a partner rather than as a vassal of the Windsor crown. But was that Curran's idea—or was he playing a deeper game as well? Was the coming world empire a mere cloak beneath which the old German-Irish alliance would move to gain revenge against Britain and the United States?

Howard broached the questions with as great care as he could, leavening his missive to Viereck with passing rhapsodic descriptions of the New England spring with the burgeoning life that turned ancient hills from their winter gray and brown to the rich green of renewed life, of the sparkling waterways of his own home city, the Providence, Seekonk, and Pawtucket Rivers, the little Blackstone that rose in the pond country across the state line near Woonsocket, Massachusetts, the narrow Ten Mile River and bustling Narragansett Bay. Howard mentioned past trips throughout Hew England and his hopes to revisit historic spots like Marblehead and Salem.

He nearly destroyed the letter, unmailed, thinking that a man of Viereck's stature and obligations would find it foolish, but finally Howard mailed it. If Viereck were to accept him, then it must be as he truly was, with all of his attitudes and interests, and not in some false *persona* devised to impress another.

The May *Weird Tales* arrives with a new tribute to Howard among the letters from readers quoted in the Eyrie. "I think Lovecraft has struck twelve with 'The White Ship.' It is one of the finest things of its sort I have ever seen. It is literature." Howard smiled at the sparse lines of praise. Once he had spurned the suggestion of writing for money at all, telling a friend that he wrote for his own satisfaction, that if a few others indicated enjoyment at his modest efforts he would be well repaid. In a way that remained his sentiment—and yet, slowly shrinking incomes from a meager family heritage forced him to turn ever more to literature as a source of sustenance, and the occasional line of acclaim from some reader was one of the high points in his own rather gray existence.

A missive arrived from an unfamiliar address in Brooklyn. Howard opened it and examined the signature—ah, it was that of the young fellow who had agented "The Colour Out of Space" for him, Julius Schwartz. Editor Sloane had taken the story, was delighted to have Howard in *Amazing*. He would use the story as quickly as he could fit it into the magazine, and hoped to present it in a manner pleasing to the author. Certainly with an artistic design, and if he could work it out in time, perhaps even a cover illustration. In the meanwhile a voucher would be forwarded to the accounting department and a check would be forwarded to Howard's agent.

All of that sounded very promising, except the part about the voucher and the accounting department. It was

Howard's experience with magazine editors that the only reliable payment was one enclosed "herewith." The proverbial voucher sent to the accounting department smacked terribly of pie in the sky by and by. He clucked his tongue and got out Waterman pen and foolscap.

The first missive he inscribed went to Schwartz, expressing his gratitude and urging Schwartz to pursue Gernsback relentlessly until the story was paid for. (And how much, Howard wondered, would Gernsback pay, if and when Schwartz did squeeze a check out of him?)

Next he penned a letter to Vincent Starrett at the rented Beechhurst cottage where Starrett was working on his novel *Seaports in the Moon*. Howard was still concerned about the world empire matter, and asked Starrett if he knew anything about connections between political figures, gangsters, and the leaders of the groups Howard was learning about. He mentioned Heinz Spanknoebel and Spanknoebel's friend Fritz Kuhn; also Father Curran (although Curran was from the East) and Curran's friend Father Charles Coughlin, who operated in the State of Michigan.

Viereck replied first. Howard was flattered by the tone of his letter. Yes, he understood Howard's concern and he agreed that some of the people they were dealing with had rather severe shortcomings. In the furtherance of a great movement like theirs it was sometimes necessary to use such individuals, and Howard might find, in time, that the likes of Evans or Spanknoebel were really diamonds in the rough. Not everyone had the advantage of a cultured heritage or fine breeding. The implied statement that Howard did possess a cultured heritage and fine breeding was not lost on its subject.

But more exciting to Howard was Viereck's proposal for a motor tour of part of the New England coast. If Howard was willing to serve as guide, Viereck and his friend Dr. Kiep of the German consular service would be pleased to survey the towns of Salem and Marblehead. They would arrive by motor car on Friday, May 13, and proceed onward from Providence, spending the weekend in New England, dropping Howard off at his home at the end of their stay and returning then to New York.

Howard wrote back to Viereck at once, accepting the suggestion. He called to his aunts; Annie was out shopping for groceries but Lillian fluttered into Howard's study from the kitchen and he told her enthusiastically of his coming trip.

Lillian fussed over Howard. Was he sure he would be all right? How well did he know these two men who were taking him off to Massachusetts? Was he sure he would be warm enough, get enough to eat, enough rest? Howard patted Lillian's hands, told her that all would be well, reminded her that he was, after all, a man whose fortieth birthday was only a few years off.

Lillian unhooked the wire earpiece of her rimless spectacles and began to clean them on her cotton apron. "Yes, I know you're a grown man now, Howard. But you're all we have now, Annie and I. Grandpa Phillips is gone, Annie's husband Edward was such a fine, promising young man but once he fell prey to the demon rum—Howard, promise that you won't let yourself come under the sway of liquor, promise me, please!"

Howard felt himself reddening. "You know, niece, that I am. T.T. and have always been."

Lillian sniffed into a handkerchief, set her spectacles back on her nose. "I know, dear," she said, "but it's so hard. My own Franklin has been gone these dozen years, Annie's boy was carried off by the consumption back during the Great War. Oh, Howard, you wanted so much to go with the AEF, and you were so bitter when we managed to keep you home. But you were the only one by then. Your own father had been gone for years, and then after the war your mother followed, my own sister Susie.

"Annie and I only have you, Howard. So I suppose we fuss a little more than we ought to, but it's all for your own good. Then someone comes along like that Russian woman and tricks you into marrying her. . ."

"Sonia did not trick me," Howard answered hotly. "She is a woman of charm and intelligence. You and Annie took to her at first—what happened later?"

Lillian wrung her hands. "You *know* what happened, Howard. That woman came here to Providence and wanted to open a millinery shop right here among our neighbors. Imagine! In trade! What she does in New York is her own business, but we have our standing to consider here in Providence. We have our standing to consider!"

CHAPTER THIRTEEN:

"I AM RELATED TO THE SALEM PHILLIPSES"

THE HUGE CAR pulled to the curb in Barnes Street shortly after Howard had finished his breakfast of fried eggs, sweet rolls, oatmeal, toast, juice and coffee. He was dressed in a lightweight suit, his valise packed and standing near the door. He heard the car's doors slam and watched from the window as George Sylvester Viereck and Dr. Otto Kiep climbed the pathway to the front door of the house.

Howard admitted the two men personally, shaking hands with each in turn, ushered them to the front parlor and presented then to his aunts. Lillian retired to the kitchen for refreshments while Annie stayed to act as hostess. Howard was eager to get away and be *en route* to the old towns, but his aunts were determined to show their hospitality to the two guests.

Finally, after a period of passing tea and cookies they managed to break away and cross once more to the car. Dr. Kiep took Howard's valise and strapped it to the luggage rack along with his own and Viereck's bags, then they climbed into the saloon and Kiep, seated at the wheel, stamped on the self-starter.

As they pulled away from the curb Howard asked what kind of automobile it was; he'd never seen one like it before.

"Nor very likely to," Viereck laughed. "There aren't more than three of these in the United States, eh, Otto?"

Kiep held his eyes on the roadway as he participated in the conversation. "This is a Horsch. Finest car built in Germany, in my opinion. Well, some prefer the Mercedes, but not I. This car was shipped over on the Hamburg-America Line; it traveled on the same steamship that brought me, the *Deutschland*. Superb craftsmanship. It has a twelve-cylinder engine, one of the finest anywhere. I have seen nothing to compare with it, although the British consul in New York travels in a Daimler which is also a very good car."

Viereck had a folding map and guidebook which he consulted from time to time, advising Kiep with directions. The diplomat managed the car skillfully, maintaining a steady pace along the Federal highway from Providence northeast, across the state line and on through the southerly suburbs of Boston.

Kiep was proud of his automobile and pointed out its features at every opportunity. As they began passing through towns on the outskirts of Boston he turned to face Howard over his shoulder for a moment and said, "Listen to this!" He turned away again, leaned forward and adjusted a series of switches on the dashboard.

To Howard's astonishment the sound of a small orchestra filled the car. After a moment Howard laughed. "You've had a panatrope installed in an automobile! How remarkable! Why doesn't the needle skip across the disk as we move along?"

"Ha-hah! You are almost correct, Mr. Lovecraft! It is not a panatrope but a radiola! I came across the most remarkable young man in New York, who works for an electrical supply manufacturer, he has devised a method of installing radiolas in automobiles, and I had him place a good one in my car. It's an Atwater-Kent, with Radio Corporation tubes. Do you see the speaker here?"

He pointed beneath the dashboard.

Howard, in the rear seat behind Viereck, peered between the shoulders of the two men. The musical selection had been completed and the announcer was delivering an advertisement for Barking Dog Cigarettes. "They're dog-gone good!" the announcer gushed. Howard was appalled.

"You see?" Kiep repeated. "Such a wonder! There is an ingenuity to Americans, I believe. German craftsmanship and precision may surpass all others, but the American engineer has a spark of originality which the rest of the world would do well to emulate."

"I must agree with you, Otto." Viereck turned halfway in his seat beside Kiep, so that he could comfortably address both the diplomat and Howard Lovecraft. "I consider the greatest advantage of the automobile radio the availability of news at virtually any time. In fact, I wonder if it is time for such a broadcast."

He consulted his pocket watch, returned it to its place. "A few minutes longer," he commented.

The radiola gave forth with music once more. The orchestra playing was one of the Negro jazz bands that Howard detested, but there was no escaping them in these times so he made no protest. Instead he asked Dr. Kiep what source of power drove the radiola.

"Very simple," the consul explained. "We use a battery-driven set, and simply attach it to the self-starter battery of the auto. The fellow who installed it for me even put in an antenna. Most ingenious young fellow with a very American name. He is called Larry Brown, of Brooklyn, New York City. He separated the layers of the running board, laid the antenna wire in a mesh there, and re-sealed the board. One would never detect this as a radio equipped car, yet it is!"

Howard laughed once again.

When the music ended there was another advertisement, this time for Gargoyle Gasoline. Viereck suggested that perhaps Dr. Kiep ought to stop the car and purchase some gasoline, at that. The news broadcast began and conversation died out among the three men in the automobile.

The leading news item of the broadcast, as it had been all week in the newspapers which Howard examined, was the topic of transatlantic aviation. Not that flight across the ocean was itself a novelty; Howard had thrilled to the 1919 flight of Alcock and Brown, between Labrador and England. And there had been a number of transoceanic passages by dirigible.

But ever since the American Raymond Orteig had offered a prize of $25,000 for the first non-stop aeroplane flight between New York and Paris, preparations had proceeded feverishly. A whole array of aircraft were assembled on Long Island, but none had actually taken the leap toward Europe as yet.

But six days ago, on Saturday the seventh of May, a daring French pair had stolen a march on all the Americans and flown up from Paris, heading westward across the ocean to make their bid for Mr. Orteig's $25,000. The Frenchmen were Charles Nungesser and Francois Coli.

Their plane, a Le Vasseur monoplane dubbed the *White Bird*, had roared aloft from Villaconblay Aerodrome, had disappeared into the blue sky to the west—and had vanished.

Reports of mystery planes, of lights in the skies, of the sound of buzzing engines came and went, but there was no sign of the *White Bird.*

And still, on Long Island, stood three planes waiting to take off and cross the ocean toward the rising dawn. Most favored was the *America*, a massive Fokker trimotor built to the order of Commander Richard H. Byrd, the famed polar exploration chief. Byrd had a crew assembled, his craft had been aloft for numerous test flights. The Byrd plane was regarded as the prototype of an aerial liner.

Then there was the Bellanca monoplane *Columbia*, to be flown by Clarence Chamberlain and Lloyd Bertrand. Smaller than the Byrd-Fokker effort, the Bellanca was owned by one Charles A. Levine, a businessman with ambitions to establish an aerial passenger-carrying business. Levine hardly needed Orteig's prize money (nor, to be sure, did Commander Byrd) but if his *Columbia* won the prize, that feat might generate sufficient public enthusiasm to launch Levine's commercial enterprise.

Finally there was the Ryan monoplane piloted by Charles Lindbergh, the young son of a minor Midwestern politician. The plane had been built to Lindbergh's specifications at the Ryan plant in San Diego. It had been financed by public subscription drummed up by the St. Louis *Globe-Democrat*. The *Globe-Democrat* had publicized its campaign as a massive display of public support for the daring scheme. Actually, most of the money had come from a single donor, Mrs. Lora Knight. Mrs. Knight was the widow of a millionaire stockbroker; she could easily afford the contribution and she got more excitement out of mothering the project than there was in the rest of her bleak widowhood.

As for Lindbergh, he took leave from a $350-a-month job flying air mail for the government—to try his luck in the transatlantic derby. If he lost, he could always go back to the Post Office Department with a story to tell his grandchildren. And if he won he'd never need that $350 again.

At any rate, Lindbergh was the last arrival at Long Island, flying his own plane in from the San Diego factory. By way of St. Louis, of course, so his sponsors at the *Globe-Democrat* could get a couple of editions worth of headlines and photos out of it. The *Globe-Democrat* rival paper, the St. Louis *Post-Dispatch* was thus stuck on the horns of a dilemma. If they featured the story they played up their competitor and if they ignored it they forfeited a colorful event and left all coverage to the competition. Either way, the *Post-Dispatch* lost out. They finally decided to cover Lindbergh but to play the story down. The *Globe-Democrat* spread headlines and photos all over its front page.

As of this afternoon, with the French *White Bird* a certain failure and its crew probably lost, the three American craft stood at the ready. Commander Byrd had already announced that he would fly in the morning if the weather was favorable. It looked as if the Orteig prize would go to the Fokker *America*, and cold supper for the Bellanca *Columbia* and the Ryan *Spirit of St. Louis*.

Other news included new developments in the Chinese civil war, where there was great excitement over the capture of Madame Borodin, the wife of General Eugene Chen's Bolshevik advisor at Hankow. She had been taken off a train by troops loyal to Chang Tso-lin, carrying a payroll to the Chen army in the field. Chang threatened to try her for conspiracy and the Soviet Russians threatened war against Chang if he executed Madame Borodin.

Chang, meanwhile, had given an interview to Walter Durant of the New York *Times*, condemning his rival Chiang Kai-shek as a Russian-bossed ultra-radical and asking the Five Powers to intervene against Chiang. Chiang himself was advancing northward through China, had defeated another warlord called Chung Tsung-chang, and had opened negotiations with Sun Chuan-fang, heir of the late Sun Yat-sen, with an eye toward legitimizing himself as the chief of all China.

In Mexico City, the Women's Club of the United States convened a Presidential debate and emerged bearing a resolution demanding that Edith Wilson, widow of the late President Woodrow Wilson, enter the 1928 Presidential election race. Mrs. Wilson could run on an experience platform, cynics and enemies suggested, referring to the fact that she had been *de facto* President of the United States for the final eighteen months of her husband's term. Woodrow had suffered a stroke while campaigning futilely for American ratification of the Treaty of Versailles and membership in the League of Nations.

Wilson survived the stroke but became a virtual invalid and recluse in his White House bedroom. Aides could not see him. Messages and questions were carried in by Edith; answers were carried out by Edith. How accurately were the messages transmitted to the sick President (or were they taken to him at all?), and how accurately were his responses announced (or did Edith Wilson simply invent the responses?).

No one knew.

Wilson had been a one-time correspondent of George Sylvester Viereck, and Wilson's closest aide, Colonel E. M. House, had turned to Viereck for ghosting services when it came time to write his memoirs. But even House had been excluded from the Presidential presence during those shadowed eighteen months. Even House did not know whether Woodrow or Edith had been President during that time.

For the inauguration of Wilson's successor, Harding of Ohio, the retiring President had been dressed and propped in the back seat of an automobile. There, silk hat jammed on his forehead, he had ridden beside the popular Harding through Washington, looking as pale and pasty-complexioned as an over-ripe corpse. Strangely enough they had got him moving a little, and carted him around for another three years, even managing to work his jaw up and down from time to time while a concealed panatrope disk spun somewhere behind him. But by that time parts were falling off with every movement and they had to keep poor Wilson packed in ice every night, and by the winter of 1924 they gave up and buried him in the Washington Cathedral.

During the year and a half that Edith Wilson had served as her husband's regent she called the arrangement "a workable system of handling matters of state."

Some critics claimed that Edith was just compensating for the fact that she was Woodrow's second wife (the first had died in the White house in 1914), and that Woodrow's first wife Ellen had borne him three daughters while Edith

was barren. But then Woodrow was Edith's second husband, too. Edith, Ellen; Ellen, Edith; the Women's Club
wanted her to run for President.

Dr. Otto Kiep guided the Horsch through the old streets
of Boston City. Sylvester Viereck, checking his pocket
watch every so often, suggested that they stop for an
early dinner, then continue on to Salem afterwards. Dr.
Kiep and Howard Lovecraft were quick to assent.

"I have been in this country a short time only," Dr.
Kiep commented, "but I have heard of a famous restaurant in Boston. If all are agreeable, may we eat our meal
there?"

Howard, as ever gracious, volunteered, "Anywhere, of
course." He heard Viereck agree as well. Howard's only
worry was whether his slim purse could afford the meals
that the others would suggest on their weekend excursion. But Viereck seemed to regard his entertaining of
Howard as a business expense (which, for the Jackson
Press, it properly was), and Kiep was presumably well
supplied with consular funds, so Howard might properly
permit himself to be treated as a guest.

Dr. Kiep growled an inquiry to Viereck in guttural German and Viereck, gesturing apologetically over his shoulder to Howard, opened his guidebook and map and consulted them, giving Kiep his answer in German as well.
Kiep, following Viereck's directions, cruised by Faneuil
Hall, turned and passed Durgin and Park hard by the old
Quincy Market, and pulled to the curb at the Union Oyster
house on Union Street. Howard held his head.

Inside the restaurant he was relieved to find that the
menu included some good, traditional yankee fare (actually, it was transplanted English fare) as well as fish.
While Kiep gorged himself on a bowl of steamed clams
and Viereck attacked a plate of Boston scrod, Howard
dined happily on roast beef and Yorkshire pudding. For
dessert he ordered a dish of ice cream drowned in chocolate syrup and scraped happily at every last drop of the
sweet remnants.

At least he'd been spared the ritual of the pre-meal
cocktail that seemed to be Viereck's habit (and that of so
many others in these theoretically dry days), but Dr. Kiep
had produced a flask during the meal and poured

schnapps for himself and Viereck. The consul had offered a glass to Howard but Howard had declined.

After dinner they resumed their journey, heading out of Boston toward Lynn, Swampscott, and Salem. Howard was in his element now, and provided a running commentary on the history and architecture of the region, pointing out the onetime home of Mary Baker Eddy on Broad Street in Lynn. Dr. Kiep made a noncommittal comment about Christian Science. Howard replied, "It is neither Christian nor scientific, but is one of the great charlatanries of all time. Have you read Mark Twain's book on the subject? He utterly demolishes the .fraudulent claims and the grasping for wealth and power of the so-called Mother Church. Pah!"

The Horsch's twelve cylinders purred along Lafayette Street into Salem; now, when Otto Kiep directed his inquiry to Sylvester Viereck, Viereck merely turned and asked Howard if he could guide them to a guest house where reservations had already been made. He gave an address on Webb Street at old Collins Cove, much to Howard's pleasure, and Howard guided them past the Salem Common where the ancient statue of Roger Conant loomed darkly.

The guest house on Webb Street was a delight. Over two centuries old, it had been built when the town itself had stood for a hundred years. A mansarded roof curved above the street, the walls were of ancient square-cut timbers of a type originally imported from England before local lumbering had developed. A false fanlight carved all of wood surmounted the doorway—Howard stood gaping at it in admiration until the old New England goodwife who ran the guest house summoned him. He ran his hands over the newel-posted banister, his eyes over the pewter-filled breakfronts.

The white-haired landlady showed them to three rooms up a narrow staircase, and Howard excused himself from any evening chatter with Viereck and Kiep to sit enchanted for hours in a black-stained rocker beneath a diamond- paned window, gazing out upon Collins Cove, its few lights swaying and blinking on the masts of sailing craft. Howard could almost convince himself that two centuries had rolled backwards and that he was a colonial gentleman sitting in periwig and small-clothes, anticipating the arrival of a packet from the mother country.

At last he sighed happily, crept beneath a huge down comforter and closed his eyes.

In the morning he was the first of the three to rise, a feat so rare that he gazed at himself in the shaving mirror and laughed.

Viereck and Kiep joined him for breakfast in the sunny front room of the guest house where their landlady served dropped eggs and fried bread with their coffee and juice. Howard was eager to show Viereck and Kiep the ancient town. Here in Salem he had laid some of his best stories, transforming the town thinly into his own Arkham (just as he altered nearby Marblehead into Kingsport). But it was witch-haunted Salem that held Howard in thrall.

Few knew, or cared to learn, that old Salem during the strange hysteria of 1692 had not been the village of today, but a far larger township encompassing Danvers (where the madness had actually begun), Peabody, Beverly, Marblehead and Swampscott. But Howard knew every detail of the story of the old slave Tituba and her Caribbean Negro husband, John Indian.

Over breakfast Howard kept up a monolog for Viereck and Kiep, condemning the cruel judge John Hawthorne and his colleague Jonathan Corwin. Hawthorne was too well known a name for Howard to tamper with, and besides, John Hawthorne had founded the line that bred Nathaniel Hawthorne in Salem twelve decades later. But Jonathan Corwin had served as the evil prototype of sinister Joseph Curwen in Howard's own recent manuscript *The Case of Charles Dexter Ward*.

Witch-cursed Massachusetts had provided the inspiration for Howard's macabre literary creations even more than his own beloved Providence. And now he was in Salem once again.

Strangely, Kiep and Viereck were less interested in the historic sites of the town than Howard had expected. They stood with him dutifully before the Conant statue, walked around the infamous Witch House where Jonathan Corwin had not only made his home but were kept accused witches for their preliminary examination, stumbled through the old burying ground while Howard crouched reading inscriptions from seventeenth century tomb-stones.

Howard explained his fondness for the old community as best he could. He showed Kiep and Viereck the ancient Gould-Pickman house near the burying ground, explained his inspiration from it for the character Richard Upton Pickman taken from old Samuel Pickman who had lived in the building in the l660s. He got Kiep and Viereck to walk with him to the Stephen Phillips house.

"I am related to the Salem Phillipses, you know, through my maternal grandfather Whipple Phillips and ancestors stretching hack to old Asaph Phillips. The Phillipses were seafaring men, and the Salem branch of the family founded their fortune on shipping as well. The Stephen Phillips house was actually built over in Danvers before 1800, and was later cut in half. Half of it was hauled here to Salem and it stands yet!"

But after a couple of hours of walking around Salem, Dr. Kiep laid his hand on Howard's arm and said, "Mr. Lovecraft, what I would most enjoy to see is the harbor nearby. You know, I am myself of an old naval family the descendent."

Howard shook his head. "I didn't know that, sir. But I can understand your interest. The sea has ever had a lure, a mystery, that fascinates Man. Some of the most charming of fantasies and yet the most chilling of myster-ies have had as their background the dark waterfront shanty, the creaking schooner, the remote island.

"Let us proceed to the waterfront, then!"

"Perhaps we could hire a little boat," Viereck inter-jected.

They walked down to Derby Wharf at the foot of Daniels Street and found an old Salem hand named Zadok Marsh to take them out into the harbor aboard his sailing shallop. Dr. Kiep managed to produce a German Zeiss miniature camera from somewhere on his person, and Viereck took notes in his pocket notebook.

They sailed on a northeasterly course, up through the Marblehead Channel into Salem Sound. Captain Marsh said that not many tourists ever hired his shallop; most of them were more interested in seeing the sights on shore, and his customers were usually businessmen from Bev-erly or Lynn out for a day's fishing beyond the channel.

"Good haddock," he said, "and cod. Course, the best eatin's lobster, for my money. But we don't get so much around here as they do farther up the coast. Salem's too far south for the cold-blooded creatures!"

They sailed as far as Misery Ledge. Sylvester Viereck asked Marsh about bottom conditions and currents; Kiep photographed islands and rocks. They beat almost due south, tacked westward at Satan Rock east of Cat Island, and made their way slowly back past Peach Point on the Marblehead Channel once again.

By the time they clambered off the shallop and back onto the Derby Wharf Howard was famished. "We missed our lunch," he complained.

"Yes. A day on the water some great hunger creates," Kiep agreed. "Do you ever encounter rum-runners, Captain Marsh?" Kiep laughed as he asked the question.

"Oh, nossir." Marsh looked away, fumbled in a pocket of his rubber jacket. He pulled out an ancient pipe and jammed it into the corner of his mouth. "You three fellers ain't Prohib Enforcers, are you? I'da never took you out to make them photos if I'd knowed that. But this boat is clean! You won't find a bottle or a barrel on my shallop!"

They dined that night at the Stephen Daniels House, a lovely shingled building dating from 1700 or thereabouts. The ridge roof and stone chimney carried the charm of centuries; inside the house Howard had to duck beneath heavy wooden beams set in place by a race shorter than his twentieth-century manhood. Great walk-in fireplaces ringed the dining room, and Howard sat in an old wing-backed chair with Viereck and Kiep, imagining himself a gentleman among gentlemen in an era long past.

When tall clocks rang out the hour they were led to their places at the long planked table and served steaming beef and long loaves of bread, hot bowls of vegetables and crisp salads.

"Tomorrow," Dr. Kiep suggested, "we can drive to the other village, to Marblehead? I would like to see more of the nautical arrangements hereabouts."

Howard said that would be fine with him.

The conversation swung around to the great Atlantic flying competition. Viereck favored Commander Byrd and his Fokker trimotor. "The others are circus performances," he said. "Any of them may succeed, although I think they're more likely to share the fate of poor Hungesser and Coli. But what point in a one or two man flight in some little toy aeroplane? Byrd's plane shows the way for a grand fleet of machines spanning the globe! There is the way for the world to go!"

Howard chewed on a slice of beef. "You are a great aviation enthusiast. And Dr. Kiep prefers the sea."

"I do," the diplomat agreed.

"Tomorrow, then, perhaps everyone can be pleased." Howard kept his knowledge of Marblehead and of the old Starling Burgess Batboat to himself.

CHAPTER FOURTEEN:

LOVECRAFT PLANS A BOOK

SUNDAY THEY drove the short distance to Marblehead, Howard Lovecraft's fictional shipping hub of Innsmouth. In Howard's stories Innsmouth, like his transformed version of Salem, witch-haunted Arkham, was a place of rotting hovels, furtive, degenerate inhabitants, gray, lowering skies by day and terror-stalked by night.

Like the real Salem, the real Marblehead was a clean and well-kept revenant of New England's remembered past, its buildings for the most part either preserved or restored, its citizens no more sinister than the run of taciturn New Englander.

Today the May sky was an unblemished blue, the briny water of Marblehead Harbor snapping into a thousand wavelets beneath a brisk, clean northeast breeze.

Howard directed Dr. Kiep along the state highway connecting the two towns, through the narrow, turning streets of old Marblehead. As they passed white-painted old houses, Howard commented, "Marblehead isn't quite as old as Salem. It was founded in 1629, three years after old Roger Conant started Salem. But it's still of historical interest. The first American warship was built here in 1775 for Captain Broughton. And during the War of 1812, Old Ironsides would probably have been captured by His Majesty's navy if she hadn't found shelter at Fort Sewall up at the mouth of the harbor."

Howard led Kiep and Viereck along the causeway to Marblehead Neck, along the length of Harbor Avenue and out to Jack Point near the Marblehead Light. He led the way to the door of an old, hip-roofed house surmounted by a widow's walk. At Howard's knock the door was opened by a grizzled oldster in rough seaman's clothing.

"Mr. Lovecraft," the old man welcomed him, "how are you."

Howard introduced Viereck and Kiep to the old man, whose name was Azor Burgess. "We'd like a ride, Mr.

Burgess. Seems like a good day for it. Think you could accommodate?"

Burgess rubbed his iron-colored mop of unruly hair. "Don't see why not. Was up on the walk myself, seems like a fine day indeed." He paused and examined the others with his blue eyes. "But it won't be a ride, Mr. Lovecraft, will be three rides. I can only take one at a time, you know."

Howard said he was sure that would be fine. He explained the situation to Viereck and Kiep, who responded enthusiastically. They exchanged a few sentences in German, then Viereck said, "I think I ought to precede Dr. Kiep, make notes and give him directions for his photographic work. How about you, Howard? Would you like to go up before Dr. Kiep and myself, or afterwards?"

"You're the guests today, I shall wait for last." Old Azor Burgess led the way from his house down to the point, entered a shed and emerged wearing long boots. He waded into the water and began clearing a canvas tarpaulin from an old, fabric-covered biplane mounted on pontoons and rocking gently on the wavelets of the harbor.

"You may find it difficult to believe," Howard told Viereck and Dr. Kiep while Burgess worked, "but during the Great War there was a little aircraft manufacturing industry right here in Marblehead. Started out building copies of English Dunne aeroplanes, then developed their own designs. Hardly any left now, but old Azor keeps this one running and gives sight-seeing rides in it. I hope you won't mind that he charges a fee for rides."

Kiep said, "Of course not. You will go first, Sylvester?" Viereck waited for Burgess to hand him a pair of oversize boots.

He pulled them over his shoes and trousers, let Burgess guide him through the shallows to the float of the biplane, then climbed carefully into the observer's seat of the aeroplane.

Burgess drafted Howard to help start the old Renault engine that powered the biplane, then climbed into the pilot's seat while Howard scrambled back onto the shore beside Dr. Kiep. Burgess waited for the engine to warm up, turned in his seat and signaled to Howard to wade out a few feet into the water again and cast off the tail-line that held the biplane in place.

With a roar and a spray of brine the biplane taxied into the harbor, turned upwind toward Chappel Ledge and Cat Island. Howard watched the plane pick up speed, skip a couple of times off the crests of wavelets, then rise into the air and begin its circling ascent, dipping once to waggle its wings over a great white yacht that stood off the mouth of the harbor, not far from the spot where the USS *Constitution* had stood off the British frigates *Junen* and *Tenedos* with the aid of the guns of Fort Sewall one hundred thirteen years before.

Dr. Kiep had photographed the biplane enthusiastically, now turned the Zeiss upon the harbor itself, the houses and quays lining its waters, the fishing and pleasure craft that dotted the channels.

When Azor Burgess brought the old aircraft circling back to land it he swept past Lovecraft and Kiep, circled over the Boden Rocks to the west, then slid in, upwind again, and taxied back to the takeoff spot at Jack Point. Viereck climbed from the biplane and conducted a conversation with Kiep while Burgess waited in his place. After the conversation and many references to Viereck's notebook, Dr. Kiep climbed into the biplane and Burgess again taxied out into the harbor for his takeoff.

"I hope you will pardon my conducting conversations with Dr. Kiep in German from time to time," Viereck apologized. "I should consider it impolite to exclude others from the discussion by using a foreign tongue, but Dr. Kiep's English is slightly limited."

"I had hardly noticed."

"You are generous, Howard. Dr. Kiep is sensitive on the point. But I wished to point out certain fascinating features to him, and I feared he would have difficulty following all of my descriptions."

Howard said it was no matter, he was only concerned that Sylvester and Dr. Kiep enjoyed their visit.

"The villages are most beautiful," Viereck agreed. "You know, although European-born I have been in the United States for over thirty years. I had been to Boston any number of times, but had never made my way to the shore resorts. Most interesting historically as well as beautiful and restful."

"Your visit, then, is purely recreational in purpose?"

Viereck reached for his cigar-case in an inside pocket. Even in his casual clothes he managed to be as well-equipped as ever. He clipped the end of the cigar, muttered the brand name (La Palina) as he slid the gold-paper band off the *belvedere claro* and drew the tobacco into life.

"In a sense, yes," he replied at last. "That is, I find the atmosphere here a great change and release from the pressures of everyday business. As, I am sure, Dr, Kiep does from his official obligations."

He drew on the cigar, squinted through his tortoise-rimmed spectacles as he located the glint of the old biplane against the cloudless sky.

"But—I emphasize that you are now privy to information which is not for general consumption, Howard—but yes, there is another consideration."

Howard blinked at Viereck, waited for him to resume.

"As you have doubtless perceived, the coming events which we together anticipate will have far-reaching effects, Howard. It is my expectation that the great New England shipping trade of past centuries will revive. Indeed, there will be a great renaissance of world commerce under the new world order. We hear so much of progress in the air, and that will doubtless flourish. But the great sea-lanes of world commerce will carry a flow of cargo and of travellers unprecedented in history."

He clenched one fist behind his back, used the other to hold his La Palina. He strode back and forth near the water's edge, smoking heavily.

"There was once a great China trade from these very ports," Howard volunteered. "My grandfather Whipple Phillips was part of it. Many of these old houses still contain porcelain and silks that came around the Horn from Asia a hundred and fifty or even two hundred years ago."

"Precisely," Viereck injected. "Of course, one expects that Asiatic ports will be more reasonably reached from America's Pacific seaports. But Europe and Africa lie before us." He stood and gestured out to sea, as if Hamburg, Le Havre, Accra were just over the horizon.

"And the virgin territories of Latin America as well. There is good reason to believe that the usurper republicans of Brazil will soon topple before the blows of a Bourbon restoration. Imagine, Imperial Brazil! Such once existed, and such may exist again! China, Russia, Germany! The tide will rise and sweep all opponents away! This is coming soon, Howard!"

~ ~ ~ ~ ~

In the observer's seat of the biplane, Howard Lovecraft turned to wave to Sylvester Viereck and Dr. Kiep. The two were bent in close conversation, their heads almost touching over the pages of Viereck's notebook. Dr. Kiep's Zeiss hung from a leather strap around his thick neck.

Howard turned back, watched the blur of the whirling propeller disk. Azor Burgess shouted at Howard and gestured, and with a shout from the biplane's engine they leaped forward, skimming the water toward the Marblehead Light. Howard felt the old craft's rough seat pressing against his back and trousers as it lifted suddenly and climbed over an exotic yacht built to simulate a classical Chinese junk.

Howard peered over the edge of the biplane and waved to the crew and guests on the junk's deck. They were sunning in bathing costume and passing a pitcher of some beverage. Before Howard could see any more the biplane had swooped past the yacht and begun a droning course toward Great Misery Island and Manchester Bay. Howard could see the boats on the sparkling water as tiny white-sailed models. Where the waters were shallow he could make out bottom features, green-tinted sands, gray rocks, darker beds of kelp. The wind screamed past his ears and he jammed his hat down onto his head to keep it from blowing away, despite the yellowed wind-screen before him.

In his mind he was composing an essay on the experience of flight and its usefulness. He never let any experience pass without turning it over in his mind for possible incorporation into a story, an essay, or at the least a letter to one of his numerous correspondents. Who would be most interested in his aerial experiences, he wondered. Paul Cook the publisher? Belknapius? Well, of course, everything was grist for young Long's unfillable intellectual appetite. What would Two-gun Bob Howard think of old Theobaldus as a modern-day Icarus? Hmm, perhaps the reference was a trifle esoteric for the earthy, energetic Texan. Starrett? Reverend Whitehead? Now there was a thought! Or perhaps Klarkash-ton, the reclusive poet of Auburn, California. He should certainly enjoy Howard's report.

Although Howard had known old Azor Burgess for some years, he'd never actually ridden in the old biplane himself. He found the experience exhilarating, and one that he wished to repeat. He thought of the old aircraft as a "hydro-aeroplane." Its ascent gave him a sense of cosmic independence from the map-like world of blue and green beauty stretched below. And yet, his antiquarian side pulling at his sentiments, Howard feared to see aeroplanes come into common commercial use, since they would merely add to what he considered "the goddam useless speeding up of an already over-speeded life." He would have preferred to see aviation preserved as a matter for the amusement of gentlemen.

By the time Burgess banked the old biplane into a final swoop over Marblehead itself, Howard's feelings had become churned into a melancholy amalgam of his exhilaration at the experience of flight, his concern over the future of his project for Viereck's Jackson Press, and a kind of free-floating *weltschmerz* stimulated by his concern over the ever-accelerating vulgarization and mechanization of society.

It took much of the rest of the day for Howard to regain his high spirits, but regain them he did. After he and Kiep and Viereck had left Azor Burgess and Marblehead Neck and crossed the causeway back to the mainland they stopped for lunch in Hooper Street near Bank Square, and Howard filled himself with a brown glazed pot full of baked beans, done with molasses and flavored with cinnamon, and after lunch they visited an ice cream parlor where Howard sampled a half dozen flavors, pronouncing them the near equal of the best ice cream he'd ever tasted.

"Actually," Howard admitted to Viereck and Kiep, "it is not easy to recall the finest ice cream parlor one has ever patronized. I was introduced recently to an establishment in Brooklyn called Jahn's which offers the most delectable concoctions. And of course the Schrafft's establishments are excellent."

He spooned a mouthful of ice cream thoughtfully. "There is an establishment in the lovely town of Warren, Rhode Island, which I visited one time with my friends James Morton and Donald Wandrei. The place advertised itself as featuring thirty-two flavors of ice cream. I fear that the three of us goaded one another on to heights of folly, or perhaps I should better say depths of gluttony."

Howard paused and laughed aloud at the recollection, then resumed telling his story. "The waitress was a lovely young woman, and since the place, Julia Maxwell's by name, was famed for the quality of its product, we ordered servings of three scoops for each of us, so that we could sample three flavors at a time. Each full serving totalled up to a pint of ice cream.

"After we had completed our servings we looked at one another and without speaking a word turned and signaled the waitress to return. We ordered once again, and consumed another pint of ice cream apiece.

"We continued until each of us had sampled twenty-one flavors. At that point poor Wandrei couldn't continue any longer. Poor chap—he's a rather good fantasy writer, you know. Lives out in the Midwest. Morton is the curator of the Paterson Museum in New Jersey.

"Morton and I pushed on for another five flavors. We managed to goad poor Wandrei into taking a little taste of each, but he showed no zest for the undertaking at all.

"Now at this point a sort of constitutional crisis arose. Julia Maxwell listed some thirty-two flavors of ice cream on her menu, and there we had sampled a mere twenty-six, and yet the waitress informed us that there were no more flavors to be had. We'd arrived too late in the day, and six flavors had become exhausted. Alas! The intrepid explorers—two of the three, at least—were quite ready and willing to continue to plunge onward into new virgin territory, only to learn that we had reached Land's End!

"But as a kind of commemorative record we prepared a testimonial certificate, duly attesting to our gastronomical achievement, and presented it to the management. To their credit I learned, when I returned to Warren on another sojourn about a year later, that Julia Maxwell had personally ordered the certificate framed and posted on the wall of the establishment. It stands there to this day."

Viereck and Dr. Kiep sat in a sort of stunned tribute to Howard's gourmandish prowess. Howard resumed spooning ice cream into his mouth. "This is really excellent stuff. Marblehead serves up a good ice cream; not a great ice cream, but a good ice cream." He permitted himself an amused cackle at his own observation.

"Your friend James Morton, Mr. Lovecraft." Dr. Kiep leaned forward slightly. "His specialty in the field of museums, it is what, if I may ask?"

"Oh, James is a mineralogist and geologist. In his modest way, a lapidary as well. One might say that he knows his rocks."

"Ah, very good. I wonder if I might from you obtain Mr. Morton's address, perhaps even a letter of introduction. If this would not be an imposition."

Howard shook his head. "I'd be most pleased to arrange an introduction for you."

They left the ice cream parlor and climbed the old Ferry Lane to Lattimer Street, to see the unusual old stone powder house where explosives had been stored as early as 1755. They turned about and surveyed the harbor, Howard pointing out the lighthouse at Marblehead Neck and Jack Point where old Burgess kept his antique hydro-aeroplane.

Before they left Marblehead to drive southward again, Viereck suggested a stop at a marine outfitter's shop, where all three purchased yachting caps and souvenirs. Dr. Kiep asked Howard if he would mind making a purchase for him. "My English is not quite that of this region," Kiep explained.

Howard agreed, and bought an official ocean survey chart of the Manchester-Marblehead area, showing the waters, channels, rocks, and depth soundings of the region.

"My thanks to you," Kiep remarked. "This region is most beautiful; these charts I will post above my desk at the consulate, to remind me of this happy visit."

En route to Providence, Viereck questioned Howard regarding his plans for *New America and the Coming World-Empire*. Howard sketched in a rough plan for the book which had been forming in his mind. He would survey the condition of the world order at the beginning and the end of the Great War. These two sections of his book would represent a huge contrast. In 1914 there was a pattern of stability, order, discipline and progress. By the end of the war in 1918 disarray had made its appearance.

The Romanoff empire had crumbled, fallen to the Bolshevists. The Ottoman Empire, for all its decadence, had still represented a unifying force; it, too, was dispersed into a dozen nations, colonies, protectorates and possessions. The proud Austro-Hungarian Empire of the Hapsburgs had gone the way of the Ottoman Empire. Even the ancient Chinese empire, although Sun Yat-sen had overthrown the Manchu's throne in 1912 rather than during the years of the Great War, had fallen into the same pattern of violent disintegration.

The next section of Howard's book would describe the various restorationist and reformist movements that had arisen since the end of the Great War. The section would be divided into two long sub-sections, one dealing with such foreign political movements as that of Mussolini in Italy, the National Socialist movements headed by Viereck's friend Hitler in Germany and Count Vonsiatsky in exile from Russia, even the potential Chinese restorationist front of Hsuan T'ung, the thirty-year-old former emperor and last of the Manchus whom Sun had overthrown in 1912. And of course there would be material on the Kaiser, Wilhelm II and the *kronprinz* pretender who might someday become Wilhelm III.

The other sub-section would deal with the domestic alliance working to bring America into this new world order: the Klan, the Social Justice movement and its potential Christian Front, the Patriotic Research Bureau and their leaders and allies.

Finally there would be a portrait of the coming world empire, its promise of renewed order and tranquility for the world.

Viereck applauded Howard's plan. "I should like you to become acquainted with a few additional persons, Howard. For one, while you have met Dr. DeLand, I wonder if you are familiar with Count di Revel."

Howard frowned and shook his head.

"Ah," Viereck resumed, "the president of the Fascist League of North America. He is a naturalized citizen, but retains his European title as a courtesy. Count Ignazio Thaon di Revel. A member of one of the oldest families of the Italian nobility, a cousin of King Victor Emmanuel, the current monarch. A splendid fellow. I should arrange a meeting for you, or perhaps you would prefer to be introduced by Dr. DeLand. Do you have her New York address? You know, she is from Kansas, but resides now at the Hotel Dixie in Manhattan."

"Either," Howard said.

"Do you find Providence a convenient location for your researches?" Viereck asked. "I understand, of course, the appeal of your ancestral home. But it seems to me that there is more activity in New York. There might be more valuable contacts available to you there."

Howard rubbed his jaw and thought about that. "You are probably right. I did live in New York for several years, and found that my own Providence is really a more congenial place. But perhaps for a period of a few months or a year at most. . . until I have completed my studies for the book. I shall give the proposal my serious consideration."

CHAPTER FIFTEEN:

THE THEOLOGICAL TERM FOR THE QUALITY

3749 North Fremont
Chicago, Illinois
April 12, 1927

Dear Howard,

You may be surprised at the above address, if you didn't notice the Chicago postmark on this letter. I was quite comfortably settled into my Long Island quarters and diligently pursuing my obligation to George B. Doran when I received an urgent summons from Walter Howey, my old chief on the Windy City *Inter-Ocean*. Walter is in dire need of a good hand who knows the ins and outs of Chicago's seamier side, as our crack crime reporter Billy Black is overworked beyond all decency, and poor Walter has no one else with the know-how to do the job. Such is the price of running an also-ran newspaper! (Don't tell Walter I told you that, although he must know it as well as anyone—the *Inter-Ocean* is staffed mainly with has-beens, never-weres, and a few bright youngsters who will in due course move on to the *News*, the *Trib*, the *Herald Examiner* or elsewhere; if Walter himself hangs around here another year I'll be astonished!)

Specifically, the *Inter-Ocean* is trying to catch up with its betters in the coverage of the bootleggers, racketeers, and gang lords of Chicago, and Walter also asked me to check up a bit on the early career of our current number one gang chieftan, Al Brown, *née* Alphonso Caponi, *aka* Al Capone-with-a-silent-E, dealer in used furniture. So I spent a few days checking out the Big Fellow's New York connection. The Five Points Gang on the lower east side, some Brooklyn activities, but nothing to suggest the genius he has exhibited since he hit the Middle West.

It was a great pleasure to climb aboard the Black Diamond (I bunked with Alex the night before and it was an easy jaunt up to Penn Station) and let a porter carry my meager bag for me. Ah—first class travel. Howard, there is nothing like it, and an expense account is the only way to pay for it (unless one inherits wealth or takes up boot-legging as a profession). As you can see from the Fremont Street address, I've even managed the temporary recapture of my old digs while temporarily abandoning my temporary Beechhurst residence. Ah, *eheu fugaces* as we used to say in poetical circles hereabouts. *Everything* is temporary, if only one has the wit to realize it! (Am I growing verbose in my old age? Must be the novelist in me overwhelming the newsman.)

I should get to the point.

You've mentioned your interest in various rightish political groupings of late, especially in some with foreign connections, and the question arises as to how the local criminal element, with its rather heavy Sicilian bias, relates to various political entities, domestic and foreign both. I should mention that Al Brown is not himself a member of the *Unione Siciliana* (although he has maneuvered his man Tony Lombardo into its presidency), nor is Brown now nor ever going to be a *mafioso*. The *Unione* and the *mafia* are strictly Sicilian outfits, and Al is an Italian. That's one thing he cannot change.

Of course Capone owns the local political structure. He took over the little town of Cicero first, to establish a "free zone" for himself, but by now he's got Chicago by the throat. Poor old Judge Dever was a weak enough reed as mayor. Now that Big Bill the Builder is back, there won't even be token opposition to Al and his colleagues. Capone owns Thompson, Thompson owns the Republican machine, and the Republicans are well in the saddle hereabouts. Governor Small isn't too happy about the state of affairs, but he's a Republican too, so he's stuck with Thompson and consequently with Capone. Pretty, hey?

I don't know that Al has any national interests, although he and his pals have their Florida interests to think about. Big Bill Thompson is playing chummy with a fellow named Long down in Louisiana, and an alliance between a demagogue (which Long surely is) and a weakling who plays cat's-paw for Al Capone is something unpleasant to contemplate.

There's an oddly mixed feeling among the local Italian and Sicilian population when it comes to the Fascists. A lot of *mafiosi* have arrived here of late. Mussolini is trying very hard to suppress the *mafia* in Sicily (it hardly has a toehold on the Italian mainland) (that's a joke, Howard), and he seems to be doing pretty well. A lot of soldiers and dons are packing up and getting out, moving to America the land of opportunity.

They don't lose any love on *Il Duce* but they still love their old country. Maybe that's because they're *mafiosi*. (Did you know that the *mafia* was originally a patriotic society? Started *anno domini* 1282 as guerrillas during a French occupation. The name is an abbreviation for *Morte alia Francia Italia anela*, Death to the French is Italy's Cry. At least, that's one theory.)

There's a local fascist organization, one Dr. Ugo Galli is the boss. Ties in with a national outfit headed by a Count Ignazio di Revel. You may come across him if you continue to look into these people.

Mainly, I'd say that the American-born Italians have a warmer feeling for the old country than this newest wave who were, in effect, just chased out. My friend Mr. Brown-Caponi-Capone is in the former class. American born, says that he got his famous scars in a machine-gun unit during the Great War.

So, Howard: Is there a tie-in here, with your political playmates? I'll have to give you a maybe instead of a yes or a no. And my apologies.

Strangely enough, the Big Fellow himself is not that unpleasant or unapproachable a person. (Not that I'd like to have him angry with me, mind you. He's not above sending somebody to visit you with a gun in his hand.)

Billy Black and I took a little tour of the South Side the other evening, and stopped in at the Midnight Frolics to have a drink or two and listen to some old musician friends of mine. A nice little band called the Wolverines run by a piano-player named Dick Voynow. They used to have a marvelous cornet player, Bix Beiderbecke. Voynow told me that he'd gone to New York to work for Gene Goldkett. Some irony! They replaced him with a young-ster named Jimmy McPartland, who's quite talented and may someday be as good as Bix although he surely isn't now. I know that the charm of jazz music escapes you, Howard, but you really ought to give it a try. You could do worse than look up the Goldkett orchestra; maybe we'll find them together when I get back East again.

Anyway, there were Billy Black and I sitting over a couple of highballs, exchanging data on the New York and Chicago scenes, and talking about Al Brown in particular, when in troop a phalanx of bodyguards, outriders, camp followers, and in the center of them all, the Big Fellow himself, replete with pinstriped suit, silken shirt, diamond rings, and broad-brimmed *sombrero*.

He recognized Billy, called us both over to the royal pavilion, and told the waiter to take away the rotgut Billy and I had been drinking and bring us some private stock! (It had been rotgut, too.)

Al introduced us to some of his party, including one Boathouse John Coughlin, who's a Republican Alderman. More about him later, Howard. Al yells at Basil Dupre, one of the musicians, to ask what tune they were playing and Basil yells back, "A Good Man is Hard to Find." Al thought that was so funny he bought a round of drinks for the entire house and gave the band hundred dollar tips!

After about an hour he turns to Billy Black and myself and says, "You boys need a story or you'll get in dutch with your editor, won't you? Well, come along and we'll do something for you."

Howard, out we march to Al's personal limo, we drive over to his headquarters in the Metropole Hotel, up to his private suite, and he says, "Anything you boys want to know, just ask."

Well, Howard, I won't duplicate the write-up that Billy and I did for the *Inter-Ocean*; see the clipping enclosed. But at one point, Al got onto the subject of politics, and declaimed on the topic of the Red menace. That didn't make the *Inter-Ocean* story, but you'd probably be interested. By my notes, Al said:

"evism is knocking at our gates. We can't afford to let it in. We have got to organize ourselves against it and put our shoulders together and hold fast. We must keep America whole and safe and unspoiled. We must keep the worker away from Red literature and Red ruses; we must see that his mind remains healthy."

Isn't that precious?

As for the man's claim about "just providing a service" (see clipping), the fact is, Howard, that it's hard to quarrel with him. Nobody has to buy hooch, nobody has to patronize his whorehouses, nobody has to play the ponies. Of course, some of the other things these racketeers are involved with *are* a different matter. The protection racket hasn't hit the East Coast very much, but it's a beauty, and the victims *do* have to kick in or they're in bad trouble. And Capone and some of the other racketeers are taking over some of the labor organizations, and that's really bad business.

But Al is a bootlegger above all else, and he doesn't make anybody drink beer who doesn't want to.

So much for Senator Sheppard and Representative Volstead.

Anyway, we finished our interview, enjoyed some hospitality, and then were given a free ride to our respective homes—Billy to his house, myself to this apartment. I must admit that I was slightly petrified with terror when Capone said, "How would you like to go for a little ride?" I must have looked pretty funny, at least if I looked anything like Billy Black at that moment.

Al doubled over laughing at us. But he meant just a ride, not a *ride*. Newsmen are pretty sacrosanct, at least so far, and Al did nothing to molest us. It was one of the most fascinating evenings of my life, to say the least!

Now, I said I'd have more to say about Alderman Coughlin. He's called Boathouse because of a little incident hereabouts a few years ago. He's a medium-distant relation of Charlie Coughlin, your friend Father Curran's priest-buddy. By the time Boathouse and I finished comparing notes, we discovered that Charlie and I, if not Boathouse himself, were boyhood acquaintances! We're both native Torontonians, you know (ay, sinister foreigners, Howard, beware their tinted hides and oddly formed eyes), almost exactly of an age (I was born in '86, Howard, which causes me an occasional moment of puzzlement at your own grandfatherly pretensions), and even roamed the same neighborhood around Oxford Street.

Half my family is Irish, as is all of Father Coughlin's, of course. (The other half of my family is Scotch.) But my Irishers are of that curious breed, Irish Protestants, so I didn't have the benefits of Charlie's ecclesiastical education. What if I had! Can you imagine *me* a priest? Ho!

At any rate, Charlie has his own parish now, although one would hardly call Royal Oak, Michigan, a major center of world influence. I visited the town, spoke with some of his parishioners (he seems to be a popular enough priest), and called upon Charlie, conveying the greetings of his umptieth-cousin Boathouse and trying to find common links in our own Toronto past. (Charles, by the way, is aware of some of the rather unsavory goings on in the First Ward of Chicago, which Boathouse co-owns with a colorful chap known as Michael "Hinky-Dink" Kenna. Charlie tut-tuts a good deal about his disreputable relation.)

Charlie's politics, to come to the point, are rather vague and contradictory. He seems to be a capitalist, socialist, fascist, liberal, reactionary, bigot, and advocate of toleration, internationalist isolationist. But I am afraid of the man, Howard! He is positively magnetic; I believe the theological term for the quality is *charismatic*. And he lusts for power! One can feel it!

Just now he is a humble parish priest. He started a weekly radio broadcast last October, out of WJR in Detroit. Mainly he seems to conduct little games and tepid homilies for children. But I don't think he plans to stop there.

As for his relationship with your friend Edward Curran, and the fact, of course, that you do not consider yourself a Christian—well, all things being what they are in this chaotic twentieth century of ours, I'm not even sure what a Christian is.

But by my Christian forebears, I don't think this man is a Christian. Not if there's any meaning left in the word at all!

At any rate, when Father Coughlin gets onto politics, the one phrase that keeps popping up through his circuitous sentiments is something that he calls Social Justice. I suppose we'd do well to keep an ear out for the phrase, and any time we hear it, at least know its source: the Shrine of the Little Flower in Royal Oak, Michigan.

Howard, beware!

Well, enough of doom-crying on my part. All is for the pretty-good in this the most mediocre of all possible worlds.

Since I am on a Ryan Special assignment rather than the *Inter-Ocean's* payroll, I was able to take a few hours off when I got back from Michigan, and I used them to hie myself up to Michigan Avenue (a mere coincidence, Howard, no play on words this time), and visit our mutual friends at the Popular Fiction Publishing Company, better known as *Weird Tales* magazine.

I received a lovely bit of news while I was up there. The management has decided to issue a Ryan Special book edition of that yarn of Birch's that they ran back in '23, and sell it cheap as a circulation builder for *Weird Tales*. But Birch's yarn (*The Moon Terror*—recall it?) isn't quite long enough to bulk out the book they want, so they're going to pad it with a handful of short stories from back issues as well, and Farnie told me that he's chosen my little parody "Penelope" for the book. I tried to talk him into using one of your own pieces, but he seems pretty well settled on yarns by myself, Tony Rud, and one of his own (the swine!). Sorry I can't congratulate you, but will you join me in a celebratory sarsaparilla when we're next both in New York City?

By the way, as you know, Ed Burroughs (whose inter-planetary Graustarks I poked fun at in "Penelope") is an old Chicago boy. He long ago deserted the Windy City for balmy California, lock, stock, and family. But he sent me a note when "Penelope" appeared in *Weird Tales* indicating vast amusement at the leg-pull. A hale fellow who can laugh honestly when he's the butt of the jape!

There was an incident while I was up at 840 North Michigan. Who should arrive as I sat chatting with Wright and Henneberger but Farnie's predecessor and Joe's one-time compatriot, Ed Baird! They've apparently yet to make their break final and complete, and while I sat embarrassed they got into a quarrel. It started over some very minor matter, I think, but soon everyone present was raking up coals from March 1923 onward.

I kept edging toward the door—I wanted no part of this sort of family squabble—but all concerned kept pulling me back. At any rate, Howard, names of all the people associated with the magazine popped up: Otis Kline, Prince Ottokar Binder, Harry Houdini, and of course H. P. Lovecraft.

Ed Baird avers that you were his prize find for the magazine. Farnie agrees that you are one of his major talents and chief drawing cards. (Your ears should have been burning during the exchange, Howard!) Baird then asked why you appear so seldom in *Weird Tales*. Wright said that you don't produce enough, and what you send him is of uneven quality. Baird said he'd yet to see a poor story by you. (You should have heard him—your greatest fan!) Wright admitted that he had, on occasion, reconsidered a rejection and taken a story after all, that he'd once passed over. Ed Baird said that if Wright had to look twice to see a talent like HPL's he'd better have his eyes examined, and that if you were ever dissatisfied with *Weird Tales* you would be welcomed any time into the pages of his current pridenjoy, *Real Detective Tales*.

Howard, I've done a number of yarns for Baird's deteckatiff book.(Perhaps you've seen my Jimmy Lavender stories, with apologies to the fine onetime gloveman of the Windy City Cubs—Lord knows I've done enough of them, and Jimmy always seems good for a quick sale and a decent check, which is more than can be said for many a more ambitious creation of mine!) My point, here, is that Baird pays better rates than Henneberger, and that he's more solidly sold on your work than Farnie Wright. So while I'd hardly suggest that you drop *Weird Tales* as an outlet for your more eldritch narrations, it would probably be a good bet to try for a few yarns with a bit more emphasis on the mysterious and a bit less on the moody, and ship 'em off to Baird.

Okay, okay, I'll mind my own business!

That's really about all that I have to tell you, old Theobaldus. Every time my poor flat wallet rebukes me for writing lengthy letters when I could be solving great fictional crimes at summiny sensaword, I begin to feel guilty, so I will close off now and try to get some shut-eye, if I can sleep through the tommy-gun battles that rage day and night in this bastion of municipal virtue.

Oh—soon as I get back East, I shall resume work on *Seaports* of course. The book is (or until my summons back to harness, *was*) making progress steadily if not too rapidly. I hope to finish it by July or so, and will probably toss an Independence Day gala out at Beechhurst. You'll be invited, and I hope you and Mrs. Lovecraft will both be able to participate in the festivities.

Yours for bigger and better Czechs
(also Poles, Hungarians, et cetera)
((That's a joke, Howard!))
Vincent Starrett

Vincent signed and sealed the letter, pulled on a cardigan sweater against the still uncertain spring evening, and strolled to the corner mail-drop to post his missive. On his way out of the apartment building on North Fremont he noticed a large new automobile parked across the street. Two men sat in it, hats pulled low, gazing at his building through the window.

As he stood at the mail-drop the engine of the car roared into life and the car made a rapid U-turn, pulling to the curb by the mail-drop. Vincent still held the letter in his hand. The passenger in the car rolled down his window and ordered Vincent to freeze. Vincent complied. In the moment he noticed both that the passenger held a sub-machine gun in his hands, and that the car was a new Buick; he marvelled at the workings of his own mind, to notice two such disparate facts at the same time.

The passenger reached out of the car with one hand. "Let me see that letter before you mail it."

Vincent handed over the envelope. The man took it, scanned the address, handed it to his companion sitting in the driver's position, then received it back and handed it again to Vincent.

"Okay, go ahead and mail it."

Vincent dropped the letter in the slot of the mail receptacle. The car roared away. Vincent walked slowly back to number 3749, made his way to his apartment, opened a bottle of whiskey and poured himself a half tumbler. He went to the sink and added the equivalent of a couple teaspoons water.

He sat at the kitchen table and drank down the contents of the tumbler. It would take a few minutes for the alcohol to reach his brain, and he used the time to change from street clothes to pajamas, brush his teeth, and climb into bed with pencil and pad. It was a funny way to get drunk, but he could feel the liquor doing its work.

He gazed at the spiral-bound sheets through wavering eyesight, jotted a few notes, and began to work on a sonnet. He could rhyme Capone easily enough. Bone, stone, moan, crone, phone, loan. Who else would go into the poem? Big Al's arch-rival, Bugs Moran. That was a tougher nut. Catamaran? No good. Rataplan was better but nobody knew what that was except drummers. Man, fan, tan, can, it was coming easier, but he liked rataplan.

Maybe he could make a play on words, compare machine-gun sounds to a rataplanning drummer. Who drummed for the Wolverines these days? He tried to remember from the Midnight Frolics but he kept seeing Al Brown's face with its one ruined cheek. He could do no more. No more. Oh, that was it, Vic More, no Vic *Moore*.

The pad slipped onto the woolen blanket, the pencil tumbled to the bare floor with a low rattle. Vincent started to reach for them but the room spun and a first warning of nausea rose from the pit of his stomach and he decided to let it ride for now. Let it slide, let it ride.

~ ~ ~ ~ ~

When he woke up in the morning he phoned Billy Black at home and was relieved to hear that Billy was all right. "Sure I am, Vince. Why wouldn't I be?"

Vincent said there was no reason, he'd just awakened with a little sense of unease and thought he'd make sure everything was okay. He hung up and asked Central for Jake Lingle's hotel suite. Fortunately Vincent knew the private line that Jake maintained; it was front desk policy to deny even that he had a room at the hotel.

Jake sounded happy to hear from Vincent. "Didn't know you were back in town. How long you planning to stay?"

Vincent said he was wrapping up business and planned to head back to New York in a day or two. Maybe they could have a drink together before he left.

Jake said that would be swell, if he got a chance for it. If not, he'd send his car and chauffeur to take Vincent to the train when he was ready to leave. Just phone the hotel any time, day or night. The private line was always covered.

Vincent thanked him and rang off.

Three days later his train pulled into Penn Station on the Lehigh Valley tracks. Vincent tipped a porter to carry his belongings through the maze of passageways to the Long Island Rail Road tracks, and headed on to Beechhurst without stopping in the city. He'd enjoyed the chance to get back into newsman's harness for a while, three cheers for the *Inter-Ocean*, its editors Harry Daniel and Walter Howey, for Billy Black, Jake Lingle, Al Brown . . .and maybe one-and-a-half for Charlie Coughlin. But he had to get back to *Seaports in the Moon* before George Doran cancelled on him and sued to take back Vincent's already-spent advance.

He arrived at Beechhurst late and managed a few hours of sleep, then rose before dawn and dressed in a pair of rumpled trousers, a sweatshirt, rope-soled shoes and a knitted seaman's cap that he pulled down, flattening his prideful pompadour. He drank half a shot of whiskey that he'd brought back from Chicago and wandered out onto the beach to smoke a cigarette.

The sky to the east was graying with impending dawn; Little Bay and Long Island Sound were black. Throggs Neck loomed against the stars and the East River (*west* of Beechhurst, of course) was quite invisible. A thick mist rose from the water and crept across the cold sand to swirl at Vincent's feet.

This would be a lovely spot for Jimmy Lavender, he thought. Too bad that Lavender and his amanuensis Gilly had been unwilling to leave their imaginary lodgings on Portland Street in Chicago, and return to Beechhurst with Vincent. Ah, but one must live in the world as it was, not as one would wish it to be. And he was not writing one of Jimmy's neo-Sherlockian puzzles now, he had to get back to work on *Seaports in the Moon* and he had to do it today.

And the puzzle that he faced was not at like one of Jimmy's who-stole-the-ruby, or who-murdered-the-playboy jobs. It was one of human psychology. What would Edgar Allan Poe and William Legrand actually have to say to each other, were they to meet in some strange universe where author and character were equally real? He tried to imagine that Long Island, New York, was Sullivan's Island, South Carolina, and that 1927 was 1843. One thing, Vincent would reread "The Gold-Bug" still again today. Should he draw the Negro, Jupiter, into the scene in *Seaports in the Moon*, or would the dramatic purity be better maintained by holding strictly to Poe and Legrand? Vincent crushed his cigarette in the pale, gritty sand, and paced.

Of all his literary acquaintances, who knew Poe the best? Probably Howard Lovecraft did. Maybe Vincent could get hold of Howard and chew over the problem for a while before he wrote the scene.

CHAPTER SIXTEEN:

NOTHING MORE DEMEANING TO A GENTLEMAN

HOWARD RETURNED to Providence and Sylvester Viereck and Dr. Otto Kiep returned in Dr. Kiep's Horsch to New York. Howard had decided that Viereck was right—he would be better able to prepare *New America and the Coming World-Empire* if he were situated in one of the centers of the national *elan*, like New York or Washington, than he would here in provincial Providence.

The move, like Vincent Starrett's *jehad* from Chicago to Beechhurst, would be an *ad hoc* operation, to be reversed as soon as the book was completed. Howard wrote to his friends Belknap Long and Starrett, to Sylvester Viereck, and to his wife Sonia announcing his intentions. Then he announced them to his aunts.

They reacted badly, and the whole incident led to as much of a real row as Howard had ever had with Annie and Lillian.

His aunts were convinced that Howard was slipping away from them, from his true home, from his Old American heritage. Those two *Germans* were bad enough, and then he would be seeing his wife again regularly, who was utterly beyond the pale—a Jewess, a Russian, and a tradeswoman. It was hard to tell which of the three marked her most blackly in the aunts' eyes, but certainly the three sins worked cumulatively to make Sonia utterly unsuitable companionship for Howard.

Besides, how would Lillian and Annie get along without Howard to support them and care for them?

Howard fumed at the sophistries. They had done perfectly well during his earlier sojourns in New York City, including the one that lasted two years. As for Howard's supporting them, the fact was that his meager earnings hardly supported him, no less providing a surplus for the assistance of needy relatives. When Howard lived with Sonia before, Annie's salary as a librarian in Providence had not only cared for herself and Lillian but had provided for an occasional small gift of cash for Howard. Annie still had her position at the library and could certainly care for her own and Lillian's needs while Lillian kept house for the two of them. And in fact could do so more easily than she could have with Howard present living his contrary nocturnal life and filling the house with his perennial flow of papers, letters, magazines and books.

He took a week to settle his affairs in Providence, shipped his most useful research materials and his ancient Postal typewriter to Sonia's Parkside apartment in Brooklyn.

There was a tearful scene with his aunts when he finally packed his meager changes of clothing and his toilet articles into his battered luggage and prepared to leave 10 Barnes. Lillian was convinced that Sonia had bewitched Howard with some Slavic magic. Annie entertained no such fantasy; she simply clung to her nephew and wept.

Howard promised to write regularly, to visit the aunts as often as he could, and to consider Brooklyn as only a temporary residence for the time it took him to complete *New America*. As soon as the book was accepted by Jackson Press, Howard would bid Sonia and the wicked city farewell and return to Providence for good. Neither aunt was happy with the promise, but both finally accepted it as the best they could hope to obtain, and Howard was permitted to exit without physical opposition.

He reached New York and headed straight for West End Avenue and the Longs' apartment.

He was admitted by the maid and found Belknap engrossed in a volume of Machen.

Belknap looked up, an innocent smile filling his round face. "Grandpa Theobald! What a surprise!"

"I wrote thee," Howard frowned. "Didst not receive my *billet-doux*?"

Belknap flushed. "Of course I did. I fear I'd become so engrossed in my reading that I utterly lost track of the hour, if not of the day."

"I didn't know you were so great an admirer of Machen's, grandchild. How come the sudden passion?"

"You share in the credit, grandsire. When you first showed me your notes for 'Supernatural Horror in Literature' I could hardly believe that anyone was as good as you held Machen to be. So I made it my business to get hold of as many of his works as I could find, and I will not only confess that you were entirely right, I'll be happy to join my endorsement, humble as it is, to yours.

"In fact," Long continued, fumbling for a cold pipe and jamming it into the corner of his mouth *sans* flame or tobacco, "I've been playing with a little verse in honor of Mr. Machen. Perhaps you'd care to look at it."

He scrabbled up a piece of handwritten foolscap from his work space and handed it to Lovecraft. Howard scanned it briefly, then said, "Well, the child hath wrought a sonnet no less! Some little verse, Belknapius. Here, let's try it upon the tongue!"

He read the sonnet aloud, beginning, "There is a glory in the autumn wood, The ancient lanes of England wind and climb. . . ." When he had finished reading the sonnet he blinked his eyes, then said, "Belknap, you outdo yourself. If I may—may I include this sonnet in 'Supernatural Horror'? Poor Cook is going to shake the rafters with his screams of protest, but I *must* have the sonnet for my essay. Say that I may, please!"

Long laid his pipe aside. "No need for such pleas, Howard. I'd be honored. By all means, take the poor thing. I only wish I could compose something more worthy of my subject!"

"Come then," Howard hurried, "let's get this copied out and into the mail at once. Poor Cook must have it as soon as possible. The pitiful chap is going to have trouble enough making changes upon changes upon changes in my essay."

On the way back from the mail-drop, Long explained, "Aside from the literary quality of Machen's work, there is the peculiar circumstance of the issue of his two Covici volumes. Those are the ones that I have, you'll notice. Picked them up in a Fourth Avenue emporium of dust-ridden veteran volumes.

"Poor Machen was mostly out of print until this Chicago newspaper man Starrett came upon him and assembled a couple of volumes of short pieces. Some really brilliant stuff. Things like 'The Shining Pyramid', 'The Mystic Speech', 'The Secret of the Sangraal'."

"I'm particularly fond of 'The Secret of the Sangraal'," Howard agreed.

"Indeed! Starrett got out a couple of volumes from his friend Pascal Covici's press. *The Shining Pyramid* in '23 and *The Glorious Mystery* in '24. Then Machen, instead of being grateful, positively blew up. Said that Starrett had no authority to act for him, denounced both books, threatened to sue. Terrible."

"Well, Starrett says the opposite. You know Vincent, don't you, Belknapius?"

"Never met the man. I've seen his stuff in *Weird Tales*, of course."

Howard burst into laughter. "Well, of all the. . . . He's a friend of mine. Living out in Queens County right now, rented a cottage on the Sound to write a novel in. He was back in Chicago recently on a newspaper job once more, but if he isn't back from there yet he should be momentarily. I'll have to introduce you to him."

Belknap grinned. "I should be grateful to hear his side of the dispute at first hand." He changed the subject. "You're going to live in Brooklyn again for a while—at least I inferred as much from your recent letter."

Howard nodded. "I should still like to make my mark as an author of macabre fiction. The tradition of Poe and Hawthorne is that which I desire to follow, and Paul Cook's plan for *The Shunned House* gives me hopes. Starrett also wrote to me about a book that Henneberger and Wright are getting out, that little novel by Birch and a scattering of short stories to pad the volume. If the book does well I would expect Joe to publish some more, and perhaps I can talk him into doing a selection of my best stories. The readers seem to like them well enough—there's hardly an edition of the Eyrie without some missive of praise for my work."

He laughed shortly. "It's almost enough to give a doddering oldster like myself a swollen bean!

"But I've got a contract from Jackson Press for a non-fiction volume that promises to be quite an important work. In addition, it should bring some much-needed shekels into the Lovecraft treasury. I despise commerce, Belknapius!" Howard's eyes blazed as he spoke. "There is nothing more demeaning to a gentleman than to be forced into common trade. But—the bills do not respect one's station. Rent, food, clothing, medicine." (He carefully gave the word its British sound, omitting the central 'i'.) "Why, I recently submitted to the ministrations of a dentist who not only gave me several of the most painful hours of my career, but then proffered a statement that positively took my breath away! I think the fellow is out to overtake Messrs. Rockefeller, Carnegie, and Mellon—and all at the expense of one poor literary scrivener!"

Belknap laughed uncomfortably.

"I do not mean to imply that your father is of the same stripe, grandchild. Surgery is another matter. This fellow in Providence merely performed what I took to be routine dental services, nothing like the advanced work that your father does. *Ahem*. Well."

They were back in the Long apartment now, Belknap seated in an easy chair, Howard pacing. Now Howard hurled himself into a chair as well, slumping with his legs stretched straight out in front of him.

"Well, at any rate, the book that I am to do for the Jackson Press is non-fiction, a study of contemporary political movements and a projection of their effectiveness into a hypothetical near-future, which is called 'the coming world empire'."

"Sounds rather like scientific romance to me," Belknap commented, "something worthy of H. G. Wells or that fellow Gernsback."

"Gernsback! Speak to me not of Hugo, child! The rascal seized a story of mine for his magazine and resists all efforts to gain payment for it! Hah! Sometimes I think that publishing is the domain of nothing but fools and thieves. Professional publishing, anyway. There are many gentlefolk engaged in amateurdom, but for all that I'd like to restrict my outlets to such gentlemanly sheaves, there I face the unavoidable fiscal dilemma once more. 'Tis a puzzle without a solution, I fear."

He heaved a great sigh. Frank Long waited for him to resume.

"But I shall spend the next several months—perhaps the rest of the year, if necessary—pursuing this book for Viereck. Sonia maintains the Parkside Avenue domicile anyway, and has indicated that I am welcome to board with her. Most of my contacts seem to center on New York. And the end product should be a respectable volume."

"You are doing this book for George Sylvester Viereck, then?" Long asked. "You've mentioned his name, of course, ever since the topic first arose last New Years. Have you and Viereck settled your differences?"

Howard heaved himself out of the soft chair and walked to the mantelpiece. He leaned against it with one elbow, a tall, lean figure out of another era.

"I cannot say that I am in *total* sympathy with Sylvester's political leanings, Belknapius. But I have found him to be a gentleman of gracious, if somewhat eccentric, manner. He is of interesting blood himself, being a sort of distant Hohenzollern."

"A member of Bill the Butcher's union?" Long asked.

"Well—I have somewhat moderated that opinion." Howard grew slightly red around the ears. "*Ahem.* And he, Viereck, moves in circles composed of a fascinating mixture of persons of class and others of—let us say, a certain primitive energy which makes them of interest. I would say, then, that while Sylvester and I may continue to differ on certain points, I would hardly characterize him in the manner of my effusions during the Great War."

Long smiled at that.

~ ~ ~ ~ ~

Lovecraft made his way by streetcar and subway to Brooklyn and used the key Sonia had provided to admit himself to the apartment at 259 Parkside Avenue. His research materials and his Postal typewriter had arrived, and Sonia had considerately arranged them for him, making a work-area at one end of the living room where Howard could maintain bookshelves, a desktop for laying out and working over materials, and a typing stand with the Postal set upon it.

She had left a note, also, instructing Howard to make himself comfortable, take any food which he wanted from the kitchen, use the radiola or panatrope if he wished, and in general make himself at home. The telephone was also at his disposal, she added.

He opened his valises and set himself up in a closet and chest-of-drawers that Sonia had apportioned to him.

Howard let himself out, purchased a Brooklyn *Standard- Union* and a New York *Post* and settled himself in a nearby park to examine the newspapers until Sonia should return from her work in Manhattan.

It was Thursday, May 19, and the papers were filled, as usual, with a mixture of the significant and the trivial, the dramatic and the absurd. The London situation was fascinating—Home Secretary Sir William Joynson Hicks had risen in Commons to explain and defend the raid on the Soviet Arcos Trading Company. Arcos was a mere sham used by the Bolshevists to spread their network of spies and agitators and promote world revolution. The Arcos spokesman Kinchuck, speaking to the press, denounced the raid as police terrorism. Prime Minister Baldwin backed Joynson Hicks.

In China—oh, Lord, there was no end nor even clarification to the tangle of affairs in China! Chiang Kai-shek was *en route* to Shanghai in a train captured from a dead rival, Pi Hsu-chen. General Feng was holding out against Chiang; Feng was the last hope of the Hankow faction against Chiang. Britain was now backing Chiang, having dropped General Chen in revulsion against Chen's associate Mikhail Borodin.

Was this somehow connected with the Arcos raid in London, Howard wondered. He whistled and turned to other matters.

A municipal election had been held in Montgomery Alabama. Mayor Gunter had stood for re-election against the Ku Klux Klan's pet candidate J. Johnson Moore. Alabama Governor Bibb Graves, another strong Klan personality, had offered Moore his personal endorsement. Astonishingly, the voters had chosen to retain Gunter.

William G. McAdoo, Woodrow Wilson's onetime Secretary of the Treasury, announced that he was not interested in the Democratic nomination for President in 1928.

An advertisement on the entertainment page of the *Post* caught Howard's eye. The headline was "Just for a Laugh." One was advised to see Lou Clayton, Eddie Jackson and Jimmy Durante at the Parody. For reservations phone CHickering 6562 and ask for Leon.

Adjacent was a notice of a performance over the weekend at the Academy of Music adjoining Tammany Hall on 14th Street. Hardeen the Mysterious would give an evening of magic and marvelous escapes. Just returned from triumphal nationwide tour.

Richard A. Lupoff

Howard smiled.

Otherwise the papers seemed endlessly full of the great transatlantic flight competition. Howard looked at the stories, thought back to his experience in the Burgess biplane and understood somewhat the excitement of the aviators. Commander Byrd's financial backer Rodman Wanamaker had offered a $25,000 reward for rescue of the lost Frenchmen Nungesser and Coli. Bertrand and Chamberlain's backer, Charles Levine, was still quarreling with his crew and threatening to kick Bertrand out of the competition. Lindbergh claimed that his Ryan Ryan Special was ready to go and that he'd be off in the morning if the weather was good. And off New London, Connecticut, a Coast Guard patrol boat had found an aircraft wing floating in the ocean. Nobody knew the origin of the fragment, but Howard looked back at the Rodman Wanamaker reward story and decided that Wanamaker's money was safe.

Howard saw Sonia walking along the sidewalk toward 259 and left his park bench. He followed close enough behind to hear her humming happily to herself, a ten-year-old popular tune that somehow struck a familiar chord for Howard. He even remembered the name of the song. "There's Egypt in Your Dreamy Eyes." Sonia stopped at the outer door of 259 and fumbled her key into the lock, switching tunes to another melody of the same era, "If He Can Fight Like He Can Love, Good Night Germany."

Howard placed his hands lightly on Sonia's shoulders, from behind, and she whirled with a gasp and a sound that was almost a little scream. "Howard!" She threw her arms around him and he drew away stiffly.

"We are in public!"

Sonia grinned at her unchanging husband. "Well, come then." She turned away again just long enough to get the building door open, then led the way into the lobby and to her apartment. As she and Howard stood in the hall briefly, getting the front door unlocked, they heard the wailing pipes of their Syrian neighbor.

Howard and Sonia both laughed.

"There is burning incense, and a sinuous dancer decked in serpent bangles and Oriental coins, and soon there will be weird chanting and eldritch entities will appear, cold,

206

slimy, malign things from unhallowed regions beyond the stars and nebulae!"

Inside the apartment Howard explained his plans for research and for the book he was planning, and Sonia asked only how long he expected to remain in New York. When Howard told her she ran across the room and kissed him warmly. Howard did not resist.

Sonia asked Howard about his travels and he regaled her with his visits to Boston and Marblehead and Salem, especially with his inauguration into the brotherhood of aviators. "Or at least of aerial travelers," Howard amended. "I suppose one should not claim the title of aviator unless one actually takes the controls of the aeroplane. Even so, merely from having traveled as a passenger, I feel a new man. A whole dimension of experience is added to one's life when once one has flown!"

After Howard had finished, Sonia chattered to him about her life in New York, her job as a milliner, a letter from her daughter Florence in Europe.

Howard interrupted. "What has she to say about the political situation—especially in France?"

"Oh, I wrote and asked Florence, but she just doesn't seem very interested. She regards French politics as a kind of game, and she is more interested in other games —making the rounds of the literary salons, making the acquaintance of expatriate Americans. She writes about poetry and the novel and sculpture, and singing and dancing and drinking all night. Her idols are Gertrude Stein and Josephine Baker, can you imagine that? And I always raised her to be a respectable person."

Their dialog was interrupted by the ring of the telephone. Sonia answered, spoke briefly, held the mouthpiece of the telephone to her soft bosom. "Howard, a wonderful invitation but I will only accept if you will come along too."

Howard raised his eyebrows in question.

"It's Theo Weiss. He's heard that Lindbergh is going to make his attempt in the morning."

"About time," Howard said.

Sonia flushed. "Theo is going to drive to the aerodrome and watch the takeoff. He's invited us both to come along with him. I can call my supervisor and get tomorrow off— once past Easter our business is slack anyway. Do you think you could come, Howard? It would be a memorable day."

Howard thought about it briefly. Finally he said, "Yes."

Sonia spoke into the telephone for a while longer, then hung the earpiece back on its hook and set the instrument back on its table.

"Theo will come for us in his automobile. He lives on 21st Street and it will be much easier for him to drive here than for us to go there."

"I doubt that I'd have bothered if I hadn't had that ride with Azor Burgess," Howard said. "I'm afraid it's turned me into something of an aviation booster."

"The only thing is," Sonia said, "Captain Lindbergh will probably leave quite early. If we're to be there and not miss the event, we'll have to leave here by six o'clock, Theo says. He says he'll have no trouble rising early, and I won't, but I know that you like to sleep into the day, Howard."

"No trouble, my dear. I shall simply stay awake reading or working, or perhaps depart on one of my prowls tonight and walk through the hours. Mayhap I can secure a few feline acquaintanceships to replace my new Niggerman and Yaller Gal of Angell Street."

Sonia responded to the suggestion with an odd look.

Howard sat up with Sonia, alternately reading, chatting, and listening to radio broadcasts on her electric set, until Sonia yawned. "Are you sure you wouldn't like to come to bed for just a few hours, Howard darling? You'll be so worn out if you stay up all night. Come, the rest will be good for you."

But Howard wished Sonia a good night's sleep and left the apartment for a good prowl, examining such buildings as survived from an older and more gracious era. He wound up, after a circuitous course, at his own former residence on Clinton Street. The building was dark by this hour of the night, and Howard stood quietly contemplating the austere brick structure until a mounted city patrolman approached and sat on his horse, watching Howard.

Howard turned when he felt the policeman's gaze. He looked up into the policeman's face and said nothing.

"Anything the matter, sir?" the policeman asked.

Howard shook his head, gestured back toward the apartment building. "I used to live there, some years ago. Just out for a late stroll, and I was thinking about former times. That's all, officer."

The policeman scratched behind one ear. "This is a pretty safe neighborhood, but it's kind of asking for trouble, wandering the streets alone in the wee hours. You weren't looking for something, by any chance?"

Howard said, "I don't know what you mean. Looking for what?"

The policeman remained still.

"You don't take me for a second-story man, do you, officer?"

The patrolman laughed loudly. "No, sir. I wouldn't take you for a burglar. Thought you might be looking for a speak, sir."

"A *speak*?" Howard thought for a moment. "Oh, a speak-easy. Hah! Hardly that. I was T.T. even before the eighteenth amendment, I'm certainly not looking for a saloon now. As I told you, officer, I was merely looking at a building where I used to live, pondering the passage of time and the effect of the years. I suppose it's sometimes difficult to accept simple truths, in an era when we expect every statement to conceal some invidious implication. But I assure you, my statement conceals no hidden meaning. It is merely as it appears. But I thank you for your concern."

Howard turned away and again contemplated the building. Behind him there was a lengthy silence. Finally he heard the policeman's horse snort once in the cool air.

"All right, sir," the policeman said at last. "But be careful. Not everyone who's out at this hour is an honest citizen."

Howard said, "Thank you. I shall be careful."

He heard the horse's iron-shod hooves clop away over the blacktop street.

After a while Howard made his way slowly back to Parkside Avenue, checking his watch now and then, and examining the sky for any sign of approaching dawn. He was back in Sonia's apartment by four o'clock in the morning. He shaved and changed to a fresh shirt and necktie, then wakened Sonia. While she dressed, Howard made a pot of coffee and they sat drinking it.

At five o'clock the lobby buzzer sounded and they made their way downstairs to join Theo Weiss for the ride to the airfield in hopes of seeing Lindbergh off on his attempt to win the hotelman Orteig's long-standing $25,000 prize.

CHAPTER SEVENTEEN:

TWO LOST FRENCHMEN

THEO EXAMINED his appearance in the glass door of the Parkside Avenue apartment building while he waited for Sonia and Howard to make their way downstairs. He was satisfied with his gray felt homburg (the precise angle of tilt was almost a matter of pride with him); his darker gray chesterfield hung properly, although he had to flick a couple of bits of lint off the black velvet collar. His shirt was well starched and the fresh collar he wore with it lay in place exactly as it ought to, but he couldn't get his necktie to behave. It was positively maddening—he'd tied and re-tied the silken thing in the popular new Windsor knot, but it utterly refused to hold the shape that the young Prince of Wales managed with his own neckwear.

He managed a final small adjustment as Sonia and Howard appeared, smiling, on the other side of the glass.

"Dash!" Sonia exclaimed, unlatching the lobby door. Theo pushed it open, took her briefly in his arms. Sonia Greene Lovecraft had appealed to him as one of the warmest and most vivacious women he had ever met, in all his travels around the globe. She brushed her full lips against his smooth-shaven cheek, giggled at him. "You're as vain as a boy of twenty-one," she exclaimed, "always preening and posing. What would you do without a mirror to look in?"

Theo reached past Sonia and shook hands with her husband, the tall, almost gaunt New Englander. As he shook hands with Howard he answered Sonia's question. "Why, I'd use apartment house door-panes, or polished belt-buckles or glass-backed rings like the card sharps. Or I'd bend over a pool like the mythical Narcissus. Or as a last resort I should have to look for myself in the eyes of a beautiful woman."

Howard Lovecraft's flat New England tones asked, "Hadn't we better be going to the aerodrome? I'd had the impression that it was quite a drive from here, and that the aviator was planning to make an early departure."

Theo checked his wristwatch and said, "Right." He led the way to his sedan, parked at the curb a short distance away. He opened the doors for Howard and Sonia, then climbed into the car himself and pressed on the self-starter switch with his boot.

"This is quite an automobile," Lovecraft commented as they drew away from the curb. "I don't believe I have seen its likes before!" He reached forward and patted the dashboard appraisingly.

"You mean my little orphan," Theo laughed. "Yes, I've only had it a short time. It's a Rickenbacker. You know, Ehrich was such a bug for aviation that I think he infected me with the fever. I bought the car because I thought that Captain Rickenbacker couldn't possibly be connected with a piece of poor engineering. And so far I've been very satisfied on that score. You know, the engine has twin flywheels, front and rear. That's why the car runs so smoothly."

"It's certainly a beautiful car," Sonia put in. "I just love the color scheme. Subdued, the cream and gray and black, but very tasteful. And the details in gold, my gracious, Theo! And these seats! You must be doing very well!"

He admitted that he was. "Not that I'm so pleased about that, Sonia. I seem to have inherited much of Ehrich's following, along with his illusions and escapes. I've been working very steadily, sometimes using Ehrich's own staff. Bess has appeared with me a few times, as well. It isn't a happy road to success. I'd rather be back in Houdini's shadow than stand in the spotlight as his heir."

He made a gesture of dismissal with his left hand. "But one accepts the will of fate, I suppose." He turned slightly in his seat. "I didn't mean to ignore you, Howard. I haven't seen you in too long a time. How is the literary business these days?"

"Well enough, thank you. I'm working on a book just now."

"Ah."

"You made a remark earlier, Theo, that intrigued me. What did you mean, that the car is your little orphan?"

Theo laughed. "I suppose I meant that Captain Ricken-backer's engineering talent may be flawless but his business sense is not quite up to par. The company that built these excellent machines went bust just a few weeks ago. This model is a '26—one of their last. I'm not sure whether they'd got out a '27 or not, before they closed their doors. Too bad, too, I say. They built a fine automobile, but that's that. I'm sure that Captain Rickenbacker will find something else to do with himself. He won't go on the dole."

Sonia nodded. "I'm sure of that!"

They had made their way through Brooklyn and into almost suburban Queens. Small houses in new little developments alternated with older, iron-fenced estates. A few luxury condominiums thrust metal skeletons into the dawn-gray sky. In tasteful small lettering their realty signs contained messages such as, "Residence restricted for the protection of your investment."

Beyond the city limits the Rickenbacker purred at higher speed. The houses that had filled much of Queens gave way to a largely rural landscape of rolling hills and dark woods, sparsely dotted with ancient wooden residences and prosperous farms. Beside Theo, Howard Lovecraft smiled and said, "Why, this is remarkable. This region is much like the New England countryside. I thought New York was all cement and brick."

"You've never been here before, Howard?" Theo asked.

Howard shook his head. "A new experience for me. Is there just one aerodrome on Long Island?"

Theo said there were several, but they were headed for Roosevelt Field. "Lindbergh has kept his monoplane at Curtiss Field, but he chose to make his flight from Roosevelt Field instead, and had the Ryan hauled over last night, by truck. A good thing I switched on my Brunswick before retiring last night, or I'd have driven us all to the wrong airfield! But there it was on the last news broadcast of the evening on WBKN."

The sky was lightening to the eastward, but a mist was falling and Theo switched on the hydraulic wiper blades to keep the windscreen of the Rickenbacker clear. There was little traffic at the early hour: an occasional pair of bright headlights would pass them, heading into the city, perhaps a commuting businessman hoping to avoid traffic and make an early start of his day; a distant red tail-reflector ahead of the Rickenbacker, picked out when the curving road ran straight briefly and the Rickenbacker's own lights probed forward and picked up the reflection.

Theo turned from the main road, guided the car onto the grassy parking area at Roosevelt Field.

There were several dozen cars parked beside the tarmac, and a crowd milled around waiting for the appearance of the solo aviator. Theo switched off the Rickenbacker's headlights and climbed from the car; they made their way to the edge of the runway, Sonia in the middle, Theo and Howard at her sides.

Theo recognized a number of members of the crowd—journalists and minor celebrities not unwilling to rise before dawn. But by now the sun was above the horizon, visible as a luminous pearl-white disk through the gray overcast.

Lindbergh's Ryan Special had already been wheeled from its place beside the runway and stood in the middle of the tarmac, lighted by a few portable electric globes. A couple of mechanics were working on the silvery monoplane. The crowd was held back by a rough rope barrier.

Lindbergh was nowhere in sight.

The mist turned to a true rain. Light but chilling, it pattered off the Ryan's wings and formed small puddles on the runway. "Do you think he can do it?" Sonia asked. "I'm afraid that we all got up early and drove all the way out here just to get wet!"

Theo shook his head. "I'm not so sure. He's a very determined young fellow. Flew his plane all the way from San Diego, all alone, with just a couple of stops. Commander Byrd and Chamberlain and Bertrand have all been here much longer than Lindbergh, and they keep tinkering and polishing and delaying. I think he'll go it if he possibly can."

Sonia shook her head doubtfully. "I don't know, Theo. Think of those two poor French boys! So young and brave! Such a waste!"

Theo spread his hands as if to say, *It's in the hands of fate.*

There was a cheer as the door of a little building beside the runway opened and a slim, youthful figure, almost effeminate in its wiry grace, strode forth. The young man was wearing a leather flying jacket and a pair of plain trousers. He carried with him a brown paper bag.

The crowd cheered and waved for Lindy. He stopped, turned toward them as if startled, then walked over and shook hands with someone. They talked briefly. Lindbergh walked back toward the Ryan and stopped again, turned and waved to the crowd. He had a shy, half-apologetic smile on his face.

He turned away again, walked to the Ryan and placed his paper bag inside, then conferred briefly with the mechanics working over the plane. He stood and looked at the sky again, gauging the strength of the sun and of the cold, light rain, then he shrugged and joined the mechanics in making their final preparations.

After a little while Lindbergh climbed into the Ryan and slammed the door behind him. He leaned out the window in the side of the plane.

"How will he ever be able to see?" Sonia asked. "There is no window in the front of the plane. Will he have to fly all the way leaning out the side of the plane?"

Theo took her hand in both of his and said, "The plane is equipped with the latest navigational instruments. It has a new Earth Inductor Compass that will not be affected by the metal of the plane itself or by the vibration of the engine. There is an artificial horizon, and there is an altitude meter. Except for feeling better about it, he doesn't even need windows at all."

"You don't mean he can fly without seeing the ground?"

"Exactly! Lieutenant Doolittle proved that over at Mitchell Field. Took a plane up, flew a preset course, returned and landed with the cockpit entirely shrouded the entire time."

The Ryan's nine-cylinder Wright engine sputtered, caught, roared as Lindbergh revved it up and down. He stood with the engine running, warming up, concentrating mainly on his instruments but occasionally glancing out the window to confer with mechanics, to throw a quick glance and a half-wave to the crowd, to turn and gaze worriedly at the gray overcast and steady rain.

Finally Lindbergh ducked back inside the Ryan, revved up the Wright engine, waited for his mechanics to pull away the wheel chocks and taxied to the downwind end of the field.

Again the mechanics placed the chocks before the wheels. Lindbergh revved the engine until its roar seemed to shake the gray overcast and bring fresh sheets of water splashing down; again the chocks were pulled aside and the silvery Ryan rolled forward, slowly gathering speed as it lumbered upwind into slashing rain. The plane seemed to gather speed reluctantly, then slowly, painfully to creep into the air. At the end of the runway it seemed hardly able to sustain itself above the earth, then slowly it gathered altitude and grew smaller as it climbed. Lindbergh banked and swung into a due-easterly path, the Wright engine's roar now a drone and now a mere buzzing.

The airplane became a child's toy and then a barely visible speck of silver-gray against the duller gray overcast.

Theo Weiss shuddered with the chill and damp. Beside him he heard Sonia Lovecraft let out her breath; how long she had been holding it he could not tell. He realized that she held his arm, her fingertips digging through the chesterfield and suitcoat into his muscle. Theo laid his own hand on Sonia's and she relaxed.

They started to walk back to Theo's Rickenbacker; a quick glimpse at Theo's Benrus showed it to be not yet eight o'clock.

Sonia said, "I suppose I'll be able to get to work today after all." She turned and looked after Lindbergh's monoplane for a moment. "It was all so quick. Now he's just— gone. Up there."

Howard said, "I am sure that Captain Lindbergh knows his business. Didn't he become known for walking the mail in repeatedly when his government plane failed? He's a competent fellow."

Sonia shook her head. "He can't walk in if his plane fails out over the sea."

Theo said, "We can only wait and see." He was startled by Howard Lovecraft's surprised cry.

"Why, there are Sylvester and Dr. Kiep!"

He pointed and Theo saw two men, one in comfortable, informal garb and the other looking like a diplomat, about to climb into a huge, foreign-built car. Theo exclaimed,

"That's a Horsch! Will wonders never cease! I haven't seen one of those since my last tour of the Continent. I never knew they had imported any."

Howard had called to the two men, and when they turned at his hail they strode back across the grass to meet Theo Weiss and the Lovecrafts. Howard made introductions, and they exchanged opinions of Lindbergh's chances. Sonia was still worried, comparing the midwesterner to the two lost Frenchmen of the *White Bird*. Sylvester Viereck was more sanguine about Lindbergh's chances, agreeing with Theo's notion that he was a competent man equipped with the most advanced machine to be had.

"As I remarked to Mr. Lovecraft during our so-pleasant tour of Massachusetts, I fear that Captain Lindbergh's choice will lead aviation down a wrong road." Dr. Kiep half-bowed, as if apologizing for his oblique disagreement with the prevailing sentiment. "I think that Commander Byrd's Fokker is a more suitable approach. Whether Captain Lindbergh succeeds or not, that is. Of course I wish him all success." He looked around at the others.

"But I must cite the work of my friend Herr Professor Rumpler. You have heard of Edmund Rumpler of Dessau? A brilliant mind. An aeroplane designer and manufacturer of many years standing. *Ja.* When I last saw him, Herr Rumpler was already making plans for an aerial liner to enter the Atlantic service. His liner is to be powered by ten engines, 1000 horsepower to each engine. Think of that!"

Dr. Kiep jabbed his hands before him as if assembling the Rumpler aerial liner in miniature.

"Herr Rumpler's aeroplane will travel at 200 miles per hour! It will carry 170 passengers across the Atlantic Ocean in just sixteen hours. Just think of it—the liner will rise from the Tempelhof Aerodrome at dawn and the passengers will have their midnight supper in New York."

"Aren't you forgetting changes in the clock?" Theo put in.

Dr. Kiep bowed to the showman. "You are absolutely correct, sir. Of course." He pulled a shiny pocket watch from his vest and examined it briefly. "We will have to learn to recalibrate our timepieces in the air. Hah! Very good!" Then, his voice becoming more serious, "But you see, Mr. Weiss, Mr. and Mrs. Lovecraft, why I have maintained that this little toy of Charles Lindbergh's is a so-bad idea. I wish him well, of course, but I fear that success on his part would lead to a. . .a *fad* of daredeviltry in toy aeroplanes instead of the proper development of the air liner."

Theo said, "Yes, I see your point, Doctor. But we shall have to simply wait and see the outcome."

On the way back to Brooklyn, Theo remarked on Dr. Kiep's Horsch. "I don't recall whether they were making them as far back as 1902. That was the first time I was ever in Germany; Ehrich must have mentioned that trip to you, Howard."

"Was that the time he had the run-in with the German policeman and wound up in the libel suit?"

"So many memories! Sometimes I jumble the tours together myself. Let me get the dates straight in my mind."

For a minute or so there was no sound but the purring of the Rickenbacker's six-cylinder engine and the hum of its modern balloon ties on the roadway. Finally Theo said, "I recall it as actually June of 1901 that we went to Germany. Ehrich was booked into the Circus Corty-Althoff. That started the whole sequence. Some petty local police official accused him of fraud, Ehrich sued for libel. Ah, what a tangle! He was in and out of Germany, in and out of court for two years over that, but in the end he was vindicated.

"Somehow in the course of all the wrangling we toured England and Russia as well."

Sonia smiled. "I remember the Russian tour. I wasn't there, of course, my mother had already taken us away from the *shtetl* and the *pogroms* and brought us to the West. But Ehrich told me about the tour. *Brrrr!* And I don't mean just the climate, either!"

"Oh, yes. And in England we had some times, too! Did Ehrich ever tell you about his run-in with that physical-culture fanatic in Blackburn?"

Sonia said he had not.

"That was—let me see—October of 1902. Just in the midst of the German lawsuit. Ehrich was having a wonderful tour, really pressing on with his escapes. He'd just developed the technique of calling for challenges, working with local police departments, and it was really going over very well. Then he came up against a fellow in Blackburn, Hopkins, Hodgkins. . .ah, Hodgson. Yes, I remember the man, William Hope Hodgson was his name."

In a startled voice, Howard asked, "Hodgson the author?"

Theo turned halfway toward Howard, keeping an eye on the roadway and the other on the man. "I don't know. I only encountered him the one time. A great, muscular hulk of a man. And cruel!"

Howard shook his head. "I wonder. It isn't a name you would likely encounter twice. The William Hope Hodgson I know—or rather, know of—wrote a number of excellent macabre tales. Ghostly tales, narratives of the sea, strange visions of the remote future. I consider *The House on the Borderland* the greatest of his works. There are a few unfortunate touches of ordinary sentimentality, but the novel, which traces the wanderings of a reincarnated soul through *kalpas* of cosmic time, is in its total effect quite extraordinary.

"His last major work was a huge novel, *The Night-Land*, which takes place in the most remote future of the earth. There is a marring effect in Hodgson's use of stilted archaisms, but once more the overall power of the book is overwhelming.

"He wrote a number of other novels and a group of short stories not without merit. All of his works appeared in the period prior to the Great War, except for a few minor posthumous pieces."

"Yes," Theo broke in, "that must be the same Hodgson. I'd heard he was killed in the war. Knocked off his horse in a cavalry charge and hospitalized. He obtained his release and returned to the front and encountered the same kind of wound, only the second time it proved fatal. I remember Ehrich's reaction to hearing that news. He felt guilty at responding with pleasure rather than grief—at the death of any man, you see—but he could not bring himself to regret the death of that man."

Again Howard Lovecraft shook his head. "What did he have against the man? I wish I'd mentioned Hodgson to your brother when he was alive. I never knew they had encountered each other."

Theo waved his hand half-dismissingly. "Oh, in Black-burn, Ehrich called for a challenge from the audience and this follow climbed onto the stage and introduced himself as the official physical culture supervisor of the local con-stabulary. He offered to place handcuffs and leg-irons on Ehrich.

"Enrich of course agreed.

"This Hodgson trussed and wrenched poor Ehrich into the most agonizing positions and clapped the devices on him. Ehrich worked for the better part of an hour, then begged to have the devices loosened just for a moment to let the blood circulated in his hands and feet. They were growing more numb, you see, Hodgson had trussed him so tightly.

"But the man refused. I remember his words to this day. It's been a quarter of a century, but I can hear them ringing yet. 'This a contest,' he insisted, 'not a love match. If you are beaten, give in!'

"The audience had been half-way won over by Hodgson up to that point. As many of them would have liked to see the great Houdini lose as see him win. But when they heard Hodgson's callous reply, the hall was filled with cat-calls and hoots. Ehrich had the hall fully behind him then, and submitted to return to work with no relief. He finally won out, too, but his clothes were shredded and his wrists were rubbed raw and bleeding. I believe he'd have chewed through his own flesh and bones rather than sur-render to that fellow!

"And the crowd were so won over by Houdini's courage and skill, and so disgusted with Hodgson's cruelty that they chased him from the theatre—it was called the Pal-ace—to the police station, and he had to take refuge in a jail-cell. Poetic justice, I'd say!"

Howard sat thoughtfully. "So there was a cruel streak in the man as well as a *fantaisiste's* talent. An oddly para-doxical individual. I shall have to re-examine his works in this light."

They had reached Brooklyn by now. The day was well advanced, the rain had ceased and the gray overcast was beginning to break up, patches of blue peeping between the slowly dissipating cloud banks.

Sonia looked from the Rickenbacker's window and said, "Well, Lindbergh should be well on his way by now. I hope the weather is improving for him as it is for us."

Theo Weiss guided the sedan to a curbside parking place on Parkside Avenue. "I am to perform at the Academy of Music tonight. Would you do me the honor of being in the audience?" He addressed the question equally to Sonia and to Howard. "Then, perhaps afterward, we could have a light supper, or perhaps visit a club and enjoy some music."

Sonia said, "Of course. I'd love to see your act, Theo."

Howard said, "It should make an interesting comparison to that of Houdini. I understand that certain of the effects you use were developed by your brother."

Theo acknowledged that they were.

"Well, it will be my pleasure."

Theo said, "There will be tickets for you at the box office. After the show, simply ask the head usher for directions to my dressing room. He will expect your inquiry."

CHAPTER EIGHTEEN:

"THEY PRODUCED SPIRIT-MESSAGES"

SONIA RODE the subway into Manhattan for work and Howard climbed to the apartment for a day's sleep in compen-
sation for his wakeful night. When he awoke he tuned the
radiola to a late-afternoon news broadcast. Captain Lindbergh's Ryan monoplane had been sighted over Newfoundland, flying steadily eastward. At its cruising speed
of 110 miles per hour the Ryan could not possibly reach
Paris before late Saturday, New York time. Newfoundland
was the last likely place of sighting. The young pilot was
now truly on his own.

When the news broadcast switched to less involving
matters—Charles Evans Hughes, onetime Secretary of
State and Supreme Court Justice, had declared himself
out of the Presidential contest—Howard switched off the
set and wrote letters for the rest of the day. One went to
Hiram Evans in Atlanta. Armed with the background information provided by Two-gun Bob Howard, Howard
Lovecraft treated the Imperial Wizard with care. He asked
him for information on the Klan and Evans' idea as to the
Klan's potential role in the world empire foreseen by
George Sylvester Viereck. Howard also asked the erst-
while dentist for the names and addresses of local func-
tionaries of the Klan. He dug Two-gun Bob's letter out of
its folder to get the proper titles to use. Ah, yes, any local
Grand Dragon or Exalted Cyclops who might be helpful in
preparing information for *New America and the Coming
World-Empire*.

Sonia arrived home and after a light meal she and
Howard dressed (Sonia in the bedroom, Howard in the
living room) for the theatre.

Theo Weiss' program(he was billed as The Mysterious
Hardeen, with lettering not much smaller explaining that
he was the brother of Harry Houdini) was in two parts.
The first was to comprise magic tricks and illusions; the
second, amazing escapes.

To the accompaniment of a pit orchestra and with the assistance of a small stage crew, Hardeen performed the Japanese Butterfly Trick, produced lighted candles from his pockets, linked a glittering series of Chinese silver rings, metamorphosed a pretty assistant from a locked trunk to an empty wardrobe cabinet, and finally swallowed an entire packet of needles, then a skein of thread, and to the strains of a loud and triumphal fanfare, pulled the thread from his mouth with the needles neatly strung along it, shining in the spotlight.

After an intermission Hardeen walked onto the stage, immaculate even for the dashing "Dash" Weiss, in formal tails. The orchestra quietened and Hardeen moved forward to the footlights and addressed the audience. He spoke of the brave man who even now was soaring through the blackness above the cold Atlantic Ocean, of the fate which awaited him beneath those icy waves should his skill falter or the droning engine of his silvery aircraft fail. He spoke of the courage that that man had shown, and of the hopes of the world that rode with him in the cockpit of his little machine.

Hardeen asked the audience to rise and join him in a moment of silent prayer.

All around Howard and Sonia a thousand men and women rose to their feet and bowed their heads.

The orchestra continued to play softly, the violins and violas carrying the main theme of a soft, almost religious melody. Then the music rose, a more cheerful and lively tune replacing the soft, contemplative air. The houselights dimmed to darkness and a single brilliant spotlight illuminated The Mysterious Hardeen still standing before the curtains.

Hardeen raised his face, smiled disarmingly at the audience. (Howard noted that Hardeen's face closely resembled that of Harry Houdini, but that the younger Hardeen had a slightly softer, rounder, more innocent expression. Perhaps in another decade he would look like the tough, seasoned Houdini; for now he did look, as Sonia had banteringly suggested, like a boy.)

"Ladies and gentlemen" Hardeen began. He explained his record of marvelous and amazing escapes. He spoke of being thrown, chained and wrapped, into rivers. . .of breaking from jail cells used to hold the most brutal of murderers. . .of triumphing over straitjackets, leg-irons, handcuffs, the infamous Maine tramp chair.

"Isn't he jumbling his biography with that of his brother?" Howard whispered to Sonia.

She pressed her face warmly to the side of his. "I think they began as a brother act, and even when they worked separately always exchanged tricks."

"I want you to understand that there is nothing supernatural in any of my escapes," Hardeen resumed, "any more than there is any supernatural force involved in the magic tricks or the illusions you have already seen. How these wonders are performed," he paused, smiled boyishly, "well, that's my own secret. But all is a matter of knowledge, skill, practice and agility. Don't let anyone tell you otherwise!"

With orchestral accompaniment Hardeen broke out of a pair of American Bean handcuffs and Lily leg irons (37 seconds), a pair of army cuffs and Russian leg-irons (one minute, 20 seconds), and a special Houdini bell-lock handcuff and American Guiteau leg-irons (2 minutes 15 seconds). The Houdini bell-lock, he explained, was the greatest test of all the manacles. It had been invented by Hardeen's brother, the late Harry Houdini, as a test of his own skill and a challenge to any self-styled "Handcuff King" who sought to match his famous exploits. The Houdini bell-lock was fitted with a bell inside its metal sheath, and would sound an alarm whenever the cuffs were locked or opened.

The challenge was not merely to escape from the Houdini cuffs, but to do so without permitting the alarm to sound.

Only Houdini himself and the Mysterious Hardeen had ever succeeded in escaping from the special cuffs.

Hardeen climaxed his performance with the famous Milk Can Escape. This was a hugely popular and dramatic escape that Theo and Ehrich had devised together. Once the escape was fully worked out, Hardeen had not waited for Houdini's death to use it—it had been a featured part of both their acts for over a decade. There had been times when imitators planned their bookings to coincide with Houdini's, cashing in on Houdini's immense skill at gaining publicity in local newspapers and on radio. Once Houdini had whipped up public interest, other performers would make their ticket sales.

Theo and Ehrich had countered that by having their own bookers, the Keith circuit for Ehrich, Klaw & Erlinger for Theo, book them opposite each other. Houdini would play to one house, Hardeen to another, capturing any overflow from his more famous brother's promotion. "Circusing," Houdini called it. He once told his friend Arthur Conan Doyle that if Doyle would only "circus" his lecture tours he'd never speak to an empty seat, but Doyle considered "circusing" undignified and went on preaching his gospel of spiritualism to half-empty halls.

At the Academy of Music, Hardeen asked his audience to draw a deep breath and hold it as long as they could. At the signal, the second-hand of a giant clock mounted above the stage began to move. At thirty seconds most of the audience let out their breaths. By forty-five, most of the rest had gone. A few lasted a full minute. No one lasted for two.

Now a regulation milk can was brought on-stage. The can was filled to the brim with water. Hardeen, wearing only bathing costume, was trussed and chained. Two assistants lifted him and lowered him into the milk can so he was completely submerged.

The giant clock was started.

The orchestra began to play.

The assistants dumped extra buckets of water over Hardeen's head to make sure that no splashing had given him airspace in the top of the can.

The lid was placed on the can, and six padlocks clamped shut around the edges of the lid.

A curtain was placed in front of the can, and the music grew louder, with a tense, exciting tempo. The clock had revolved through a full minute.

The audience shifted restlessly in their seats.

There was a subdued thumping from behind the small curtain; Hardeen's two assistance disappeared to the edges of the stage for a moment and returned bearing fire axes—just in case they had to smash the padlocks and rescue their master from the bizarre drowning.

The clock hand had revolved through two minutes. There was an undercurrent of conversation in the audience. The music grew louder and more strident.

Hardeen's assistants exchanged worried glances. There was a loud thump from behind the small curtain and the milk can rolled into view of the audience. The two assistants exchanged another look, laid down their fire axes and set the can upright again.

The clock had marked off three minutes.

Somewhere in the rear of the audience a man jumped to his feet and shouted, "Get him out of there! He'll die!"

A chorus of mixed agreement and denial ran round the auditorium.

One of Hardeen's assistants ran to the footlights so he could see the clock face. He was turned half-way from the audience, so his face was still visible. He showed an expression of agitation close to panic.

He ran and seized his fire axe again and began to swing it at the padlocks on the milk can.

The other assistant grabbed his arm and stopped him. They exchanged remarks that were inaudible to the audience. One of them ran to the edge of the stage and crouched over the orchestra pit. He shouted something to the conductor and the music faded away.

The clock showed five and half minutes gone.

An assistant ran to the curtain and flung it aside with one blow of his fire axe. The padlocks lay in a neat circle around the milk can. The lid flew into the air and rolled, clattering, across the stage. The dark-haired head of Hardeen popped from the can. He sprang erect, showed his free hands, flung his opened manacles to the boards and climbed grinning from the can.

The orchestra burst into a triumphal rendition of "Anchors Aweigh."

Hardeen strode to the footlights and bowed graciously to his audience, water dripping from his arms and face. Suddenly he slumped; only the quick move of his two assistants prevented his toppling into the orchestra pit. He was helped from the stage. The curtains closed, the houselights and the music rose simultaneously, and the audience began to make their way out in Fourteenth Street.

Sonia and Howard found Theo in his dressing room, seated before his mirror removing stage makeup from his face. He turned and smiled broadly as they entered the room.

"Come on in and sit down for a few minutes. I hope you enjoyed the show. A fair house tonight, I think everyone is a little distracted by Captain Lindbergh. It's hard to hold an audience who are thinking about something beside the show."

"Do you really believe that the prayers of the audience tonight will have any effect on Lindbergh's flight?" Howard asked.

Theo was leaning toward his mirror now, but he kept eye contact with the reflections of his guests. "Who knows? Who knows what forces there are at play, eh?"

Howard shook his head. "As a militant atheist, I can hardly approve of mass public prayers. Besides, after all the time and effort that your brother placed in his campaign against spiritualism. . ." Howard gestured as if shoving something aside with his hands.

Theo smiled again. "That's really a strange thing," he said. "Ehrich was placed under threats and curses by more spiritualists than any man in history. But, you know, he never actually stated that there was no 'other side.' He simply said that he'd never seen convincing evidence that there is communication with the beyond. If it exists, that is. He investigated hundreds of mediums, and found them divided between frauds and hysterics. The latter, of course, were the hardest for him to deal with. Their own sincerity and desire to believe could be heartbreaking. And some of them, even—oh, let me offer you some. . ."

He went to a corner of the room and lifted a pot of boiling water from a gas ring. "Would you like a cup of tea? The milk can escape always leaves me chilled. I've tried it with warm water but that doesn't help very much and it's always hard to get the temperature right. I almost boiled to death one night before I abandoned that idea!"

He found cups and packaged tea bags and poured cups of tea for Howard and Sonia.

"I was afraid for you tonight, Theo." Sonia put down her tea and reached to place her hand on Hardeen's silk-gowned arm. "The clock—you were submerged for six minutes! I thought you had drowned!"

"I'll tell you a little secret. I'm sure you already know this, Howard, from your conversations with Ehrich. I could have been out of my bonds in thirty seconds and out of the can in another thirty. There's nothing to it."

"I should say there is!" Howard interjected.

Hardeen nodded, smiling. "Well—if you know how to do it. If you have the equipment and the skill there's nothing to it. I would hardly expect a beginner to succeed." He spread his hands wide. "That's why there are so many bad imitators and so few good ones! They either don't have the knowledge or the equipment or the skill.

"But if you can do the trick, you can do it quickly," he went on. He was standing before Sonia and Howard now. "But if I just went into the milk can and came out again— what kind of show would that be? It's all in the timing, in the suspense, in the showmanship. That's something that the great magicians and all great showmen have always known."

Howard Lovecraft shook his head. "Still, Mr. Weiss, you *were* submerged for the full six minutes, were you not? There was no fraud concerned? You had, for instance, no concealed air supply with you?"

Theo's expression grew serious. "You are right on that score. There is no fraud concerned with any of my escapes. The illusions—magic tricks—are of course a matter of sleight-of-hand. Did you ever look up the etymology of the word prestidigitation? It's one of my favorites! It means fast-finger work! That's what stage magic is, to a large extent.

"But my escapes are all authentic. Legitimate. There have been many fraudulent escape artists and self-designated handcuff kings. But neither Ehrich nor I have ever used any fraudulent methods in our escapes. It is a matter of knowledge of the equipment, skill and practice and physical conditioning.

"Yes, the six minutes submergence, Sonia, was absolutely real. With proper understanding, physical conditioning and practice, one can do without oxygen for remarkably extended periods of time. Ehrich did very extensive work on that subject before his death. There was no secret about it, either. You may recall his experiment with the coffin in the swimming pool?" They both did. "Well, you see, that's the same technique that I use in the milk can.

"If I just popped out, it would be a trifling achievement. But by building tension and suspense in the audience, I make the escape the climax of my show." He smiled deprecatingly. "I'm afraid that the collapse at the edge of the stage, though—you might call that fraudulent."

Howard Lovecraft put his cup down. "You mentioned earlier your brother's attitude toward spiritualism. And of course I am intrigued by your assertion that Houdini never denied the existence of the beyond."

"That is correct. My brother was fascinated throughout his life with the notion of there being some form of survival of the personality, the consciousness, beyond the occurrence of physical dissolution. Did you know that in the early days of their marriage Ehrich and Bess were themselves spiritualistic mediums?"

"That is indeed news to me. And I must say, distressing news."

Theo pulled a wire-backed chair in front of him, turned it and sat with his arms crossed over its metal curves, the cup of tea balanced in his hands. "I'm certain that if Ehrich had recovered from his injury and had pursued the writing projects he'd hoped to get your help with—he'd have mentioned this to you. It wasn't the proudest phase of Ehrich's and Bess's life by a long cast, but they did not deny it.

"They produced spirit messages, table-raisings and the rest. As part of a traveling show in vaudeville at the turn of the century. They'd bring greetings to farmers in Kansas from their departed relatives, standard stuff. Ehrich always held that their object was entertainment, not fraud, and he and Bess were always unwilling to perform private séances or otherwise promote belief by fraudulent means. But they were never quite comfortable with the practice, even so. They dropped it quite early.

"But in an odd way it was very important to Ehrich's later work. He was able to expose mediumistic frauds because he already knew their tricks—he'd used them on the stage!"

Hardeen's tea had grown cold while he talked. He strode to a small sink and dashed the cold liquid down the drain, then poured himself another cup. "Are you in a rush? Howard? Sonia? We should be going shortly, but I like to relax for a while before leaving the theater.

"All right? Good.

Richard A. Lupoff

"The frauds used to send Ehrich into a rage. Especially after the death of our mother. Ehrich was always most attached to her, and time after time a medium would claim the ability to bring Ehrich into contact with her. All frauds. It was like having his heart broken, over and over and over."

Howard interrupted with a gesture and a word. "All?"

Hardeen echoed him. "All? All what, Howard?"

Lovecraft grew pink in the face. "All frauds. You said that Houdini found the spiritualists who claimed to have contact your mother to be all frauds. Yet I recall a rather different attitude toward Lady Doyle. Was there not a controversy over a message received through her?"

Theo slumped heavily into his chair again. "That was indeed a different matter. You're absolutely right. I should have said that Ehrich found all the mediums he'd examined to be frauds or hysterics. Lady Doyle was certainly not a fraud, and it was difficult for Ehrich to suggest that she was an hysteric. You know, Ehrich had the highest regard for both Arthur and Jean. And the manifestation Lady Doyle produced—a rather lengthy written message—was very impressive.

"And, yes, the entire incident took place under conditions of great emotional stress. Both of the Doyles are convinced, absolutely convinced, of the reality of spiritualistic manifestations and of the authenticity of Lady Doyle's mediumship. And both wished desperately to convince Ehrich.

"As for Ehrich. . . he was highly skeptical, especially after his many encounters with fraudulent mediums. Yet he wanted with all his heart to be *able* to believe.

"Then when the message arrived, there in that hotel room, why, Ehrich was emotionally overcome for the moment. He almost believed. Maybe he *did* believe, for the moment. But the more he analyzed the occurrence, the less was his belief sustained.

"The message was headed by the sign of the cross; as you know, our family is descended from a line of rabbis. Our mother was a devout Jewess throughout her lifetime. She would never have used such Christian symbolism.

"And then the message itself was in English." Here, Theo paused and smiled almost sadly. "Our mother never knew English, you see. She spoke German, mainly. She

230

knew Hungarian also, and Yiddish, and some Hebrew. But not English. We always spoke to her in one of the other languages, usually German or Yiddish. The two are somewhat related, you know.

"But you see how the Atlantic City message simply fell apart once it was calmly analyzed.

"Then Lady Doyle provided her own rationalization, strongly supported by Sir Arthur. She claimed that the crucifix was her own mark, a sort of personal good luck charm against mischief from the spirit world. And as for language, she claimed that the spirit of my mother had communicated with her in some direct, psychic manner, and that the language was her own used in recording the message.

"Well. . ." He rose and arched his back, collected the empty cups from Sonia and Howard and washed them carefully in the sink. "That's a nice notion, but it makes the whole incident so very fuzzy. I'm certain that the message was authentic in a sense; Ehrich was convinced of this also. He told me so, in so many words. It was authentic in the sense that it 'came' to Lady Doyle. She did not make it up—consciously.

"But where did it come *from*? Jean and Arthur believe that it came from the spirit world. But Ehrich concluded that it came from Lady Doyle's unconscious, created there by a desire to convince Ehrich, poured out into Lady Doyle's automatic writing. If there was a fraud, it was committed by Lady Doyle's unconscious mind against herself!

"Oh, but come." He looked at his watch. "I'm so sorry to keep you this late. And we were all up so early this morning. It seem a year ago!" He excused himself and stepped behind a screen to don his street clothes.

"I'd thought we would all go on for some refreshment after the show tonight, but perhaps we'd better make that another time, when we can get a more reasonable start. But may I give you a lift home? My car is ready outside."

Sonia put her hand warmly on Theo's. "I think you're in love with your little orphan automobile. But if you and Howard want to go on, I can ride home in a cab."

"No, no, absolutely."

At Parkside Avenue he dropped them, promising to phone in a few weeks. He was to set out shortly with a touring company, but the tour was a relatively modest one and Hardeen would not be away from home for a very long time.

Howard and Sonia climbed to the apartment and prepared to retire. Even Howard found it late enough to sleep, and was shortly beneath the quilt of his makeshift bed in the living room. Sonia emerged in her nightgown and robe and sat on the edge of the couch, beside him.

"I had a lovely day, Howard, and a lovely evening."

"The Weiss family are a remarkable tribe. I must concede that. If Sir Arthur Conan Doyle can accept Houdini, I suppose that I can do the same." Howard sat upright, leaning against the padded arm of the couch, his legs still covered by the quilt.

Sonia ran her fingers down his arm. "I can't understand, Howard dear, I just can't understand. How can you be so pleasant to Jews and still hate the Jews? I can't sort you out."

Howard exhaled loudly, almost a snort. "If for no other reason, Sonia, then a man of my sensibilities must despise Jews and Judaism by reason of Christianity."

"Howard!" Sonia gasped. "You haven't fallen in with those anti-semites who call us murderers! Christ-killers! Howard, I grew up beneath that scorn and that hatred. At least—all of my years in Russia were like that. Things were better in England, but we Jews had to keep to ourselves to be left alone. Have you fallen prey to the poison of thought that leads to pogrom and persecution?"

"Do not misunderstand me." Howard pointed a finger for emphasis. "It is not for the killing of Christ that I despise Judaism. It is for spawning him and his weakling, slave's philosophy that I curse the Hebrew race. What philosophies were displaced by Christianity, for which we have the Jews to thank?

"The two great forces in the Western world before Christianity's advent were the classical culture of Greece and Rome, and the vibrant dynamic pantheon of the Nordic barbarians! What two more splendid and beautiful cultures have ever emerged on the face of the globe?

"The Greeks created and the Romans transformed the early nature deities and their children the Titans. Phorcys, Enyo, Pemphredo, Dino; the Gorgons and the Titans themselves, Chronus, Rhea, and their children Hestia, Demeter, Hera, Hades, Poseidon and Zeus.

"What splendid figures and what splendid tales are told of the Olympians! Such were the subject of the dreams of my boyhood. Artemis, Apollo, Pan were all as real to my boyish mind as were the prophets and the archangels of my mother and my teachers at the First Baptist Meeting House on College Hill!

"And the Teutonic pantheon, for all its lack of the grace and polish of the graeco-roman—perhaps because of that lack of polish!—carries with it a sense of pure energy that exhilarates the soul! Thor! Odin! Fria! Njord! The brilliant but treacherous Loki! The Aesir and Vanir and the great Midgard Serpent! What conceptions!

"And all of these, ground beneath the heel of the puny, sniveling Jew-god Christ! Pah! That is why I despise Jewry—not for causing the death of Christ, but for giving him life!"

He stopped, panting with his own exertion, the passion of his outburst.

Into the silence Sonia said, "You are as eloquent as ever, Howard, and as silly." She climbed to her feet and disappeared through the doorway.

CHAPTER NINETEEN:

DRIVING COLLECTORS TO DISTRACTION

SATURDAY WAS a day of vigil for Howard, as it was, it seemed, for all the nation. Howard rose in the early afternoon, many hours after Sonia had left the apartment for her work in the millinery department of Russek's department store in Manhattan. There had been no communication following their quarrel of the night before—a dismal ending to a fascinating and rewarding day. Somehow Sonia simply could not understand that she was the possessor of a personality, a nature, an intellect of her own, aside from the collective identity of her race. So was Samuel Loveman the poet whom Howard liked and admired so greatly, and so in fact were the publisher Gernsback and the young literary agent Schwartz. That did not prevent them from being fine and admirable individuals (or Gernsback from being a scoundrel pennypincher), nor did it prevent their race from possessing such characteristics as it did. Good grief, the Jewish race had produced the composer Felix Mendelssohn and the mathematician Einstein! Were their achievements to be ignored because they happened to be Jews?

It was very hard for Howard to understand Sonia's lack of understanding. He shook his head and switched on the radiola in hopes of receiving word of Lindbergh and his aeroplane. He found a news broadcast on station WMCA but there was no word of the flier.

Howard dressed and ate and went for a stroll in the mid-afternoon sunlight. The spring was well advanced, the sun warm and the air balmy. Near the water he could almost believe that he was back in Providence, strolling near the familiar Seekonk. His spirits rose at the thought.

He needed an equal, an intellectual compatriot, to talk with, and tried to work out a list of candidates. First to come to mind was of course young Long, but Belknapius' very youthfulness was an obstacle to full intellectual exchange.

Ah, but Howard was fond of the lad! Could he but se-lect his own style of living, it would probably resemble that of Belknap more closely than that of any other. The youngster's needs were met, his education had been at-tended to, he had achieved by the age of twenty-two as many appearances in the magazines as Howard had in fifteen more years, and had further a book of his own in print. Well, that, at least, should be equalized within the year!

But Belknap simply lacked the intellectual common-ground of shared experience that Howard required. Belknap had no recollection, as had Howard, of the old century with its pre-mechanized manners. Belknap had grown up in the age of the electric lamp and the automo-bile; Howard, in that of the gas light and brougham. It came down to that in the final summation: Howard and Belknap could be best of friends but they could never be full equals.

He thought of Clark Ashton Smith, but Klarkash-ton was far too remote geographically. There was Henry S. Whitehead, the Episcopal churchman and *Weird Tales* writer, but he was at his post in the distant Virgin Islands; and Two-gun Bob Howard was stuck perennially (or so it seemed) in Cross Plains, Texas.

That left. . .Vincent Starrett, and George Sylvester Viereck. Howard succeeded in obtaining the number of Starrett's Beechhurst retreat by telephoning Alexander Laing in New York, but there was no answer on Starrett's line. Surely he was back from Chicago by now—but he might be off, almost anywhere, since he wasn't at home working on *Seaports in the Moon*.

Finally Howard gave Central the number of Viereck's Riverside Drive residence and learned that Viereck was visiting his friend Count Revel. Mr. Viereck had left word that Mr. Lovecraft would be welcome to join the informal gathering at the Count's home, should he happen to call.

Flattered, Howard jotted down the address given for the Count's residence, and set out by subway. As he en-tered the Parkside Avenue BMT station he stopped to ex-amine the display at a newsdealer's kiosk. The June *Weird Tales* had gone on sale and Howard fished a quarter from his pocket and purchased a copy before descending the stairs and paying his nickel for the ride. He scanned the pages of the magazine, first as he waited on the platform, then as he sat jouncing on the wicker seat riding into Manhattan on the train.

It seemed a very run-of-the-mill edition of the magazine, with little to leaven it aside from a very amusing poem, "Advice," by Belknapius. Howard made a mental note to congratulate the young fellow when next he spoke with him. "Carouse, my friend, with such as these," Howard reread the concluding lines of the poem, "And shun the bloated things that wheeze!" Ho!

The Eyrie, as usual, contained a reference to Howard himself. He scanned the letter—or rather, the single sentence—attributed to a John B. Woodhouse aboard the Hamburg-American steamer *Deutschland*. "Such stories as 'The Woman in the Wood,' 'The Night Wire,' 'The Atomic Conquerers,' 'The White Ship,' and 'The Last Horror' are worthy of book form and a wide circulation."

Good company—Woodhouse had an admirable story sense, whoever he was. Probably a businessman or wealthy tourist whiling away the hours in mid-Atlantic by reading pulp magazines. Howard remembered every story that Woodhouse mentioned, all of them very recent. "The White Ship" was of course Howard's own work. The others were by Abraham Merritt, H. F. Arnold, Edmond Hamilton and Eli Colter. Merritt was the only one of these whom Howard had actually met, but all were excellent writers. Hamilton in particular was a master of the weird-scientific school, just as Merritt was of the lush (not to say over-ripe) sensuous fantasy. Woodward's nominees might not make a bad book at that, should Henneberger's project for *The Moon Terror* succeed and a successor be called for. Of course what Howard would truly prefer would be a collection of his own tales, but that was another matter.

Walking the few blocks from the subway exit to Count Revel's address in Manhattan, Howard noted that the midtown crowds were not their usual bustling selves. The Saturday shoppers were out in smaller numbers than usual, and everywhere that radio shops had loudspeakers set up, groups of people would stand listening for word of Lindbergh.

Howard rode the elevator to Count Revel's apartment, and was admitted to find not only George Sylvester Viereck visiting the fascist leader, but Dr. Kiep and Dr.

Maude DeLand as well. Viereck introduced Howard to the Count, a tall, distinguished man in proper afternoon clothing. He wore his gray hair brushed back to both sides of his face, and kept a neatly trimmed moustache and small, pointed beard on his thin face. Howard was delighted with the Count, finding in his distinguished appearance and gracious manner a marked contrast to the callow Russian Count Vonsiatsky. Only Revel's crude accent marred the overall impression; Howard did his best to overlook the comic dialect speech and to converse with the Count purely on the level of the content of the latter's statements.

Viereck and Count Revel had risen at Howard's entry; once the introduction had been accomplished they returned to their seats; all five—Viereck, Dr. Kiep, Count Revel, Dr. DeLand and Howard—sat on elegant satin-covered Renaissance period chairs about a low, elegant table. The table was set with light refreshments.

Viereck immediately spotted Howard's copy of *Weird Tales* and commented on it.

Howard was embarrassed to show the lurid, red-covered pulp magazine with its crude cover illustration of a skeletal revenant, but Viereck encouraged him and finally quoted the Woodhouse letter aloud to the group.

Dr. Kiep remarked, "An amazing coincidence!"

Howard said that he did not understand the comment.

Viereck explained. "Dr. Kiep is to return home shortly for consultations with his government."

"Quite routine," the diplomat interjected.

"And as I have plans for a new series of interviews with leading figures of the European scene—Mr. Hearst has asked me to undertake the series, and the editors of *Liberty* magazine have also been after me for material—I have coordinated my travel plans with Dr. Kiep's."

Viereck smiled. "We shall sail during the first week of June, and we have booked cabins on the *Deutschland*. Who knows, your admirer Mr. Woodhouse may have left some old copies of *Weird Tales* in the ship's library!"

Everyone laughed. The conversation turned toward Viereck's planned series of interviews. "What with the Nungesser and Coli flight, and of course Captain Lindbergh's, and with the other aviators planning various feats, I shall investigate the state of aerial development in Europe."

"You will visit Eddie Rumpler," Dr. Kiep put in. "I will personally arrange your introduction."

"That will be my pleasure," Viereck nodded. "But just to get the other side of the argument, I have already arranged to interview Count von Eckener. I met him when he visited the United States in 1924 in his Zeppelin. Captain Lindbergh's flight has of course the greater drama to it, but Hugo Eckener, I am confident, will continue to make a case for the Zeppelin rather than the aeroplane as the great hope for the future."

Dr. Kiep said, "I think that Eddie Rumpler will disagree with that contention."

"All to the best," Viereck said. "Let them both make their cases. It will make for better reading, and it will also bring about the best results in the long run."

The conversation was overcome for a moment by a loud strain of music coming from a radio speaker in a corner of the room. "I hope you do not to this music object," Dr. Kiep said. He walked to the radio set and lowered the volume. "We are awaiting any bulletins that may come over the transatlantic telephone wire to the broadcast studios. There may be an interruption to the music at any time with word of the Ryan monoplane."

"Please, Dr. Kiep," Maude DeLand replied, "don't lower that lovely music on our account. I just love that fine music, don't you all?"

"It is Strauss," Dr. Kiep said.

"Oh, the great waltz compose?"

"Nien, nien," Kiep shook his head. "That was Johann Strauss, this is the great Richard." (*Reek-hard*, he pronounced it.) "They are playing *Des Helden Walstatt* from his great composition of 1899, *Ein Heldenleben*. I consider him the greatest composer since Wagner.

"Are you fond of music, Mr. Lovecraft?" Kiep asked, turning toward Howard.

"I am afraid that my musical education was somewhat neglected," Howard confessed. "I do remember as a child, my mother singing to me as I was put to bed each night, what I assumed were ordinary lullabies. Only in later years, hearing the melodies again and recognizing them quite clearly, did I learn what they were. They were the melodies of Sir Arthur Sullivan.

"My mother was a great admirer of Sir Arthur's, and of William Gilbert as well. She told me in later years that she never missed a performance of Richard D'Oyly Carte's touring company when they would bring each new operetta to the United States. Her favorites, I believe, were *Iolanthe* and *Utopia, Ltd*.

"As for myself, I do have a certain fondness for Wagner, particularly the orchestral music for *Lohengrin*, and some of Chopin's nocturnes."

Count Revel said, "Perhaps, Sylvester, you will find time to visit Italy on your journey. You should make it your business to see the great Toscanini in Rome. He is the great interpreter of Wagner!"

Viereck smiled. "If there is time, Ignazio. But I expect to be very busy. I must talk with Count Luckner in Germany, and I hope to see both President von Hindenberg and Chancellor Marx, as well as Hitler. I must pay at least a courtesy visit to the Kaiser at Doorn. I plan to visit Vienna and renew my friendship with Dr. Freud. And I hope to enter Russia again."

Dr. DeLand asked, "Didn't you go there several years ago?"

Viereck nodded. "Unfortunately, I was unable to obtain an audience with Ulianov. Lenin, you know. And now he is gone. But perhaps I can reach Djugashvili and Trotsky, or at least Premier Rykoff. Count Vonsiatsky and the Grand Duke Alexis have predicted the overthrow of the Bolshevist regime, and this may be a last chance to meet its leaders.

"They're so embroiled in their falling-out, I suspect that they may not need to be overthrown—they may topple themselves within a short time!" He burst into laughter.

The Strauss music was cut into abruptly, and a voice spoke from the radio apparatus. Dr. Kiep jumped from his chair and raced to the control panel of the receiver and turned the volume of sound upward.

The announcer, speaking from the studio, stated that Captain Lindbergh had landed safely at Le Bourget aerodrome, near Paris, at 10:24 PM, French time. He was safe and well, although tired, and had been met by a cheering throng of thousands of French citizens.

Richard A. Lupoff

At the end of the bulletin, Dr. Kiep switched off the radio and disappeared from the room for a few minutes. He returned bearing a tray, glasses, and a towel-wrapped bottle.

"Pardon my performing as butler," he apologized. "For so intimate a gathering, I thought servants superfluous."

He unwrapped the bottle and removed its cork with a loud pop.

"If you please."

He handed around glasses of champagne and the assemblage toasted the success of Captain Lindbergh.

Howard Lovecraft accepted a glass and joined in the toast.

Sylvester Viereck, the electric lights of the room reflecting from his polished spectacles, said, "Whether the bonds of empire are forged by steamship, airship or aeroplane, they are nonetheless being forged with each passing day. Captain Lindbergh has made his contribution to the coming world empire."

They drank a second round of champagne to Viereck's sentiment.

Slowly the party began to break up. Viereck and Howard Lovecraft left together, Viereck offering Howard a ride in his automobile. Howard accepted the offer, mentioned Belknap Long's address on West End Avenue.

"Why, that is almost my own neighborhood," Viereck exclaimed. "Fine."

They climbed into his front-wheel drive Cord and Viereck started the engine. Viereck asked Howard his impression of Count Revel.

"I rather like the man," Howard said. "It's a terrible shame that he speaks English with so poor an accent. But he seems to be a cultured gentleman, which is of course by far the more important."

Viereck nodded emphatically. "He is a close associate of Il Duce himself. I am most pleased that you are well impressed with Revel. He is going to be an extremely important man in the future.

"Now," Viereck continued, "I believe that you have met as many leaders of new American movements as you need do. I do not expect to return from Europe for some two months. During that time, will you need any assistance from me?"

Howard frowned and said he would not.

"That's very good. I hope you will have at least a partial manuscript prepared when I return. Do you think I might see one in August?"

"I should think so," Howard replied. The answer was not an easy one to give. In fact, to have a partial manuscript by August would present no difficulty, but Howard disliked the whole mechanism of deadlines and schedules. His conception of the gentleman artist was that he would write when his mental state was correct, when inspiration was present, when the proper combination of mood, talent, and appropriate subject matter presented itself.

The whole notion of promising to deliver a manuscript —even a partial manuscript—by a specific date distressed him. It smacked of commercial trade rather than gentlemanly enterprise. But he managed to make the commitment.

"If you incur any expenses and require reimbursement, please communicate with my office," Viereck went on. "There is Jackson Press money available. And in continuing your work with any of the groups you've been in touch with—Dr. Evans, Father Curran, Heinz Spanknoebel and the rest, don't hesitate to use the Jackson Press name or mine. All right?"

Howard promised to do so.

Viereck pulled the Cord to a halt before Belknap Long's home. He turned in his seat and extended his hand to Howard. "I shall be in contact immediately upon my return, Howard. I wish you a successful summer. Great things are in the offing, I assure you!" He grinned broadly.

Howard took his hand and wished him a pleasant sailing. "If you run across my friend Mr. Woodhouse aboard the *Deutschland*, please thank him for me, for the kind letter in *Weird Tales*."

They both laughed, and Howard stepped from the Cord onto the sidewalk and made his way into Long's apartment building. Even in the few seconds that Howard was on the sidewalk he detected an unusual mass exhilaration in the air. Passers-by smiled, stopped and exchanged jubilant reactions to the successful landing of the *Spirit of St. Louis* at Le Bourget.

Upstairs, Howard found Frank Belknap Long, Jr., in a jubilant state. Long's first words to him were, "Have you heard about Lindbergh?"

"Oh, it's all over town," Howard replied. "Quite an exploit. I suppose you got the news over the radio, the same way I heard it."

Long's eyes sparkled with excitement. "I expect we'll all be swooping around the heavens like a squadron of Richtofens and Rickenbackers in before long, and blasting off for deep space and alien worlds like some figures from a Verne novel in a while after that. Quite an exploit indeed."

Howard smiled tolerantly. "Some day we will visit remote planets, of that I have no doubt. Probably for the purpose of spreading the filth and corruption of so-called civilization while we are at it. But as for swooping around the heavens, I wonder if you are deceived into thinking that Captain Lindbergh is the first person to fly the ocean."

"Is he not?"

"Not at all. Ah, Belknapius, thou child. Well, I have taken a greater interest in contemporary affairs of late than had earlier been my wont. Thus to the arsenal of recollection have I been adding the ammunition of research. I suppose thou hast never heard of Commander Albert Read? No?" The effort recollection brought lines to Howard's tall brow. "On May 8, 1919, a squadron of three naval aeroplanes left the United States, headed for the Azores. Two of them failed, but Commander Read's Curtiss succeeded. That was the first recorded aerial crossing of the ocean.

"Within weeks a single-engined Sopwith left Newfoundland on a similar attempt—Read's Curtiss had been a large, four-engined craft. The Sopwith failed, but shortly after that two more of His Majesty's airmen tried again, using a Vickers bombing craft left over from the Great War. They flew from Newfoundland to Ireland successfully —Captain Alcock and Lieutenant Arthur Whitten Brown.

"Dirigible flights go back even further. Britain sent the TROTZKY.34 to the United Colonies in 1918! The German Count Eckener—apparently a close friend of my associate Mr. Viereck—duplicated this feat in 1924. I think that Viereck expects Eckener to open a great world-spanning air service with his Zeppelins at any moment. Well, perhaps he shall."

Belknap shook his head, smiling ruefully. "I don't understand, then, Howard, why all the uproar over Captain Lindbergh's flight. "Aha! 'Tis the common herd in action, grandchild. Only the cultured few truly understand the value of achievement in its own right. The ordinary run of mortals are aware only of vanity and of material wealth. This hotelier Orteig—does the name sound mildly Semitic to you as it does to me?—offers his prize of $25,000, and suddenly the hounds leap and slobber at the ends of their leash! Orteig, I suspect, has notions himself of establishing a commercial aerial service linking New York with the Continent. What better way to spur interest than to fabricate a contest certain to grasp every headline from the New York *Times* to the *Daily Graphic*? I'll give the fellow credit for slyness if not for class!"

Before Long could answer the telephone rang elsewhere in the apartment, and a uniformed maid entered with notification that there was a call for Mr. Lovecraft.

"Remarkable," Howard exclaimed. "Who could know that I was planning to visit you, Belknapius, when I myself did it only upon the spur of the moment!"

He followed the maid to the telephone and raised the earpiece of the instrument to hear who had called. As soon as Howard had identified himself the caller said, "Howard, this is Vincent Starrett. I need some expert assistance, and you are the person I thought most likely to be able to help me out."

Howard smiled to himself at the compliment. "I appreciate the research work you did for me in Chicago and Detroit, Vincentius. The very least that a gentleman could do in the circumstances is to reciprocate. What is the nature of the service you require?"

"It's simply some information. Or—more, I suppose, your opinion, your educated guess as to what might happen in an imaginary situation. It involves Poe, you see, and I consider you the number one Poe expert among my circle of friends."

"I should be most pleased, Vincentius. Is it something I can provide over the telephone? Or shall we foregather to invoke the shade of the sainted Baltimorean?"

Starrett was silent for a few seconds, then he said, "I think it would be more fun and more useful as well if we could chew this out for a while. As I mentioned, I don't need a *fact* as such. It's more in the line of an insight, I suppose.

"Listen, Howard, I've been planning on a little book prowl one day soon. Suppose I come into the city on Monday. Will you be free Monday afternoon?" Howard would.

"Okeh, then let's meet—how about Fourth Avenue. You know the antiquarian book shops there."

"Of course. Isn't that where you got your lovely *Blondeville*?"

"Don't rub it in, will you?" He suggested an hour and a shop where they would meet, and Howard asked if it would be acceptable to invite a friend along. Starrett said it most certainly would be, and the pact was sealed.

Howard dropped the earpiece back onto its hook and sought out Belknapius. He invited the younger man to join himself and Starrett the following Monday and Long announced his pleasure at the prospect.

"Very well. I think I shall take my leave, then, grand-son. Oh—before I go—have you seen this as yet?" He displayed the red-bordered issue of *Weird Tales* containing Long's poem, "Advice."

"No, I hadn't received my copy as yet. Why, are any of our circle represented this month? You know, Pharnabus isn't too reliable when it comes to notifying authors and readers of his schedule of material. I suppose he sells a few extra copies that way and keeps Joe Henneberger happy."

Howard opened the issue with a flourish and began to declaim. "Down the stairs and up the street / The kobolds go on silent feet. . ."

"That's 'Advice,' " Long exclaimed. "Do you know how long Farnie had that little effusion of mine in his inventory?"

Howard closed the magazine and shook his head. "I don't know but I can guess. He's never been one to rush things into print while still fresh from the egg. I suppose he feels that literature like fine beef needs to age a bit before it is served."

"Well," Long replied, "I'm glad that he finally got around to using the little thing. Have you sent him any verse of late? Or anything at all? I seem to find your name regularly in the Eyrie but nowhere else in the magazine. Surely you haven't stopped producing tales, I hope."

Howard said, "Actually, I get a little discouraged sometimes, but no, I haven't stopped producing. Farnie has turned down a few pieces of mine, but he has one or two awaiting his use. And I've a few more at home, aging in my own little pantry.

"And at the moment, of course, I am preparing my book for Viereck. It is not quite in the line of the fantastic, or—well, in fact it does involve a certain amount of prediction, or projection of social forces to describe a future circumstance. But the objective is not the fictional one of creating a pseudo- or counter-reality. Rather, it is one of anticipating a potential state of affairs which is the logical outcome of actual movements."

Howard stood still, chin in hand, looking somewhat distracted.

"Well," Long filled the silence, "I am certain that you will bring to the project all the skill that you do to anything you undertake. But I still would hope to see further tales from you."

~ ~ ~ ~ ~

The bookshop occupied the ground level and basement of a hundred year old building not far north of the famous Cooper Union on Fourth Avenue. Howard Lovecraft, striding through the May afternoon warmth from the BMT subway exit, met Belknap Long emerging from a tobacconist's shop nearby, and they strolled the rest of the way, Long adding cloudlets of blue aromatic tobacco smoke to the gasoline fumes that filled the canyons of the city.

Inside the shop they halted at a wooden counter and greeted the proprietor, a scholarly looking young man with a heavy, dark moustache and round glasses. They all knew one another slightly from past book-prowls of Howard's and Long's. Howard asked if a tall, dignified, fortyish man with a huge pompadour had been in looking for him.

The bookman stepped from behind the counter and walked to the head of the stairwell. He called downstairs to his partner. "Jack, is that Poe fellow still downstairs?" There was a muffled reply and the bookman returned to the counter. "He'd down in the fiction. You can go down there, it's all alphabetized."

They went downstairs and found Starrett immobilized beneath a dim electric bulb, studying the copyright page of a small gray volume. Howard put his finger to his lips, winked at Belknap Long and tiptoed up behind Starrett. He hissed into the Chicagoan's ear, then asked, "Want to buy a nice copy of *Blondeville*, cheap?"

Starrett whirled, surprised, then burst into laughter, throwing a mock punch at Howard's prominent jaw. "Once more," Starrett growled, "and I shall present that poor orphan volume to you with my compliments."

"No need," Howard said, "what would I do with a second copy of Volume I and only a single set of II through IV?" They both laughed, than Howard introduced Starrett and Belknap Long. "That doesn't look like Poe," Howard commented with regard to the gray column, "unless you've come up with an edition unfamiliar to me." Starrett grinned and turned the book so its narrow spine was visible. "No, I looked at their Poe but this is something a bit more modern that I just happened to be looking at. Fitzgerald. You ever read him?"

Howard made a sour face. "The Princeton fellow? I've looked at a few of his things, but he's really not to my taste. I found *This Side of Paradise* one of the few convincing arguments for the suppression of books that I have ever seen."

Starrett laughed. "No, I didn't really expect you to be an admirer of his. But this recent novelette of his—*The Great Gatsby*—might have something in it to titillate you."

"What would that be?"

"Why, your friend Mr. Viereck. What you've told me about him, at any rate. And a few of the other sentiments in the book ring a familiar tone as against some of your own writings."

"I do not pretend to the role of expert in regard to the works of Mr. F. Scott Fitzgerald, but from the little reading of his works which I have done, I cannot imagine any such relevance." Starrett grinned a great Barrymore grin and flipped the pages of the slim gray volume. Lovecraft watched him intently, almost glaring, while Belknap Long smoked his pipe in bemused observation of the pair. "Very well," Starrett broke the silence. "Here. Listen to this:

" 'You make me feel uncivilized, Daisy,' I confessed on my second glass of corky but rather unimpressive claret. 'Can't you talk about crops or something?'

"I meant nothing in particular by this remark, but it was taken up in an unexpected way." ("That's Nick Carraway, the narrator, speaking," Starrett interpolated; Howard's only comment was a noncommittal *hmm*.)

" 'Civilization's going to pieces,' broke out Tom violently." ("That's Tom Buchanan, Daisy's husband," Starrett inserted.) " 'I've gotten to be a terrible pessimist about things. Have you read *The Rise of the Colored Empires* by this man Goddard?'

" 'Why, no,' I answered, rather surprised by his tone. " 'Well, it's a fine book, and everybody ought to read it. The idea is if we don't look out the white race will be—will be utterly submerged. It's all scientific stuff; it's been proved.' "

"Sounds like Alexis Carrel to me," Howard said. "Nothing very new or startling there. But go on, Vincent, go on."

" 'Tom's getting very profound,' said Daisy, with an expression of unthoughtful sadness. 'He reads deep books with long words in them. What was that word we—'

" 'Well, these books are all scientific' insisted Tom, glancing at her impatiently. 'This fellow has worked out the whole thing. It's up to us, who are the dominant race, to watch out or these other races will have control of things.'

" 'We've got to beat them down,' whispered Daisy, winking ferociously toward the fervent sun.

" 'You ought to live in California—' began Miss Baker, but Tom interrupted her by shifting heavily in his chair.

" 'This idea is that we're Nordics. I am, and you are, and you are, and—' After an infinitesimal hesitation he included Daisy with a slight nod, and she winked at me again. '—And we've produced all the things that go to make civilization—oh, science and art, and all that. Do you see?' "

Vincent Starrett closed the book, holding his place with one inserted finger.

Howard Lovecraft said, "That's plain common sense. It pleases me to see even a debauched sybarite like Fitzgerald writing something sensible and important for a change. Although I've never heard of his writer Goddard or his book. I wonder if that's all a fabrication. Well, no matter. It's good sense anyway."

Starrett frowned. "Now, you told me a few things about Herr Viereck. Plus what I recall reading about him during the Great War. He made a few headlines at one point, you know.

"Anyway, listen to this little passage from Fitzgerald." Again he searched out a page. " 'Well, they say he's a nephew or a cousin of Kaiser Wilhelm's. That's where all his money comes from.' They're talking about Gatsby himself now. And listen to this." (He turned a few leaves.) " 'He was a German spy during the war.' Gatsby again.

"Of course, later in the book it turns out that that's all false, his family were American and he was in *our* army, not the Kaiser's. But still and all, isn't that uncanny, Howard? Long, what do you think?"

Belknap took his pipe out of his mouth and slipped it into a side pocket of his tweed jacket. "Rather," he commented.

Howard said, "It is a remarkable similarity. Maybe Viereck and Fitzgerald know each other, or maybe Fitzgerald just recalled the uproar of a decade ago and borrowed some of it for his character Gatsby. I'll have to ask Viereck about it if I remember."

Starrett reached for a shelf crowded in just under the old building's low beamed ceiling and slipped the book into a narrow opening between two identical spines. "Hmph, Fitzgerald seems to be a drug on the market."

"Off it as well, I'd say." Howard adjusted the gray fedora that he still wore in the basement. "But come, you didn't say that you wanted to spend the day discussing modern decadents. What's this about Poe? Now there is an author worth discussing!"

Starrett suggested a more comfortable setting and they left the bookshop. (Oddly, the only purchase was made by Belknap Long: a slim volume of Baudelaire.) They strolled southward to Lafayette Street, then west to

Washington Square and found a comfortable bench near the fountain.

"I do appreciate your help," Starrett told Howard Lovecraft. "As I may have mentioned, *Seaports in the Moon* is a sort of fantasy wherein I've been mixing some real historical figures with others out of literature. I've got Ponce de Leon in there, and Queen Isabella, Cyrano and d'Artagnon, Alex Pope. Now I want to put in a chapter where Ed Poe meets his hero from 'The Gold-Bug,' Legrand. I have my own notion of what they'd say to each other, but I'm interested in your opinion."

"You don't mean a discussion of 'The Gold-Bug,' the story? There's an interesting background to that, you know. There is good reason to believe that Poe lifted it."

"No," Starrett exclaimed with a delighted grin. "That's marvelous! Where did he get the story?"

"Well, I wouldn't exactly say that he plagiarized, mind you. But there's an earlier tale by Washington Irving, called 'Wolfert Webber.' Webber seems to have been the prototype for William Legrand. There's a comic darky like Poe's Jupiter, a lost treasure, a cryptogram to be solved. The whole thing is very similar." Starrett frowned. "And the locale?"

"Also an island. Only Poe used Sullivan's, near Charleston, while Irving used this island." He pointed to the soil of Manhattan beneath their feet. "Of course Poe's tale is superior to Irving's, and Poe's cryptography is quite brilliant. He'd actually done an essay on the subject for *Graham's Magazine* in 1841—two years before he wrote 'The Gold- Bug.' "

Vincent said that was marvelous, but questioned that Poe and Legrand would discuss Poe's literary career and sources should they have met.

"I'm not so certain," Belknap Long contributed. "Poor Poe. Howard, most of what I know of him I learned from you, but didn't he get bad reviews most of the time? Poor chap! It must have crushed him. *He* knew he was doing important work, but the world pretty well ignored him. He died early and poor. I should think that he'd have talked about reviewers, and rather bitterly at that!"

Howard Lovecraft stroked his chin. "You may be right at that, grandchild. Say—" he exclaimed, "—is that not the mellow chime of an iced cream vendor's cart?"

He leaped to his feet and led the way to the cart, buying a double confection for himself. Long and Starrett each bought a more modest treat. They strolled through the park, pausing to watch a mime briefly while they continued their conversation.

"I do think that they would discuss cryptography," Howard volunteered, "although not necessarily Poe's article in *Graham's*. Although they might make mention of it at that."

"I notice that you put references to various occult works into your own stories, Howard. Real as well as invented ones, eh? You must drive some collectors to distraction, not to mention bookmen who receive orders for books they can't locate for love or money!

"Anyway," he went on, "I've been thinking of setting the scene in a Baltimore hotel or inn of some low sort. It's near the end of Poe's life, and you know he was really down and out, the poor wretch. Sick—dying, in fact—penniless, obscure. If only he could have come back fifty years later to see what high regard he warranted! Well, there they are, Edgar and William. You think they'd discuss cryptography, eh? Not a bit esoteric?"

"Actually," Howard wiped his mouth fastidiously, swallowing a gob of confection, "if Poe was in that bad shape—which, you're correct, he was—he might well have put the bite on Legrand, as it were. Legrand was a Southern gentleman. Down on his own luck at one point, but Captain Kidd's treasure set things right for him."

"That's delicious!" exclaimed Vincent.

"What, the ice cream?"

"No! Hah! Poe borrowing money from his own creation."

"Well—or if not money, then he would certainly have tried to cadge a meal from the man. A meat pie, a bottle of absinthe, a fine cheroot or several of them. And if you've got them meeting in a hotel, Vincentius, he might have gone all out and worked poor Legrand for the price of a night's lodging."

Starrett slapped his thigh. "I knew I came to the right man, Howard. You are a story doctor *par excellence*. I can see it now, I can hear the dialogue with my mind's ear."

"I'd like to add a suggestion," young Long said. "Howard, you've told me that Poe was tormented by strange dreams and nightmares throughout his life. Do you think he'd mention them to Legrand? Do you think they inspired his stories?"

Howard finished his ice cream and carefully wiped his lips with a paper napkin, then deposited it in a trash container. "I'm not certain of that," he frowned. "He had nightmares and I'm sure that they inspired many of his stories, but—would he speak of them to a stranger?

"A stranger!" he challenged himself. "Of course, Legrand would be no stranger. He was a figment of Poe's mind, possibly of those dreams. He had the dreams, and they were real and awful dreams, even as. . ." He stopped speaking. Even as Kadath? he thought. Or—even as the death of Madeiros? The strange hospitality of Joseph Morelli on Federal Hill?

He shut the thoughts from his mind. "I suppose he would discuss his dreams with Legrand," he said.

CHAPTER TWENTY:

FUNGI FROM YUGGOTH

AT A FAREWELL PARTY for Dr. Kiep and George Sylvester Viereck, Howard encountered the fascist leader Ignazio Thaon di Revel again, and was introduced to a friend of Viereck's, Kurt Luedecke. Luedecke was a German citizen, visiting the United States on a tourist visa, but in heavily accented words he told Howard, "The new leader of Germany, the head of the National Socialist party, has asked me to represent his interests in North America."

Howard admitted that he was unaware of a change of government in Germany.

Luedecke, punctilious in wing collar and morning suit, laughed. "Ach, no, you are quite correct, sir. The old Marshal remains as president and Chancellor Marx clings to power. But a puff of wind and Hindenberg will be gone. A tremor of the earth, and the tree will quiver. The prize will fall into our hands."

He gestured with immaculately groomed fingers, cupping his hands as if to catch some invisible golden apple dropping from the bough of an intangible tree.

Count Revel joined Lovecraft and Luedecke with a polite half-bow. "You are a spokesman for Herr Hitler, then, Herr Luedecke?" The German nodded stiffly.

"I wonder what future you see for the collaboration of fascist and National Socialist forces."

Luedecke, squinting, asked, "In which country? Italy, of course, gives full allegiance to Signor Mussolini. Herr Hitler is an admirer of Il Duce of many years' standing. It will naturally be Germany's policy, under the National Socialist government, to remain uninvolved in the internal affairs of a friendly power."

"Certainly! And equally, Il Duce will do nothing to interfere with Herr Hitler's exercise of power. There is no conflict. Il Duce has made clear that he has no greater ambition than to restore the proper rights and prerogatives of Rome."

"You mean," Howard interjected, "that Mussolini will take control of the entire Mediterranean?"

Count Revel smiled. "Our historic hegemony extends only as far eastward as Asia Minor, southward into Africa, and no farther to the west than Spain."

Luedecke bowed. "My mission, understand, is concerned with our friends in the New World. I am not privy to the details of the *fuhrer's* plans for Europe. But he is, I know, dedicated to the most advanced principles of scientific racism. His plans are for the introduction of eugenic principles as matters of State policy in the new Reich, and in all lands ruled by the Reich.

"The Nordic peoples, after all, are the progenitors of all that is noble and advanced in our civilization. Science, art, discipline. We must be on guard or we will drown in a sea of inferior blood. The dark, inferior races—Jews, Slave, Negroes—will utterly swamp the fair Nordics if we permit them. Principles of scientific eugenics will be applied throughout Europe under the leadership of the new Reich. And in the western hemisphere—we will shortly establish a Swastika League of America. We will work hand in hand with native groups of like sympathies.

"Herr Viereck," he interrupted himself as Viereck passed by.

"You will visit the *fuehrer* shortly?"

Viereck smiled amiably.

"Please, you will bring him greetings from me and inform him that contacts have been established and the work is going forward."

"I will do that. Of course I have a very busy schedule ahead of me, but I wouldn't miss an opportunity to pay my respects to Herr Hitler."

He spoke to Howard. "I'm very pleased that you were able to come this afternoon. You will continue to press onward with your work in my absence, of course?"

Howard acknowledged that he would.

"Have you made your plans for Tuesday, Signor Lovecraft?" Count Revel asked.

Howard shook his head, puzzled. "It is the American Memorial Day," the Count explained. "Many observances are planned."

"Oh, yes," Viereck contributed. "There's to be quite a Klan parade out in Queens County. Jamaica. I had a little note from Hiram Evans about it. And of course the local Klunker will be out in force."

"Klunker?" Howard's brain raced, trying to recall the term from Two-gun Bob's letter about the Klan and its organization. "What in heaven's name is a Klunker?"

Viereck laughed. "I think there's no such thing. I was teasing. You know those Klansmen and their love of pageantry and alliteration—anything that starts with the letter K they enjoy." He shook his head and clucked his tongue.

"You know, Sylvester, I don't think you quite take the KKK seriously." Howard Lovecraft pulled his earlobe, trying unsuccessfully to resemble a New England yokel. "En't thet saow?" he asked.

Viereck laughed. "Well, to tell the truth, I do think that there's a good deal of silliness about the Klan. But—" His expression became serious. "—they can marshal a good deal of manpower, and they wield a great deal of influence—a *great* deal—in many parts of the country. How well they'll do in Queens. . . well, let's just wait and see.

"Of course, I won't be here to observe. I shall be well out on the high seas, enjoying the *haute cuisine* of the liner *Deutschland* by next Tuesday. But I'm sure I shall receive reports."

"Well, I understand your feeling about the Klan," Howard pressed on. "What about some of these other groups? What about your own American allies, Herr Luedecke? I assume you have been in communication with the Friends of New Germany? People like Herr Spanknoebel and Herr Kuhn, of Mr. Ford's staff?"

The German let out a breath explosively. "They are crude, would you not say so?"

Howard nodded vigorously. "To say the least. Crude." Luedecke appeared pensive for the moment. "As a matter of fact, Mr. Lovecraft, I have not as yet met either Herr Spanknoebel or Herr Kuhn. But from all that I have heard, your assessment of them absolutely correct is. But you see—" He made a gesture with both hands, as if exposing some hidden sacrament to the eyes of anyone able to see it. "—Crudity and vigor are often associated, is it not so? Sophistication sometimes goes hand in hand with decadence, I am frightened. But the muscular, the fearless, the ruthless—the crude often also is. You see?"

Howard conceded the point, only in part grudgingly. "At any rate, Signor Lovecraft," the Italian recaptured the conversation with a diffident bow, "on Memorial Day there will be a parade of our American associates. You have heard of the Blackshirts? We will be marching from the group's headquarters. Not my own office, you understand, but the Blackshirt headquarters, on 45th Street. If you could be persuaded to be present, as an observer, of course—?"

Howard made a note of the time of the parade and the address of the Blackshirt headquarters. A steward passed by carrying a tray of *hors d'oeuvres* and Viereck spoke to him briefly in German. The steward offered the tray to the men in the group and Howard took several small sandwiches. Balancing the sandwiches precariously he excused himself from the conversation and crossed Viereck's First Class cabin to stand looking out the porthole.

It was still late afternoon—the *Deutchsland* was to sail with the evening tide—and the lengthening shadows of the New Jersey palisades hung far out over the Hudson, turning the yachts and commercial craft on the river into studies in pale blue, faint gray, dim white.

There was a small burst of voices from behind Howard and he shoved the last of his *hors d'oeuvres* into his mouth and turned to see Dr. Otto Kiep of the German consulate surrounded by a group of questioners. They were speaking German but at the sight of Howard, Kiep switched to English and the others followed suit.

Kiep had been at the consulate until a few minutes ago; that was the cause of his late arrival at the *Deutchsland*. Cables had been received giving the European itinerary of the hero Lindbergh. The flier had already been received by the President of France, Gaston Doumergue, and been presented with the Order of the Legion of Honor. The biggest problem of the occasion had been Lindbergh's lack of clothing other than the flying suit he had worn in the *Spirit of St. Louis*, but the son of American ambassador Herrick had loaned the flyer a set of clothes reasonably near his own size, and Captain Lindbergh had worn them for the ceremony.

He had also visited the grieving mother of the lost pilot Charles Nungesser, an admirable gesture; had received the plaudits of both Orville Wright, the first man to fly a heavier-than-air craft (his older brother Wilbur had been dead for fifteen years), and from Louis Bleriot, the first pilot to cross the English Channel. Foreign Minister Briand and the great Marshals of the late war, Ferdinand Foch and Joseph Jacques Joffre, had added their own praises.

Lindbergh had stunted over Le Bourget aerodrome in a 300 horsepower Nieuport, and had endorsed the Benrus watch and the Waterman pen.

Now he was off to visit the crowned heads of Belgium, Holland, and the United Kingdom before returning to the United States.

To Howard Lovecraft the news of Lindbergh's plans was a matter of only mild interest; he was unable at first to understand the agitation of Dr. Kiep, the paleness of George Sylvester Viereck and the reddening face of Kurt Luedecke which met the announcement. But his puzzlement was quickly dispelled.

"See how he avoids the Reich!" Luedecke blurted angrily. "His own blood means nothing!" Dr. Kiep was almost visibly jumping up and down. "He is a German-American, not so is it?"

Viereck, grave in manner, shook his head. "I recall reading a biography of the more senior Lindbergh, some years ago, when he had published a book of political nature. The ancestry of the family is Swedish rather than German. But still—this is Nordic blood. Have you seen photographs of the captain? A perfect type, blue eyes, light complexion, fair hair. A perfect Nordic type," Viereck reiterated, "yet he avoids all of the Nordic countries! Especially Germany!"

There was a moment of silent tension in the cabin. Howard Lovecraft noted that a ray of sunlight coming through the porthole had been focused into a perfect oblong and was shifting slowly across the surface of a small writing-desk at one side of the plushly-furnished cabin. There were a few grumbled exclamations in German, then the Italian-accented tones of Count Revel asked, "Why do you believe he is doing this, gentlemen?"

Three voices responded at once. The harsh, powerful tones of Kurt Luedecke quickly overrode the others.

"This Lindbergh a very young man still is, *nicht so*, Herr Graf?" Revel nodded dubiously.

"He does not his own plans control. A boy, a boy, a child. Powerful forces at play are, Hauptmann Lindbergh the lead of others follows. Consider: the money he takes from Herr Orteig, the clothing even from Herr Herrick. This not is any incident. . . co-instance. . . *ach*, Sylvester, *ubereinstimmung*, eh?"

"Coincidence," Viereck supplied.

"*Danke*. Graf Revel, this any coincidence is not. A slap he delivers to Germany!"

Another steward arrived, cutting through the growing tension and excitement with bottles of *schnapps*, Rhine wine and champagne. He offered the beverages with words in German, but to Howard Lovecraft and Ignazio Thaon di Revel, the only persons present who spoke no German, the message was amply clear.

In a calmer voice Luedecke resumed. "Have you read the great book of National Socialism? Herr Lovecraft? Graf Revel? In German it is called *Mein Kampf*. Written by Hitler himself with the aid of Rudolf Hess. You know Hess, *wissen sie* Hess, Viereck? *Ach*, no? You must meet him! And Ludendorff! In 1923 and 1924, Hitler the book created."

"I suppose I ought to examine the tome," Howard said. He exchanged a glance of agreement with Viereck. "If it is really all that important."

Luedecke nodded jerkily, barely able to contain his physical energy and his renewed excitement. "National Socialism the. . . the. . . *ach*, Viereck, *unwiderstehlich*—"

"Irresistible."

"—force is. Germany will it sweep, all of Europe will it sweep. The day soon is coming!"

Howard Lovecraft, a glass of Rhine wine in one hand, spotted a tray of *petit fours* and reached for a few of them with his other. He jammed one in his mouth, chewed it as the Germans and Count Revel continued their conversation.

Before much longer a steward marched through the companionway sounding a gong, leaning into each cabin and warning passengers that the ship was being cleared, sailing time was approaching. Viereck's party began to disintegrate. Dr. Kiep offered Howard a lift from the pier in his Horsch and Howard gratefully accepted, asking to be let out at the nearest BMT entrance kiosk.

"We will see you on Tuesday, then," Revel said in parting.

"I shall present myself at your office," Howard replied. He checked the time, entered the station and paid his nickel for the ride back to Brooklyn. Sonia was not yet home from Russek's so Howard settled down to examine the mail forwarded from Providence while he brewed a pot of coffee for himself.

There were letters from any number of friends and colleagues, the most urgent missive being a brief dunning note from Farnsworth Wright. If Howard was going to be so slow and unprolific with regard to new stories for *Weird Tales*. . .Howard threw down the letter with a furious exclamation. Slow and unprolific indeed! Wright was the guilty one, not Howard Phillips Lovecraft! Wright was the one who took weeks or months to read any submission, who rejected anything at all original and out of the ordinary, who had to ask for second readings and third readings of stories he'd already returned as unsuitable before changing his mind and accepting them, and who then held them in inventory until the very paper on which they were typewritten flaked away with age, before he got around to putting them into print!

Maybe Starrett had been smart to follow Ed Baird over to *Real Detective Tales*, and maybe Howard ought to listen to Starrett's advice and do the same. Create some silly series hero like Starrett's James Eliot Lavender and produce an unending torrent of silly and repetitious tales for a steady and remunerative market! Come to think of it, Howard *had* created such a character years before, for Julian Houtain and his odd magazine *Home Brew*. Houtain had paid little and late (a familiar situation!) but he *had* paid—Howard's first experience as a professional author, and a strange mixture of having lowered himself to *trade* tinctured with pride at actually earning real money for his effusions, had been Howard's reaction.

The hero, Herbert West—Reanimator, had been less than a fascinating figure, and the stories, half a dozen of them written for a fixed rate of $5 apiece, had been far from Howard's favorites among his own works. But he had done it. He had created a series character and produced the six stories as promised, and he should certainly be able to do again what he had done already. But that was something to be considered at his leisure. For the moment, what could he send to Wright?

He spread his files of commercially-unpublished materials on the brocade-covered couch and began to sort through them. He'd promised Wright some more poetry and now he reread and rearranged a group of sonnets selected from his files, some of them previously published in amateur journals, others present only in manuscript.

He'd been interested for years in the limits of the Solar System; one of his earliest published works, an article in the series he'd done for the Pawtuxet Valley *Gleaner* in 1906, had treated of exactly this subject. The onetime "outermost" planet, Uranus, had been discovered by William Herschel in 1781; thereafter the only suspicions of additional bodies had been the false notion of "Vulcan," the supposed intra-Mercurian worldlet, and the equally false idea of "Counter-Earth," the fabulous body supposed to share Earth's orbit, 180° out of phase with the Earth and consequently forever hidden in the glare of Sol.

Then, some sixty years later, the British astronomer Adams and the French Leverrier had independently calculated the source of odd perturbations in the orbit of Uranus, and had discovered their source: Neptune.

Was this the end? There were still unaccounted oddities in the movements of the outer planets. Perhaps there was still another; the American astronomer Percival Lowell believed that there was. Howard had paid tribute to Lowell in his writing of 1906, and although Lowell had died in 1916, others were continuing to search the heavens for a sight of his elusive ninth planet.

Howard Lovecraft's imagination had been seized in 1906 by the notion of that mysterious, remote planet, its dark and frigid face forever turned toward a sun so distant that it appeared no brighter than a minor star and its surface untouched by life or warmth for countless billions of years. Howard named the planet Yuggoth, and penned a cycle of poetry in its honor. The sonnets of this cycle he dubbed "Fungi from Yuggoth," and he now selected the ten sonnets that he considered most successful and copied them out painstakingly on his old Postal typewriter, and sealed them with a covering note to send to Pharnabus. There, let the gawking fool use those and be damned to him! Howard was fishing now in deeper waters, and had reason to believe that he had hooked a far weightier fish than Farnie Wright or Joe Henneberger, in Sylvester Viereck!

~ ~ ~ ~ ~

Sonia came through the door of her apartment singing a two-year-old song that had stuck in her mind, "Keep Your Skirts Down, Mary Ann," and found her husband busily working in the living room. She bustled past him into the kitchen to deposit the brown paper bags of groceries she'd purchased on her walk from the subway, then returned happily to the living room and bent over Howard to give him a kiss on the cheek.

She didn't say a word until he'd sealed the envelope he'd been stuffing with sheets of manuscript, then asked how his day had been, what he had done after arriving home.

"This is just some light verse for Pharnabus," He waved the envelope disparagingly. "You know the old fool. When I send him material he doesn't like it and when I don't send him material he doesn't like *that* even more! Baird should never have left."

Sonia said she was sure Howard would find his way to superior markets in time; his book, after all, should open important doors once it was published.

"Oh, yes!" he rejoined. "And keep them open, if they use it an a doorstop! Say, that last time I was down on Fourth Avenue with Belknap Long and Vicentius I wandered up and down the aisles of dead books like a ghoul in the shadows of a giant mausoleum! Novels and tales, essays and verse, history, philosophy, drama, jokes. We toil away our wretched hours at the quill, and what is the result? A quick day in the press—if we're lucky; not even that if our stars are ill!—and then on, to the remainder table, to the bookman's stall, to the two-for-a-nickel bin and eventually to the rubbish heap. Julian Houtain, where art thou now?"

Sonia ignored the outburst. Sometimes she saw Howard in a moment of real despair and offered all the warmth and sustenance that her womanly nature could provide to a suffering man, but at other times (like today) she knew that Howard was indulging in a momentary wallow of self-pity, half-mocking himself all the while, and rather than play to his gambit she ignored it and turned the subject elsewhere.

"I thought you were going to a farewell party for your friend Sylvester on the *Deutchsland*," she said.

Howard had cleared his files from the couch and returned them to the corner of the room set aside as his work space. He sat now on the couch and Sonia sat opposite him, her ample comeliness balanced on a padded stool.

"Yes, I went to the party. The *Deutchsland* is quite a ship. I must credit the Germans with great efficiency in the building and furnishing of liners, and in the service provided on board."

"Was it a good party?"

"Some interesting people there. I met one Kurt Luedecke whom I'd not known before; otherwise it was the usual Viereck crowd. Mostly European, and mostly German. Dr. Kiep from the consulate. Count Revel, the Italian."

Sonia smiled. "What about Herr Luedecke? Did you hit it off with him?"

Howard rubbed his jaw and hesitated before answering. "I'd not put it quite that way," he said at last. "There was a great deal of agitation about Captain Lindbergh."

Sonia was astonished. "Why would that be, Howard? I should think that Lindbergh would be the most popular man in the world just now. And you say this man Luedecke was distressed?"

"Everyone was," Howard replied. "All the Germans, anyway. Count Revel didn't seem to be at all distressed. Dr. Kiep came marching in from the consulate complaining that Lindbergh's itinerary had been announced, and that he was visiting Britain and Belgium and the Netherlands, but not Germany. At once there was an uproar. Everyone is convinced that there's a sinister plot under way to snub Berlin."

Sonia shook her head. "Well, that's all of no matter. Come, how's your appetite, Howard dear? I brought home a surprise for dinner and I'll change and start it now if you can eat. Or was there something else about today?"

He patted his pockets until he brought forth his notebook. "There's a book by this new German leader Hitler that was recommended to me. Thing called, ah, *Mein Kampf.*" Howard put the notebook away. "Something about a party program hatched in prison after Hitler had been arrested in a beer hall or something of the sort. Sounds like a speakeasy raid to me. Maybe the drys have sent Izzy and Moe off to Europe now."

Sonia looked very serious. "I know that book. *My Struggle.* That's the English title. It is a vicious book. Hitler blames all of the ills of Germany and Europe on the Jews. He ought to get together with Henry Ford. They're birds of a feather. Are you an admirer of his? Are you seriously becoming involved with the American branch of his party?"

"I'm not one to join any political party. As for involvement, I suppose it depends upon how one defines involvement. There is a certain affinity of thought between Viereck and myself, and certain of his associates. Others are mere ruffians, thugs, little more than criminals operating in the guise of politics.

"From what I've seen of Hiram Evans—and from what Two-gun Bob Howard writes out of Texas—the KKK is a money-making racket at the highest level and an excuse for hooligans and vigilantes at the lowest. A far cry from the worthwhile and constructive association headed by Nathan Bedford Forrest half a century ago!

"The Germanically-oriented groups—have I mentioned the names Spanknoebel and Kuhn before? Good!—seem to be crude and vulgar. So does Hitler's emissary Luedecke.

"But Viereck himself is a cultured and sensitive gentleman. I must say that my opinions of him formed during the Great War have been substantially altered through personal contact. I may not be in total agreement with him on all political questions. I still feel that he exonerates the Central Powers in general and the Kaiser in particular to a greater extent than is proper.

"I find his restorationist sentiments most compatible with my own feelings. Count Revel also is a fine gentleman—a Roman of the highest type who would not be out of place in the Senate of Marcus Aurelius' time—not a greasy, garlic-spewing wop of the type so common today!

"As for the Russian Count, Vonsiatsky—we have already discussed him. I know of the low regard in which you hold him, Sonia, and while my scorn for him is less than your own, I cannot call myself an admirer of the Count's. Yet, if he is to be the instrument for the removal of the Bolshevists and the restoration of the rightful imperial regime, he may yet prove the agent of more good than harm."

Sonia heaved a great sigh. "Well, Howard, this all has to do with that Hitler book. I suppose you will make it your business to obtain a copy."

"At the earliest opportunity."

"Perhaps that will be a good idea after all. When you've read for yourself not only the bestial and disgusting ideas that he pushes but the crude, almost hysterical way he has of expressing himself. . .it should help you to understand what you're dealing with."

Howard shrugged. "I understand that his wrath is directed against inferior races. Slavs, Jews, the same swarthy mongrels that I despise."

"No, Howard, that's wrong." Sonia shook her head. "He says that he hates only certain races, but let me tell you something. I, who know at first hand what that racial hatred means. What it grows from. It grows from hatred of self, Howard. It grows from a feeling that he is an inadequate, thwarted man, or less than a man. It grows from the feeling that one has failed, that one's life or one's state or one's race has been beaten by the challenge of human existence. That leads to a seething rage. Howard, I have seen this in the flaming eyes of Cossack rapists in Itchno, in the dark glaring looks of peasant traders in Konotop.

"Believe me, Howard. A man like Hitler may say he hates only Jews, but in his heart he hates all men, and in his innermost heart of hearts, Howard, he most bitterly of all hates himself."

CHAPTER TWENTY-ONE:

LOVECRAFT MEETS A PRINTER

HOWARD SET an alarm clock in order not to miss the Black-shirt parade in Manhattan. He managed to drag himself from between the sheets and join Sonia for breakfast, a rare occurrence. She had the food ready by the time he arrived at the table, and he gulped most of his first cup of black, syrupy coffee before speaking a word.

Not that the apartment was silent. Sonia had tuned the radio console to WBRS and the corner speaker was pouring forth popular tunes like "Clap Yo' Hands" and "Someone to Watch over Me," and Sonia was chattering over the music, trying to convince Howard to spend the holiday with her. The employees of Russek's were holding their annual picnic at Cunningham Park in Jamaica, Queens. It was warm and a pleasant breeze lifted the light curtains from before the Parkside Avenue apartment windows. They could travel to the picnic by streetcar and omnibus, without having to venture into the city, and were bound to have a wonderful time surrounded by trees and ponds and hilly meadows not unlike those of some parts of New England.

Howard forked half of an egg into his mouth, washed it down with a mouthful of coffee, and smiled across the table. "You go on, my dear, and enjoy your outing. I have work to do this day."

Sonia pleaded, trying to convince Howard to come along. "I'm so proud of my wonderful husband, I want to show you off to my friends. They all know about you and they think it's the most wonderful thing that you're a famous author, Howard. Everyone is dying to meet you. Please, dear!"

He shook his hand. "It cannot be helped. I have a commitment to meet Count Revel." He paused and examined his watch to see the hour. "I've quite a bit of traveling to do, at that, if I'm not to miss my appointment. It's a good thing that we are not to meet at the Count's own office, which is all the way up at 187th Street. We're to meet instead at the Blackshirt organization's headquarters, in midtown, and then observe the Blackshirt parade. "I have spoken of the Count before, have I not? A Roman of the highest type. I have long felt that Caesar was not only the noblest Roman of them all, but perhaps the greatest man in history. It was a pity that the Romans permitted unlimited, or virtually unlimited, immigration, from all corners of their empire. It was the inferior strains entering Rome from her more easterly possessions that both brought about the moral and political degeneracy of the empire and the decay of her fine racial stock. Only the countering influence of Nordic strains in later years partially offset the degenerative influence of the eastern immigrants, and rescued some simulacrum of both Roman civilization and the Roman race."

Sonia left the table and stood with her back turned, working over the kitchen stove for some time. She returned with a fresh platter of crisp bacon and toast with butter and jam.

"You mustn't go off to meet your Count without a belly full of good nourishing food, Howard," she said.

He cleared his plate, refilled and cleared it once again, and after downing a couple of glasses of fruit juice and one more cup of coffee, rose from his chair and sought his gray fedora. "Please make my apologies to your colleagues, my dear, and do enjoy your outing."

Sonia put her hands on Howard's shoulders and planted a small kiss on his cheek before he left the apartment.

As he crossed West 45th Street on his way from the BMT exit kiosk to the address Count Revel had given him as Blackshirt headquarters, Howard encountered a familiar, somewhat swarthy figure of a young man. The younger man was walking with a man Howard had never before seen, a huge, brutish looking individual with a broad flat face, wide shoulders and a protuberant belly.

The swarthy man's eyes widened when he saw Howard and he hurried forward, extending his hand and grasping Howard's with it. "Mr. Lovecraft! What a coincidence. You remember me, I hope? We were introduced by Sylvester Viereck at his little party a few weeks ago. I'm George Pagnanelli."

Howard swallowed, returned Pagnanelli's handclasp. "Of course, so happy to see you once again. Are you headed in my direction?"

Pagnanelli fell in beside Howard. "I'm on my way to meet Count Revel. Let's see, he's to be at—" He pulled a notebook from one pocket and consulted it. "—number 145, West 45th. That's just another block or so. Oh, pardon me, I've forgot my manners. I don't think you've ever met Peter here."

He halted and swung around so that the three of them—Howard Lovecraft, George Pagnanelli, and the hulking heavyset man—stood on the sun-baked sidewalk in a rough triangle. "This is Pete Stahrenberg. Peter, Howard Lovecraft. Howard is a novelist, I believe. Is that correct, Mr. Lovecraft? We've only met once."

"A gentleman littérateur and *fantaisiste*, I should hope."

"Peter here is my printer. Turns out the *Christian Defender* for me, and a good many other patriotic publications of a very, very worthwhile nature."

"Yeah," Stahrenberg gripped Howard's hand in a rough paw and mashed it for a while. "You need a printer for your stuff, Lovelace?"

"Lovecraft. Not just now, thank you, sir. But I shall be pleased to keep you in mind should I require the services of a tradesman in your particular line of work." He accepted a messily printed business card from Stahrenberg and slipped it into his pocket.

They resumed walking and found 145, an office building of indeterminate age and undistinguished architecture. Together the three men rode the elevator up to the headquarters of the Blackshirts and Pagnanelli rapped on the glass-paneled door. Before the knock could be answered Stahrenberg reached past the smaller man and rattled the knob in one huge hand. It was locked, but almost at once Count Revel personally admitted the visitors.

The office was a beehive of uniformed figures; Revel and the three newcomers were the only ones in mufti, and Stahrenberg turned to Pagnanelli once they were inside, saying, "George, I got to get into my other clothes." He disappeared into a warren of shoulder-high partitions to get a Blackshirt outfit.

Count Revel, correct and immaculate as usual, bowed slightly to Howard and Pagnanelli. "I was unaware that you gentlemen were acquainted. It gives me pleasure to see that I was mistaken."

Pagnanelli asked who was expected at the demonstration and Revel reeled off a list of names. They were unfamiliar to Howard but Pagnanelli nodded repeatedly and smiled. "A fine turnout," he commented.

"Yes," Revel agreed. "You see, the *fascisti* are heavily supporting the gathering of the day, but we are far from alone. Many of Herr Spanknoebel's *Freundes* will be with us, and even a few of Father Curran's associates will be in black today." He grinned at the image. "In fact, we had hoped for a very large turnout, but the Klan had already made commitments to hold a parade of their own in Queens County. But our show of solidarity will include a few Klansmen marching with the Blackshirts and *vice versa*. A little sprinkling of salt in the pepper, and a few peppercorns among the crystals of salt, one might say."

Pagnanelli nodded and grinned. "Excellent imagery, Count." The exchange was interrupted by a pimply-complexioned youth in black shirt and tan jodhpurs who grasped the Count's spotless shoulder and whispered earnestly into his ear. The Count's face grew pale, his expression sobered. "If you will excuse me, please," he half-bowed to Howard and Pagnanelli. "I must—a very urgent matter."

He turned without waiting for a reply and ran across the office to take a telephone call, clutching the receiver with whitened knuckles and pressing the earpiece hard to his head. Howard watched him, nodding and gesturing as if he could see the party on the other end of the line. The Count sat down and scrabbled on a desk-top for pencil and paper, carefully wrote down a few lines and read them back into the telephone for confirmation.

After the call was ended he climbed onto the desk, standing in uncharacteristic disarray, and waved his hands for attention. "Comrades! Fratelli! Fascisti!"

The stir and activity in the room quietened and dozens of men in black shirts and tan jodhpurs turned to give their attention to the elegantly garbed nobleman.

"I have received terrible news from Fascist headquarters. Two of our fratelli, our brothers, have been murdered. Giuseppe Carrisi and Nicola Amorroso. Do you know them?"

There was a rumble from a few of the men in the room. A voice called out, "What happened?"

The Count consulted the piece of paper he'd scribbled on during his telephone conversation.

"You know Turini's restaurant?" the Count asked. Again a few voices grumbled that they did.

The Count studied the sheet of paper. Comrades Carrisi and Amorroso were just climbing the steps to the El at 183rd Street, on their way from Fascist headquarters to come here. Two men came out of Turini's and approached our comrades. One man pulled a gun and shot Comrade Amorroso. The other, he pulled a knife and stabbed Comrade Carrisi. Both dead. The killers ran away."

"Who did it?" a voice shouted. Others took up the cry, answering "Commies! Bolshies! Reds!" One voice yelled "Kikes!"

Count Revel waves his sheet of paper in the air until the yelling stopped. "The two killers," he shouted, "wore flaring red neckties!"

The room exploded into pandemonium. Shouts and curses at the killers and their allies filled the air. Finally the Count, waving and shouting, regained control.

"Comrades! We will gain our vengeance! We will find the murderers and make them pay! But for today, we must show our strength and our discipline! The Blackshirt parade must take place exactly as planned, without incident unless we are attacked!"

The Count went on giving instructions to the Blackshirts. Howard Lovecraft, standing with Pagnanelli, saw Pagnanelli's printer Pete Stahrenberg return to the room decked out in full Blackshirt regalia. Stahrenberg waved to Pagnanelli.

"I don't suppose the Count will have much time for social discussions after this," Pagnanelli said to Howard. "Would you like to come over to my place after the parade?"

Howard accepted, and they filed out of the rabbit-warren of Blackshirt offices along with the uniformed figures, dozens of black-shirted, tan-jodhpured men with a scattering of uniformed Klansmen moving among them, contrasting like snowballs tossed onto the open back of a coal delivery wagon on a bright winter's day.

Outside the building the Blackshirts marshaled their rank and file (the group who had assembled in the headquarters office were the leaders and parade-marshals of the group) and they moved off, to the sound of a row of snare-drummers. "About four hundred, I'd say, what do you think?" Pagnanelli asked.

Howard, unused to estimating the size of crowds, agreed. They followed the small parade, keeping to the sidewalk as the Blackshirts, drummers, Klansmen and Count Revel, stepped down the center of the street. They moved the width of Manhattan, from Blackshirt headquarters on West 45th Street to the East River, then broke into angry little knots of men discussing the killing of Carrisi and Amorroso and gesturing angrily. During the march, police had kept the Blackshirts separated from public observers. There had been an occasional smattering of applause as they marched past clusters of spectators, and more occasional catcalls and hoots. At one point a spectator had thrown an egg and hit a Blackshirt. A contingent of marchers had taken after the spectator, but a policeman had got to him first and hustled him out of the way. The Blackshirts had angrily returned to their formation and continued their parade.

Now, with the parade over and the formation dispersed, a pair of Klansmen strolled past Howard Lovecraft and Pagnanelli. Howard acted on a bizarre impulse as the Klansmen passed and called to them, "Ayak?"

The two white-robed figures halted and peered at him through the eye-slits of their white pointed hoods. "Akia," one of them replied, "Capowa?"

Howard said nothing.

"Cygnar? Capowa?" the Klansman repeated. "Cygnar?" Howard made a gesture toward Pagnanelli with his head. "Sanbog! Sanbog!"

The two Klansmen nodded their hoods and bowed shallowly to Howard. "Potok," Howard said, and "Kotop" the Klansmen replied in unison and walked away.

As soon as they were beyond sight or hearing Howard doubled over in laughter.

George Pagnanelli said, "What was that all about?" Howard laughed until he wept, pulled a white handkerchief from his pocket and wiped his eyes. He blew his nose and put the square of linen away.

"Come along, George, and I'll tell you all about it." He refused to say anything further until they reached Pagnanelli's tiny apartment in a brownstone at 100 West 86th Street. "A lovely spot," Howard commented. "Between the park and the river, you must enjoy living here greatly."

Pagnanelli, visibly close to bursting with curiosity, demanded to know what Howard's dialog with the Klansmen had meant.

Howard, slumped into a dusty overstuffed easy chair, alternately giggled, explained to Pagnanelli what he'd learned of the Klan through both the Viereck circle and Two-gun Bob Howard's investigation, and wept tears of mirth. "So much for General Forrest's noble order," he wound up. " 'Twas a glorious Invisible Empire in the last century, and a retreat for charlatans, mummers and fools in this. Oh, oh, George, it was worth it to play those fools for the poor fish they are. The money they spent to purchase their lovely gowns is keeping Hiram Evans in luxury. Oh, oh, oh!"

Pagnanelli paced back and forth.

Howard's eyes ran over the furnishings of the little apartment. A bed, a lumpy sofa, a dusty easy chair, a rickety desk with a Smith-Premier typewriter almost as ancient as Howard's familiar Postal, a wooden stool. The only luxury in the place was a small radio apparatus marked with the Grebe-Synchrophase logotype. The set seemed lacking a loudspeaker, but a pair of earphones were connected to the chassis by a lengthy cable.

The desk-top was covered with books and pamphlets of a political nature, all of them reflecting the general outlook of the Viereck circle, and the walls of Pagnanelli's dwelling were almost invisible behind the membership certificates and credentials from dozens of organizations. Pagnanelli was apparently a member of the Christian Mobilizers, the American Patriots, the Crusaders for Americanism, Inc., the Paul Revere Sentinels (An All American Patriotic Non-Profit Membership Corporation), the Anglo-Saxon Federation of America (Howard raised his eyebrows at that one, flicked his glance from the certificate bearing the very Mediterranean name to the swarthy owner of that name and back to the certificate), the American National Socialist Party, the Yankee Freemen (Think Yankee, Talk Yankee, Act Yankee), and the Christian Front (Howard had not known that Pagnanelli was a member of the Curran-Coughlin movement).

"I've put some water on the hot-plate for tea," Pagnanelli broke in on Howard's ruminations. "Will you have a cup of tea? Would you like a cigarette?"

Howard declined the tobacco, said that he would enjoy a cup of tea. He remarked, "You appear to be quite a joiner, Mr. Pagnanelli."

The younger man gave a grunt of assent. "There are a lot of organizations working toward the same goal, Mr. Lovecraft. They may differ in details of orientation and interest, but they agree on the need for a free and liberty-loving America, clean of the dominating influence of the British- *Bolshevist*-Zionist clique that presently exercises power behind the scenes in Washington." (He pronounced the nation's capitol city *Wore-shington*.)

Howard started to protest the linking of Great Britain with the Red and Jewish influences that Pagnanelli opposed, but the other anticipated his objection.

"That's where many of our differences arise. Some people don't think that England is part of that alliance. They see the Prince of Wales when he comes to town on a good-will tour, they hear of his playing drums in a jazz band or falling off a horse or dancing with all the girls at a party, and they're charmed. And there are undeniable cultural links between Britain and the United States, of course.

"But we have to see past these things. Some of our people place heavy emphasis on the Papist menace, and yet we have members like Father Curran who is as true-blue and loyal an American as he can be. And of course we have to keep down the blacks. Everyone agrees on *that* threat to a brave, strong, white America!

"At any rate, I feel that I can best produce my paper, the *Christian Defender*, and can best contribute to the movement, by keeping in touch with as many groups and individuals as I can. That's why I'm interested in you, Mr. Lovecraft, and in your work."

Howard mentioned that he was doing a book for the Jackson Press, under Sylvester Viereck's sponsorship. Viereck hadn't mentioned any need to keep secret his work on *New America and the Coming World-Empire*. "So I have to perform a research task not unlike your own work as a self-appointed liaison officer," Howard explained. He walked over to a spot on the wall beside a window that overlooked bustling 86th Street with its markets and shops. "This organization is one I have never heard of, but that surely rings a bell with me." He pointed to the Yankee Freemen membership certificate bearing Pagnanelli's name.

"Think Yankee, Talk Yankee, Act Yankee," Howard quoted the motto that appeared in old-style italic type beneath the name of the organization. Beside the words on the off-white parchment certificate was embossed a royal blue Maltese cross. "The organization is not specifically Christian," Howard commented, more in question than in assertion.

"No." Pagnanelli shook his head. The water had begun to boil on the hotplate, the tin pot in which it had been heated giving off a shrill whistle. The young man turned off the hot-plate, poured water over tea bags for himself and Howard Lovecraft and handed a cup to Howard. "The Yankee Freemen are not a religiously oriented group. They're a patriotic and educational organization dedicated to the restoration of traditional American values in the face of attacks by alien and disloyal elements."

Howard rubbed his jaw, his gaze moving from the Yankee Freemen certificate to the traffic passing in 86th Street below. An electrified street car had stopped at the corner; now the conductor sounded his bell and pulled the lever and the car moved off eastward, toward Central Park.

"You might have guessed, Mr. Pagnanelli, that I'm somewhat of a Yankee myself, although I cannot go along with the anti-British element of so many of these groups. I certainly agree with most of their aims, and I favor a reuniting of the Nordic races in Britain, America, and the Continent of Europe."

"The coming world empire of your book?"

"Precisely that. Sylvester Viereck's ideas are largely in line with my own, except for his great sympathy toward the Kaiser and the German cause which I do not wholly endorse. Yet reconciliation between the branches of the great civilizing race is most assuredly to be sought. Perhaps you are familiar with the works of Mr. Houston Stewart Chamberlain?"

Pagnanelli removed a stack of loose papers from beside his Smith-Premier typewriter and uncovered a thick, black-covered volume. "*Foundations of the Nineteenth Century*," he announced its title. "Virtually a bible. A book of importance almost on a par with Hitler's *Struggle*. Did you know Chamberlain?"

"I know nothing about him personally, only his great book." Pagnanelli laid the book down beside the type-writer and propped himself on a wooden stool beside his desk. "A great man. He died just two years ago, a German of English ancestry. There's your reconciliation right there. He was a close friend of the Kaiser's."

"That is fascinating," Howard returned from the window. "Sylvester has never mentioned Chamberlain, but they must have been acquainted. Sylvester is himself a close friend of the Kaiser's, and claims a certain blood relationship with the Hohenzollerns."

Pagnanelli sipped his tea, waiting for Howard to continue about Chamberlain, but instead Howard asked about the Yankee Freemen. "Is the group headquartered in New England?"

Pagnanelli scrabbled among the papers on his desk until he produced a letter on Yankee Freemen stationery. "Let's see, there's a George Hornby who's an officer. The president, though, is Edward Holton James of Yonkers. I've never met the man."

"Well, of little import." Howard shook his head. Pagnanelli asked Howard to excuse him while he switched on his radio receiver. "We can hear any late news reports. I'd like to follow developments of that double murder of the *fascisti* at Third Avenue." He consulted a listing of radio broadcast schedules clipped from a morning newspaper, then switched on the Grebe-Synchrophase radio set. He lifted the earphones and disconnected them from their headpiece, passing one to Howard and pressing the other to his ear.

"I'd like to have a loudspeaker instead of phones, but the good ones are terrifically expensive. Anyway, I suppose I'd be less likely to offend my neighbors using the earphones. There's a family above who play a panatrope so loudly at times that I think there's a live marching band and chorus up there!"

Howard took the proffered earphone and pressed it to his ear as Pagnanelli did with the other. He winced at the squeal of sound as the younger man adjusted wavelength and frequency. Finally a voice announced that station WMCA was about to present its regular news broadcast.

There was considerable news about the day's memorial observances. A contingent of 200 Civil War veterans had paraded in the city under the banner of the Grand Army of the Republic; mention was made of Count Revel's Blackshirt parade but not of the egg-throwing incident. The announcer reported on the murders of Carristi and Amorroso and read a statement by Fascist headquarters demanding a police roundup of Reds and a return to the Mitchell Palmer policies of suppressing radicals and anarchists.

In Jamaica, Queens, there had been a near riot as 1000 Ku Klux Klansmen and 400 women's auxiliaries had paraded. The marchers had been heckled by Negroes and Jews in the crowd of spectators and when paraders charged into the crowd to punish their tormentors they had been restrained by police.

The Grand Dragon of the State of New York had issued a demand that Governor Smith take action against the police. Dominated by Irish Catholics, the police had obviously used the incident as an excuse for unleashing their bigoted Papist sentiments against the Protestant Klansmen.

Several Klansmen and spectators had been injured in the scuffle and taken to nearby hospitals for treatment.

Howard dropped the earphone. "My God!" he exclaimed.

"What is it? What's the matter?" Pagnanelli asked.

Howard clutched at the edge of the table. "Sonia! Do you have a telephone? I must place a call at once!"

Pagnanelli indicated that there was a telephone in the hallway.

Howard ran from the apartment, found the telephone and rummaged up a nickel from his dark suit trousers. He dropped the coin into the telephone slot and asked Central for the number of the Parkside Avenue apartment.

After a long pause the operator at Central informed him that there was no response at the other telephone.

Howard ran back to Pagnanelli's apartment, mumbled a quick and incoherent apology, and ran out once more, jamming his felt hat down around his ears as he did so. He made his way back to Brooklyn as rapidly as public transportation would carry him, and ran panting up the stairs to Sonia's apartment.

When he flung open the door and charged into the foyer he found Sonia seated at his Postal typewriter, tapping out a letter to a friend. "Sonia!" Howard cried.

She turned and looked up at him. "Oh, Howard, I hope it's all right for me to use your typewriter. I'd have asked if you had been at home, of course, but. . ."

For the first time in well over a year, Howard Lovecraft embraced his wife and kissed her lips. The incidents of Memorial day had repercussions ranging from the tragic to the trivial. The slaying of the fascists Carristi and Amorroso brought demonstrations and protests from around the world. The bodies were embalmed and seen off from New York by Count Revel, addressed to Rome where they were to be met and orated over by Il Duce personally. Meanwhile an organization was founded in Jamaica, Queens County, City of New York, under Ku Klux Klan sponsorship.

The Klan had protested police action at their parade, seeking aid from Governor Smith against the police in retaliation for the pro-Catholic, anti-Protestant actions of the latter. Governor Smith answered politely that the Governor's office had no control over the city's police. A more proper course of redress would be either to petition the office of Mayor Walker or to go to court. The Governor made no mention of his own religion (Roman Catholic) in his response to the Klan petition.

The Klan's Ryan Special fund, "Protestants Against Roman Catholic Police" (P.O. Box 57, Jamaica, NY), collected a total of $13.86, several semi-literate letters of support, a roughly equal number of threatening notes, and a rusty Hughes & Fairbanks campaign button attached to an illegibly scribbled card, before being closed out as more trouble than it was worth. Imperial Wizard Hiram Evans said that the entire incident was further evidence of the rottenness that had spread through America and needed to be cleaned out like decayed matter in a once-healthy tooth.

Howard Lovecraft stayed close to home during the early weeks of June, studying daily newspapers and reading the books that he had obtained earlier from George Sylvester Viereck. To these he added a copy of Hitler's *Mein Kampf,* and wrote to his aunts in Providence to have them send his copy of Chamberlain's *Foundations of the Nineteenth Century.* He had read the book years before, and was familiar with Chamberlain's theories (with which he agreed) concerning the contribution of the white race, and particularly the light-haired, blue-eyed Nordic stock, to the furtherment of world order, and the importance of preserving the purity of that race and its position of dominance over lesser breeds. But George Pagnanelli's emphasis on the book had made Howard wish to read it again. Something about Pagnanelli kept bothering Howard. He spoke to Sonia about the young journalist, trying to pin down the cause of his unease. Something just didn't ring true about the man. His appearance was that of a typical Mediterranean; he claimed to be Italian, which matched up all right, but his accent was not Italian. And he belonged to *so many* patriotic organizations. Maybe he was, simply, a "joiner." Howard had encountered plenty of those in the ranks of the National Amateur Press Association and its sometime rival, sometime collegial, organization, the United Amateur Press Association.

There were those who would join such organizations and pursue their goals with energy and dedication—and other who seemed interested only in obtaining certificates, credentials, the right to claim membership. Maybe Pagnanelli was a man who simply got a thrill of sorts from being a Christian Mobilizer, American Nationalist, Crusader for America, Yankee Freeman and so on.

No. Howard shook his head. No. He just wasn't *convinced.* He'd been at the point of calling Pagnanelli on just that issue when the radio broadcast had sent him scurrying for Brooklyn, frightened that Sonia had become involved in the Klein struggle in Jamaica. He would have to sound out Pagnanelli again the next time they met.

Howard noted a newspaper item involving the steamship *Transylvania.* Her captain, David Bone, reported sighting a mystery plane headed east over the mid-

Atlantic. Lindbergh had long since completed his flight and was being lionized in Europe—hobnobbing, in fact, with the British royal family of George V, Queen Mary, and young David the Prince of Wales, once the formality of the award of the Air Cross was out of the way—and Byrd's and Chamberlain's planes were still sitting on the ground in Long Island, awaiting the proper combination of favorable weather conditions, good mechanical order, and proper psychological auguries. What, then, was the identity of the plane Captain Bone had seen?

Howard clipped the news story, marked a question mark in the narrow margin, and slipped the sheet of paper into a file folder marked *Aviation*.

He had by now given up trying to keep all the information he gathered in his head; despite an exceptional memory he found it more practical to keep things in paper form so he could file and sort them into significant patterns.

He purchased a set of manila folders (first phoning the Jackson Press for an advance against the cost) and set up files for such subjects as *Monarchist Restorations, Bolshevism, China, Christian Front (Coughlin-Curran), National Socialism, Ku Klux Klan, Fascism*.

Now he could spend a day pleasantly, any time he felt disinclined to leave the apartment, with a stack of newspapers, a pair of scissors and his files. When he came across an item which bore on several of his topics he jotted down cross-reference notes for all the folders save the one in which he placed the actual clipping. Thus the news that Chiang Kai-shek and Feng Yu-hsiang had formed an alliance against Chang Tso-lin was noted in the *Bolshevism* and *Restorations* files; the clipping itself went into *China*.

On Saturday, June 4, Clarence Chamberlin finally piloted his Bellanca *Columbia* into the air above Long Island and headed eastward for Europe. The quarrel between the airplane's sponsor, Charles Levine, and Chamberlin's navigator Lloyd Bertrand had not been settled; Bertrand had finally quit (or been fired) and Levine personally took over his job.

Chamberlin and Levine had refused to announce their objective. The Orteig prize had already been claimed by Lindbergh so there was little point in the *Columbia's* heading for Paris. Speculation arose as to whether the Bellanca would fly to London, Rome, Berlin. . .or even Warsaw or Moscow. The latter cities were discounted on grounds of fuel limitations, but once the *Columbia* was airborne the puzzle of her goal became the major topic of discussion.

Howard filed the *Columbia* item under *Aviation*. He added a minor story datelined Berlin. A Dr. Engelbert Zaschka had built a strange kind of aircraft with a sort of giant overhead fan or propeller instead of wings. Borrowing ideas from Juan de la Cierva's auto-gyroes and George de Bothezat's even earlier experiments with models lifted by powered rotors, Zaschka created a machine called a helicopter. It worked.

Colonel James Churchward's book *The Lost Continent of Mu: The Motherland of Man* was published by Rudge and reviewed in the New York *Times*. Howard read the review and was tempted to try to purchase the book with Jackson Press money, but decided that it would be stretching a point. Churchward's notions dovetailed oddly with his own imaginary city of R'lyeh that Howard had written about In his story "The Call of Cthulhu." What a trial he'd had with Pharnabus over *that* one! At last Farnie had accepted the manuscript, although he'd never actually used it in *Weird Tales*. That was an occasion for which Howard could only wait impatiently as the magazine appeared, month after month, with readers in the Eyrie crying out for material by Howard, and with Editor Wright sitting on unpublished manuscripts and filling his pages instead with material by (it seemed) just about anyone who had ever set words on paper *except* H. P. Lovecraft.

He ground his teeth, threw down the newspaper and invited Sonia to join him in an expedition to Jahn's ice cream parlor. A multi-flavored and multi-syruped concoction at Jahn's never failed to raise Howard's spirits, and while the treat threatened his always slim purse, Sonia managed on most occasions to pick up the cost of the sweets. "Oh, don't bother, Howard dear, I happen to have the exact amount handy." Or, "All of these coins are pulling my handbag out of shape, Howard, please let me get rid of them."

Following the exploits of Chamberlin and Levine was like reading a serial story in a magazine. The suspense of their destination was broken when they landed in Germany; a little town called Eisleben was their first point of contact, and having refueled there they set off once more for Berlin (where American Ambassador Schurman waited at Tempelhof) only to stop again, at Kottbus, to replace a damaged propeller.

Their landing made them heroes throughout Germany where Lindbergh's snub had been bitterly received. In Berlin the fliers were presented to President von Hindenberg, Premier Marx, Papal Nuncio Pacelli. From the Presidential Palace they were paraded to the City Hall, greeted by Burgomeister Boess and invited to sign the Sacred Golden Book of the city.

Even before leaving Germany Levine announced his plan to establish a $2 million airline between Europe and America, Chamberlin to serve as director of operations.

Other aviation enthusiasts announced more and more ambitious projects; the aviation craze promised to grow even greater than that for radio.

Guiseppe Bellanca, who had built the *Columbia* for Levine, set out to build a fleet of trimotors for New York-Chicago and New York-Miami travelers.

Dornier Metallbauten GmBh of Friedrichshafen began work on a 50-ton flying boat that would carry 100 passengers on the Atlantic run.

The US Army announced that a daring team would attempt to fly from Oakland, California, to the Territory of Hawaii.

The Army also announced that a series of tests would commence for the selection of a new bombardment craft. Glenn H. Curtiss, Glenn L. Martin, and Anthony Fokker had all submitted plans and built prototypes of new bombers. All had advanced features; Curtiss's *Condor*, for instance, a biplane of 90-foot wingspread powered by two engines of 600 horsepower each, could carry a crew of six, three machine-gun nests each fitted with twin guns, and an 8500 pound useful load for 700 miles at 105 miles per hour.

Howard duly clipped the story, filed it in *Aviation*, wondered how far the technology of war could be developed before man blasted himself back to the use of rocks and clubs.

The same file contained a quotation from Hugo Eckener promising to modify his LZ-127 Zeppelin to use gas as a fuel and then fly around the world in 300 hours. Now *that*, Howard thought, would be an experience to be envied. His enjoyment of the short seaplane flight at Marblehead had been so great—think of sailing majestically in a great Zeppelin, far above the mundane world, passing through clouds, droning onward both day and night for nearly two weeks, stopping to visit and sight-see in the famous and the exotic capitals of the world!

He sighed and filed the clipping.

Lindbergh was due back in the United States—returning safely on board a cruiser dispatched by President Coolidge, Howard noted!—and radio station WOR would send Swanee Taylor aloft to broadcast Lindbergh's triumph from the air.

Howard closed his *Aviation* folder and opened the one marked Ku *Klux Klan*. It was a weekday evening, the meal had been completed and Howard was seated comfortably in his makeshift office working on his compilations while Sonia completed her postprandial duties in the kitchen.

He felt her hand placed warmly on his shoulder as he carefully scissored the story from the *Times*, then wrote carefully in the margin, *Discuss with Evans—or Two-gun Bob. . .*

Sonia smiled. "Is that an interesting story, Howard? I hardly get to look at newspapers these days. The radio broadcasts are a lifesaver for me, but I think I must miss most of the details you see."

Howard looked from the clipping to his wife. "It's an amusing little incident from the South. Seems that—" he consulted the paper for details "—two Negroes were accused of shooting a white man named Clarence Nichols. The niggers were brothers named Fox. They were arrested and imprisoned but the sheriff, a fellow named Permenter, feared for their safety and set out to take them to a larger city with a more secure jailhouse."

Sonia pulled up a lightly padded chair and sat, listening to Howard's paraphrase of the news story.

"A party of 1000 citizens, however, felt that justice must not be delayed, and near the village of Louiseville, seized the prisoners and tied them to a telephone pole, where they were drenched with gasoline and immolated." Howard closed his Ku *Klux Klan* folder. He shook his head disapprovingly. "However little one may sympathize with the brothers Fox, the incident smacks dangerously of anarchism. One cannot approve of that!"

CHAPTER TWENTY-TWO:

HIS NAME ON THE CONTENTS PAGE

WHEN HOWARD grew restless with his researches he diagnosed the problem, accurately, as cabin fever, and phoned friends to arrange an outing in the city. At Howard's instigation he and Vincent Starrett descended on Frank Belknap Long when the New York *Times* predicted, late in June, the appearance of the Pons-Winnecke comet. The object had been absent from the skies since 1921, and on its return, the newspaper's resident expert on astronomy predicted, it would brighten the northeastern quadrant of the sky with a glow rivaling that of a full moon.

His spirits bounding at the prospect of a night's sky-watch, Howard varied his route from Parkside Avenue to West End Avenue with a detour on the Brooklyn City Rail Road; New York could, if approached selectively, be a delightful place after all. This was a feeling that Howard had experienced before, when he moved to Brooklyn for the first time in 1924. Only gradually had the noise and dirt, the crowding and above all the noisome and oily immigrant mongrels who teemed in the city's streets, turned it from the wonderland it had first seemed, to the horror-chamber depicted in Howard's stories "The Horror at Red Hook" and "He."

Now he watched the borough's old houses and tree-lined streets receding from the windows of the Brooklyn Rail Road's cars and slumped happily into his seat.

In Manhattan he switched to a surface car, pausing at the site of a deep excavation where the new Eighth Avenue subway would someday run. He watched the progress of the work for a while, then stopped to examine the new arrivals at the nearest newspaper and magazine kiosk. The July *Weird Tales* had made its appearance, and Howard purchased a copy and turned to the contents page to see if Wright had finally got around to using any of the material of Howard's that he was holding. Of course there was no chance that the "Fungi from Yuggoth" would be in the magazine yet, but Wright also had his short stories "Pickman's Model" and "The Call of Cthulhu."

Disappointed at not finding his name on the contents page, Howard turned to the Eyrie to see if he had at least received his monthly allotment of ego gratification from some reader; instead, there were two!

A fellow named Ralph Raeburn Phillips wrote, "Your contributors are splendid. I especially like Greye La Spina and H. P. Lovecraft." Howard liked Greye La Spina's stories himself, and was pleased at the comparison.

But the great treat came from one Jack Snow in Dayton, Ohio. "I am taking this opportunity to thank you for the March issue of *Weird Tales* which contained Lovecraft's 'The White Ship.' It was a beautiful, exquisite little story, as remotely unreal and Lovecraftean in character as his terror-striking masterpiece 'The Outsider.' I wonder how many of your readers truly appreciate beauty of this sort. Certainly your publishing material like this raises the magazine many points as an artistic and worthwhile journal."

Howard whooped with delight and bounded into the air, then pulled down the brim of his fedora and crimsoned with embarrassment as strangers turned at his unusual display. Still. . .still, he grinned to himself as he strode toward the car stop, he *was* appreciated, his work was not worthless, his efforts were not all in vain!

He wondered if this fellow Snow realized what old material he was praising. Although *Weird Tales* had run both stories within the past year, "The White Ship" had been penned originally in 1919, when Howard was still in what he himself often called his Dunsanian period. And "The Outsider" dated from 1921, a transitional year for Howard, when he was moving away from the gossamer Dunsanian fantasies into the moodier horror vein, more influenced by Poe than Dunsany but most of all emerging with his own style and sense of atmosphere.

He arrived at the Long apartment and waved the red-bordered magazine before the bespectacled eyes of his protégé. Long backed away and returned waving his own copy of *Weird Tales*, as happy for his older friend as Howard was for himself at the praise his stories had received.

"You'll have a book of your tales yet, Howard!" he grinned. "Sometimes appreciation comes quickly and sometimes it takes a long time, but the deserving artist emerges eventually into his own!"

"Why, Belknapius," Howard laughed, "you sound like old Grandpa Theobald himself, giving encouragement to some gloomy fledgling all a-snivel in the Slough of Despond at the receipt of his first rejection notice!"

"Do I? Do I? Well, I suppose I've received my pep-talks from Grandpa himself, I'm qualified to deliver the same sentiments back to their originator. But in any case, may I render my most profound congratulations." He paused and examined his wrist watch. "If the good Mr. Starrett will only make his appearance, we shall set to at the groaning board of Long's literary library and first-class eating emporium."

With Starrett's arrival the three authors made their way to the dinner table. The senior Longs were absent for the evening, and Belknap offered pot-luck to his guests, a meal comprising chiefly chopped steak and fried potatoes. Howard Lovecraft coated his food thickly with ketchup and set to happily. Between mouthfuls he interrogated Starrett as to the state of *Seaports in the Moon*. "Your Poe data fit beautifully, Howard." Starrett gazed balefully at a glass of water before sipping. "I couldn't fit in *all* the facts you provided, of course, but they gave me plenty of information to pick around in. I think the confrontation between poor Edgar and Legrand is one of the best scenes in the book, now. Funny and poignant at the same time. A touch I'd striven for throughout the novel. I don't know how many scenes quite achieve that touch, but this one does. I call it 'An Author and his Character.' A little *double entendre* right there, eh? The scene is designed to expose Poe's inner nature as well as show off his creation."

Howard said that sounded good. And how was the general condition of the book?

Vincent said it was virtually complete. The Poe sequence was one of the last chapters; he was wrapping up his narration now, tying all of the loose threads together and bringing the main theme to its climax.

"Do you think it's really vital to tie all the loose threads?" Belknap Long inquired. "I mean to say, real life seems often to be made of nothing *but* loose threads. If fiction is to be representative of reality, should it not leave at least a few threads hanging loose at the end of a narration? To represent those unresolved, ah, vectors in the everyday life of actual men and women?"

Howard Lovecraft put down his knife and fork with a small but distinct clatter that drew the attention of Starrett and Long to himself.

"Fiction is not a mere representation of reality," he asserted. "If it were, it would comprise not creation but mere journalism. In the creation of art, one seeks the portrayal of graceful and symmetrical patterns, significant concatenations of events and development of characters, so as to gratify the aesthetic sensitivity at the same time that the emotional responses of the reader, viewer, or auditor are affected.

"As well create a musical composition fraught with unresolved themes, paint a canvas showing only half the face of its subject, or pen a 'sonnet' of thirteen lines, as produce a fictional narrative in which thematic elements remain dangling at the end of one's manuscript like soiled and tattered threads at the bottom of a carelessly hemmed garment."

Howard picked up his knife and fork and resumed eating his chopped steak, pausing to turn each load of beef in a deep pond of crimson at the edge of his plate.

"Well, that's that!" Starrett conceded. "I suppose that some of our more advanced authors will have a different opinion. My fellow Chicagoan John Dos Passos, for instance, seems to be trying to hybridize fiction and journalism, exactly as you suggest, Howard. Have you looked at his novel *Manhattan Transfer*? Very interesting book. He seems almost to clip little bits from various sources, street observations, news items and so on, and create of them a mosaic. Very, very intriguing. Then there was that play of his last year, *The Moon is a Gong*, did you see it? No, well, here's one for you. You know the original name of that work? He meant to call it *The Garbage Man*. What do you think of that? Hah!

"I don't know him very well, of course, but last time our paths happened to cross out in Illinois he mentioned that he was pushing on toward some sort of massive trilogy of novels that represented years of effort. He's a supreme naturalist—what you call a mere journalist, okay."

"You were in Chicago recently?" Long inquired. Starrett reiterated the story of his interview with Alphonse Capone and his visit to Charles Coughlin in Detroit. "Did you ever follow up on that, by the way?" he asked Howard.

Lovecraft shook his head. "Not exactly, although it's all part of a book I'm working on. I suppose I'm doing something like your friend Mr. Dos Passos. Picking up clippings and observations and sorting them out and putting them together. But I hope, before I am finished, to make a significant pattern of them. There are as many threads in a grand tapestry as there are in the worst of mares' nests, Vincentius. it is the artist's talent and applications that will make those threads into a tapestry as great as those designed by Rubens or Raphael."

After dinner they packed Belknapius' portable telescope into the elevator and rode to the roof of the building. While Belknap set up the instrument Howard Lovecraft lectured to him and to Starrett on the history of the Pons-Winnecke Comet and the general development of astronomical knowledge.

The great comet was already visible in the northeast, and Long pointed the barrel of the telescope in that direction, over the rooftops of Harlem and the Bronx. Finally adjusting the eyepiece he invited the others to view the glowing object. Howard took a quick sighting, then yielded his place to Starrett, continuing his monolog as he directed the Chicagoan's attention first to the comet's semi-solid head ("It is probably made up of millions of bits of metal and rock ranging in size from the smallest of pebbles to boulders of considerable massiveness,") and then to the glowing tail ("A streamer of finely distributed gases millions of miles in length, pressed away from the sun by the very pressure of light particles so that the tail precedes the head during the comet's recession from Sol only to swing about and follow the head when the comet curves at its apogee and begins its long and lonely return journey to the brighter regions of space").

When Starrett had gazed through the telescope for a while he pulled his eye away from it and straightened up. "Unh! Life after forty, Howard, is no bargain! Day by day you seem the same man, but the bones are drying and the joints grow stiff. Oh, my poor back! One little while crouching over that telescope is as much strain on the sacroiliac as a whole day leaning over a typewriter!"

He walked in a circle, swinging his arms to limber himself while Frank Long fixed his own eye to the optical instrument.

"I mean to ask you, though," Starrett resumed, addressing Howard Lovecraft, "how you come to know so much about comets. Or are you secretly a visitor from the void yourself? You didn't ride in on the back of one of those things, did you?"

Howard laughed at the notion. "No," he said seriously, "I've never been to the realms beyond this little planet of ours, except at times in dreams. I sometimes wonder if those dreams are not the true reality and this mundane existence the illusion. You know, 'Am I a man dreaming that I am a butterfly, or a butterfly dreaming that I am a man?' " he quoted.

"A man, I assure you. And not dreaming at all." Starrett rapped on the cement-topped wall of bricks that surrounded the roof at waist height.

Howard heaved a deep sigh. "In that case, I suppose that I learned what bits of astronomical lore I have got in the halcyon days of my Rhode Island boyhood. I had been a student of mythology as a small child, and through a perusal of the Greek legends of the zodiacal figures developed an interest in the heavenly objects themselves. I even put out a little hand-written scientific paper in my childhood. *The Rhode Island Journal of Astronomy*, I called it, with all due seriousness.

"Yes," he went on, "in childhood I had planned to make my career in that field. Through elementary and secondary school I rather assumed that I would one day attend Brown University in Providence. My home for some years was next door to the library on College Avenue in that city! I intended to concentrate upon the study of the heavens, and become in time a professor of astronomy. It seemed to me that an academic career is permissible to a gentleman, where one of trade is of course foreclosed."

He walked to the waist-high wall and stood, hands closed on the rough, gray edge of the cement.

"But during my senior year at the Hope Street High School, my health underwent so severe a deterioration that I was forced to withdraw from enrollment. I was a semi- invalid for several years thereafter. In time I recovered, of course, but by then my contemporaries had long since obtained their diplomas, gone on to whatever higher education they could assimilate and afford—and begun to make their various ways in the world.

"I did contemplate the possibility of returning to Hope Street for the brief period requisite to obtain my own credentials needful to gain admission to Brown, but it all seemed quite fruitless by that time. The moment had passed, you see, Vincentius. The turning of the road had been missed, and there was no retreating to an earlier year in my life. More's the pity, eh?

"Say, Belknapius, you've had a long time at the eyepiece. What prospect for Grandpa to get another peep at our friend Pons-Winnecke?"

~ ~ ~ ~ ~

Starrett left after the sky-watching session, to bunk in at Laing's apartment and return to Beechhurst the following day. He carried with him a plea from Howard Lovecraft to Laing, to try and press T. O'Conor Sloane, the editor at *Amazing Stories*, and/or his boss Hugo Gernsback the publisher, for Howard's money due him for "The Colour out of Space."

Howard was surprised to be awakened before noon the following day by a telephone call; he'd stayed over at Long's and wondered who would call him there. Even more to Howard's surprise, the caller was Dr. Sloan himself. He expressed his pleasure once more at the story Howard had sent to the magazine, and urged Howard to write more tales for *Amazing*.

To this Howard responded by asking when Mr. Gernsback intended to pay for the story he already had.

"I can tell you definitely now, that 'The Colour out of Space' will be in our September number," the aged Sloan replied. "Mr. Paul, our chief illustrator, has created a most striking design for use with your story. Unfortunately we were unable to schedule a cover design to accompany your contribution, but by a curious happenstance Mr. Paul's cover design, although associated with another tale than your own, "The Malignant Flower,' is thematically suggestive of 'The Colour out of Space' as well."

"Perhaps I failed to make myself clear, Dr. Sloan. I meant to inquire, not when you plan to publish my story but when you plan to *pay* for it." Howard clenched his teeth waiting for Sloan's reply.

There was a momentary silence, then, "I have sent a purchase voucher on to the accounting department, sir. It was my impression that your check had been dispatched. If it has not, I shall inquire in your behalf."

Howard sighed and thanked the old man and ended the call. With Belknap Long he boarded a downtown car and debarked near the new subway construction site at 45th Street.

"Quite a lot of excitement for a bit of routine construction, Howard." Long pointed ahead of them.

Roughly-dressed workers were milling about, pointing and voicing exclamations, calling for their superintendents and signaling to the operators of heavy machinery to pull back from an excavated area. A blue-uniformed policeman was working his shining bay through a growing crowd *of* onlookers, trying to reach the point of excitement.

Howard and Belknap Long followed in the mounted officer's wake to the edge of the excavation. Howard gave an exclamation of surprise and Long gasped, "Look at that! There are more of them, too!"

The workmen, turning away the ground with shovels and pickaxes where the heavier machines had gouged off the bulk of earth, had uncovered a corner of a wooden case, then another and another. Even as the two writers stood with the other curious onlookers the workmen cleared away the dirt from the lids of the boxes. Based on their size and configuration Howard surmised that they were coffins. Long peered around his taller friend and quickly agreed.

The mounted policeman ordered the superintendent of the construction project to have his men cease work in the area of the boxes while both a higher officer and a police ambulance were summoned.

Taking his older friend by the elbow, Belknap Long pushed his way to the police officer and announced, "I'm Doctor Long and this gentleman is my assistant. I propose that we take charge here until the coroner's ambulance arrives."

The policeman assented eagerly and moved away to clear the excavated area of workers and onlookers.

Howard turned to Long amazed and said, "What kind of story is that? What are you trying to do?"

Long covered a chuckle with one hand and said, "Well, I'm Doctor Long's son, anyway. We won't do anything; I should certainly not open those boxes in any case. But what a situation to build a story from! Come, let's examine the boxes."

Now it was Howard's turn to suppress his laughter at the uncharacteristic bravado of his friend. "Marvelous, Belknapius! The world may never learn of this exploit, but we shall remember it forever. Come."

He advanced to the exposed wooden lid of the box closest to them. There were eight in the row, and Howard knelt beside the first, heedless of the condition of his neatly-pressed trousers. The lids of the coffins were of plain wood, roughly hewn and roughly fitted to the boxes themselves. "Do you think these things were built by George Birch?" Howard heard Belknap ask.

He was barely able to suppress a guffaw at that. "Looks like it, does it not?" he replied. "If anything, this is a more macabre sight—and site—than my own setting for 'In the Vault.' So art falls short of reality still again, Belknap! Yes, if George Birch built these coffins, I suppose we should find Matt Fenner footless inside, waiting his chance to gain revenge. As it is. . ."

He ran his fingers over the crude wooden lid. It was partly rotted away with age and with the effects of the damp soil in which it had lain. "I would estimate that these boxes have lain here for a century or more. What stories could they tell, were they able? Whose remains lie within? In all probability this is the burying ground of some local farmer, where generations of bucolic bumpkins were laid peacefully to rest at the ends of their natural terms.

"But perhaps the story is far more lurid than that!" He climbed to his feet, brushed the clinging dirt from his knees as best he could and then wiped clean his hands with a handkerchief. "My, my," he muttered, "Sonia will certainly scold me for this little escapade. Well, all in the name of research, I suppose." The shorter Belknap looked up at Howard Lovecraft. "You think the story of these coffins is a lurid one?"

Howard shook his head. " 'Tis all a matter for conjecture, grandchild. Unless the coroner opens the boxes and finds evidence within. A skull with its parietal bone crushed in or with *numerous tiny penetrations* of the frontal structure, eh?" He rubbed his hands together, perhaps to clear of them of any residual earth or perhaps to mock the gesture of a melodramatic fiend.

"Or perhaps a revenant with an antique rusted blade still between its ribs," Long provided.

An older and more businesslike voice asked, "Dr. Long?" Belknap turned and looked into the gray-mustached face of a well-dressed, middle-aged man. "Yes, sir," the youth responded.

"Well, you're quite a young man to have your degree, doctor. I'm Dr. Davis of the coroner's office. Have you commenced an examination of the cadavers?"

Frank grinned as best he could and said, "No, we have not opened the boxes or anything. I just thought that there should be medical supervision until you could be summoned. My assistant and I haven't touched anything. Well, I'll be very happy to turn this over to you and leave you in complete charge here, doctor.

"Well, good-bye."

He reached and took the older man's hand, shook it once, dropped it and turned to Howard Lovecraft. "Come along. We have an appointment." He scrambled up the side of the excavation and onto the street, Howard close behind.

As soon as they reached the rear of the crowd they collapsed in mutual laughter. After a few minutes they strolled eastward.

"That was marvelous, Belknapius." Howard patted Long on the shoulder, grinning. "You youngsters and your never-ending pranks! Well, I shan't soon forget this one!"

"But, Howard—we never did find out anything about those coffins."

Howard shook his head. "I'm sure it will be in tomorrow's press, and I'm quite sure that the verdict will be that they've been there a long while, and quite innocently.

"But if anything does develop of an unconventional nature, we shall have been in on it from the start. Eh, grandson?" Howard halted.

"Well, what are your plans now?" Long asked him.

"I'm for Brooklyn, a clean set of clothing and a warm dinner. I thank you for an excellent dinner and a most enjoyable jape. Also, for a good look at the Pons-Winnecke last night. Who knows what mysterious realms *that* caller has been visiting, eh? Well, I'm off!"

CHAPTER TWENTY-THREE:

ONCE THE KIKES INFILTRATE

SONIA SET the pot of beef stew with barley on the rear burner of the gas range and set the flame for a low-simmer, then returned to the parlor and switched on the radiola console. WEAF was broadcasting some melodious music and she turned the volume control to a pleasant, unobtrusive level.

She returned to the couch where she had spread the newspapers—the Brooklyn *Daily Times*, the New York *Post* (which she had bought because she knew that Howard admired its dignified appearance and restrained literary style as well as its conservative political attitudes), and the *Daily Graphic* which she found hugely amusing in its own earthy vulgarity even if a poor source of information.

The letter from her daughter Florence, the child of her previous marriage to Stanley Greene, she placed between the embroidered cushion and the armrest of the couch, leaving the corner with its bright European stamp exposed as a kind of marker. The new modern clock in its polished aluminum case ticked away on the mantelpiece. It was one of Sonia's rare indulgences in advanced fashion, and it was one of Howard's indulgences, she knew, not to condemn her for it, for all that Sonia knew he would really prefer an old-fashioned chain-driven timepiece, if not an hour-glass.

The long, June twilight was barely darkening when she heard Howard's key grate in the lock of the front door. He eased the apartment door shut behind him, dropped his fedora on the old mahogany chiffonier that stood in the foyer, and entered the parlor. Sonia stood up and when Howard joined her at the couch she leaned over to give him a welcoming embrace.

"You had a good time, Howard dear? The comet was not a disappointment? It must have been good viewing, you were gone overnight and all of today. How is little Belknap? And your friend from Chicago, Mr. Starrett?"

Howard described the appearance and explained the structure and orbit of the Pons-Winnecke Comet and narrated the history of Vincent Starrett's projected book for George Doran. "Vincentius claims that the novel is very near completion, and his general attitude toward it seems to be one of satisfaction. He is concerned, however, about a rumored sale or merger of Doran's publishing house with one whose management might prove less receptive to the book."

With a shake of his head Howard went on. "I assume that Doran is a gentleman; at least, Vincentius so depicts him to me. This being the case, he would surely be bound by honor to include in any arrangement of sale or merger, the provision that obligations undertaken by the present management be honored by their successors.

"Not that publishers are universally of such an elevated breed."

"You mean Gernsback," Sonia suggested.

"I most emphatically do! I sent a plea for payment on 'The Colour out of Space' via Vincentius' friend Laing, and in return received a telephoned communication from Gernsback's minion Dr. Sloan. He was most gracious and appreciative of my work until I forced myself to dun him for payment—a most distasteful act, Sonia; the driving of a gentleman to such necessity should itself be a whipping offense!—whereupon he became mysterious, distracted and remote, and indicated that he would make enquiry of the accounts department in my behalf.

"In my behalf! As if I were a mendicant rather than a gentleman requesting the fulfillment of a clear obligation!"

Sonia stroked his hand, and after a momentary wince he left it on the couch between them and permitted her to continue. "My poor Howard! My poor, poor dear Howard! Did that spoil your whole outing? I hope it didn't."

"It got today off to a very ill start, I'll own to that." Sonia saw Howard, even as he spoke, draw his eyes away from hers to as to scan the newspapers laid out before the couch. "But young Master Long accompanied me part way home, and a most fascinating incident occurred *en route*. I wonder if any report of it appears in the newspapers." He looked over the pages to which Sonia had opened the dailies, commented, "Hmph, nothing but travel notes," picked up each newspaper in turn for a cursory examination, then laid them back, opened as he had found them. "I don't suppose there was time as yet; there shall probably be something in them tomorrow."

He narrated the incident at the construction site, finishing with a comment that, "There will presumably be a mysterious 'Short Dr. Long and his somewhat longer assistant,' in the coroner's report, and dire speculations as to the fate and true identity of the enigmatic medico for years to come."

Sonia laughed appreciatively at the narration, then Howard leaned past her to retrieve Florence's letter from the end of the couch. "What's this? What's this?" he asked.

Sonia said, a letter from Florence. She urged Howard to read it and he carefully fitted his wire-armed, rimless spectacles onto his nose before commencing to read. After a few moments he handed the letter back to Sonia. "I'm afraid that her penmanship utterly defeats my fiercest efforts. Do you think you could read it to me?"

Sonia said that the handwriting was a formidable obstacle for her as well, but in view of her longer experience with Florence's script she would get through it.

"Dear Mother," Sonia began, "You shall have to forgive me for not writing sooner or oftener or at greater length, but Paris is a whole new world for me, and I find myself totally involved in it. I've done some dispatches for Hearst, of course—I hope you've seen them in the *American*—but the real wonder of Paris isn't *news* in the sense that newspapers mean news.

"It's the spirit of the place. It's the air when you wake up in the morning and throw open your windows and look out to see this whole city with its ancient buildings and crooked streets glowing in the sunlight like a gold and brown canvas by some Dutch painter, with mist rising from the Seine and a thousand and one smells on the slightest breeze, most of which are *almost* the same as you'd smell at home on the morning air, but they're all just a *little* different in the most subtle way.

"My little walk-up isn't exactly what you'd call luxurious, and I would be happier with better sanitary facilities than the *pension* offers (or most of Paris for that matter—the French seem to care distressingly little about such things; for men at least there are the *pissoirs* in the streets, but what's a girl to do?)

"You wrote and told me that Howard had asked about the political and cultural climate in France these days. Please tell him for me that there is very little political climate here at all—or maybe, as one of my friends says (a Ukrainian S.D. who fled Moscow when the November revolution prorogued the constitutional convention) *everything* is politics and I don't notice it because I'm immersed like a fish in water.

"The *official* politics here is in the hands of a bunch of senile degenerates to whom *nobody* pays any mind; the general feeling is that the Republic won't last another ten years. Whether the country then becomes a Fascist state like Italy or a Red one, is anybody's guess.

"In the meanwhile, everyone laughs at the Russian Whites. They preen and pretend that they are going back and overthrow the Bolsheviks, and everyone knows that this is an empty charade. As typical of these fools, their leader is some clowning old fraud who claims to be a Romanoff cousin and calls himself the Grand Duke Nicholas Nicholaevitch. A penniless fraud who dresses up in old Russian Imperial uniforms and sponges off French plutocrats who use him as entertainment at their *grande bals* and laugh behind his back. Each think they are fooling and exploiting the other!

"I met a lovely young Frenchman at Sylvia Beach's book store recently, who is more interested than most of the people I know here. His name is Louis-Ferdinand Destouches, and he says that the course of history lies inevitably in a *Bolshevist* order. He is going to go to Russia himself and see what things are really like under the new government there. When he comes back I will find out the truth about Bolshevism.

"In the meanwhile, I do spend a lot of my time at Sylvia's because so many fascinating people congregate there. There's a little photography studio upstairs and the man who runs it (an American) has invited me up a few times to visit. He is a Dadaist photographer, if you can imagine such a thing. Says that he started as a painter but no one would look at his canvases so he switched to photography and seems to be making a living at it. But he says that a few people may have heard of some of his earlier works, and when I told him that you were married to an author, Mother, he opened up a little and told me about his projects. Did you (or rather, ask Howard if *he*. . .) ever hear of a unique *object d'art* (isn't my French getting good?) called 'The Enigma of Isadora Ducasse,' or one called 'Pain Peint.' Very enigmatic!

"I don't know if this letter really tells you all that you wanted to know, Mother, or all that Howard wanted you to find out from me. Somehow America seems so remote and unreal to me here in Paris that even writing this letter is very hard to do. It's like trying to talk to some of the strange and alien beings that Howard writes about in his stories.

"But do stay in touch with me, and I'll try to write to you whenever there seems anything worthwhile to write about, other than the things I do for the *American*.
"With love,
"Florence."

Sonia folded the letter and slipped it back into its envelope, then looked up at Howard.

"She seems to have calmed down a little," Howard commented. "Perhaps she'll get over her flapper ways yet."

Sonia smiled wistfully. "It must be wonderful, to be a young girl living in Paris as a correspondent for an American newspaper. But is this letter useful? Did she give you the information you need for your book? You can have it for your files." She held the envelope toward him and Howard accepted it, crossed to his stack of manila folders and slipped it into the one marked *Bolshevism*.

"She might have gone into more detail, my dear, but I suppose this is better than nothing. Of course there is whatever information appears in the press, and I'm sure that Sylvester Viereck will have a good deal to say when he returns from his little tour of the Continent.

"But Florence does give us a little bit of the atmosphere."

For a moment the sound of a reedy piping broke into the apartment. Howard made an annoyed face and crossed the room to turn up the volume of the radio set. "That damned Syrian again!" he complained. The loudspeaker in the corner of the room drowned out the eastern piping with the sounds of an orchestra playing a three-year-old popular tune, "Baghdad."

"It's a conspiracy!" Howard shrieked, but laughed at himself at the same time that he uttered the words. He walked back to the table before the couch where Sonia sat, and pulled an armchair forward. "Well, I've seldom seen you concentrate to this degree on current events. Was there some particular item in the news that made you wish to read three versions of the report?"

"No. Actually I was looking at the travel pages. Fourth of July is coming, and I thought I'd ask for part of my annual vacation then and we could have a nice little trip. I was just comparing the various travel accommodations that are offered."

"I'm afraid that my *exchequer* is somewhat depleted," Howard said.

Sonia smiled. "I wasn't thinking of a very expensive vacation for us, Howard. Maybe we could go up to New England—"

"That is always a *most* welcome suggestion!"

"Yes. And maybe visit your aunts in Providence."

"Our accommodations would then be provided. *Hmmm.* Well, and had you any other thoughts?"

"Well, you know I make a good salary, Howard. If you could just think of it as *our exchequer.* You are always generous in sharing your earnings. It isn't your fault that publishers are so unreliable, and pay so poorly when they do pay. I'm quite willing to share my earnings with my husband, just as you share yours with your wife."

Howard puffed out his breath. "It is not the same thing. The moneys of a gentleman are his by right, and the support of his dependents is his duty. Whereas the moneys which you obtain in *trade*, Sonia. . ." He spread his hands, half disdainful. "Still, it is an attractive prospect. And if we could afford a side-trip or two. . ."

"I know you enjoyed showing Marblehead and Salem to your friends," Sonia smiled. "And there's always Cape Cod, and I have a soft spot in my heart for Boston, Howard. The city where we first met. I'll never forget it."

"Nor I, Sonia," Howard replied after a moment's pause. "Well, I suppose we'll just take the train as usual."

"I thought it would be more fun to go by steamer. See—" She turned the paper so the advertisements would be right-side-up for Howard. "One means of transport seems about as dear as another. The motor bus would be very convenient, we could board just at the Prince George without having to leave Brooklyn.

"But what I'd really love is the overnight steamer. See, the Fall River Line charges only $5.50 per person, less than the bus! But for a dollar more we can take the Eastern steamer, oh, Howard, let's just splurge and pay the extra fare. Look," she pointed to the advertisement, "we sail from Pier 19 in the early evening, and we have our dinner on board. There is music and dancing, and we get to sail through the Cape Cod Canal, and arrive in Boston the following morning. We could spend all day in Boston and then go on to Providence in the evening and not have to stay over if you'd rather not, in Boston. Wouldn't that be grand?"

Howard held his head in his hands and mulled over the proposal. Certainly it would be a wondrous break to his present spell of residence in New York, his exile from his beloved New England. With Sonia's salary they could afford the trip, and no one need know whose money was paying the expenses. Well, someone would know, did know already. Both Howard and Sonia knew. Yet Sonia didn't mind, and she made a good case for the mutual sharing of resources between husband and wife.

At length he consented to the trip, and proceeded directly to his desk to write to his aunts while Sonia retired to the kitchen to prepare dinner.

The decision made and Howard's letter written, the evening meal became a virtual celebratory feast. Sonia chattered away in her usual outgoing manner; sometimes Howard found this annoying but for the moment her warm enthusiasm made a pleasant background for the meal. Sonia even offered to make their travel reservations and purchase their tickets during her lunch hour at work. Howard questioned the necessity of taking the Eastern Line at $6.50 per passenger when the Fall River Line offered the same transportation for $5.50, but Sonia insisted that the music on the Eastern Line was worth the extra dollar. ("Ah, but then the supposedly free music is not truly free, is it?" Howard countered, but more for the sake of his rhetorical pride than in serious objection.)

For dessert Sonia served ice cream with hot fudge syrup and whipped cream that she prepared while the fudge was heating on the gas range. Howard downed several dishes of the concoction along with cups of sweet coffee, then excused himself and strolled happily around the block to settle his meal while Sonia cleared up the debris of dinner.

~ ~ ~ ~ ~

Howard and Sonia obtained booking for the Eastern Line steamer to Boston leaving Saturday evening, July 2. In lieu of a sailing party they celebrated the prior evening by meeting in Manhattan after Sonia completed her work for the day. Howard visited young Long during the afternoon, laughing again over the incident of the mysterious young doctor and his assistant. The incident had appeared in the newspapers, but no mention had been made of the mysterious "Dr. Long" and Howard and Belknap decided that the coroner's office and the police had been too embarrassed to make a public announcement concerning that particular aspect of the matter.

The coffins *had* turned out to be a hundred years or so in age, and the remains they contained were unexceptional in nature—no crushed occipital bones, no rusted poignards lying between dry ribs, and certainly no feet separated at the ankle and tossed into the box to permit a procrustean accommodation.

Howard Lovecraft, reluctant to end the enjoyable afternoon, invited Long to join himself and Sonia for the evening, and they traveled downtown together to meet her. The three of them dined at Keene's Chop House, their conversation alternating between Howard and Belknap's literary discussions and Sonia's bright anticipation of the coming vacation. The news of the day was an almost laughable anticlimax to the whole Nungesser-Lindbergh-Chamberlin aviation competition. Commander Byrd and his crew had finally got off in their Fokker trimotor *America*, the craft billed as "the first air liner to Europe," and wound up lost, out of fuel, and having to splash into the Atlantic and abandon their aircraft, completing their journey ignominiously by life-raft. The New York press gallantly tried to play the four men up as heroes but they were more nearly a laughing stock.

After dinner Howard and Sonia and Belknap strolled eastward through the deepening dusk, the heavy automobile traffic with its flashing pairs of headlights making a brilliant background of the city streets. Howard had planned a climax for the evening and held his intention back as a surprise for the others.

At the Cameo theatre he halted and suggested that they attend a show. The featured photoplay was a seven-year-old revival, but one that none of the trio had ever attended, the German impressionist drama *Das Kabinett des Dr. Caligari*.

"I refused to see this production in 1920," Howard commented. "The Great War was then too recent an event, and all things German were anathema to me. But an adequate number of years have passed and sentiments and relationships have altered sufficiently that I believe the film may be judged purely upon its artistic merits, and not condemned solely because of the political history of the nation in which it was produced."

Following the film they strolled along Broadway, stopping to peer into shop windows, chatting idly about the picture. After a while Frank Long suggested that they stop for a snack and they entered an Italian restaurant. Sonia ordered coffee; Belknap, a slice of Italian cake; and Howard, a plate of spaghetti with meat balls.

When the food arrived Howard pitched in.

"I didn't care too much for the film," Sonia said. "I thought the cast were excellent, especially the old hypnotist."

"Werner Krauss," Belknap supplied.

"But the whole feeling of the film was so confusing, it was nightmarish."

Around a mouthful of spaghetti, Howard countered, "But that was the entire idea behind the film." He paused and washed down his food with a sip from a heavy cup of tan chinaware. "The atmosphere was very much that of a nightmare. Perhaps those mortals blessed with tranquil slumber might miss the point.

"But I have had very much the kind of experience—in my dreams—that Herr Wiene and Herr Hameister achieved in this photoplay." He was reading the names from the play program he had folded and slipped into his inner pocket at the Cameo.

"You call it confusing, Sonia, but to the haunted dreamer there was a bizarre and familiar reality to that confusion. I would venture that Director Wiene at least, and possibly the others involved in the production, are long experienced in the realm of nightmare. Most impressive were the strange angles assumed by the streets and walls. Did you notice the sets, Sonia, Belknap?"

Frank Long smiled behind his spectacles, fished his cold pipe from a jacket pocket and gazed into its empty bowl abstractedly. After a period of absolute silence he broke his moment of abstraction and slipped the pipe back into his pocket.

"Strange angles, indeed," he said slowly. There was still a look of unusual concentration on his face. "It was as if there were something unnatural, something *wrong* with those angles. As I watched, I half-expected something . . .some. . .I don't know what, to bound from out of those strange angles and attack the somnambulist, or perhaps to join him in seeking victims. It was most strange. It was something that I think will stay with me for a long time."

Howard Lovecraft smiled at the younger man. "I know that look and that feeling, grandson. I think you've got a story coming on."

~ ~ ~ ~ ~

The Richard Himber Orchestra were playing a medley of two-year-old sentimental tunes, most of them from Broadway shows, and the couples were moving slowly around the deck beneath widely strung electric lights. Howard had as usual been reluctant to dance, claiming a general debility and inaptitude for matters physical, but Sonia had coaxed and flattered him until he finally consented, and once engaged in the undemanding romantic dances he had actually admitted that he enjoyed the activity.

"I'll be loving you, always," the male vocalist with the orchestra crooned over the sounds of saxophones and violins, the throbbing of the ship's engines and the lapping of the waters of Buzzard's Bay.

"We'll have Manhattan, the Bronx and Staten Island too," the female vocalist responded as the music segued from melody to melody.

"If you were the only girl in the world, and I were the only boy."

"Remember the night, the night we met."

"Just a cottage small, by a waterfall."

"Moonlight and roses."

And finally, "Show me the way to go home, I'm tired and I want to go to bed." The next line of the song, "I had a little drink about an hour ago and it went right to my head," drew an appreciative round of snickers from the dancers, for hip flasks had been in plentiful evidence through the evening, but neither Sonia nor Howard had been so supplied, and when adjacent couples had offered a neighborly nip now and then, the Lovecrafts had politely declined.

With the ending of the music, couples began drifting off to their staterooms and in quick order the deck was nearly deserted. Howard remained at the portside rail watching for the occasional glimmer of a yacht's running lights and the even more occasional blink of illuminated buildings or flashing automotive headlights from the Connecticut shore not far away.

Sonia stood at Howard's side, her chiffon gown fluttering in the soft breeze. The night was balmy and the sea breeze carried a tang of salt that pleased Sonia's nostrils and seemed at least not to offend Howard's.

The dinner served earlier had been an unexceptional meal, and the Eastern Line steamer was a good deal smaller and far more Spartan in accommodations than Howard had anticipated. He had little standard for comparison; by contrast to Sonia's girlhood recollection of crossing the Atlantic in a steerage crammed with European emigrants seeking a new life in the New World, Howard had been aboard only tiny New England shore vessels—plus the great Hamburg-America liner *Deutschland* where he had gone for the farewell party in honor of Viereck's current European tour.

The air seemed to cool before long, and Sonia gently urged Howard to take her to their room, but he replied that he was eager to see the Cape Cod Canal, and gallantly stripped off his suit jacket and draped it around her shoulders even though he was shortly uncomfortable himself from the chill. To keep his mind off the cold he narrated some of the history of the canal; in typical fashion he had studied it in the public library before making the trip.

"The canal was begun by August Belmont in 1909, not only to shorten the distance between New York and Boston harbors, but to permit shipping to avoid the dangerous waters of Cape Cod Bay. In the first two decades of the present century there were nearly a thousand wrecks in Cape Cod waters, ranging from small pleasure and fishing craft to major shipping.

"Belmont was a good marine engineer but his project ran into financial troubles and under wartime conditions the government undertook to complete the work, accomplishing this in 1918. The only significant Cape Cod town that the canal passes is Bourne, a village some three centuries in age. Once we pass into Cape Cod Bay we shall sail by the historic village of Plymouth, Massachusetts, followed by Brockton and Quincy before entering Boston harbor." The canal itself was a quiet, sea-level passage and Howard was finally convinced to come to bed with Sonia. She had to wake him in the morning, but Howard for once expressed gratitude at the sight of Cape Cod Bay under the early light, a few wisps of fog and mist rising from its surface; the panorama of New England waters, bright July sky and sun, drew expressions of joy from him.

In Boston they spent the day sightseeing, resting on the Common in the afternoon, idly perusing a newspaper that Howard had bought. Sonia was interested in a continuing story out of Brooklyn, which even the Boston *Globe* managed to carry, while Howard was impatient with the report and intrigued more with a dispatch datelined Adelaide, Australia. He had always been fascinated with the ancient desolation of the island continent, he said, and thought that the sere and unpopulated desert of Australia might have as much potential for use in a tale of ancient mysteries as had the pyramids of Egypt or the ice fields of remote Antarctica.

Sonia's story concerned a scandal that had arisen at Kings County Hospital. The first reports had been of the hazing of young interns and resident physicians, but ugly racial overtones had erupted as the story developed.

A group of young Jewish doctors had been made prisoners, doused with water, daubed with shoe polish and otherwise humiliated; they were forced to take their meals in a segregated section of the staff dining room; several had been forced to leave the hospital. Investigation showed that the recent incidents had been only the latest in a series dating back more than a decade.

Spokesmen for the doctors accused of the hazings pointed out that Kings County was the only city hospital with a non-Jewish staff majority.

Mayor Walker demanded more information.

Dr. Mortimer Jones, the superintendent of the hospital, said that he didn't consider the dining facilities segregated; people liked to be with others of their own kind, that was all.

The plaintiffs said that the most severely hazed physician at the hospital had been a Dr. Oldstein, back in 1917. Mayor Walker asked for Oldstein's testimony but it was learned that Oldstein, driven to resign from the staff at Kings County, had enlisted shortly thereafter in the AEF and been killed in action.

Dr. Shields of Kings County found this history in accord with his own theory. "Good Jews," Dr. Shields was quoted as saying, "can be found only in cemeteries."

One George W. Harris, the editor of the New York *Negro News*, joined the dispute with an appeal for better treatment of black doctors. At present, he said, they were permitted to serve only on the staff of Harlem Hospital.

"You see," Howard commented idly, "once the kikes infiltrate, niggers follow close behind."

Sonia laid the paper down with a sigh and turned away to look at a graceful elm tree.

Howard read the Adelaide story. It was regrettably brief and lacking in detail, but the sparse information that it provided was enough to pique his curiosity and gratify his love of the odd. "This is really intriguing, Sonia," he said to her back. "Broadcast station 5-CL in Adelaide produced a drama of an aerial invasion of that region of the continent. By utilizing a broadcast style similar to that of their regular news reports, they hoped to gain a sense of verisimilitude in the dramatization.

"Unfortunately, many of the listeners, especially those who switched on their receiving sets after the drama had begun, mistook it for an actual news broadcast and fled their homes in panic, many citizens seizing firearms with which they hoped to form an impromptu militia brigade and defend themselves against the invaders."

Sonia made no comment.

CHAPTER TWENTY-FOUR:

THE OLD GHOSTLY CARRIAGE

THE VISIT to Providence was a mixed experience for Howard and Sonia. They arrived in the evening and were welcomed to Barnes Street by Lillian Clark and Annie Gamwell. Lillian had returned to an old hobby, the painting of landscapes and still-life compositions, and had several canvases to display. Howard admired them in tones reflecting his usual reserve; Sonia showed greater enthusiasm. This produced small gratification in Aunt Lillian who had clearly hoped to obtain a strong response from her nephew, and who had little interest in the reaction of his wife. Annie Gamwell reported that she was still happily employed in the public library, and that the Phillips household finances (for the sisters still regarded themselves as Phillipses) were in satisfactory if not robust condition.

Sonia and Howard took a cold supper and then at Howard's urging traced the old pathway along Angell Street toward the river. Howard carried a few scraps of cold poultry in case any old friends should be encountered, and reacted ecstatically to the appearance at the usual corner of the reincarnated Nigger-man and his consort Yaller Gal. The cats showed no diminished enthusiasm for joining Howard and Sonia on their exploration, and were suitably grateful for the midnight supper when Howard knelt on the sidewalk to serve it to them. Sonia stood smiling as the cats, ignoring her, circled Howard, tails raised and halfway fluffed, rubbing against his legs and his hands.

After the felines had consumed the last scraps of their treat Howard spoke to Sonia of the old days when both Susie Lovecraft and Grandfather Whipple Phillips had been alive and the family had dwelt comfortably in the big Angell Street house. Before his almost hypnotic whispers and gestures the old ghostly carriage and team, coachman and passengers, rolled again, the coachman's whip cracking in the air above the horses' rumps, the tall iron-tired wheels crunching over graveled ways, the child riding happily between his beautiful mother and the grizzled old sea-captain.

They strolled back to Barnes Street and retired, rising late in the morning of Monday, July 4. There was nearly a quarrel that day, over the question of American independence. To Sonia the whole matter was more nearly ludicrous than serious, yet Howard insisted on taking it with deadly seriousness. "The American war of rebellion was an illegal undertaking, and those responsible were nothing better than traitors to their lawful sovereign."

He was willing to admit that George III had been a tyrant and his minister Lord North a fool. The colonists had been provoked almost beyond toleration. Their protests had gone unheeded and against all warnings the King and his government had pushed the colonists toward violence.

"Still," Howard insisted, "it is the ultimate duty of the citizen to submit to his sovereign. Circumstances may mitigate the crimes of Washington, Jefferson, Franklin and the rest, but they cannot turn guilt to innocence. Washington was a noble officer of his majesty's colonial army before he became a rebel. Franklin was a staunch New Englander and one of the towering figures in the history of human striving after knowledge, but he too sided with the rebels.

"Only think of what a splendid community we should today inhabit, had that rebellion never taken place, or had its leaders been punished and its rank and file chastened by defeat! There would be a community of Old and New England spanning the ocean. Canada and these more southerly colonies would alike pledge their fealty to the Union Jack. Travel would be unhampered and immigration from the mother country encouraged, to the exclusion of those noisome lesser breeds who flock like vermin to the bright shores of this westerly continent. North America would be one, from Hudson's Bay to the Rio Grande, and that one would be united with the mother country yet, learning at the knee of wisdom and supping at the fount of experience. God save the King!"

The explosion of disagreement was avoided by the simple practice on Howard's part of delivering his opinion in a manner little short of a formal orator's, then retiring to his own thoughts, giving little attention to those who disagreed with him.

The family passed the day quietly, Howard nervously departing from their house to take short strolls through the neighborhood on College Hill, Sonia attempting with severely limited success to ingratiate herself with the two aunts by volunteering her assistance with whatever household tasks were conveniently available. The evening meal was taken in a somewhat restrained atmosphere, and as the evening settled over the ancient hill Howard, Sonia and the aunts walked together toward the Narragansett Boat Club at the easternmost tip of Angell Street, to watch the fireworks display over the dark waters of the Seekonk River.

Howard asked Sonia's opinion as to whether he ought to contact the Providence police department regarding the Madeiros killing in which he had become unwillingly involved those long weeks before. Sonia reminded Howard of his last contact with the police, and of the odd visit to the Morelli home on Federal Hill (which Howard had described to Sonia in detail). She suggested that a call to the homicide department would be futile at best, dangerous at worst. Howard grunted his assent.

~ ~ ~ ~ ~

Sonia bought a Boston *Herald* in the Union Station at Providence, and carried it with her as she and Howard boarded the northbound train. The entertainment page confirmed that Hardeen the Mysterious was appearing in Boston, and in fact that his engagement at the Globe Theater was about to end. When the Lovecrafts arrived in Boston they proceeded directly to the theater to leave a message for Theo, and were surprised to find him there.

He had come to check on his equipment, he told them. You could never be too certain of the equipment used in an escape act. Every factor must be controlled. An error, a faulty piece of gear, an unexpected influence in the course of a magical illusion could lead at worst to embarrassment for the performer. But a faulty escape device could cost the showman his life.

"You're familiar with the milk-can escape?" he asked.

"We had the pleasure to witness its accomplishment at the Academy of Music recently," Howard reminded Weiss.

Theo nodded. "Ehrich and I worked that out together, a good many years ago. I recall telling you that we'd tried it with warm water for a time to avoid the chill, but couldn't get the temperature right and decided it was safer to put up with the cold than to risk being boiled alive. But I didn't tell you that one time we had a challenge from a brewery while on tour. It was Ehrich's act at the time, and as a stunt the can was filled with beer instead of water.

"Poor Ehrich! He was a lifetime teetotaler, you know. During those minutes locked in the container, he inadvertently swallowed a good deal of beer, and it made him so dizzy and nauseous he was barely able to make good the escape. Well—" He cut off the topic with a chopping gesture of one immaculately manicured hand.

"Here I've been gabbling on about myself. How are you both? Have you plans for the afternoon? Do you think you could join me for a little surprise?"

"We are actually *en route* to Marblehead," Howard told him. "We are on a modest vacation trip and merely stopped for a brief visit as we were passing through Boston *en route* from Providence, where we had paid our respects on my two aunts at the ancient hill."

Sonia reached past her husband a laid her hand on Theo Weiss's forearm. "Tonight is your last night in Boston, Dash. Do you have to go right back to New York? Why don't you join us at the shore, we could have such fun there!"

Theo said, "What a wonderful idea! My assistants can move all the equipment. I don't have any engagements after tonight." He reached inside his summer-weight jacket and extracted a notebook. "No, I'm free for the rest of the week. Done!"

He shook hands heartily with both Sonia and Howard. "But now, for this afternoon, I'll have a little treat for you. Sonia, I know you're a great lover of photoplays. Howard, unless I miss my guess you're interested in pictures with a macabre or fantastic turn, rather than any bit of fluff."

Howard admitted that that was a fair assessment of his attitude. "Then come," Theo insisted. He took them each by the elbow and propelled them along the sidewalk to his shiny Rickenbacker Super Sport sedan. They climbed into the carefully polished machine and Hardeen kicked the engine to life, drove them through the streets of old Boston until they reached a neighborhood just showing the first evidence of going to seed.

They climbed from the Rickenbacker and Hardeen pointed to a motion picture house halfway up the block from them. The marquee boasted that the theater was showing *The Man from Beyond* starring Harry Houdini.

"You've never seen this, have you?" Theo asked.

Neither of the Lovecrafts had.

"I thought not. Well, you're in for a treat. It's the kind of story you'll enjoy, Howard. It has the touch of the fantastic to it all right. And romance, Sonia. If we'd all known one another back when Harry made *The Man from Beyond* I'm sure he would have asked you to take a part in the story, Howard. He was a great admirer of your writing, and he would have asked you for help with this one. But that was back in '21. Well, come along."

They went into the theater and found that their timing was fortunate. The house was half empty and the matinee showing of the film was about to begin. The auditorium darkened and the screen grew bright. The photoplay was well received by the audience, and Howard and Sonia both enjoyed the film hugely.

As they left the theater Hardeen looked at his watch. "Do you have to reach Marblehead tonight?" he asked. "If not, won't you stay over? We could have dinner together, then you could come to the Globe tonight, and we could go on in the morning. In fact, we've enough of a crew for the show that we have a hotel suite blocked off for us. I'm sure we could accommodate two more, and just drive to Marblehead tomorrow."

Sonia accepted for herself and Howard.

At dinner they discussed *The Man from Beyond*. Howard inquired as to who had written the story for the film, and Theo informed him that Enrich had done that himself. It was an intriguing notion, Howard ventured. A man frozen for a hundred years, reviving to fall in love with a reincarnation of his lost sweetheart.

"Not what one would call startlingly original," Howard went on, "in view of the works of Rider Haggard and others of similar bent. But nicely handled."

"I think the biggest admirer of *The Man from Beyond* was Sir Arthur Conan Doyle. He attended the opening, you know, and afterward he said that the photoplay was a great contribution to culture. Hmm. But I've always suspected that his judgment was ideological rather than artistic."

Sonia asked him to expand on that statement.

Theo smiled. "You know, Sir Arthur never did give up his hope of converting Ehrich to his own beliefs regarding spiritualism. When he saw *The Man from Beyond*, I think he interpreted the theme of reincarnation as a crack in the wall of Ehrich's skepticism. You know, Ehrich never did find any evidence of communication with the beyond that convinced him. Sir Arthur thought that the film meant Harry was swinging around.

"Not that Sir Arthur is exactly a reincarnationist. The theories of reincarnation and spiritualism are a bit out of agreement. But at least the basic ideas are similar."

Howard held a glass of water before him, peering into its contents. "What was Houdini's response to this interpretation?"

Theo shook his head. "He told Sir Arthur that the film was a sheer fantasy. Nothing more nor less. I'm afraid that it was a disappointment to the great Dr. Doyle. Sometimes Harry was more honest than I think he needed to be. At least he could have given Sir Arthur a noncommittal answer. But Ehrich considered it a matter of principle to be entirely truthful about his beliefs. Even about his uncertainties. And he would not mislead Doyle, even by withholding a statement, no less saying something he didn't believe."

~ ~ ~ ~ ~

They breakfasted together at Theo Weiss's hotel, room service providing steaming hot viands on white-linened rolling tables. A fresh linen napkin and a folded morning newspaper were placed beside each dish.

Howard breakfasted on bacon and eggs, rolls and sweetened coffee. He scanned the newspaper and laughed at an item that he summarized aloud. "Poor Byrd! He's so chagrinned at his ignominious standing in the great New York-Paris prize competition that he has now announced his plans to fly to the South Pole, making an expedition of two airplanes filled with dog-teams. Hah!"

"I thought you had an interest in the South Pole," Sonia said to her husband.

"In a way, yes. It is a form of literary legacy. You know the great Poe's unfinished novel, *The Narrative of A. Gordon Pym*. This involves an expedition to the Antarctic —by sailing vessel, of course, Poe having written the book in 1837, when it was first serialized.

"Poe's tale ends on a most enthralling and most enigmatic note. There are great portents. Huge walls inscribed with titanic Egyptian letters, shrouded giants and snow-plumed birds guarding a cryptic cataract of mist. Writers have been fascinated for ninety years by the unfinished story. Jules Verne wrote a sequel to *Pym* attempting to explain Poe's mysteries, but Verne's book was a poor one.

"I should like to assay the task myself some time, yes. I shall not permit Commander Byrd to pre-empt my territory."

Theo Weiss helped himself to a couple of fried eggs, then mentioned a story from his paper. (The hotel management had thoughtfully provided a variety of dailies— the Boston *American* and *Traveler*, the Providence *Journal*, the New York *Morning Sun*.)

"Do you see that Henry Ford has backed down in his dispute with Sapiro and Bernstein?"

Sonia leaned forward eagerly; Howard carefully raised a steaming cup to his lips, watching Theo over its rim.

"This is absolutely amazing!" Weiss took a forkful of egg, chewed and swallowed as he examined the article, washed down his food with a swallow of fresh orange juice. "He says directly that he was wrong, absolutely wrong to attack the Jews. He calls his own charges nothing but exploded fictions. Listen to this, Sonia. 'There are black sheep in every flock, but it is wrong to judge a people by a few individuals.' Can you imagine Henry Ford saying that?"

Sonia shook her head in amazement. "It's hard enough to believe, but I suppose anyone can see the light. So much for the Dearborn *Independent*. Does it tell what the *Independent* says about this? Do they have a quote from the editor of the paper?"

Theo examined the story once again. "Here it is. William J. Cameron, editor of the Dearborn *Independent*. He says, 'I can't believe it.' That's all they have from him. Hah! I wonder if he's going to need a job now. Well, let the poor fellow tighten his belt a few notches, for my money!"

"Anything else?" Sonia asked. "There's something here that you will want for your files, Howard. But is there anything else on Ford? Theo?"

Hardeen, still grinning, said, "Sapiro has accepted Ford's apology and dropped his suit. The *Jewish Tribune* editors, Mosessohn and Bernstein—no comment from Bernstein, Mosessohn is profoundly gratified. Well, and so should we all be! What did you have for Howard? I see he isn't really too concerned with the Ford story."

"No." Sonia smiled at her husband. "There's a quotation here from *Pravda*, Howard. You might want to clip it for your files."

Howard asked what the clipping concerned. "*Pravda* has admitted that the Soviet policy in China has failed. I suppose your friend Count Vonsiatsky will be interested as well. Poor Comrade Borodin will have some explaining to do when he gets back to Moscow.

"And there's quite a fight going on in *Bolshevist* circles over who is to blame. Trotzky, Radek and Zinoniev have put out a statement blaming Stalin, Litvinoff and Rykoff for the failure. Stalin and company haven't replied yet. I don't see how they can all stay in the party, fighting with each other like that."

"I think you are right on that score," Howard agreed. "All the reports indicate a final showdown between Stalin and Trotzky. An article recently in the *Times* predicted August for the final resolution of affairs."

"But what *is* happening in China?" Sonia asked. Howard spread his hands. "That, Mrs. Lovecraft, is one of the great mysteries of the modern world. Not even Hardeen the Mysterious could unravel the enigma of China."

"I wouldn't want to try," Hardeen said. He reached for the platter of eggs and helped himself to a few more. "Delicious food here. I always put on weight when I'm on the road, and diet when I get home. My poor wife says that if I toured any more than I do, I'd never fit back through the front door at the end of the trip! Would you pass me the sweet rolls, Howard?"

~ ~ ~ ~ ~

The tan-and-gray Rickenbacker Super Sport sedan rolled down the old country highway through Saugus, Lynn, Salem, and on into Marblehead. As the Massachusetts landscape fell away toward the harbor Sonia half-quoted Howard's description of witch-haunted Arkham and ancient Innsmouth with its rotting wharves and decrepit gambrel-roofed houses.

Theo asked what Sonia meant; the names Arkham and Innsmouth seemed vaguely familiar to him, but he couldn't place them. Sonia explained Howard's renaming of the towns in his moody, dark-tinted stories. Theo wondered why Howard didn't simply give the towns their proper names.

"Your question is not really a bad one," Howard said. "In some cases I do use real place names. Providence, Red Hook. But for this particular set of tales I have sought to establish in the reader's mind a reality of my own, dislocated from that of his everyday surroundings, and yet corresponding to those surroundings in such a manner that he does not feel that he is reading pure fantasy, as would be the case with a tale set in some wholly invented locale like Kadath in the Cold Wastes.

"Fantasies of the latter type are of their own validity, and are not to be dismissed out of hand, but my efforts in the tales which I locate in Innsmouth, Arkham, and Kingsport—all of these, neither pure reality nor total fantasy, but something which might be called *transformed reality*—are of a type intentioned to achieve a peculiar and *haunting* effect on the reader, as if a reality not the same as *our* reality were beating at the doorposts of the mind, seeking to enter there and to replace the comfortable and secure world to which we are accustomed."

Theo swung the Rickenbacker into town on Pleasant Street beneath a crystal-like blue sky with the smallest and whitest of clouds drifting indolently high overhead. Seeking accommodations for the party, he followed Howard's recommendation, guiding the car along Washington to Orne Street, and to the old Spite House where they entered from the lower side and asked for two upstairs rooms.

Assembling in a few minutes, they looked down from the old building, over Fountain Park the Gas House Beach, to the low crags of Orne Island and Gerry Island, and the Atlantic Ocean just beyond the mouth of Marblehead Harbor.

Theo exclaimed at the beauty of the view, "But this is one of the strangest buildings I have ever set foot in!" he said. "Not one but *three* separate entrances and sections of the building. There are no doors between them, the architecture is completely different in each. It looks like the work of a lunatic!"

"So it does," Howard grinned, "but the explanation is other than one of lunacy. "The house was built fairly recently by Marblehead standards, only about two hundred years ago. The plot of land on which it stands was owned conjointly by three brothers, hard-working fishermen all. They were an independent-minded and stubborn type, and when they set out to build their house each one had his own ideas of how it should be laid out, and none would yield an inch to the others. So each built his own section to his own liking, with the unique result we see today!"

Hardeen shook hie head, barely able to believe the tale.

They took a light luncheon, strolled around the old burial ground above the Spite House and Fountain Park below it, then decided to hire a shallop for a sail around the harbor. "You know," Hardeen laughed, "I've seen many a harbor from bridges and wharves, but once I'm in my shackles and straitjacket and they throw me into the drink, there's no time for sightseeing. It's strictly business!

"So I look forward to the opportunity to sail around in the afternoon sun and just enjoy myself! I hope you don't mind!"

"On the contrary," Sonia said. "I know that Howard loves everything about these old towns. Howard, for all that you say your heart belongs in Providence, I believe that some even greater reservoir of joy and vitality for you lies here in these villages."

"Perhaps," Howard grunted.

"In any case, *I* can certainly see far more beauty here, and I know that a little sail will be wonderful for us all!"

They hired a shallop out of the Little Harbor above Fort Sewall, and had the crusty old seaman who owned the boat sail out north of the Marblehead Light where great yachts basked in the July sunlight and hardworking fishercraft beat toward known schools of fish. They passed southward of Cat Island without incident but near Satan Rock a trio of motorized trawlers were drawn into a large triangle. They had apparently dropped anchor for some reason and lines and ladders were dropped over their sides.

As the shallop neared the first of the trawlers a deck hand hailed them and the New England sailor shouted back. The hand on the trawler spoke with a thick accent. The New Englander shouted that they were out for a pleasure ride and merely wanted to sail by Satan Rock. The deck hand ordered them to stand off.

In the shallop the grizzled New Englander cursed beneath his breath and guided the little boat ahead on its original course.

The hand on the trawler shouted again, then raised an object that glinted in the sunlight. As Hardeen shouted, "He's got a rifle," a puff of smoke appeared from the weapon, followed by a crack as a bullet splintered the gunwale of the shallop.

On the deck of the trawler an officer appeared suddenly, ran to the deck hand and struck his rifle aside. He raised a pair of field glasses and gazed at the shallop, then shouted, "Are you all right?"

"Damned right we are, you Hun!" the New England sailor shouted back. "And the harbor master's going to get an earful of this!" He started to bring the shallop about but the officer shouted again, asking him to stand to and wait for him.

Howard and Theo both urged the sailor to comply. "I'd rather stay here and find out what this means," Hardeen said, "than turn tail and run crying to the harbor master."

The officer had left the deck of the trawler. A dinghy had been lowered and the officer had himself rowed toward the shallop by a crew of hefty sailors.

Speaking in heavily accented English he apologized to the New Englander. "We are conducting delicate soundings and other scientific experiments here. Traffic in our immediate vicinity can bad interference with our work cause. So the crew men on guard we set. We do not wish to have our work disturbed, and also some danger to you there is.

"But he should not have shot at you. I will see to the man's discipline. Also, we will indemnify you. What is the value of the damage, please?"

The old sailor finally settled on a payment for the bullet through the shallop's wooden gunwale, and they sailed back toward Little Harbor.

Sonia, Howard and Theo entered a wharfside restaurant for dinner that night, still talking about the odd incident. "What kind of work did he say they were doing?" Sonia asked. "Some kind of soundings?"

"He didn't say," Hardeen answered.

They were seated at a corner table, surrounded by diners feasting on baked lobsters, scrod, oyster stews, an occasional steak. Sonia asked Howard if he was certain that the sea food didn't distress him and he replied that it was quite all right as long as *he* was not expected to partake.

"As a normal matter," he went on, "soundings are taken by Coast Guard ships and published by the government. Sometimes scientific expeditions do supplementary or specialized work, but I have never heard of foreign craft being permitted to do such work in our coastal waters!

"What! Here comes someone I know!"

Sonia asked who it could be and Howard indicated a roughly-dressed man pushing between the tables toward them. "His name is Luedecke," Howard told Sonia and Theo. "I met him at Viereck's sailing party."

The German halted at their table and bowed rather clumsily. "Herr Lovecraft!" he said. "From across the room I recognized you! Perhaps you do not remember me. Kurt Luedecke."

Howard said that he recognized Luedecke very easily. He introduced Sonia and Hardeen.

"Madame Lovecraft! A great pleasure. And Mister—" he paused for an almost imperceptible moment, "--Weiss. Do you mind? May I join you?" Without waiting for a reply he drew a fourth chair up to their table and seated himself.

"A remarkable coincidence," Howard commented. "I didn't know that you were fond of our New England sea-coast."

"Ach, very much so fond, yes. The region is most beautiful. But not entirely a coincidence my finding you is. I have heard of the regrettable incident of today. I wish to extend my apologies to you all three."

Hardeen said he'd always heard that word traveled fast in small towns.

"Oh, no," Luedecke smiled, "that it is not. I was on board one of the trawlers. If I had known there would never have any shooting been. When afterwards I learned, from the description of you I recognized. I so pleased am that no one was injured."

Hardeen shook his head. "I'd still like to know what was going on out there. What kind of expedition is that? They're not just fishermen, that's for sure."

"No, no," Luedecke said. "Scientific work. *Ach*, my English so poor is, I apologize. *Unterseeisch studieren, schwerr arbeit des bauen.*

"*Ach*, forgive me. Please, you have not yet eaten? Have not I eaten, also. Please, you will permit, I the host shall play."

Later Luedecke departed, and Howard, Sonia and Theo found themselves sipping cocoa before a roaring fire in the lobby of the Spite House.

"I don't think that fellow Luedecke realized that I speak German," Theo said. "You remember his comments before dinner?"

Sonia lowered her cup. "I picked up a few words of it. When I was very small we spoke Yiddish and Russian, and I can pick at German just a little He was talking about *studieren*, studies, and *arbeit*, work. I didn't get the rest."

"*Unterseeich studieren,*" Theo quoted from memory, "*schwerr arbeit des bauen*. I think he told us more than he wanted us to know. His pride was making him show off, saying things in German that he'd never have told us in English because he thought none of us understood German.

"*Unterseeisch studieren* are underwater studies. That was easy enough anyhow, and he told us that much without hesitation. But *schwerr arbeit des bauen* is hard work of constructions. Well, I should translate a little less clumsily. But they must be building something there on the ocean floor. I wonder what!"

~ ~ ~ ~ ~

"My curiosity is still piqued," Theo said. He reached for a marmalade dish and spread the orange preserves on the top of his stack of hotcakes. From a dish of dropped eggs that had been placed in the center of the table he removed a few and placed them besides the hotcakes. "I'd never have guessed that these would be what I always called poached. I thought they were going to be damaged goods!"

"That isn't what piqued your curiosity," Sonia said.

"No." He reached for the pitcher of maple syrup and poured a generous brown pool over the marmalade.

"Is that really good that way?" Sonia asked.

"Delicious! What I'd like to find out is what those trawlers were doing. What kind of soundings and what kind of construction. I don't think they'd be building breakwaters that far from the shore. Besides, there's a fine harbor here already. Very odd. One thing for certain, they're not welcoming sightseers. No point in taking a boat out there again. I wonder if the water is clear enough to see from overhead. Maybe we could get Mr. Lindbergh to help us out!"

Howard lowered his fork. "Mr. Lindbergh may be engaged, but I should think that Mr. Burgess of Marblehead Neck would be quite inclined to substitute for the Lone Eagle."

"Burgess?" Hardeen repeated.

"Old Azor Burgess." Howard made a vague gesture in the direction of Marblehead Harbor and the Neck beyond. "Used to work in the aeroplane manufactory during the Great War. He still has an antique hydro-aeroplane in which he gives sightseeing rides for a small fee."

Hardeen chewed a slab of breakfast steak thoughtfully. "Do you suppose he'd take us up? You could point out the proper directions to the area where we saw the trawlers yesterday. What was the area called?"

"It was between Cat Island and Satan Rock. But Azor's hydro-aeroplane only carries one passenger at a time. I don't see how we could do it. But Azor could take you to the place easily enough."

Theo absently sliced off another bit of steak and dipped it in the yolk of a dropped egg before placing it in his mouth. He washed it down with a drink of orange juice before speaking again.

"I'm sure I could fly a Burgess. I recall them from the war. Could hardly be an old Burgess-Dunne, it has to be the 'H' model. Good aircraft, nice little air-cooled Renault engine. I didn't know they'd been fitted with floats, but of course that's reasonable. Come, let's ask Mr. Burgess if he'll entrust his prize to two visitors. How well do you know the gentleman?"

Howard said he knew Azor moderately well. He was surprised to learn that Hardeen was a qualified aviator.

"Oh, I learned to fly years ago. Back before the Great War, Enrich and I took lessons in France and Germany. Ehrich even bought a Voisson biplane—we thought it was very modern and daring back in those days. By today's standards, it was a little box-kite. Well, hardly modern, but certainly daring!

"Ehrich had the biplane shipped to Australia by steamship, and he had the distinction of being the first man ever to pilot an aeroplane on that continent. That was back in 1910. It was quite an event—there was a sort of competition, not unlike the race for the Orteig prize that young Lindbergh won this year. There was no cash award in Australia, just publicity value, but you know Harry was a bug for headlines and he competed fiercely against an Australian daredevil named Banks.

"Harry won the title of first, and the colonials were so impressed they presented him with a beautiful leather flying jacket and helmet as mementoes. They were made of kangaroo hide! I've kept track of them, in fact. Bess still has them, in New York. But anyway—I'm running on—I learned to fly also. I'm sure a Burgess would be easily handled, especially over water—you don't have to worry about hitting mountains!"

~ ~ ~ ~ ~

"There is Cat Island," Howard Lovecraft shouted, pounding Hardeen on the shoulder and pointing down from the

Burgess biplane. Hardeen nodded his understanding and banked the aircraft into a gentle descending curve.

"And there's Satan Rock! Now. . ."

In a moment the three trawlers were visible, still drawn up in their triangular formation. Sailing yachts and fishing boats as well as a few steam yachts looking like miniature ocean liners dotted the harbor and the ocean beyond.

Hardeen circled over the area bounded by the island, the rock and the trawlers, peering down and trying to penetrate the water to see what was going on beneath. The ocean was clear and the bottom was somewhat visible, but the water was also fairly deep at this point, reaching to ten fathoms at the deepest point between Cat Island and the gray, jagged point of tiny Satan Rock.

Activity was clear on the decks of the anchored trawlers. Deck hands worked over lines and hoses, pumps and compressors, and slung loads of equipment through hatches from their holds, over their sides in winch-lowered nets, and down into the work area in the center of the triangle formed by the three trawler hulls.

Hardeen shouted something to Howard that sounded like "Capper's Flow;" Howard shouted back that he couldn't understand and Hardeen shouted again, gesturing to indicate that the hearing was hopeless in the little Burgess biplane and that he'd have to tell Howard after they landed.

He circled the trawlers once more, trying to make out the activity on the sea bottom, but although large shapes were visible there was no way of telling precisely their nature, or the nature of the activity going on around them.

Deck hands began pointing at the little aircraft and with a scurrying of dark figures glints began to appear on the trawlers' decks. Howard and Hardeen must have spotted the new activity at the same moment, for they shouted at each other simultaneously (and incomprehensibly) and Hardeen swung the Burgess away from the trawlers before any tell-tale puffs of smoke appeared. The aeroplane roared over Cat Island, its 70-horsepower engine at top pitch and its wooden propeller clawing at the clear air. Hardeen bore straight on, crossing Gray's Rock, then swung inland, flying the length of Marblehead proper, swung through a 180° turn and headed eastward, over the Little Pig Rocks, Devereux Beach and the causeway once more, and setting the little plane down on its floats just off the shore where Azor Burgess and Sonia Lovecraft waited.

Once they had settled up with Azor Burgess and climbed back in Hardeen's Rickenbacker sedan, Howard asked what *Capper's Flow* meant.

"Oh, I wasn't saying Capper's Flow," Hardeen answered, "I said Scapa Flow. You know, where Cox and Danks are doing their work."

Howard Lovecraft shook his head. "I don't know what you mean."

"Do you remember that, Sonia?" Theo asked.

Sonia leaned forward from the comfortable rear seat of the Rickenbacker so Howard and Theo could hear her. "I remember that the German fleet was scuttled there. It's way up in the north of Scotland, isn't it? In the Orkney Islands. I remember because the event was odd."

Howard turned in his seat to pay closer attention to Sonia's words.

"Most of the German Imperial fleet was there and surrendered to the British at the end of the Great War. They were impounded there and everyone just sat around waiting to find out what they were going to do. What the peace settlement would tell them to do with a whole navy. And they just stayed there."

Theo supplied the time of the impoundment. "Till June 21, 1919. I remember it very clearly."

"Then there was a Red uprising among the German sailors and they seized control of several ships. The officers were afraid of what would happen next so they scuttled the whole fleet. Everybody got to shore—some escaped in small boats, some were rescued by the English fleet standing picket duty, some even swam. That was the end of the German Imperial navy."

"Ahah! Not quite!" Hardeen gestured with one hand. "Both the British Admiralty and the German government— the Weimar government, that is—tried to raise the scuttled fleet, but both attempts were utter failures. The British government claimed title to the fleet since it was scuttled in British waters. I don't know the legality of that, but they tried to get commercial salvagers to take it over but everybody said it was impossible, even Wijsmuller, the Dutch salvagers."

He pulled the sedan to the side of the road and parked. "What about a little snack?" he asked.

Howard and Sonia assented, and they entered an inn beside the old Marblehead Town House on Mugford Street. Sonia ordered a cup of tea; Howard, a pot of New England style baked beans; and Hardeen, a small steak and eggs. Then he resumed his story. "Finally, after everybody had given up, a fellow named Ernest Cox came out in a small boat to look at the fleet. You could see the hulks just lying there on the bottom, a whole navy. Cox knew nothing about marine work, he was a scrap iron dealer, he and his partner Danks.

"Cox decided that he could raise the ships one at a time, and cut them up for sale as scrap metal. Of course they're all obsolete by now as warships. He had to borrow the money to raise the first ship, succeeded and raised enough money from that success to raise another, and so on. He's been at it ever since!"

Howard swallowed a mouthful of baked beans sweetened with molasses and dark sugar.

"I was unaware that you had made so thorough a study of marine salvage techniques, Theo."

Hardeen chewed a piece of steak, smiling. "Ehrich and I have done a good deal of underwater escape work. As I've said many times and as Harry said many times to journalists who wanted to believe there was something mystical about our work, it's purely a matter of knowledge and equipment. Well, and practice to develop the skill you need to use your knowledge and equipment.

"It's very much my business to keep abreast of technical developments. In fact, Harry and I worked out a method for divers to escape from their own diving suits. Normally, you know, someone has to undog the copper diving helmet from its ring and lift it off the diver's head. Harry wanted to be able to get the helmet off himself for an escape he was developing, and I worked with him until we developed a modification to the locking dogs so the diver himself can get out of the suit. It worked for the escape, but it may also same some diver's life someday!"

"But, Theo," Sonia shook her head, "I don't see what all this has to do with those trawlers. What actually did you and Howard observe from the aeroplane?"

"Unfortunately, we didn't observe very much. The water is fairly clear but it's just too deep there for much light to penetrate, although there was a little. It looked to me like some kind of salvage operation. That's why I yelled 'Scapa Flow' to you, Howard. But neither of us could make out very much, Sonia, except that they're doing something on the sea bottom there, that looks like some kind of salvage or construction work. Howard, maybe you'd better check on that with your friend Herr Luedecke."

Howard said that he would do that. Actually, his thought was more of bypassing Luedecke and consulting Dr. Kiep, who should be returning imminently from Europe, or better yet, with Sylvester Viereck when he returned from his series of interviews on the Continent.

CHAPTER TWENTY-FIVE:

ITS WHIPLIKE ANTERIDIA

BACK IN New York, Sonia resumed her daily work. Theo Weiss, Hardeen the Mysterious, returned to his own career, leaving the investigation of the Marblehead trawlers to Howard. Howard Lovecraft himself picked up the threads of his own routine. He visited Frank Belknap Long, Jr., on West End Avenue and saw the proofs that Paul Cook had sent of Long's introduction to Howard's little book, *The Shunned House*.

"You see," Long told Howard, "recognition is coming to you."

"I'll believe it when I hold the book in my hands," Howard replied.

"But here it is. Take it, hold it!"

Howard shook his head. "Proofs are all very well, grandchild, but a book is not a book until it is completed. Not even unbound sheets make a book. One must have the final product before it is real. Of course, the writing of *The Shunned House* was a rewarding experience in its own right. And the appreciation of one's friends—most emphatically including yourself, Belknapius—is reward enow.

"But I do look forward to holding a book, a real book, and reading upon its spine the author's name, *H. P. Lovecraft, gent.*"

Long clapped the older man on the shoulder. "It will happen, Howard. Patience, confidence in oneself, faith in the future. You will be recognized."

Howard smiled, the restrained expression covering stronger feelings of gratitude than a stranger could possibly have guessed.

He returned to Brooklyn via subway, stopping to buy a set of dailies *en route* and setting them on the table before Sonia's couch along with his set of manila folders. Before commencing his perusal of the newspapers he attempted two inquiries by telephone. The first, to the

Gernsback office, brought an embarrassed Alex Laing onto the wire.

"Didn't get your check, hey?"

Howard said that he had not.

"Who'd you talk to last time?"

"Dr. Sloan."

Laing made a sound somewhere between a growl and a harsh laugh. "Good old Doc Sloan. He means well, Lovecraft, but he's at least 200 years old and he doesn't really swing much weight around here. Look, you sit tight and I'll see what I can do."

Howard asked if he might speak with Mr. Gernsback directly, but Laing told him that the publisher was not available. "That doesn't mean he isn't here, you understand what I mean?"

Howard acknowledged bitterly that he did, and clicked off. His second telephone call went to the New York consulate of the German Republic; when a courteous individual answered the telephone Howard asked to be connected with Dr. Otto Kiep.

The familiar voice of the diplomat came across the wire. *"Ja, Kiep hier."*

Howard introduced himself and Dr. Kiep switched to English. Howard asked politely about Kiep's visit to Germany, then switched the subject to the Marblehead trawlers, seeking as delicately as he could to find out whether there was any connection between the odd activity and the German government. Dr. Kiep denied all knowledge of the matter.

Howard mentioned having met Kurt Luedecke in Marblehead, and Luedecke's acknowledgement of his own connection with the trawlers. He said nothing about Theo Weiss's translation of Luedecke's comment, in German, concerning the hard construction work going on, on the sea bottom.

There was a lengthy silence on the wire. Just as Howard was beginning to wonder if the connection had been lost, Dr. Kiep said, "You are undertaking this investigation in behalf of Herr Viereck, are you not?" Howard said yes.

"I suggest that you postpone your inquiry until Herr Viereck returns to the United States. Then ask him. Yes? For now, I will say to you only that Herr Luedecke is not a representative of the German government. You understand, sir? Herr Luedecke is the personal representative of Herr Hitler, and of the NSDAP—the National Socialist German Arbeiters, ah, Workers Party. You understand, Mr. Lovecraft? As a consular official I cannot speak for Herr Luedecke. Please consult Herr Viereck upon his return.

"And I thank you again, Mr. Lovecraft, for the excellent visit to Massachusetts." He closed the call.

Howard paced and fumed, finally placed a third call, to Viereck's office on 42nd Street. The receptionist there told him that Mr. Viereck was expected back shortly after Labor Day. Would he care to leave a message, or was there something that someone else might handle for him? Howard said no to both questions and rung off.

He clipped newspapers and filed stories for a while, then went to the lobby of the building and brought up the latest mail delivery. The only item of interest was a letter from Florence Greene, Sonia's daughter, to Sonia. Howard put it aside carefully and returned to his work.

He opened the *Aviation* file and placed several clippings in it. Lindbergh's flight and its sequels, Chamberlin and Levine's flight to Germany, Commander Byrd's ill-fated attempt, and Hegenberger and Maitland's flight from California to Hawaii, still filled column after column of space with direct reports, sidebars and related stories. Hegenberger and Maitland had succeeded, but the daring aviators seeking new achievements and greater notoriety with each day were as often unsuccessful as the opposite, and of these the fortunate minority wound up safely pulled from the sea or from the wreckage of crashed aeroplane. The others were simply lost.

The Italian government was sending a flight of planes on a good-will trip around the world. Howard looked for the name of Count Revel in the reports, to see whether the story should be cross-indexed under *Fascism*. Oddly, while Revel's name was absent from the report, Howard found the familiar one of Alphonse Capone on the list of dignitaries designated to welcome the flight to Chicago.

Howard looked up at the sound of a key grating in the lock, and saw Sonia come through the doorway. She recognized the foreign envelope and French stamps at once, and ran to examine Florence's new letter. "Why didn't you open it, Howard?" she asked.

Howard shook his head. "It was not addressed to me. I wouldn't *think* of examining mail addressed to another!"

Sonia opened the envelope and scanned the lines while she sank into a chair facing Howard.

"Besides," Howard added, "after Florence's last letter, I made a firm resolve not to force myself to cope with her penmanship unnecessarily."

Sonia laughed half-attentively. "Well, I'll read it aloud, then, if you'd like. Florence certainly reveals little of her personal life in these letters, but she has some things to say about the way the world looks from Paris."

"That is all that I wish to learn from her, my dear Mrs. Lovecraft."

The paper crackled slightly in Sonia's hands. "Dear Mother," she read, "You mustn't expect very frequent letters from me. I'm just dreadfully busy here, and of course as you know I've never been much of a correspondent. How you and Howard and all the other members of that circle of yours keep up that incessant flow of mail is way beyond my little mind. It seems to me that just *living* takes up so much of one's time and energy—that there's none left over for things like keeping diaries or publishing those little magazines that the members of the 'Lovecraft Circle' seem to dote on."

Sonia looked up from the letter and locked eyes momentarily with Howard, but the message she received was one of passive attentiveness only. She returned to Florence's letter.

"Besides, I have to keep up my dispatches for the *American* or Mr. Hearst will simply hire somebody else to replace me, and there will be one more penniless American wandering around Europe, more concerned with how she is going to pay for her dinner tonight and where she's going to lay her head than with the beauties of European culture or the oddities of postwar politics.

"But I know you're interested, or rather that Howard is, and that as a good and dutiful wife you make your husband's interests your own. So here are a few observations on the events of the day. Oddly, they concern America more than they do Europe anyhow, but maybe the perspective of a few thousand kilometres will add something to the clarity of the picture."

Howard cleared his throat for attention and Sonia paused in her reading to hear what he had to say.

"Hmph, she certainly takes her time about getting to the point. Why doesn't she just say what she has to say, especially if she is as busy as she says she is!"

Sonia leaned forward and patted Howard's hand. "You're right, of course, but we must be patient with youth, don't you think?"

"I think that Irish rascal Shaw was right for once in his cursed life!"

"Well! All right, Howard. I will resume reading. "The only things that anybody pays attention to nowadays are the aviators and the anarchists. You must have heard all the excitement when Charles Lindbergh flew here from Long Island. Paris was hysterical with love for him. The only sadness to the event was the loss of Nungesser and Coli the week before. Every time there was a report of some chunk of wreckage found at sea, or some mysterious object seen overhead or some buzzing in the night, everybody would gather around and whisper that maybe it was the *Oiseau Blanc* but of course it never was and everybody really knows that we'll never hear of the fliers again.

"Anyway, everybody loved Lindy, especially when he turned out to be such a boy, if you know what I mean, Mother. Things like having to borrow the ambassador's son's suit to be presented to the President in. He was so modest and polite and reserved—I tried to get an interview with him for Mr. Hearst but he was much too rushed, but I at least got to shake hands with him and say 'Howdayadoo' at the press reception. Everybody guesses that when he met the Prince of Wales, Lindy must have been scandalized at David's worldliness and David must have been astonished at Lindy's *naïveté*. I wish I could have been there!

"Anyway, he's back in America now, probably off making a movie like Babe Ruth or Red Grange. Then when Charles Levine and Clarence Chamberlin flew to Germany, there was the whole thing all over again. I took the overnight sleeper to Berlin to see the ceremonies for them, and if the *American* ran my dispatch you can find it in their back issues. (They never send me clippings of my work for *months* afterward, and sometimes not at all, so that half the time I don't know whether they use my dispatches or throw them in the trash can!)

"I must say that I was most impressed with old President von Hindenberg. He's such a noble-looking old man, and it seems as if the people really love him, and *vice versa*. A unique politician!

"The other thing that has France in an uproar is the Sacco and Vanzetti case. They're going to be executed next month, aren't they? Every time there's a new committee, appeal, review, postponement, or anything else, it only adds to the turmoil. They ought to execute them at once and get it over with, or cancel the execution once and for all. Think of those two poor men, sitting in jail, waiting to die, and constantly having their deaths put off for another few days, another few weeks, and never knowing whether the latest postponement is the last one.

"*Brrrr!* You and Howard can talk about your creepy monsters and your horror stories, but this is *real*, and I think I'd rather meet a flying octopus or whatever the latest invention calls for, than exist the way those poor Sicilians are forced to live!

"Can you imagine their feelings when the Governor himself went to visit them in jail, personally, and then came away and said there was no change! Over here, even old Captain Dreyfus emerged from obscurity the other day and issued a statement calling for mercy for the poor men. I don't know if you read about it in Brooklyn or not. Over here, nobody likes to think about poor old Dreyfus. The French wish that he would just somehow go away so they wouldn't be reminded of what they did to him. You can be sure that if America executes Sacco and Vanzetti they'll haunt the nation's conscience for a hundred years!

"Well, there are a few little political things going on in Europe that might prove useful for Howard's researches. (What kind of book is he writing? I thought all he produced were those horrid little fantasies about people being eaten by giant piles of gooseberry jam!)

"They had a little revolution in Austria recently. The Palace of Justice was burned out and Parliament itself became a battlefield. There were hundreds of people killed, mostly in Vienna, some out in the countryside. Everybody says it was a Bolshevik uprising, trying to establish a Soviet republic, but of course it failed. The Premier (he's a *priest*, Mother—shades of Richelieu!) has clamped down an iron fist on the country.

"But the whole incident made Jules Sauerwein (he's an editor for *Le Monde*) predict an *anschluss* of Germanic countries—Germany, Austria, Czechoslovakia."

"*Ahah!*" Howard interrupted Sonia's reading. She asked why he had exclaimed and he said, "Sylvester Viereck made the same prediction months ago, that's all. Please continue."

"The politicians in Austria and Czechoslovakia don't like that idea very much. Siepel, Benes, Masaryk. Of course not. Everybody knows that if *anschluss* happens, Berlin will call the tune for the new country. The Soviets don't like it either. Premier Rykoff, who seems to be everybody's candidate for a nice safe 'front man' while Stalin and Trotzky fight it out for *real* power, says that if *anschluss* occurs there is bound to be war. Of course the Soviets seem to pick fights with everybody these days—the Poles over the Volkoff assassination, the British over the Arcos raid (now talk about the crook blaming the cop who caught him!), the Chinese over the Borodin matter. . .By the way, did the American papers carry the story that Borodin finally gave up and went back to Moscow?

"The Rumanian crisis, in contrast, is more like a Sigmund Romberg operetta than a world problem. Old King Ferdinand dying in the arms of Queen Marie while the Crown Prince Carol wines and dines his commoner sweetheart Magda Lupescu against the background of glittering Pah-ree. Meanwhile, back in Bucuresti (that's the Rumanian rendering, anyway!) the cold-eyed Premier Bratiano and the widowed Queen install the little five-year-old Prince Mihai as King with themselves as co-regents. It's all too quaint! I'd swear it was some odd version of *The Student Prince*. Even the names are charming!

"Well, I may not write often, but looking back over this letter I realize that once I get started there's no stopping me. So I must stop myself. There's to be a *soiree* in a little while, and I want to get ready for it now. There's quite a colony of Americans over here, including some very good writers, and I enjoy their company and their talk. I suppose it's the same thing that attracted you to Howard Lovecraft, Mother.

"With love,

"Florence."

Sonia folded the letter and placed it back in its envelope.

Howard asked Sonia if she had prepared anything as yet for dinner, and when she said that she had not he suggested that they dine out. Sonia was delighted.

They made their way to a small Greek restaurant and were seated amidst decorations of Hellenic themes. Wall tiles and miniature statuary illustrated scenes from Grecian myths—the fauns and satyrs, dryads and godlings of long ago. "I find it comforting to return to my earliest loves," Howard commented, "when the frantic pace and the bizarre stupidities of the modern world grow too great to bear, I can always find peace in the contemplation of that great culture that flourished centuries ago in rocky and arboreal Hellas."

"Did Florence's letter upset you so?"

Howard let out a deep breath and shook his head. "There are times when I wonder at the futility of all the petty strivings and ambitions of man. More and more speed, more and more power, more and more dehumanizing mechanization. Man seems incapable of achieving a stable and gracious way of life. Such was the civilization of the Hellenes, and such again in the England of the great Elizabeth and that of the first two Georges, before the third of that line wrought such unremedied mischief with his arrogance and obtuseness.

"A stable society functioning under the benevolent guidance of a trained and unselfish aristocracy—there would be the ideal form of human organization. Instead, what do we see? On the one hand the rule of the mob swayed and bullied by its worst members; on the other, dictatorship by crude and ambitious men who can lead eventually to nothing but holocaust.

"Well, perhaps the new leaders, Mussolini and Herr Viereck's friend Hitler, preferably in association with a restored monarchial state, will lead part of the world to better things.

"Of course, in the ultimate sense, all human striving can be nothing but futile, for we are but ephemeral maggots crawling about on the face of a tiny blob of mud, that spins briefly about a flickering spark called the sun, all of it but the most trivial mote of dust floating in an infinite blackness. Soon all will be darkness again, man will be less than a memory, the sun and the stars themselves will be cold cinders, and the whole silly mummery will have come to its close."

Sonia clutched the edge of the white tablecloth. "Oh, Howard, I wish you wouldn't speak that way. You make everything seem so—hopeless. As if there were no point to *anything*."

"My dear, there is not."

"Then why do we live? What point is there in all of. . . of. . .this?" She gestured around them.

"I suppose there is point only to the extent that we believe there is point. In the view of the cold and uncaring cosmos there is no more point in the life of a mayfly than in that of a Copernicus, and no more in that of Copernicus than in that of an ant. But man alone of earthly creatures can define his own horizons, and by setting for ourselves limitations in time and space, we can establish a setting in which there is purpose, or at least the illusion of purpose."

"And that is why you are pursuing this book for Mr. Viereck instead of the stories that you always used to write."

Howard reddened. "I would like to think that the book will have value in its own right, but chiefly it is to be my entree into a literary world greater than that of the tawdry pulp magazines. I am not interested in the money that It brings, but in achieving the standing and recognition that an artist must always strive after. I write mainly for my own entertainment and self-expression, and for the amusement of my friends, but it would be pleasant to be able to enter a book shop or a library and find one's works shelved with those of Dunsany, Machen, and Poe, rather than to see them—almost to *hear* them screaming at one—between the gray-jawed mobsters and the scantily-clad flappers featured on the covers of the pulp magazines on sale at every subway kiosk and cheap news dealership in the city."

Somehow, between segments of Howard's diatribe the waiter had taken Howard's and Sonia's orders, and by now the food arrived. Howard tore into the *feta* salad and flat eastern bread, then the main course of lamb marinated in olive oil, baked and served with rice pilaf alongside a portion of yellow chick peas. For dessert he ordered a double portion of *baklava* and downed the twin triangles of thin, honey-drenched pastry layers and ground nuts along with several cups of black, sugar-saturated coffee.

Howard wiped his lips with his napkin and said, "Please pardon me for a moment. The honey is sticky." He rose and proceeded to the washroom, returning in a few minutes.

When he seated himself at the table again, Sonia said, "Oh, the waiter brought the check while you were away. I hope you didn't mind my paying it—he said he was going off shift and couldn't leave until the check was settled."

"That was very thoughtful of you," Howard replied. "Here, I shall reimburse you." He started to reach for his wallet but Sonia gestured him to stop.

"Don't bother, Howard. It's such a minor thing."

She took her purse under one arm and Howard retrieved his hat before they left for home.

~ ~ ~ ~ ~

Belknap Long answered the door-chimes himself, correctly expecting to see his friend Howard Lovecraft. He took the taller man's hat and placed it on a bentwood coat-tree that stood near the door and led the way into his own den.

"You said you had to discuss a problem with me, Howard, that wouldn't do to discuss by telephone. I hope there's nothing seriously amiss."

Howard Lovecraft placed a brown paper envelope of some size upon Long's desk. "Have you been to the newsstand today, sonny boy? Then I've a couple of things to show you. But first, yes, there is a little conundrum concerning which I might well utilize an objective view."

Long picked up a cold pipe and fingered it self-consciously. "Anything I can do, of course." He put the pipe into his mouth, drew on it absently, then slipped it into the side pocket of his casual jacket. "Don't know that my callow *Weltanschauung* will have very much to offer an older and wiser sage like yourself, but of course, anything I can do."

Howard smiled. "I knew thou'd not let me down, child. I assume that you are familiar with the case of the two Massachusetts anarchists who are shortly to be meted out the punishment for their murder of a payroll guard some seasons ago."

"You mean Sacco and Vanzetti."

"Precisely."

"And what is the problem, then?"

"Ah," Howard leaned forward, "as you are doubtless aware, vast agitation has arisen over the matter, mostly from radical and anarchistic circles, and among the ranks of the foreign-born and mongrel element of our populace. This has led to repeated delays in the execution of the malefactors, each such delay and legalism leading only to further agitation and bizarre courtroom maneuverings.

"The Governor of the Commonwealth of Massachusetts has done all that any reasonable man might be called upon to do in the situation. He has permitted the criminals interviews and visitors in their place of confinement. He has repeatedly stayed their execution in order to permit them to conduct extensive legal appeals. He has even stayed the execution of another man, one Celestino Madeiros, whose guilt in *another case* is unquestioned, solely on the remote possibility of his having to give testimony in some hypothetical new trial of these two dagos!"

He rose angrily to his feet and paced to and fro. "He appointed the blue ribbon panel comprising two university presidents and a high judge, and as the final gesture of reason and mercy combined, has journeyed to the prison himself and sullied his person by interviewing the two killers *viva voce*."

"Yes, yes," Belknap prodded, "I'm reasonably familiar with the case, what is the problem?"

"Patience, child!" Howard hurled himself into his chair again. "As you are also aware, I am engaged in preparing a book—now moving from the stage of research into that of manuscript preparation—dealing with contemporary and projected political trends in the United States and the world at large. I consider the case of the two guineas well applicable to that volume."

"Yes," Long nodded.

"Now it happens that Mrs. Lovecraft is also concerned with the matter, and is preparing to absent herself from her place of employment this coming Wednesday, in order to travel to Boston and partake in a vigil against the hour of midnight, when the two men are to be electrocuted at Dedham Prison. Mrs. Lovecraft has invited me to join her in the excursion, and this is the crux of my dilemma. While it would surely be a source of valuable material for my literary endeavor, to be present at the place of a political demonstration of this sort might jeopardize my standing and conceivably lend support, or be so interpreted, to a cause toward which I feel a most violent antipathy."

Long nodded his head sympathetically. He pulled his pipe from its place in his pocket, reached for a jar of tobacco and packed the bowl of the pipe. He struck a match and started the tobacco, then looked at Howard and apologized. "I was so intent—forgot that you dislike tobacco smoke, Howard."

"No matter."

"Hmm. Well then, regarding this Sacco and Vanzetti thing. In all honesty, Howard, I don't understand all the fuss. They're convicted of murder, not political unorthodoxy, aren't they? Then they're either innocent or guilty, they either killed this—whatever his name is—"

"Alesandro Berardelli."

"Thanks. Anyway, what is the cause of all the distress?"

"You're wrong on that score, Belknapius. Their political unorthodoxy is not incidental to the case, it is the very heart of the case. The anarchists maintain that these men are being executed because they are a danger to society, spreaders of revolutionary doctrines, and their actual guilt or innocence regarding Berardelli is of no import. And I'll tell you something, young man. For once these radicals are not incorrect. It is precisely because Sacco and Vanzetti have become symbols of the entire anarchistic and revolutionary movement that they must be executed. Also, regardless of whether or not they actually slew some other wop!"

Long nodded thoughtfully. "Well, in that case, I can see your great interest in their fate. And I should think, certainly, there is no reason *not* to go to Boston, if only for purposes of research."

"You don't think my motives would be misinterpreted?"

"By whom? Do you expect to know many others in the group?"

"By Jove!" Lovecraft slapped his knees enthusiastically. "You're absolutely correct. I will be among strangers, one more face in a faceless multitude. I shall exert extraordinary efforts to remain inconspicuous, and none shall be the wiser. And I shall obtain what they call local color on a most interesting event. Very good, very good!

"Now that *that* is settled, let me show you two periodicals. He reached into the large paper envelope and extracted the familiar red-bordered *Weird Tales*, this time the issue for August. "Wright didn't send you this?" he asked. Long shook his head.

"Well, then, behold!" Howard opened the magazine to Long's story "The Man with a Thousand Legs." "What do you think of that?" he asked. " 'Someone rapped on the door of my bedroom,' " Howard quoted the opening of the story. " 'As it was past midnight. . .' " He grinned at his friend.

"Oh, that's delightful," Long exuded. "You know, Pharnabus doesn't regard me in the same light that he does you, Howard. I don't get the treatment of advance copies and the like. When a piece of mine is there, I find out about it the same way that thousands of others do—I see it in the magazine.

"Well, well, what else of interest in the issue? I see the infamous Senf is missing from the cover for once; whose work is the pleasant-looking little *tableau* in the Egyptian tomb?"

Howard Lovecraft graciously handed the bulky magazine to his friend.

"Hmm, Hugh Rankin, is it. Never heard of him. But it's a rather nice rendering, don't you think? For a story by brother Kline, 'The Bride of Osiris.' Well, that should bear looking into. Now let's see if Ec'h-Pi-El has got at least his usual bit of publicity via the Eyrie, if not a place on the contents page."

He turned to the letter section of the magazine and scanned the readers' comments therein. "Ah, Miss Cathryn M. Banks of Staten Island. 'Could one read anything ghostlier than "The Outsider?" ' I don't know." He looked at Lovecraft and grinned impishly. "Could one?

"Ah, and one D. E. Helmuth of Cleveland, Ohio. 'From time to time you have given us stories which have made a strong impression on me, like "Drome" or the Lovecraft tales.' You know, Howard, you've quite a following all over the country. It's a pity that no one has seen fit as yet to issue a volume of your tales. Not just the little Cook project, but a full collection. It seems to me that there should be a market for such a volume."

He returned to his perusal of the magazine. "Ho! Now I see why your grins are so broad today. Pharnabus is finally going to use 'Pickman's Model.' Well, it's about time. Let's see what the editor has to say." Again he quoted from the magazine. " 'Thrill tales in the next few issues. . . "Pickman's Model" by H. P. Lovecraft. . .An eldritch tale of the cellars in a New England city, and unutterable monstrosities that crept from behind the crumbling walls—a horror tale by the author of "The Outsider" and "The Rats in the Walls." '

"Well, that's not so bad at all, is it? And what other surprise have you brought along to spring on me?"

Howard reached into the brown envelope and extracted another magazine, one as large as the old giant-format *Weird Tales*, and passed it to Long, face downward.

Long turned it over and gazed pop-eyed at the cover painting of a gargantuan orchid clutching a topee-and drill-khaki-clad man in its whiplike antheridia. "Why, it's the legendary *Amazing Stories* supposed to contain 'The Colour Out of Space.' The picture does resemble a scene from your tale, or at least suggest one such thematically. Quite amazing."

Howard laughed briefly at the unintentional pun, joined after a moment by Belknap.

"Let's see what they did with your work, Howard." Long consulted the contents page, then turned to the story by his friend. "Oh, my, that drawing is a mess, isn't it? That's the one Dr. Sloane was so proud of, is it? Well, let's see what he has to say. Hmm, 'Here is a totally different story that we can highly recommend to you. We could wax rhapsodic in our praise, as the story is one of the finest pieces of literature it has been our good fortune to read. The theme is original, and yet fantastic enough to make it rise head and shoulders above many contemporary scien-tification stories. You will not regret having read this mar-velous tale.'

"Well, that is praise indeed! One expects an editor to praise the stories he runs, but is this not more than the usual *pro forma* puffery? I think you've got an admirer there, and a good alternative market if you want to avoid dependence on Wright!"

Howard pursed his lips and nodded once. "Everything you say is true, grandchild. The only problem is Dr. Sloane's employer. Gernsback *still* has not paid, I cannot reach him by telephone, and 230 Fifth seems intent on giving me a polite but emphatic dose of the old Twenty-three Skidoo!"

Long was still leafing through the magazine. "Well, look here, Howard. It says that Mr. Gernsback speaks every Tuesday at 9 P.M. from WRNY on various scientific and radio subjects. I've never tuned to that station. It might be interesting to do so some Tuesday." He flipped the pages again. "Hmm, 'All About Television' by H. Winfield Secor and Joseph H. Krause, fifty cents. Looks interesting also. You say that fellow Alex Laing is a minion of the in-sidious Mr. Gernsback? Can't he do something in your be-half?"

Howard shook his head. "He's tried. Everything gets re-ferred to the accounting department, and once entered there, there emergest no man's enquiry. You know that I hate commerce, Belknap. But one must meet one's obli-gations nonetheless. And it is a matter of principle as well—amateurism is amateurism and trade is trade, and one not ought to carry out one of these in the guise of the other!"

CHAPTER TWENTY-SIX:

QUAHOG, CORRECTLY PRONOUNCED *QUOG*

BECAUSE Vincent Starrett agreed to join them on the ride to Boston, Howard and Sonia prepared to entertain the Chicagoan at the Parkside Avenue apartment. Arriving like a love-smitten swain, Starrett strode through the doorway and made a sweeping bow, then rose and presented Sonia with a box of Fannie Farmer miniatures and a bunch of deep red American Beauties.

"My dear Madame Lovecraft," he intoned, his high pompadour swaying slightly, "I am overwhelmed to meet the helpmate of the most esteemed Lord Howard of Providence Plantations!"

Sonia burst into laughter and accepted the candies with her left hand so she could shake hands with her right. "I feel as if I'd known you half my life," she told Starrett. "Howard used to quote from your letters and show me your stories, and lately he's told me about your marvelous book. *Seaports in the Moon*, isn't it? All about d'Artagnan and Cyrano and Alexander Pope. . .?

". . .and Edgar Allan Poe," Starrett continued for her. "Thanks to our resident authority on the great Eddie. I've never known any man with the breadth of knowledge and the depth of understanding of literature—at least, the literature of the macabre and the fantastic—that Howard has."

Lovecraft, standing behind his wife and observing the interchange between her and Starrett, asked, "How is your book coming along, Vincentius?"

"Completed, I'm partly happy to report."

Howard grinned. "Partly happy? Why not entirely—are you dissatisfied with your efforts?"

"It isn't that. Of course, I suppose we always have a few doubts about our books. Only the author knows what he was *really* trying to achieve, so only he knows how closely he has approached his goal."

"Or how distant from it he has halted!" Howard countered.

Sonia tried not to interrupt the flow of conversation as she grasped Starrett by one arm and Howard by the other and steered them both away from the front door, into the living room, and into a pair of comfortable chairs separated by a low deal table. At the first pause she asked Vincent (and her husband) if anything was desired—tea, coffee, a cup of broth, a sandwich or other snack. Starrett said that a slice or two of toast would be most welcomed, and asked for a glass containing an ice cube or two.

Howard said he'd love a cup of coffee or tea, either would do equally well, and wondered if there might be any ice cream lurking in the ice box.

Sonia strode off to the kitchen, asking the men to raise their voices while she was out of the room. "I'm not a real literary personage like either of you, but I'd like to hear the news!"

Howard fixed Starrett with an inquiring look. "Well, and what are you going to do now? Have you shown *Seaports* to Doran as yet? Have you decided on your course over the coming months?"

Starrett ran long fingers, their tips oddly blunted and muscular from pounding out thousands of pages of copy on heavy office-model typewriters over the years, through his gracefully waved hair. "Old George is a canny fellow. I took the manuscript to his office the other day and he shook my hand, offered me a cigar, bought me a drink out of his personal cache of old-stock hooch, took me out to lunch, brought me back to his office, loaded me down with complimentary copies of recent books—some nice ones, by the way, Howard, I'll show them to you some time—and sent me on my merry way. Stuffed, tipsy, loaded down with an armload of the objects I love most in the world—first edition books.

"I was too overloaded, both internally and externally, to face the trip out to Beechhurst, so I freeloaded upon my friend Laing, and it was only when Alex asked the key question that I realized I'd had no response from George regarding *Seaports*. The man just waltzed me and finessed me right out of his office without giving me one word on the thing that really mattered. Some hard-bitten newshawk I am!"

Howard felt the impulse to guffaw at Starrett's discomfiture, and had only partial success in suppressing it. He was still giggling and gasping at the story when Sonia reappeared bearing a blue-mirrored serving tray. "Ice cream and coffee for you, Howard. Tea and toast for me. And for you, Vincent, also toast and a glass of ice. Although I can't imagine what you want a glass of ice for."

"Ah, my dear, innocent Mrs. Lovecraft!" Starrett reached inside his jacket and pulled forth a hammered silver flask. "May I offer you a tot of rum, either of you?"

Sonia declined politely; Howard, rather sternly, explained that he was a teetotaler and a supporter of Prohibition, but that he would not presume to dictate the conduct of a guest. Starrett gave him a slightly puzzled look but poured himself a glass of iced rum and drank a wordless toast to the Lovecrafts.

Sonia looked at the aluminum-cased clock. "We'd better get on our way to Clark Street. The bus leaves the Prince George Hotel in a little while and we don't want to have to hurry into Manhattan for another."

~ ~ ~ ~ ~

As they made their way from the bus terminal to the Boston Common, Sonia said, "I think it was worth the ride to be here. The Emergency Committee called a mass rally in New York, too, at the *Jewish Daily Freiheit* building in Union Square. But it's more important to be here in Massachusetts."

They were walking in a milling crowd of people, most of whom had been on the same bus with them from Brooklyn. On the long ride there had been impromptu speeches and mass singing of anthems in several languages. When Sonia joined in a song in Yiddish, Howard had grown so agitated that she had had to stop singing and speak quietly to him until he calmed down.

There were leaflets being handed out; home-made cardboard placards fixed to wooden staffs were waved over the mixed crowd, calling for a new trial or for the outright release of the convicted murderers.

Grinding his teeth, Howard demanded to know why the protesters included so many Jews and Slavs. "What do they care about the fate of a couple of greasy wops anyhow?"

Sonia touched Howard on one hand. "People who have been victimized and persecuted feel for each other, Howard. We haven't all had the good fortune to come from a distinguished Old American family like yours. If we don't help one another, who will help us? Certainly not the Cabots and the Lodges!"

Rumors flew through the crowd and slid into welcoming minds or crashed against hostile listeners. Government buildings and commercial temples had been blown up in New York, in Baltimore, in Paris. Sacco and Vanzetti had killed themselves with poison smuggled to them in their cells. The Italian ambassador in Washington had transmitted a letter to Governor Fuller from Premier Mussolini pleading for mercy for the two.

The last report reached Howard Lovecraft and he snorted angrily. "The Duce would do no such thing! There is a throwback to the finer Roman type, a close relative of the strong Nordic stock, who has mastered the sniveling mongrel hordes of today's squalid Mediterranean rabble and will restore at least a modicum of the classic discipline and culture of the Augustans. The last thing he would do is appeal in behalf of two such as those!"

In the Common itself there was more singing and speech-making. The crowd was confronted by lines of Boston City policemen and Massachusetts state officers. "At least they learned something from Coolidge," Howard muttered.

Late newspapers and verbal repetitions of news reports broadcast by radio stations rippled through the crowd again. A document had been signed pleading for the men; the late Woodrow Wilson's daughter Margaret had joined the other signers, so had the intellectual Carl van Doren and the Negro athlete and baritone Paul Robeson. An attempt had been made to reach Chief Justice William Howard Taft to appeal for a stay of execution but the former President had retreated with an armload of his favorite reading matter (detective thrillers) and crossed the border into Canada. Here he could rest and relax undisturbed by official duties, since he believed that his office extended only to the American border and outside the United States he was only a private tourist.

Vincent Starrett's smooth voice rose above the songs and speeches and mutters of the crowd and Howard Lovecraft realized that the Chicagoan was saying something into his ear. "Over there," Starrett pointed with one blunt-tipped finger, "some people I'd like you to meet, Howard. You've heard of Dorothy Parker—drama critic. She put out a little volume of verse last year.

"That's John Dos Passos with her, in the spectacles. . . the portly fellow."

The crowd was swaying and surging; Howard had no idea how they could make their way through it to the people Starrett had indicated. But he said, "Passos—he's the all-loose-ends man you mentioned."

Starrett had to shout his reply. Again there was a surge of the crowd. The Common was sparsely lighted against the star-scattered August night; the hour was approaching the scheduled midnight execution.

Somehow at the edge of the Common the demonstrating crowd and the police line collided. The police charged into the edge of the crowd, some of them mounted, the remainder striding forward in closed ranks. A few officers strayed from the ranks of their fellows. With truncheons raised they began rounding up men and women and herding them off the Common, into Tremont Street, then marching them up the street to the State House.

As Howard Lovecraft watched, Dorothy Parker marched up to the line of police and said something to the officer nearest her. He reached out with his truncheon as if to prod her but she slipped past the club, through the police line, and voluntarily joined the group being herded off down Tremont.

Dos Passos, seeing the police truncheon extended toward himself, turned and began to run. His spectacles flew off and he stumbled, half blinded, against a Massachusetts trooper. Bouncing off the trooper he flew backwards into the waiting arms of a city patrolman and was dragged off, struggling and digging his heels into the grass of the Common.

Within minutes the group of arrested demonstrators— roughly two score—had disappeared in the direction of the Massachusetts State House. The police had retreated to a more passive attitude of watchful waiting at the edge of the Common.

A well-dressed civilian had emerged from the State House and walked to the edge of the Common. He gestured to the commander of the police squads and said a few words to him. The police commander waved his hands at the crowd, asked the other man something, listened to the reply, then took off his broad-brimmed military hat and handed it to a subordinate. He pulled a bandana from a voluminous pocket and mopped his brow, then sent a trooper scurrying off, to return from a police van in seconds with a huge cone-shaped megaphone.

The police commander was helped onto the hood of an official vehicle, then climbed to the roof, megaphone in hand. He waved the megaphone in the air and hundreds of demonstrators pointed and shouted until the crowd noise was reduced to a steady hum like the sound of a vast flight of honey bees.

"I've just received word," he began. There was a shout from the crowd and something flew through the air and missed the police commander, falling harmlessly into Tremont Street. The commander looked around nervously, caught the eye of the well-dressed civilian official and lifted his megaphone again.

"I have received word that the Governor has issued a stay of execution. He signed the order at eleven twenty-one pee em. Word was telephoned to Warden Hendry at Dedham Prison. The executions are stayed. Sacco, Vanzetti and Madeiros are all safely returned to their cells. So you can all go home and sleep now. Please go home and sleep now."

He started to climb down from the roof of the van. Questions were shouted from the crowd. "How long a stay?" "Will they be freed?" "Will they be tried again?" But the police commander continued to climb down.

Songs were taken up again in the crowd—one in Italian rising in one section of the Common; one in Russian, in another. Howard Lovecraft asked Starrett what would happen next; Lovecraft had never before witnessed a public demonstration of any sort, no less participated in one.

"To the people they arrested? Nothing. They'll probably book them for disturbing the peace or some such charge. Maybe unlawful assembly. Then let them go and quietly quash the whole matter. Boston won't want the publicity of trying masses of people, especially if the defendants include prominent individuals like John Dos Passos and Miss Parker. I'm just sorry we couldn't get to chat with them before."

"Hmph." Howard pondered for a moment. "And what will happen here?" He stretched out one hand to indicate the throng that still filled most of Boston Common.

"Oh, they'll drift away. Somebody always climbs on a rock or a statue and starts trying to convince everyone that they ought to march on the City Hall or the State House or the local newspaper office, but it never happens. Inside an hour there won't be more than a dozen souls left here." He grinned and linked elbows with Howard and Sonia, and the three of them began slowly to make their way from the crowd.

"I just hope, Vincentius, that my presence will not be accounted as lending support to the radical objectives of this multitude. I am in total disagreement with their goals. I think that the stay of execution was an error, a surrender of lawful authority to the howls of a mob of mongrels and curs.

~ ~ ~ ~ ~

Sonia sought to take the first means back to New York. "I can't afford to miss more work than is unavoidable. You know, Russek's isn't any little private business, it's a big department store and they'd as soon throw you out and hire somebody else as put up with any problems. Will you join me—I suppose the train is actually the fastest way home."

"I'm rather at loose ends," Starrett said. "*Seaports* is all finished, and I suppose I'm waiting for a response from George Doran—in theory, anyway. But those merger talks that were rumored keep recurring, and I have a feeling that he's going to remain noncommittal until he's got a settlement one way or the other.

"So I expect that I'll just cool my heels for a little while, maybe try to get out a couple of Jimmy Lavender yarns to keep the pot boiling. Then if I still haven't heard, I shall hie myself to the depot and entrain for Caponeville. There are some editors I'll try and hit up for a job. A good newspaperman can generally find work if he isn't too particular about hours, working conditions, or rates of pay."

Howard halted abruptly and turned about to face the others. They were off the Common now, and standing in the street. Lamps burning on tall stanchions gave the thoroughfare a ghostly illusion of pallid daylight, and the rare vehicle that passed through swerved to avoid the three figures chatting obliviously in the center of the roadway.

"Sonia, we shall see you off on the first New Haven train. Vincentius, neither of us has pressing business in New York. Since we are this far north anyway, suppose we undertake a brief holiday amidst the colonial buildings, the ancient hills and sparkling watercourses of old New England."

~ ~ ~ ~ ~

Sonia's train pulled out of Boston's North Station, headed south to New York. Howard and Vincent walked back to the out-of-town newsstand where Vincent bought an armload of dailies from across the nation, concentrating on those published in his adopted home town, Chicago. He carried them to the waiting room, then on, along with Lovecraft, to the Boston & Maine tracks where they boarded a train that would carry them on the little spur line past Lynn and on to Marblehead.

Howard lectured on the geography and history of the region, and the transformations he had put the towns and countryside through in the creation of his stories of Innsmouth, Arkham, Kingsport, Dunwich. Vincent listened for a while, then asked Howard whether he planned to return to the writing of fiction after he finished his political book for Sylvester Viereck.

"I hope to complete the thing by year's-end," Lovecraft said. "I've voluminous notes and files in Brooklyn now, and have been working up fragments of the actual text, so that there is already a sizeable manuscript in existence. Of course, once past this book, I will still have the obligations of my work as a revisionist to occupy my efforts."

"That's something I don't really understand," Starrett said. "You've mentioned revision work before. You mean freelance editing?"

"More or less. Of course, Henneberger tried to hire me as a full-fledged editor a couple of times." His eyes seemed to focus on some distant scene, as if he were contemplating a path not taken. "But he wanted me to live in Chicago and work from there. With all due respect, my dear Vincentius, I could never be happy in that raw, uncultured, frontier town. Two-gun Bob Howard, you know, might do well in such an environment, although it is my impression that he is as reluctant to leave Texas—at least on a permanent basis—as I am to leave my beloved New England with its white steeples, its fanlighted Georgian homes with their gambrel roofs, its old by-ways and its intimate associations with that older, more leisurely-paced, more courtly and in the final analysis more civilized manner of conducting daily life."

He gestured somewhat stiffly, in a vague effort to emphasize his words. "There was another project of Henneberger's—the unhatched egg of *Ghost Stories*—which it appeared he was willing to permit me to edit from New York. I cannot say that I feel the same enthusiasm for Gotham that I hold for Providence, or for such other New England strongholds as Boston or Salem, but I felt that the congeniality of the assignment, the not-altogether obnoxious surroundings of New York, and the geographical proximity and ease of transportation between New York and New England, would make it possible for me to accept Henneberger's offer, and I so informed him.

"But then his financing failed to materialize as anticipated, and it was back to Chicago for him, and back to the blasted typewriter—God! How I hate being turned into a mechanician! Could Swinburne have written *Atalanta in Calydon* on a damned Remington Upright?—for old Humphrey Littlewit Lovecraft!

"Well, as for my revisions, I suppose one might characterize them as freelance editing. For some reason not easily fathomed my little effusions in *Weird Tales* and the amateur journals seem to have attracted to me a small following of tyro *fantaisistes* who think that the magical touch of the Theobaldian Waterman can work wonders upon their manuscripts. They send me their crude efforts, I work over them to the best of my poor ability, and the original begetter of the work then sells the result, paying me a share of the receipts for my own little assistance.

I've performed these poor services—usually, but not always in anonymity—for the likes of the late Harry Houdini, for Madame Sonia H. Greene (who is now Mrs. H. P. Lovecraft), and for some score or so of lesser lights."

Starrett waved frantically until he could get Howard to interrupt his monologue. "I'm sorry," Vincent said, "somehow we've got off the subject. I mean to ask, Are you planning to write more stories? Of your own. Not revision-work."

"Hmm." Howard nodded vigorously. "Inasmuch as my other obligations leave me time for such indulgences, I should like to pen a few more tales of my own. Some dreams, some notions, some vivid images of my days and nights, cry out for embodiment in fictive form. I wish I had a better and more reliable outlet for them. Wright is such a peculiar fellow to deal with."

"I wrote to you about Ed Baird, didn't I?" Starrett asked. "He's as high on you as ever, Howard. He'd welcome your stories." Howard made a sour face. "Baird holds my admiration and good will, but really, a sensational detective story pulp, featuring the tough visages of brutal gangsters, the rolled stockings of gin-soaked flappers, the smoking muzzles of brutal firearms—I could hardly permit my work to appear in such a form.

"Once again, I commend to you—and Ed—the products of Two-gun Bob Howard. He is a producer of amazing prolificity and versatility, as agile with the adventures of a practitioner of fisticuffs as with those of a pirate swashbuckler, a muscular barbarian reaver or a Yankee soldier-of-fortune. My own talent, modest as it is, I fear is further limited by its very narrowness and specialization. Without meaning in the least to denigrate such versatile practitioners as yourself and Two-Gun, I feel that I could never bring myself to produce the commercial hackwork that seems to be the requirement of the run-of-the-mill pulp publisher."

By now the train was pulling into the little station just off Pleasant Street in Marblehead, and Howard and Vincent climbed down through puffs of moist steam onto the Spartan platform.

"So this is famed Marblehead Mass," Starrett exclaimed, pronouncing the name of the Bay State as if it were a Catholic religious observance. "I must say that it's a nice-looking town, from the first glimpse." He pointed toward the northeast, where a tall spire drove upward into the brightening morning sky.

"That," Howard Lovecraft replied, "is old Abbott Hall. The structure dates from the centennial year of the unfortunate war of rebellion against George III. In fact, then, you see that the building is relatively modern by the standards of the region. I have studied its lines and construction many times, and must say that I find it a rare exception to the noisome architectural excesses and gingerbread of the nineteenth century. The Gothic forms with their spires and pediments, their arches and stained-glass windows which give the structure a misleading suggestion of ecclesiastical utilization, the careful brickwork and multiple roof lines, combine to produce an effect both unique and striking."

The strolled down through the town, Starrett still lugging the sheaf of newspapers he had bought in Boston, Howard Lovecraft happily lecturing the Chicagoan on the history of the town. "Did you know that Marblehead even has an official town anthem? 'The men of old were heroes, who fought by land and sea,' and so on. Usual militaristic bombast, as is typical of anthems. But there is a certain swing to it."

Starrett stood and sniffed the ocean air. "You know, we've been up all night and I don't even feel drowsy. Must be this invigorating setting. But I must say that I have an appetite. What would you say to a meal?"

Howard said he wouldn't mind one a bit.

"Well then, suppose we make our way down to the water's edge. I can just see one of those famous New England shore dinners rising before me. Although, at this early hour, I think I'll settle for a pot of steamers." He noticed the sour expression spreading across Howard's face. "What's the matter?" Starrett asked, "Did I say something wrong?"

"Merely an idiosyncrasy of mine, Vincentius. I love the sea—it's in my veins, of course, inasmuch as I am descended from an old sea dog named Whipple Phillips. But I cannot abide sea *food* in any form."

Starrett gave a hearty laugh without breaking stride. "Remarkable, my dear Lovecraft. We must resemble the famous Spratt family of nursery rhyme fame, you and I.

Whereas I positively dote on steamed clams, broiled lobster, filet of flounder and all the rest of Father Neptune's
bounty, I cannot abide the sea itself. Oh, it's pretty
enough to look at, I'm positively charmed with this little
village, but swimming is an art quite beyond my ken, and
as for travel by water. . .

"Why, you know, I've made ocean voyages to both
Europe and the Far East, the first such as a sort of sea-
going cattleman many years ago. I was hardly more than
a child. Positively hated it, and I've never been able to set
foot on board ship without my stomach going queasy on
me.

"But come on, if you don't mind sitting opposite me
and ordering some dish that rests more comfortably with
you. . ."

"Not in the least!" Howard directed their steps toward a
dockside cafe near the Town Landing. "One can obtain as
fine a bowl of bacon and beans in Marblehead as anywhere in New England. We shall have a positive fiesta of
the gustatory art!"

~ ~ ~ ~ ~

They stepped through the old wooden-framed door with
its summer panels of screen and let it creak closed behind
them. Howard's attention was arrested by a quintet sitting
around one table, finishing a meal with pie and coffee and
conversing earnestly. There were four men and a woman
in the group.

Two of the men wore rough sailor's garb, one of them
a dark woolen shirt, jean trousers and heavy boots; the
other, a thick, rib-patterned black sweater, a pair of
patched and spotted drill trousers that must once have
been white, and thick-soled, high-top shoes. Both wore
hats as they ate; the first, a knitted sailor's hat; the
other, a grimy peaked cap.

The third man wore a crisply pressed suit, a white shirt
with wing collar and dark cravat, and a monocle.

The others, apparently a couple, comprised a young
man with lank blond hair and a sallow complexion, and a
woman apparently double his age and substantially
greater in bulk. The two were garbed in fashionable resort
outfits; a green-tinted panama hat apparently belonging

to the man surmounted a near-by hat-rack, while a silver-handled walking stick leaned against the post.

Howard Lovecraft felt himself jabbed lightly in the ribs. "Do you know those people?" Vincent Starrett asked him softly.

Howard ushered Starrett across the wooden-floored cafe and introduced him to four of the five people. They were Dr. Otto Kiep of the German consulate in New York, Kurt Luedecke the American agent for the NSDAP, and Count and Countess Vonsiatskoy-Vonsiatsky. Dr. Kiep rose before any of the others and introduced the fifth member of the group to Lovecraft and Starrett. He was Fritz Kuhn, Heinz Spanknoebel's closest associate in the *Freunde des Neuen Deutschlands*.

The heavy-set Kuhn left the table and dragged another to it so Lovecraft and Starrett could join the larger group. "I heard about you from the Count," Kuhn commented to Howard Lovecraft. "Who's your pal?"

"Starrett? Why, he's a literary man of outstanding merit. I'm surprised you are not familiar with his name. Surely so meritorious a poet and scrivener—"

"I don't read that junk," Kuhn grunted.

Count Vonsiatsky pressed Kuhn's arm and got him to sit down again at the table. "This is remarkable incidence," he said, "meeting people we know in town like Marblehead." He picked a half-smoked cigarette made with pastel paper and gold-colored mouthpiece from an ashtray beside his dish. "But I recall, Viereck said you were New Englander, Mr. Lovecraft."

"Apparently the only such among us," Howard replied. "Oh, I beg your pardon, Countess. You are from Connecticut stock, I recall your mentioning to me."

"Quite so, Mr. Lovecraft."

A waitress appeared and took Howard's order for beans and bacon, Vincent's for steamed clams and broth.

"Starrett and I didn't mean to insert ourselves into a private gathering," Howard said. "If your plans are firm, please do not permit us to interfere with them."

"How'd ya like a boat ride?" Kuhn rasped.

Howard saw both Count Vonsiatsky from one side and Dr. Kiep from the other move their hands as if to stop him from asking the question, but both were too slow to prevent it, and Kuhn was obviously too oblivious to anyone else's ideas to pay attention to them.

"I am afraid that boat is very small," Vonsiatsky tried to cancel the invitation, "can hold only few persons."

"That's loony," Kuhn gritted. "The *Alpdrucken* can take half a hunnert people easy!" He pronounced the name of the craft as if it were spelled *Owlp-drunken*.

"If you're concerned over too many passengers," Starrett volunteered, "I'll be very happily counted out. I was just telling Howard that while I appreciate the sea as an esthetic object and as the source of most excellent meals, I invariably suffer for my indiscretion when I venture out in a boat of any sort."

Howard, watching the interchange, saw a look of relief spread over most of the other party.

"Besides," Starrett resumed, "this is such a lovely town, I'll be very satisfied to spend the afternoon wandering around its streets. No need to miss a boat-ride on my account, Howard."

"Well then," Howard began.

Countess Vonsiatsky said, "Mr. Starrett, the Count and I were not planning to join the *Alpdrucken* party either. Perhaps you would like to join us. We were planning to motor up to Newburyport for the afternoon."

"Please," the Count added, "I will show my Duesenberg. Is model SJ, Starrett, 320 horsepower. Won Indianapolis race this year. Also 1925 and 1924."

Starrett, eyes shining, said, "It sounds marvelous." He carefully picked the hot morsel from a white-shelled steamer, dipped it in rendered butter, then more briefly in the hot clam broth before popping it into his mouth. He chewed with a blissful expression, then swallowed the grayish meat. "Best clams I've ever tasted," he commented.

"Properly, I believe, they are designated *quahogs*," Countess Vonsiatsky corrected him. She pronounced the word *kwogs*.

Howard Lovecraft scooped a forkful of beans, speared a chunk of bacon and conveyed the food to his mouth. He smiled approvingly at the Countess's pronunciation.

"Kwogs hell," Starrett commented, "I say they're clams and I say they're heavenly. But—" (addressing his friend) "—you're sure you wouldn't mind, Howard? I don't want to deprive you of your boat ride, but it would be sheer agony for these old bones and I'd love to have a cruise in a Duesenberg SJ. Make an interesting comparison to Alphonse's Cadillac in Chicago."

Howard insisted that Starrett have his ride with the Count and Countess. "Besides, Newburyport is a most attractive settlement, you shall assuredly enjoy the outing. By all means, see the old burying ground there—some of the markers bear fascinating inscription: And the Old South Church in that village, dating from 1756. A most admirable survival of Georgian architecture, kept in perfect preservation.

"And I shall enjoy an afternoon in the old whaling and shipping port of Marblehead."

CHAPTER TWENTY-SEVEN:

LOVECRAFT DONS A COPPER HELMET

THE TRAWLER *Alpdrucken* had not docked, and perhaps Count Vonsiatsky's lame excuse about the smallness of the boat had been more valid than it seemed. Kuhn, Luedecke, Dr. Kiep and Howard Lovecraft climbed from the old wooden pier down a crude ladder and into a dinghy. Without discussion the heavily muscled Kuhn seized a pair of lengthy oars and prepared to row the little craft out into the harbor. Kurt Luedecke stood in the prow of the dinghy and cast off the line that held the boat to the pier. Dr. Kiep and Howard Lovecraft sat side-by-side in the stern.

"Mr. Viereck places great confidence in you, Mr. Lovecraft," the diplomat told Howard as the dinghy moved slowly across the calm summer water. "I have had a communication from him. He says that in September he will be back in New York. On the liner *Bremen* he sails."

Howard made a neutral response regarding Viereck and the latter's journalistic tour.

"It is fortunate that Count Vonsiatsky could offer your friend a ride. I can show you a very interesting sight today, thanks to Sylvester's latest letter. But I could not have shown Mr. Starrett because him I do not know."

Howard shook his head. "This is somewhat difficult to understand, Dr. Kiep. How did you know I was going to be in Marblehead today?"

The German laughed. "*Ach*, no, I did not know that. It is only a coincidence. But you would have been invited soon, in any case. It is only *geschehen-ereignis. . . ach—* happening that we today encountered. But everything is fated."

"Perhaps."

The heavy-shouldered Kuhn pulled the dinghy toward the mouth of the harbor, then past it, gliding between ancient Fort Sewall at the southeast corner of the town proper and the Marblehead light at the farthest point of the neck. He continued into the calm ocean waters where yachts stood to (the yacht *Gossoon* had won the annual Marblehead yacht race a few weeks earlier and the annual influx of wealthy boatmen and their parties was in full swing), drawing occasional glances from yachtsmen and waves from busier fishermen.

Between Cat Island and Satan Rock, where the triangle of anchored trawlers had held off shallops earlier in the year, a single dark-hulled craft stood at anchor. Kurt Luedecke stood in the prow of the dinghy and shouted to the trawler until a ladder was unfurled over the railing and dropped to the water line.

Luedecke and Fritz Kuhn steadied the dinghy and aided first Howard, then Dr. Kiep, in getting up the rope-ladder; then crewmen aboard the trawler lowered davits. Kuhn and Luedecke dogged them onto the prow and stern of the dinghy and climbed up the ladder while the dinghy was hoisted to the deck of the trawler.

On a life-preserver hanging against a cabin bulkhead, Howard made out the lettering, *Alpdrucken*, *Hamburg*. Luedecke led the way into a large cabin and offered the others wooden ship's chairs.

"You have ever diving been, Herr Lovecraft?" he asked.

"I paddle about a trifle, but I'm afraid that my bathing costume is well packed away in camphor upon the ancient hill in Providence."

Luedecke looked puzzled by the response. The cabin was silent for a moment, Luedecke, Kiep, Kuhn and Howard sitting in a rough square, then Kuhn burst into crude, vigorous laughter. "He don't mean like Gertrude Ederle, Mr. Lovecraft. He means like Commander Ellsberg, Julius Furer, people like that. Wearing Siebe suits."

To Howard it sounded like *see-bee*. He asked what kind of suits those were.

"Augustus Siebe he refers to," Otto Kiep supplied. "An Englishman." He spelled the name. "Almost a hundred years ago the diving suit he invented. Like so." He crossed the room and opened a large door. Inside hung a row of canvas-and-rubber costumes designed to cover their wearers from neck to ankle. The storage room also held a number of dull copper helmets with thick glass windows in them, and sets of heavy boots with metal weights clamped to their soles.

"You want me to dive in one of those?" Howard's voice rose to a near squeak, something that it rarely did, and then only in moments of extreme surprise or agitation.

"Oh, there nothing to it is," Dr. Kiep said. "Everyone on his first dive upset becomes, but a little calmness solves all. Even I have done it," he said proudly.

"But for what purpose?"

"Only a friendly observer I am," Kiep replied. "Herr Luedecke in charge of the operation is."

"Ja, the captain of this *Alpdrucken* and the *grundstruckvorhaben—ach*, Kiep, in English. . ."

"Bottom ground, *ach*, sea-bottom project."

"*Danke*. The captains, Herr Lovecraft, I command. Herr Viereck has sent word that you our *vorhaben-arbeit*, our project work, may see."

Howard thought that over for a little. "Very well," he said at last. He stood up and walked toward the cabinet containing the diving apparatus. Shortly, aided by Luedecke and a few sailors summoned from the trawler's deck, all four men were outfitted with the diving suits and heavy, weighted footgear. Each carried a copper-and-glass diving helmet under his arm as they clumped from the cabin onto the deck of the trawler.

Howard asked how they would make their way to the sea bottom—did they just climb over the side of the trawler and sink?

"No, no," Luedecke laughed. "We use *ein tauchenbahnsteig*—Kiep!"

"A platform-diving."

"*Ja.*"

Before they climbed onto the platform—actually, little more than a metallic grid with end-railings and an overhead hook attached to a motor-winch—each diver had his helmet carefully fitted onto the metal collar of his canvas suit and dogged into place. Howard stood on the metal grid then, holding onto the end railing with one hand. Lines were attached to each diver's helmet—an air hose, a telephone line, and a life-line to be used in hoisting the heavily-suited men should they not get back to the platform for any reason.

The platform was winched over the railing of the *Alpdrucken*; Howard felt a flash of panic as they splashed from bright Massachusetts sunlight into the blue-green

Atlantic water. At first there was plenty of light and he had no trouble in seeing the other three divers, but as the platform was slowly lowered the water became increasingly murky. Again, Howard felt a rush of panic but he fought down the impulse to call out, clutching the railing of the diving platform.

Through his helmet telephone he could hear conversation between the deck and the other divers. The dialog was in German, with only an occasional recognizable noun, but the voices were confident, matter-of-fact, which in itself increased Howard's feeling of security.

For a brief time the platform descended through total darkness; Howard's mind flew back through the years to one of his early stories, "Dagon," and to another semi-juvenile work, "The Temple," both involving submarine themes. His life was imitating his art, a bizarre happenstance, but he expected no weird or supernatural events to befall him. Still, with the voices in his helmet speaking a language unknown to him, with the water surrounding him in utter darkness, it was like entering a dreamland where time was suspended and normal laws had no effect.

A vague blur or light appeared below the platform and grew in brightness and clarity as the metal grid settled slowly to the ocean floor. The light moved forward and Howard recognized it as a lantern of some sort, adapted to use under water.

The light-bearer led the four divers across the ocean floor, beneath the lip of a metal structure resembling an inverted cup. They climbed laboriously up a flight of metal stairs; after the first few steps Howard's helmet broke into air and he climbed onto a lighted, dry platform. The four divers were helped out of their helmets and suits, stepped through a pair of heavy metal doors.

Howard found himself inside a room that was a cross between a fortress and a ship's cabin. There were heavily-glassed ports but nothing could be seen outside due to the depth of the ocean. Men in rough sailors' garb moved around, in and out of the large room; occasionally someone would appear in naval officer's uniform without the expected insignia.

"This is our project, Mr. Lovecraft," Dr. Kiep said. "This is what the trawlers were beginning when you first saw them above." He looked at Kurt Luedecke as if seeking permission to continue.

In the momentary lapse of conversation Howard became aware that a mélange of sounds formed a continuous background in the metal room: the hiss of compressed air being steadily and slowly fed into the atmosphere, the hum of exhaust fans drawing off used air for recycling, the lower-pitched tone of diesel engines and the whine of generators providing the background of power for all the other devices.

"Herr Viereck," Otto Kiep resumed, "has told you of the expectations of us all, for the bright world of tomorrow. Once the treacheries and injustices of the past decade have been corrected, a new world order will arise."

"I have researched exactly this theme, Dr. Kiep. But perhaps you would care to explain to me the precise function of this rather odd installation." Howard indicated the structure where they stood.

"Perhaps another might speak more appropriately than I," Kiep replied.

"Ach, when the new order comes," Luedecke supplied, "in case any resistance we meet, then it we must—Kiep, *zersmettern, zerquetschen, vass*?"

"Overcome, *meinherr*."

"*Ja, danke*. We it must overcome, Herr Lovecraft. Prepared to overcome we must be. This is our place of preparing."

The background noise of machinery in operation rose with the loud whine of large electric motors and the rumble of an airlock door opening to the sea. The traffic of work-clad sailors through the metal room increased, all of them headed in the same direction.

"Great timing," Fritz Kuhn burst in. "You think it's the boat?" Howard was not certain to whom Kuhn addressed his question, but Luedecke and Kiep both indicated that they did think it was the boat.

There was a resounding thump that sent a tremor through the floor of the metal room, and a grinding sound of metal against metal. More mechanical noises followed, then the metallic clanging of watertight compartment doors being undogged, opened, shut and dogged shut once again.

With a sound of almost military precision a party of men stepped into the room where Howard still remained with Dr. Kiep, Fritz Kuhn and Kurt Luedecke.

The newcomers were, for the most part, dressed in unmarked but militarily cut gear that gave the distinct impression of their being members of the officer class. A few of them were more conventional civilian outfits. Of these men, Howard recognized one, the sponsor of his book *New America and the Coming World-Empire*; George Sylvester Viereck.

Luedecke, Kiep and Kuhn stepped forward to shake hands and exchange greetings and introductions with the members of Viereck's party. To Howard Lovecraft, sensitively attuned to nuances of social stratification, it was clear that Luedecke, Kiep and Viereck were members of the same stratum, their precise seniority a matter of delicate balance. Luedecke and Viereck were almost precisely equal in rank; Viereck bore messages and instructions, and his attitude was somewhere between that of a mere courier and that of a man issuing commands in his own right.

Dr. Kiep's attitude was more that of a close friend and associate of the others, but of one who is not included in the chain of command.

Hanging back from the group, Fritz Kuhn clearly played the part of a henchman, a flunky of use for his brutal strength and blind obedience, but of no authority whatsoever.

After a few minutes of conversation in the German language, Viereck looked up from the group surrounding him and smiled his acknowledgement of Howard Lovecraft.

Howard stepped forward, mumbled a brief greeting to Viereck. Sylvester introduced Howard to the other members of his party; their names, all with heavy Germanic tones, were unfamiliar. Howard shook hands with each, muttered how-do-you-do's, was surprised, in fact bemused, at the militaristic heel-clickings and half-bowings of the dark-clothed Germans.

"You must excuse us, Howard," Viereck said. "I am delighted to see you here, but also a trifle surprised."

"And I also," Howard answered. "I had been under the impression that you were not due back in New York for another month."

Viereck nodded his head vigorously, the artificial lights of the metallic room glinting on his horn-rimmed spectacles. "I will ask you to make no mention of this encounter. In fact, this entire project—what did they tell you it was called, by the way, the *grundstruck-vorhaben*?—that just means sea-bottom project—we must ask you to tell no one about it for the time being."

To Howard's serious-visaged puzzlement, Viereck laughed lightly. "We're afraid of the prohibition enforcement people!"

Now Howard smiled, too. "One hardly expects Izzy and Moe to burst through the doorway there at a depth of—how many fathoms?"

"Ah, I believe—" he turned to one of the naval officers nearby and asked a question in German, received his answer and said to Howard, "ten fathoms."

"Well," Howard spread his hands.

"Ah," Viereck countered, "you're right, of course, in that one would never expect a knock at the door, a face peering through the porthole. That was an oddity of the design of our *grundstruckvorhaben*, by the way. There's never any light down here except that which we provide. Someone miscalculated and put in 'windows.' Ha-ha.

"But the prohibition agents work with the Coast Guard, and we would be most unhappy to find the Guard sending divers down to investigate our activities. So—I am sure that your discretion can be counted upon."

"Of course," Howard said. "But as for yourself?"

"Ah," Viereck smiled wistfully, "I would so enjoy to visit my family in New York. . . even to spend a pleasant evening dining in one of the most excellent facilities here in Marblehead. The days that I spent here and in Salem with yourself and Dr. Kiep are such lovely memories for me, Howard; I hope that the time will come when we can again visit the historic sites which you so thoroughly explained to us.

"But for the time being, it is best that my presence here not be known. I will be returning to Europe in a few days on the boat—the *unterseeboot*—to make a report, to complete my program of interviews, and then to return to

America by steamer. I do look forward to the luxury of a few days' relaxation aboard the *Bremen*. Life aboard any *unterseeboot* is quite rigorous, as you surely understand."

Howard indicated that he did.

"But come along," Viereck continued. "Have you been here long? Just a brief while, eh? Then you have not had the opportunity to tour our modest facilities. The *grundstruckvorhaben* is far from completed; we have fortunately been able to part with the trio of supply ships that stood above us. Too much curiosity was caused by them, too many yachtsmen and fishermen and sightseeing boats wondered what was going on. Now we have only the single tender, the *Alpdrucken*, which does not have to remain overhead at all times. Most of our supplies arrive by *unterseeboot* now. With the airlocks of our *grundstruckvorhaben* the boats can dock directly with the project. We can land supplies, rotate work crews, and so on.

"But now, let us examine the facility."

He led Howard through the project. It was like a ship inside, more than a building, with metal bulkheads for walls, dark portholes mounted with thick glass instead of windows, heavy water-tight doors separating compartments.

The project was astonishingly large. Not only did it contain living quarters for its staff, but complete equipment for sustaining life, storage bays, airlocks for docking submarine, a well-stocked armory, a radio room.

"Car you operate a radio from the sea-bottom?" Howard asked Sylvester Viereck.

"We are trying, but so far without success. We can run a line up to the tender," he pointed one finger straight up, "and use the ship as a relay station. That is a reason for keeping the *Alpdrucken* here. Also we are trying to develop a system to send our antenna up on a float. We have had some success, and we work at that still. If we succeed, we can then dispense with *Alpdrucken*."

They completed the tour. Howard questioned Viereck about the functionings of the project, and about the need for an arsenal. "If the prohibition enforcers do find you out, what use is a cache of weapons? You don't plan to go to war with them, do you?"

Viereck smiled oddly. "No, no. The arms are just for— let me say, long-range potential. It will be years before

any use is made of our *grundstruckvorhaben*. By then—
who knows? But as for prohibition—come." He examined
his watch. "You will want to return to Marblehead before
night, I assume?"

"One loses track of the hours in a place like this," Howard said. "In fact, a friend of mine is off picnicking with
the Count and Countess Vonsiatsky. I imagine that they'll
be getting back from Newburyport before long. I should
be in Marblehead when they arrive, or at least not too
long afterwards."

Viereck led the way back to the first room that Howard
had entered in the project; it was as close to a parlor as
the undersea structure contained. "We do violate prohibition just a little bit," Viereck said. "Might as well be hung
for a sheep, eh?"

He invited Howard to sit. The other members of the
shore party who had traveled with Howard reappeared:
Fritz Kuhn, Kurt Luedecke, Otto Kiep. Luedecke and Dr.
Kiep sat with Howard and Sylvester while Fritz Kuhn bus-
ied himself at a locker, returning in a few minutes with a
tray, glasses, and a bottle of *schnapps*.

"Fresh," Viereck announced, lifting the bottle and slit-
ting the seal around its cork. "From Deutschland I
brought this myself." He pulled the cork, poured drinks
for them all, lifted his glass in the air. *"Prosit!"* he said,
and drank.

"Well, Howard, I have meant to ask you, how is your
own labor progressing?"

"New America? I've an extensive portion of the book
completed. I have no doubt that it will be ready for your
perusal by the end of 1927. The book is not in the least
sensational, but with the material you have provided me,
in addition to my own observation and researches, I am
certain that it will represent an outstanding contribution
to the comprehension of world relationships and historical
doctrines.

"I cannot say that I have been wholly favorably impressed throughout my studies. The Ku Klux Klan in particular has proved a disappointment. The original Klan of
General Forrest was a very different organization from the
present agglomeration of opportunists and thugs."

"Hey, wait a minute!" Fritz Kuhn started to challenge Howard's opinion, but Kurt Luedecke barked a few words at him and Kuhn subsided.

Viereck ignored the outburst. "Well, and have you finished your study of *Mein Kampf*? You did obtain a copy, at my recommendation?"

Howard nodded. "I found a number of the ideas expressed to be most appealing, and I should be pleased to discuss the book with you at length. In particular, Herr Hitler's notions of racial advancement, the negative effects of certain strains upon the development of national cultures—a fascinating work."

Out of the corner of his eye, Howard could see the bulky Kuhn, still smarting over Luedecke's earlier rebuke, begin to thaw. Luedecke himself, as well as Viereck and Kiep, seemed pleased with Howard's comments.

"However," he continued, "I must state that I found the tone of the volume overly bombastic and emotional."

"It was dictated in prison, you know," Viereck explained.

"And the logic," Howard said, "perhaps because of difficulties in translation, of course, one must always be cautious in judging works read in translation, but with that proviso mentioned, I must say that the logic at times baffles me. The author seems to leap from premise to conclusion, or simply to assert his conclusions, without fully demonstrating the logical process which leads from the accepted factual departure point to the terminus of the argument."

Again, Fritz Kuhn began to object but was silenced by Kurt Luedecke.

Viereck said, "I must concede that you make telling points, Howard. Perhaps at a later time we shall find an opportunity to examine the book at length. I am convinced that *Mein Kampf* will become one of the pivotal documents of modern history. One must learn to penetrate such a work beyond the superficial criteria of merely literary criticism, and understand the impassioned expressions of the soul, the will, the national fervor, that it embodies.

"For now, however. . ." Again he consulted his watch. "If you wish to reach the shore before darkness falls. . ."

Dr. Kiep, Howard, and Fritz Kuhn rose and moved to retrieve the heavy diving gear in which they had descended from the *Alpdrucken*. Viereck and Luedecke rose also, but shook hands with the others, indicating an intention to remain behind. "I am still 'touring Europe,' and will be for another month or so," Viereck smiled. "In fact, I do have a number of interviews yet to be performed, in Bavaria and Austria. And I must return to Munich for further consultations with Hitler and his associates. A splendid group—Hess, Eckart, Gottfried Feder, Albert Rosenberg—"

Howard Lovecraft lifted an eyebrow.

"Is there something—?" Viereck asked.

"Albert Rosenberg," Howard repeated. "An odd name, I should think, for an associate of Hitler's, in view of Hitler's comments regarding Karl Lueger and his general attitude toward Jews and other inferior strains."

Viereck laughed. "Albert is kidded a good deal about his name, but he is Aryan, I assure you; his name means 'rosy mountain', an almost Rosicrucian reference, eh? You are familiar with the Rosicrucian Order and their pseudo-history?"

"Oh yes. Different branches of the movement claim a lineage dating to ancient Egypt, Atlantis, Mu—Ignatius Donnelly and Colonel Churchward, Madame Blavatsky—they all tie together, somehow, and all amount to little more than a method for fleecing the innocent lambs of their wool. Certainly their influence is no more pernicious than that of Christianity, however, with its puling, weakling so-called saviour.

"But I suppose that such movements give comfort, of a sort, to minds too lacking in strength or in courage to face the realities of an indifferent and ultimately meaningless universe. And some of them do achieve a beauty of a sort. In their vestments and architecture, their ceremonies and liturgical music, if not in their absurd doctrines."

Again Viereck looked at his watch.

Lovecraft, Kiep and Kuhn shook hands again with him and with Kurt Luedecke, then were helped into their diving costumes and shown to the airlock. A sailor from the *grundstruckvorhaben*, also in diver's equipment but with an air-hose running back to the project, carried a submarine lantern and guided them to their diving platform. They reconnected their air, telephone, and life lines to the lines left at the platform, and were soon hoisted back to the *Alpdrucken*. Howard was happy to don his normal clothing once again.

~ ~ ~ ~ ~

On the train back to New York, Vincent Starrett finally got to examine the newspapers he'd bought at the Boston North Station. He mumbled a single word repeatedly until Howard Lovecraft demanded to know what it was.

"Ah, scope, Howard. It seems there is no avoiding the syllable today. Look here."

He produced a news story concerning the opening of a new film, *Wings*, produced by a man named Hughes and dealing with the aerial exploits of the Great War. "You see?" Starrett pointed out. "Magnascope. The size of the screen is doubled to give the audience a sensation of being surrounded by the action instead of merely witnessing it.

"And here's another. Students in New Jersey have found a sunken submarine complete with periscope, buried in six feet of dried mud. They examined old records and found that the inventor escaped the disastrous experiment but the machine was irretrievable. Hah—1870!

"And still another. What were you doing out there all afternoon while I was off with that Russian phony and his social-climbing sugar mama? Traipsing around the sea-bottom in a brass hat? You should have been in communication with Mr. John L. Baird, the inventor of television over in bonnie Scotland."

"Eh?" Howard reacted. "I thought television was an American invention. Did Secretary Hoover not inaugurate the service?"

"Everybody claims it." Starrett rustled the newspaper and paraphrased the overseas report. "Meestair Baird has been running experiments in Britain with grand success, and claims to have devised a thingumbob called an—oh, I beg your pardon, Howard. I read this as a *noctoscope*, but actually it's a *noctovisor*."

"Well, what does it do anyway?"

"Hmph. Meestair Baird claims that it permits him to pick up television images in the dark, in thick smoke or fog, or even undersea, and transmit them as successfully as if he were in a lighted theater."

Howard said, "We could certainly have used one of those devices this afternoon! What a Hades-like place the sea-floor is. Ah, well. I shall have to mention that device of Mr. Baird's to my friend Hardeen the Mysterious. I don't know if it would be of use to him in his stage presentation, but he seems to have a predilection for subaquaeous escapes and I imagine that he would feel curiosity if nothing more for each advancement in the state of applicable technology."

Starrett shuffled the newspapers some more.

"Hah, here's one that won't effect me but might be of interest to you, Howard. I'll be headed back to Chicago shortly but you keep an eye on Broadway, I know."

"Eh?"

"The theater."

Howard snorted. "Hardly! If I attend once in two years it's a record-setter for me. The last performance I attended was *Outward Bound* in 1924. Went with the late Harry Houdini."

"I beg your pardon. There I thinking you were a regular stagedoor Johnny. Well, look at this anyway—list of openings for the new season. Here's *The Intruder* by your chum Mr. Viereck and someone called Paul Eldridge. Billed as 'another Salome.' I wonder what that could mean. And here's *If* by Lord Dunsany."

"A fine fellow! Now that, Vincentius, An' I can but accumulate the price of a ducat, I shall make it my business to attend. Any more?"

Starrett frowned over the list. "The usual run of song-and-dance trivia. A new *Zeigfield Follies* with Eddie Cantor, something called *Funny Face* with that brother- and-sister team, the Astaires, and here's one I know you'd like to see, considering your love of fantasy and antiquity. Rodgers and Hart have done a musical version of *A Connecticut Yankee*."

Howard Lovecraft combined a small laugh and a rueful shake of his head. "Oh, my aching bank account! Most of those will simply have to get along without me, much as I shall regret to miss them. However, I expect to be holed up over most of the autumn completing my book anyway. So perhaps it's just as well that I have not the wherewithal to play the patron of the theater. I'd never finish my work!"

"Of course you're right," Starrett agreed. "Then I won't bother you with this straight play that's coming to the Horace Liveright Theater."

Lovecraft gritted his teeth. "Tormentor! Out with it!"

"I'd go myself, but I'll be back in Chicago by then. Too bad. Well, maybe they'll get up a road company, or even make a film version of the thing. I'll write to you about it, Howard, if they do and I get to see it."

"At the peril of thy gizzard, Vincentius, deliver the straight infor!"

"Hmm, very well then. *Dracula*, play by John Balderston, based upon the novel by Abraham Stoker."

CHAPTER TWENTY-EIGHT:

THE STEAMING AND RANCID STEW OF RACES

BACK IN New York, Howard kept to his resolve, spending days and weeks on end sealed in the Parkside Avenue apartment, covering page upon page of foolscap with his spidery dark-blue script. Sonia kept the apartment well supplied with food, tended to Howard's needs by way of laundry and office supplies. From time to time Howard would finish a chapter of *New America and the Coming World-Empire* and set it aside for typing; half the time he performed that hateful task himself, reading glasses perched on the bridge of his straight nose, a shaded floor-lamp placed to shed its light on the old Postal standard machine. Other times, Sonia would relieve him of the task, putting in an hour or two in the evening after completing her day's duties at Russek's on 36th Street, just uptown from the Waldorf-Astoria, or devoting half of a Saturday or Sunday to the task.

On occasion Howard would grow stale at his task of study and correlation and writing. One source of variety was correspondence; he'd switched most of his incoming mail from Barnes Street to the Brooklyn apartment, and devoted many late hours to writing to Two-gun Bob, Klarkash-ton the wizard of Auburn, W. Paul Cook in remote Athol. He wrote even to Samuel Loveman, his poet-friend from Cleveland who was now residing in New York, and to Frank Belknap Long; it seemed easier to draw a sheet of foolscap from the shelf where he kept blank paper and cover it with writing than it would have been to walk to the nearest BMT kiosk and ride into Manhattan to visit them.

When he felt the need for escape from the apartment he strolled across Parkside Avenue and wandered the knolls and pathways of Prospect Park. This latter activity was almost always conducted in the late hours, after he had completed his day's (or more properly, night's) work. He would don a light topcoat and his dark fedora (Sonia had made him buy another; counting the replacement for the hat he had lost in the Seekonk, that made two new headpieces in a single year: an unprecedented extravagance for Howard), let himself out through the deserted and echoing stone lobby of 259 Parkside, and cross the deserted thoroughfare to the park.

Usually he remembered to carry scraps of meat in case of chance encounters with feline residents of the neighborhood, and lumps of sugar for the horse of a mounted patrolman or pre-dawn delivery wagon. Once he met a cat and discovered that he had forgot to bring food; he sped back to the apartment, let himself in and sacked the ice box without awakening Sonia, and returned to the park, relieved to find the cat patiently awaiting its treat. The Parkside area proved rich in feline nocturnal prowlers. Howard became fast friends with a number of them. His favorite was a wraithlike black torn whose stubby tail and uneven fangs marked him the veteran of tough encounters. Howard dubbed the tom Nigger-man III and felt fully repaid for proffered victuals when he received a vigorous butt from the tough old tom.

His daily routine was always highlighted by the arrival of each morning's and afternoon's mail delivery, and by a perusal of a selection of the day's newspapers which Sonia brought home each evening. The papers, as ever, carried a mix of the trivial and the profound. President Coolidge, vacationing in the West, announced that he did not intend to seek the Presidency again in 1928. Radicals protesting the approaching execution of Sacco and Vanzetti bombed the 28th Street subway stations on Broadway and on Lexington Avenue.

The warring Chinese factions continued to chase each other up and down the railroad lines that provided the shaky infrastructure of that huge, feeble nation. Another Sacco and Vanzetti bombing occurred, this time in Baltimore. Roger Francezon, Chairman of the Industrial Workers of the World, issued a statement to the press accusing capitalist plotters of the act.

One Lewis Landes of the International Broadcasting Corporation brought a court action against Hugo Gernsback's Experimenter Publishing Company alleging that Gernsback had reneged on a commitment to lease his radio station, WRNY, to Landes. Howard Lovecraft made a

Richard A. Lupoff

face at the item, phoned Alexander Laing at his Greenwich Village apartment and received a gratifying description of the discomfiture at 230 Fifth Avenue. If Gernsback was unprepared to keep his promises, at least he could be made to wriggle unhappily over such betrayals.

Mrs. Augusta E. Stetson, 85-year-old excommunicated Christian Scientist predicted that she herself would never die, and that Mary Baker Eddy, founder of the Mother Church and dead for seventeen years, was planning to be resurrected. The Central Committee of the Communist Parity of the USSR condemned Trotzky and Zinonieff but failed to expel them. Doubleday, Page issued *Gerfalcon*, a strange fantasy by Leslie Barringer, giving Howard Lovecraft renewed hope for his own works' eventual appearance in boards. Chiang Kai-shek, despondent over conditions in China, resigned his Kuomintang posts and entered a Buddhist monastery in Fenghwa County, Chekiang Province.

Michael A. Musmanno, acting for Sacco and Vanzetti, appealed to Supreme Court Justice Louis Brandeis for a stay of execution. Brandeis expressed sympathy for the condemned men but explained that his wife's friendship with Mrs. Sacco might prejudice his actions and disqualified himself from acting. Paul Winters, a field organizer for the Ku Klux Klan, announced a recruiting drive for the Kamelias (female Klan members) and the American Krusaders (an affiliated body for foreign-born citizens not eligible for regular Klan membership).

When the three convicted killers were finally executed in Dedham, Massachusetts—the night of August 22, or, more precisely, early on the morning of the 23rd—it came almost as an anticlimax to the series of trials, convictions, appeals, demonstrations, panels, stays, reports, statements, charges, and denials, that had gone on for more than seven years. Celestino Madeiros went first, his last words (if any) unrecorded by the press; Nicola Sacco went to the electric chair at 12:19 that Tuesday morning, a dedicated man to the end, his last words (*long live anarchy*) widely reported, although different journalists claimed that he had spoken them in English or in Italian; poor Vanzetti, always the follower, was left alone for only seven minutes. Without his stiffer-spined comrade to prompt him at the end, he died proclaiming his innocence rather than spouting political slogans.

Sonia Lovecraft had risen and left for her job at Russek's hours before Howard's awakening that day, so he did not hear of the execution as Sonia did, on the early morning news broadcast. For him the major occurrence of the day was the arrival in the morning mail of the September *Weird Tales*, but even that was more of a letdown than anything else. Wright had announced "Pickman's Model" in the August issue; true enough the story was only promised for "the next few issues," but that usually meant the following month. In this case, Pharnabus had left the story out, and Howard had not even the consolation of his accustomed mention in the Eyrie. As far as this copy of *Weird Tales* showed, Howard Phillips Lovecraft did not exist.

He left the apartment for a rare daylight stroll through Prospect Park, and stationed himself finally on Sonia's route home so they would meet as he returned to the apartment. The snub he had received in the new *Weird Tales* left Howard badly in need of some sympathy and cheer, and Sonia, instead of providing these in her usual manner, acted upset and preoccupied.

They returned to the apartment in silence, then Howard demanded to know the cause of Sonia's uncharacteristic manner. She told him that everyone was concerned with the Massachusetts executions; this was the first news that Howard had of them. His comments were concerned chiefly with the involvement of the Morelli gang in Providence. Apparently Celestino Madeiros had been silenced by the murder of his brother—more members of the Madeiros family remained at large, subject to retribution if Celestino said too much, and so he had gone in silence to his death.

Sonia prepared only a light dinner and left most of her portion uneaten. She retired early and Howard returned to his work, pushing *New America and the Coming World-Empire* toward its completion. He was eager for the return of Sylvester Viereck from the latter's European tour. Howard wanted to discuss the latest situation with Viereck before finishing up his draft manuscript, but in the meanwhile he had made extensive notes for his section on the role of Germany in the new arrangement of world powers.

Howard still had some difficulty in erasing the last of his ill-will toward the Kaiser and the German nation, but he felt that he had found a kindred soul in the German-Austrian Hitler who had written *Mein Kampf.*

The fellow's prose was far from stylish, at times vague; at others bombastic and melodramatic But many of the sentiments were virtually interchangeable with ideas that Howard himself had embodied in essays for the amateur press, in letters, or even in his own stories. Too, Hitler was opposed to the use of alcohol and of tobacco, as was Howard; and the German-Austrian's loss of his parents, the thwarting of his earliest ambitions, his sense of historical displacement from an era of culture and of heroism into one of vulgar materialism, all produced in Howard a sense not only of agreement with Hitler's philosophical outlook, but of personal kinship approaching brotherhood.

Hitler's book was bulky and rambling—almost 400 pages of heavy if not murky prose, with a publisher's slip enclosed promising the issuance of a second volume. The first alone seemed sufficient. Howard discussed the book and its impact on his own work with Sonia. She said that she had always been highly interested in Howard's work and eager to read his writings, whether essays, letters, or fiction. As for his section on Hitler, though, she pointed out that her own European experience had been divided between Russia and England. Perhaps Howard would do better to discuss the subject with one of his German-born friends—Kiep, Luedecke, Spanknoebel, Kuhn, the printer Stahrenberg he'd met through George Pagnanelli, or Sylvester Viereck himself.

Howard pointed out that not all of those men were German-born, although all were of German blood. But he preferred to discuss the material with Sonia anyway, both because she knew and understood him and his work better than any of the others, and because she was herself a Jewess.

Because Hitler made certain very serious charges against the Jewish race, it would temper Howard's commentary to have a Jew rather than a Gentile examine his draft, even challenge it.

Sonia consented at last, after a final suggestion that Howard add others to the discussion group—Theo Weiss, for instance, or the poet Samuel Loveman. When Howard still demurred, Sonia agreed to act alone.

Howard retired to his alcove with his copy of *Mein Kampf* (by now heavily annotated in his cramped, spidery hand) and a sheaf of foolscap. He emerged hours later with the following document only to find Sonia still seated on the couch, sewing in her lap, asleep.

~ ~ ~ ~ ~

When Adolf Hitler, born in the Austrian village of Braunau just a year before the present writer entered upon the worldly plane in Providence-Plantations, was growing into his youth, he traveled to visit Vienna, just as the present writer, in slightly later years, traveled to such cities as Boston and New-York.

Young Hitler's comments on his visit strike a most sympathetic chord. He says, "The purpose of my trip was to study the picture gallery in the Court Museum, but I had eyes for scarcely anything but the Museum itself. From morning until late at night, I ran from one object of interest to another, but it was always the buildings which held my primary interest. For hours I could stand in front of the Opera, for hours I could gaze at Parliament; the whole Ring Boulevard seemed to me like an enchantment out of *The Thousand-and-One Nights*."

Later, Hitler says, "I believe that those who knew me in those days took me for an eccentric. Amid all this, as was only natural, I served my love of architecture with ardent zeal. Along with music, it seemed to me the queen of the arts: under such circumstances my concern with it was not 'work' but the greatest pleasure. I could read and draw until late into the night, and never grow tired."

This dedication of the German-Austrian to the field of architecture is clearly indicative of a sensitivity and understanding of one of the highest fields of human endeavor, for in architecture are combined science and art in a manner which not only rewards the grandest aesthetic faculties of the most finely attuned mind, but also serves the practical requirements of diurnal human enterprise.

Herr Hitler's appreciation of traditional values and time-honored modes of expression give the lie to charges that he is of a radical bent and indicate clearly to the discerning eye that he is, in fact, a conservative with regard to such values. His judgment of "modern" politico-literary documents gives clear evidence of the soundness of his approach:

> "Only our decadent metropolitan bohemians can feel at home in this maze of reasoning and cull an 'inner experience' from this dung-heap of literary Dadaism, supported by the proverbial modesty of a section of our people who always detect profound wisdom in what is most incomprehensible to them personally."

The present writer's familiarity with the meaningless and insulting effusions of Messrs. Tzara, Arp, and Ball, Dr. Huelsenbeck, Messrs. Duchamp, Aragon, Eluard, Soupault, Ray and their disciples, leaves him faced with the choice between a totally nihilistic philosophy on the one hand and a Marxist revolutionary outlook upon the other; Herr Hitler is unchallengeably correct in his condemnation of the movement.

Mein Kampf is of course filled with expressions of its author's dedication to the preservation of the superior races from contamination by lesser strains of humanity; his identification of Slavic, Jewish, and other inferior influences and their destructive effect upon Aryan civilization are forceful and compelling. In particular, one is struck by Herr Hitler's anecdotal recitation of his experiences in the evolution of his racial awareness:

> "Once, as I was strolling through the Inner City (of Vienna – HPL) I suddenly encountered an apparition in a black caftan and black hair locks. Is this a Jew? was my first thought.
> "For, to be sure, they had not looked like that in Linz. I observed the man furtively and cautiously, but the longer I stared at this foreign face, scrutinizing feature for feature, the more my first question assumed a new form:
> "Is this a German?"

And again, in describing his reaction to the polyglot population of Vienna, Hitler expresses himself thusly:

"I was repelled by the conglomeration of races which the capital showed me, repelled by this whole mixture of Czechs, Poles, Hungarians Ruthenians, Serbs, and Croats, and everywhere, the eternal mushroom of humanity—Jews and more Jews. To me the giant city seemed the embodiment of racial desecration."

Only an individual of gentle breeding with roots traced to the finest and eldest stock of the higher races and possibly appreciate the horror and revulsion which must have been felt by Herr Hitler in the moment he describes. The resident of white-steepled and tradition-bound communities such as are found primarily in the New England region of the United States, and in few other locales (such as Charleston, South Carolina), and then forced to submit to the steaming and rancid stew of races and languages encountered in such bohemian quarters as Greenwich Village in New York City or the populous Red Hook section of Brooklyn, can fully understand the fury felt by Adolf Hitler at the racial and cultural desecration which he observed visited upon the cities of Europe.

Advocates of so-called "democracy" and "universal suffrage"—in fact, of rabble-rule and the tyranny of the vulgar and easily-swayed mob with its whimsical and changeable favor—have the effrontery in these days to voice praise of precisely such degenerate programs and demagogic appeals as the repulsive concept of the "melting pot," "industrial democracy" and similar such vile sloganistic catch-phrases. Herr Hitler crushes this pernicious nonsense with the following argument:

"Mustn't our principle of parliamentary majorities lead to the demolition of any idea of leadership?

"Does anyone believe that the progress of this world springs from the mind of majorities and not from the brains of individuals?

"Or does anyone expect that the future will be able to dispense with this premise of human culture?

"Does it not, on the contrary, today seem more indispensable than ever?

"By rejecting the authority of the individual and replacing it by the numbers of some momentary mob, the parliamentary principle of majority rule sins against the basic aristocratic principle of Nature, though it must be said that this view is not necessarily embodied in the present-day decadence of our upper ten thousand."

Another fallacy of much degenerate modern thought is the notion that universal peace is not only a desirable but an attainable goal. The present writer wonders which of these paired absurdities is the parent, which the offspring, of the other. Does the fool who considers the momentary respite and luxuriation facilitated by the temporary state of affairs known as "peace" create, through a fantasy of wishful thinking, such chimerae as the flaccid and irresolute League of Nations? Or does the soft-minded and idealistic supporter of the League follow the path of his own mad reasoning to the illusory conclusion that such a senseless body can overcome the innermost nature of mankind—in fact, of all species—which is competition, the triumph of the powerful and the resolute, and the ultimate extinction of the weak and the degenerate, whose blood, if not eliminated from the heredity of the race, will in time serve only to weaken and threaten with extinction, all of the species?

Once again, the present writer finds in Herr Hitler's works a passage which crystallizes precisely the principles and attitudes needful to the comprehension of the problem:

"No one can doubt that this world will some day be exposed to the severest struggles for the existence of mankind. In the end, only the urge for self-preservation can conquer. Beneath it so-called humanity, the expression of a mixture of stupidity, cowardice, and know-it-all conceit, will melt like snow in the March sun. Mankind has grown great in eternal struggle, and only in eternal peace does it perish.

"Was it not the German press," Herr Hitler inquires, "which knew how to make the absurdity of 'Western democracy' palatable to our people until finally, ensnared by all the enthusiastic tirades, they thought they could entrust their future to a League of Nations?"

Fortunately, a small band of wise and selfless Senators, rising above the usual pettiness and self-seeking of political hacks, were able to prevent the United States from entrusting *its* future to that League against which Herr Hitler rightfully rails. Let the weak and foolish nations in their decadent self-indulgence entrust their protection to this sham, while the virile and vigorous States rely upon their own strength, self-determination, and will to defend their interests against all threats, to preserve them against the storms and earthquakes of international competition!

As early as the year 1915, the present writer, in an essay titled "The Crime of the Century," pointed out the true tragedy of the European War of 1914-1918. This was not a struggle of ideologies, for all political ideologies are but the transitory trappings beneath which the nations of the globe carry out their struggle for territories, for resources, and for influence with the inferior races and minor nations of the world. Above all, war is the ultimate testing ground and crucible for the races of mankind, in which the strains which are unsuited to continuing existence are weeded out, those which are of a viable but inferior nature are subjugated to the will and guidance of their betters, and those of the most advanced type are offered the opportunity of placing banners upon the mountain peaks and their heels upon the necks of those lesser breeds ultimately fitted by Nature only to play the role of hewers of wood and fetchers of water.

The present writer is in enthusiastic agreement with Adolf Hitler in reaching the inescapable conclusion that the two most dangerous of the inferior races, the one because of their insidious cleverness in infiltrating and undermining Aryan societies, the other by the force of their simple brute forces, are those two products of the Oriental spawning ground of the Middle East and eastern Europe, the Jew and the Slav. By contrast, the most advanced, the most cultured, the most sensitive, the most virile, the most warlike, the most intelligent, the most forthright, and the most courageous; consequently, by the dictate of Nature, the dominant and most worthy of survival of the races of mankind, is the Nordic or Teutonic race found in the British Isles, in the Scandinavian peninsula where the blue-eyed and yellow-bearded Vikings once roamed fjord and forest and where their heirs carry yet the blood of those enviable savages, and in Germany.

Herr Hitler accurately and painstakingly analyses the errors which led to the outbreak of the Great War, "The Crime of the Century," in paragraphs to which the present writer would proudly have affixed his own name; knowing that the Jew owns no land in his own right, Hitler leaves the weeding-out of this pernicious elements to a later time, turning his attention first to the subjugation of the swarming Slav:

"If land was desired in Europe, it could be obtained by and large only at the expense of Russia, and this meant that the new Reich must again set itself on the march along the road of the Teutonic Knights of old, to obtain by the German sword sod for the German plow and daily bread for the nation.

"For such a policy there was but one ally in Europe: England.

"With England alone was it possible, our rear protected, to begin the new Germanic march. Our right to do this would have been no less than the right of our forefathers. None of our pacifists refuses to eat the bread of the East, although the first plowshare in its day bore the name of 'sword!'

"Consequently, no sacrifice should have been too great for winning England's willingness. We should have renounced colonies and sea power, and spared English industry our competition. . .

"There was a time when England would have listened to reason on this point, since she was well aware that Germany as a result of her increased population had to seek some way out and either find it with England in Europe or without England in the world."

How different would the history of the past thirteen years have been, had the Kaiser and his ministers, no less the Habsburg regime in Austria, had available to them the wise counsel of *Mein Kampf*! The Great War, The Crime of the Century, might have been averted. The two great branches of the elevated Nordic Race, the Anglo-Saxon and the Teuton, instead of turning upon each other in fratricidal carnage, might have turned to the East and swept away the ever-looming threat of the Russian bear.

Not only would the Slav have been thrown back upon the mountainous borderlands of his Oriental breeding-place, thus retarding if not wholly eliminating the pernicious influence of the decadent Tsarist Empire, but that scourge of civilization, the Russian *Bolshevist* regime which replaced the evils of the Tsar with the even greater malignity of the Commissar, might well have been snuffed out *in utero*. Where the despicable Romanoff dynasty was eliminated only to present to the world the monstrous new succession of Ulianov, Trotzky, and Djugashvili, there might instead have been established a firm and uncompromising but nevertheless culture-bearing and just colonial regime headed by some carefully chosen representative of the great royal-blooded tribe of the cousinly House of Windsor-Hanover-Hohenzollern.

It is already known that the decadent Romanoffs were in fact a lesser branch of the Royal Houses of England and Germany. In the grand and admirable war of Teuton against Slav which might have transpired in place of the tragedy of 1914-1918, Nicholas II and his Tsarina might peacefully have abandoned their prerogatives in favor of a more virile and dynamic branch of the family, and retired to an honorable exile either in a more remote region of their former realm, or in a congenial clime such as that of the French or Spanish Cote d'Azur. Instead, they faced their ultimate tragedy in the infamous cellar at Ekaterinburg.

As Herr Hitler points out over and over in his volume, the rivalry of nations is ultimately a manifestation not of political differences but of the racial struggle for domination, supremacy, and ultimately survival. Following the establishment of an Aryan dominion in the regions currently populated and governed by Slavic mongrels of every description, the succeeding and far more difficult task will be the purification of the white nations by means of the identification and removal of such inferior stock as has infiltrated, ingratiated, often dominated, and most regrettably of all, interbred with the superior Aryan strain.

The most obvious and most pernicious because most extensive instance of this infiltration, is that of the Jew. Hitler points out most compellingly the fact that the Jew, while permeating the body of all of the great nations of Europe and America, and living off those nations as does any parasite off the strength and substance of its host, in fact has nothing whatever of the two ingredients which mark any race of entitlement to consideration, respect, or preservation: a culture and a state. Herr Hitler says:

"Since the Jew—for reasons which will at once become apparent—was never in possession of a culture of his own, the foundations of his intellectual work were always provided by others. His intellect at all times developed through the cultural world surrounding him.

"The reverse process never took place.

"For if the Jewish people's instinct of self-preservation is not smaller but larger than that of other peoples, if his intellectual faculties can easily arouse the impression that they are equal to the intellectual gifts of other races, he lacks completely the most essential requirement for a cultured people, the idealistic attitude.

"In the Jewish people the will to self-sacrifice does not go beyond the individual's naked instinct of self-preservation. Their apparently great sense of solidarity is based on the very primitive herd instinct that is seen in many other living creatures in this world. . .

"That is why the Jewish state—which should be the living organism for preserving and increasing a race—is completely unlimited as to territory. For a state formation to have a definite spatial setting always presupposes an idealistic attitude on the part of the state-race, and especially a correct interpretation of the concept of work. In the exact measure in which this attitude is lacking, any attempt at forming, even of preserving, a spatially delimited state fails. And thus the basis on which alone culture can arise is lacking.

"Hence the Jewish people, despite all apparent intellectual qualities, is without any true culture of its own. For what sham culture the Jew today possesses is the property of other peoples, and for the most part it is ruined in his hands. . .the Jew never possessed a state with definite territorial limits and therefore never called a culture his own."

While Herr Hitler's book serves many functions in a single volume, standing as an autobiographical recitation, a historical analysis of the period leading up to the Great War, a chronicle of the author's experiences in that war, a record and observation of the postwar period in Germany, a very extensive and oft-times eloquent exposition of Herr Hitler's philosophy of race and culture, and a delineation of the founding of the German Workers Party, its metamorphosis into the National Socialist German Workers Party, and its program for the acquisition and exercise of power, it is possible that the greatest value of *Mein Kampf* lies in the author's explication of the respective roles of the politico-philosophical theoretician (such as the present writer) and the practical politician (such as Herr Hitler), and the interrelationship of the two:

> "It is not the task of a theoretician to determine the varying degrees in which a cause can be realized, but to establish the cause as such: that is to say: he must concern himself less with the road than with the goal. In this, however, the basic correctness of *an* idea is decisive and not the difficulty of its execution. As soon as the theoretician attempts to take account of so-called 'utility' and 'reality' instead of absolute truth, his work will cease to be a polar star of seeking humanity and instead will become a prescription for everyday life. The theoretician of a movement must lay down its goal, the politician strive for its fulfillment. The thinking of the one, therefore, will be determined by eternal truth, the actions of the other in his correct attitude toward the given facts and their advantageous application; and in this the theoretician's aim must serve as his guiding star."

The present writer has found no clearer statement of the true purpose of theory or the role of the theoretician in over thirty years of broad and extensive reading. The entire purpose, in fact, of *New America and the Coming World-Empire,* is magnificently summed up in the words of Adolf Hitler. The practical tasks which may be assumed by a broad coalition of organizations and movements, whether they be the Social Justice Movement, the Christian Front, the Imperial Fascist Association, the All-Russian National Socialist Labor Party, Friends of the New Germany, various monarchist restorationist movements in widespread nations, the Ku Klux Klan here in the United States, the Patriotic Research Bureau, or any and all other allied bodies, will find in *New America and the Coming World-Empire* their not a road but a goal; a polar star of seeking humanity.

CHAPTER TWENTY-NINE:

AN EXPLOSION IN BROOKLYN

FARNSWORTH WRIGHT at *Weird Tales* was another problem.

At least Gernsback and Dr. Sloane at *Amazing Stories* had not badgered him to alter "The Colour out of Space." If only Gernsback had dealt more honorably with Howard in regard to payment for the story, this might have made for a very useful relationship. Wright and his employer Henneberger at *Weird Tales* were always honest when it came to making payment. Not that they were prompt or generous; seldom either. But one or the other always apologized and explained the necessity for delays, and ultimately they always did produce the promised check, for however small an amount.

Howard found his thoughts drifting. Well, he would get *New America* into shape for Viereck (who was due back from Europe shortly) and deal with any requests for changes in the book when the appropriate time came. There was no point in suffering distress over the matter now.

Howard rose from his work-table and stretched cramped muscles. He crossed the room and stood before Sonia's art deco clock, making a wry face at the polished aluminum case and fantastic modernistic design of the timepiece. In a strange way he found himself growing fond of the thing! It was still as ugly an artifact as ever, but there *was* a certain sense of optimism and energy to it, like something out of one of the futuristic cities that the artist Paul designed for Gernsback's magazines.

A momentary impulse to show his completed manuscript to Sonia gripped Howard; not that she could be expected to read or even to scan the many pages just now, but simply that it would be something to share for a moment. But the clock indicated the nearness of dawn; not an unusual hour for Howard to be completing his work, but hardly a convenient one for Sonia whose daily obligations made a regime of early retirement and early rising mandatory. Not *this* early, Howard could almost hear her murmuring in her sleep-laden voice.

Instead of waking Sonia, Howard put on his fedora and a light topcoat against the pre-dawn coolness. He stood before his work-table, gazing at his newly-completed manuscript like a mother watching a newborn child. Unable to separate himself from the new work he stuffed the pile of foolscap into an oversized manila envelope and tucked it under his arm. He felt that he was acting in a foolish manner, but it was almost as if the book were real only as long as he had it with him. Is a rock real if I do not see it, Bishop Berkeley had asked, and Samuel Johnson, striking his foot on a boulder, replied, "Thus I refute Bishop Berkeley!"

But Howard tucked the manuscript under his arm nonetheless. He crossed the avenue and strolled through Prospect Park, sitting on a rock atop a small knoll to watch the sun rise behind the trees and rooftops of the Scott Fitzgerald country farther east. The air of Brooklyn held a warmth and moisture redolent of life. Even here, in the midst of the metropolis with its noxious mongrel crowds and malodorous gasoline fumes and industrial stench, life not only persisted but throve.

The morning dew had not yet evaporated from the thick grass surrounding Howard's rock, and as he watched a splendid brown-and-red robin swooped upon an industrious earthworm and carried it off in triumph, for all the world like an illustration from some saccharine children's book come to life.

On his way back to Parkside Avenue, Howard passed among the earliest of the city's workers on their way to their places of employment: stevedores with deadly- looking hooks slung carelessly on their muscular shoulders, factory hands with their lunch-boxes clutched under their arms. . .and occasional party-goers, overdressed and bleary-eyed from their protracted revels, wandering home to their beds.

Mingling with this strange heterogeneity, Howard stopped at a tiny eating place at the edge of the park. He counted the change in his pocket and decided that he would treat himself to an early breakfast of ham and eggs and coffee. He bought a Brooklyn *Eagle* and scanned the stories in its first few pages. It wasn't really what Howard would call a trashy sheet—certainly not in the miserable class of the daily tabloids Sonia seemed to favor—but it was hardly a paper of the sort that Howard normally preferred. He wished that he'd bought a morning *Sun* or *Herald-Tribune*, but the die had been cast.

To Howard's despair the *Eagle* carried such trivia as sports news in its front pages, as if such things mattered. But overhearing the conversation of laboring-class diners around him he realized that such insignificant events were taken with great seriousness. One group of men were debating the probabl outcome of the Dempsey-Tunney boxing match to be held next week. Howard sliced a triangular chunk off his slab of grilled ham and conveyed it carefully to his mouth, listening to one curly-haired, swarthy-complexioned longshoreman of probably Sicilian descent telling another dock-worker of square, chunky countenance, that Tunney had beaten Dempsey in their earlier bout by fancy trickery and that Dempsey could not possibly be prevented from knocking out his opponent in the return. On the opposite side of Howard a youthful couple, he in formal tails and she in gown and stole, drank coffee and discussed baseball! The local team, the Brooklyn Robins, and their rivals from Manhattan, a club apparently known as the McGraws, were both the victims of hard luck this season. But the Bronx entry had set an incredible pace and was destined for the World's Championship, while two members of the team, Gehrig and Ruth, were both threatening the all-time home run record of 59 in one season.

Howard shook his head, forked up a large serving of fried egg, and turned his attention back to the Brooklyn *Eagle*. The most interesting news, and hence that receiving the least space, was from Europe. A large party of AEF veterans headed by General Pershing had sailed to France and were touring the battle-sites of the Great War. Meanwhile the political situation in Germany—Howard's recent reading of *Mein Kampf* had given him an increased understanding as well as a heightened interest in the doings of the German nation—had come to one of those curious situations in which an entire mélange of questions were subsumed into a single and intrinsically insignificant issue.

President von Hindenberg had several ceremonial functions on his official calendar. Toward the end of September he would dedicate a war memorial at Tannenberg in East Prussia, and then at the beginning of October would celebrate his own eightieth birthday. Von Hindenberg was himself a popular figure, acceptable to all elements of the German nation. To monarchist-restorationists he was a temporary figurehead, one of the last and greatest military heroes of the old regime, a man in whose hands the spirit of the nation was safe pending the re-establishment of the *Kaiser-Reich*.

To liberal republicans he was a constitutional symbol of the state, in his own right without power but spiritually the guardian and preservator of the republic. To nationalists of a more extreme stripe he was still the Marshall, symbol of military leadership and strength. Only the German *Bolshevists* scorned him.

The question into which the divergent ambitions of these groups were subsumed was that of the colors to be used in the bunting with which cities like Tannenberg, Weimar, Berlin itself, would be decorated for the ceremonial appearances of the President. Monarchists and nationalists stood in *ad hoc* alliance in demanding the use of red, white, and black bunting. Republicans (with limited support from the *Bolshevists* who really would have preferred solid red) insisted that the bunting be of red, gold, and black.

Red, white, and black were the colors of the old Reich.

Red, gold, and black were the colors of the new republic.

That was how the question of Germany's destiny was crystallized into a decision over the colors to be used in decorating a reviewing stand.

Howard put down his fork, sopped up the last remnant of egg with the last remnant of toast, and rose from the oilcloth-covered, padded counter stool. He placed a small stack of coins beside his empty dish, folded his Brooklyn *Eagle* under his arm, retrieved his fedora and topcoat and left the little restaurant. Outside, the gray and pink of dawn had yielded to a pure blue summer sky. The air had picked up a fresh tang and Howard inhaled happily before turning to walk back to the apartment.

Without warning there came a loud sound, a combination of a hard thump and a bass rumble. For the moment Howard could not detect the direction from which the sound had come, then, as the rumble persisted for a few seconds he turned and homed in on it.

The sound had come from downtown Brooklyn.

Several other customers came tumbling through the door of the little restaurant, accompanied by a short-order chef in white cap and apron, spatula still clutched in one hand. They stood looking around the bright morning street, asking one another what the sound had been, where it had come from. Someone suggested that two heavy motor-trucks had collided; another, that a train had been derailed. A dark-complexioned man with a stevedore's hook slung from one shoulder—Howard recognized the Sicilian sports fan—suggested that someone had set off a bomb. The young woman in the gown and stole, no longer bleary-eyed, asked if he meant an aerial bomb, like those used in the Great War, and the Sicilian said No, he meant a bomb planted or thrown, like that in the Haymarket case.

There was no further activity until several police cars and ambulances roared past, gongs sounding.

Once the excitement quieted, Howard resumed his walk home. By this time, he knew, Sonia would have left for Russek's and he would have the apartment to himself. He almost gloated over the prospect of having no obligations: his book was completed, at least in draft form, and he would not concern himself for the moment with the possibility of having to make revisions in it. He could empathize with his friend Houdini's friend Arthur Conan Doyle, at the moment (recorded in Doyle's autobiography) when he wrote the final lines of an early novel and flung his pen across the room, shouting in exuberance. The splattered ink, Doyle recorded, had remained on the wall for many months afterward.

Howard climbed the stairs at 259 Parkside and let himself in the front door of the apartment.

He stood, gaping and appalled, at what he saw. The apartment had been rifled. Drawers were dumped on the carpeting, Sonia's radio apparatus had been overturned (although apparently not damaged—the intruders had been searching, not performing malicious damage), the carpets themselves had been turned back, closets were opened and their contents strewn about; in the bedroom Sonia's mattress and box-spring stood on end; wherever a chair or sofa was fitted with slip-covers and cushions these had been stripped away and tossed aside.

Howard checked the apartment quickly, concentrating on his own research files and manuscripts. These had obviously been examined; they stood about in varying degrees of disorder. But nothing appeared to have been removed or destroyed.

Howard went to the telephone and asked Central for the number of Russek's Department Store in Manhattan. When he reached Sonia he told her rapidly what he had found in the apartment. She asked if there was any sign that the intruders were still about and Howard said No, that they had apparently kept watch in the early-morning hours, noted first his own departure, then Sonia's, and made their raid as soon as they knew there was no one in the apartment.

Sonia told Howard just to remain in the apartment and not try to put anything back in place. She would contact the police from Russek's, then return home on the subway. Howard agreed and ended the conversation.

He paced around the apartment, going from room to room studying the evidence left by the intruders. They had certainly made no effort to conceal the signs of their work, yet nothing was apparently missing or damaged. Had they been searching for something, and failed to find it? Or was the rifling of the apartment done deliberately, as some sort of warning? Was this an act comparable to the Madeiros killing in Providence, something designed to frighten Howard into some course of action? Out of something? If so, he didn't even know what he was supposed to do!

He felt waves of emotion sweeping over him in heightening degrees of intensity. First shock at the invasion of the apartment, then anger at the men who had done the act, then fear—apparently that was the purpose of the rifling, to frighten him—and with that realization, a renewal of his anger. He clenched his teeth and pounded a fist into the palm of his other hand in an outflow of his indignant but futile rage at the unknown men who had done this to him.

He strode to the telephone and stood holding the instrument in one hand trying to decide whom to call about the incident.

Frank Long?

The boy had a fine brain and a good nature but he lacked the years of maturity needed to deal with this. Annie Gamwell or Lillian Clark?

They would twitter sympathetically over the wire from Providence but in the end they would only scold Howard for his foolish and headstrong behaviour in leaving Providence after his past bad experiences in New York; he certainly wanted no vice-maternal lecture at this point.

Vincent Starrett?

But Vincentius had returned to Chicago and it would be a struggle to find him by telephone, a struggle that Howard did not feel up to attempting just now. Sam Loveman?

Howard nodded to himself. Loveman was a late riser and late retirer like himself. That meant that Samuelus, a man of mature years as was Howard and of congenial literary interests, was almost certainly abed at this moment, and he would probably be willing to come to Parkside Avenue and help Howard to deal with the crisis.

But in the precise moment that Howard's fingers closed around the earpiece of the telephone he was shocked nearly into dropping it by the shrill sound of its electric bell. He stood staring flabbergasted at the telephone for a few moments, hearing the shrill and insistent sound of the bell, until he realized that someone had coincidentally placed a call to him just as he was about to have Central ring up Loveman for him.

He lifted the earpiece and heard a cool female voice ask if Mr. Lovecraft could come to the telephone. He said that he was Mr. Lovecraft; the voice asked him to hold for a call from Mr. Viereck.

Viereck said that he had returned to the United States the preceding day, and was back at work. He started to comment on the situation in Europe and to ask about Howard's progress when a key ground in the apartment door and the superintendent of the building entered surrounded by uniformed figures.

Howard interrupted Viereck to say that the police had arrived; he would have to end the call and contact Viereck later.

Viereck began to ask puzzled questions but Howard repeated what he'd said and clicked off. He turned to confront the New York City police. The building superintendent hovered in the background of the group for a few minutes, then disappeared from the apartment, pulling the door shut behind himself.

Howard sat down with a police sergeant. The uniformed man apologized for delay in responding to the call from Sonia. "Is Mrs. Lovecraft here?" he asked. Howard explained that Sonia was on her way home; She had telephoned from her place of business in Manhattan and might be on her way from BMT station even now. "We'd have been here sooner," the police sergeant explained, "but so many squads were called down to the bombing, the precinct is down to a skeleton crew."

"Then it was a bomb!" Howard exclaimed.

The sergeant raised his eyebrows.

"I heard the explosion earlier," Howard said. "I was coming out of a restaurant. Everybody ran out, someone thought it was a train derailment but a wop longshoreman said it was an anarchist's bomb—an anarchist or a *Bolshevist*!"

"They're all reds, don't make a difference, Mr. Lovecraft. They blew up the Supreme Court and the Hall of Records, down at Livingston Street. What a mess! Nobody got killed, a miracle, sir!"

"Mad, nihilistic mongrels," Howard grumbled.

"Yes, sir, they are that. There is no sign of forcible entry, Mr. Lovecraft. Do you know if anyone has a key beside yourself and Mrs. Lovecraft, sir, and the building of course? They seem to have come right through the front door. No, well then either someone has a key you don't know about, or we've got a burglar here who is a locksmith as well. Can you tell what's been taken away, sir?"

Howard explained that nothing had been taken—or apparently nothing had been taken.

The sergeant stroked his fleshy jowls. "That's funny."

"I don't see why."

"Oh, it's just that we had one exactly the same not far from here, just the other day. Careful entry, apartment ransacked, nothing taken."

Howard's ear perked up. "Do you recall the identity of the victim? You say it was near here?"

The sergeant nodded, a look of deep concentration creasing his brow. "It made an impression on me, sir, because the victim was a very interesting fellow. A place over on 21st Street. He was traveling when it occurred, came all the way home from California and found he'd been burgled. Let's see, he's some famous Jew-boy magician, something like that fellow Houdini who used to do the trick escapes. I saw his show once, like to lose faith in my own equipment, the way he got out of locked cells and irons and cuffs. Let's see now, this fellow on 21st Street, what was his name?"

"Hardeen?" Howard supplied.

"That's it! That's the fellow. Gave his legal name as Mr. Weiss. Just like your own experience, Mr. Lovecraft, sir. Do you think we're going to have a rash of breaking-and-enterings with nothing taken? Very odd. Why would anybody want to do something like that? It just don't make any sense, sir." Howard shook his head.

"Well, sir," the sergeant resumed, "if you'll just accompany me on a tour of the apartment, we'll get some notes on just what's been done here."

While they were taking inventory of the burglars' handiwork, Sonia arrived. She ran to Howard, embraced him (much to his embarrassment, for all that the policemen seemed to ignore the exhibition of intimacy), gained his assurance that he was unharmed. They both completed brief statements for the police; the sergeant said there was no present need for them to come down to the station house although they might be asked to do so if a suspect were apprehended.

The police left.

Sonia set about restoring the apartment to its usual order; while she worked, Howard told her that Theo Weiss's home had been similarly raided without the removal of anything. Sonia said she couldn't understand that; neither Theo nor Howard had any enemies, had they?

Richard A. Lupoff

If Theo's sister-in-law, Harry Houdini's widow Beatrice Rahner Weiss, had been the victim, that would have been more understandable. Not that Sonia and Bess were close friends, but an amiable acquaintanceship had developed through Howard Lovecraft's relationship with Ehrich Weiss, and Sonia had stayed in occasional communication with Bess since Ehrich's death.

Houdini had carried out a much-publicized campaign against fraudulent spiritualists in his later years, with Bess's close help. Since Houdini's death, the work had been continued by other members of the magic community who seemed to feel that they had a Ryan Special responsibility to expose those who perverted their art, who used its tricks not to entertain audiences and carry them to lands of wonder and mystification, but to deceive and rob them.

Recently Carnegie Hall had seen a debate between Howard Thurston, a collegial friend of Houdini's, and the Reverend Arthur Ford, one of the world's most famous spiritualists. In the course of the debate Ford had claimed that Houdini himself had sent messages back to his widow. At the dramatic moment a petite, white-haired woman had risen in the audience, identified herself as Beatrice Houdini, and denied having received any such messages.

Houdini had been cursed repeatedly by spiritualists; if such forces were behind the odd burglaries they might have been directed against Howard Lovecraft because of his work with Houdini, against Bess Houdini or Howard Thurston. By why Theo? He had taken over much of his brother's magic and escape act, and had worked on these in earlier years with his brother. But he was not strongly identified with Ehrich's anti-fraud campaign.

Sonia Lovecraft lifted the telephone and waited for Central to come onto the line.

While Sonia placed her call, Howard left the apartment to check the brass-doored mailbox in the building lobby, against the morning's delivery. He found a letter there from Vincent Starrett, once again using the North Fremont Street address.

"Good news!" Starrett's letter said in part. "Since you have a stake in the success of *Seaports*. I'm sending you word before any other. I do ask, though, that you hold off any public statement until the merger announcement is made.

"You'll remember, Howard, that I exhibited some nervousness over the reception *Seaports* would receive, in view of the merger rumours circulating about Doran. Well, when I arrived at home here in Caponeville, what should await me but a *billet-doux* from Mr. George B. Doran himself. (Now why do people act like that? He had me at his beck and call for half a year and wouldn't tip his hand; as soon as I left town he wrote me *everything*. In the words of my very favorite burlesque comedian, Monkeys is the craziest peoples!)

"In a nutshell, Howard, Doran has completed his merger talks and we are to be presented with a new tripartite publishing enterprise including Doran, the present Doubleday, Page (Nelson D'day is George's chief associate in the new firm; what happened to poor Page deponent knoweth not), and the venerable English firm of William Heinemann.

"Georgie states that he specifically discussed *Seaports in the Moon* with Nelson Doubleday. Nelson was willing to accept the book, along with the rest of Doran's inventory, for the new firm. But Doran insisted that Doubleday look over my manuscript and respond to it, which was done, and the book is formally accepted for issuance by *Doubleday, Doran* in the new year of 1928.

"So—my thanks again for your sage advice concerning the handling of Messrs. Poe and Legrand (I think one of the best passages in the book); and of course a suitably inscribed copy will be coming your way as soon as the thing is bound.

"As for me, it's back to the beat and the deadline, at least for a while, but I shall turn my hand to fiction again sooner or later, rest assured."

~ ~ ~ ~ ~

Howard smiled broadly, folded the letter back into its envelope and stuck it in his pocket, then made his way upstairs once again.

CHAPTER THIRTY:

A CASE FOR DR. DOYLE

HOWARD AND Sonia met Theo Weiss at the Greek restaurant they frequently visited. Sonia had phoned Theo and asked him to join them, then had called her supervisor at Russek's and explained that she would return to work the following day.

At the restaurant, all ordered lunch, then Sonia and Howard, speaking alternately, described the morning's incident. "The policeman told Howard that you had been raided recently, just as we were. I thought there might be something we could work out together, Dash. You and Howard and I, to find out what's going on. I wouldn't have minded an ordinary burglary so much—well, yes I would, to be honest. But I think this bothers me even more.

"What could they have wanted? Why didn't they take anything? Who would go to the trouble of conducting a raid like that, yet take nothing away? The police seem totally baffled, of course."

"I cannot avoid the suspicion that there is some connection between this and the Madeiros murder in Providence," Howard supplied.

Dash picked up a double-layered piece of round Greek bread and tore it open, filled it with chick peas and bits of feta cheese, and took a large bite. He chewed meditatively.

"I gave the police a theory of my own," he said after swallowing. "I told them that the burglars might be rivals, looking for the secrets of my escapes and illusions. I was in Oakland, California, when the burglary took place—at least, that is as near as I can come to putting a date on it, since I only found the mess when I reached home at the end of my tour.

"I told the police that my most preciously guarded secrets are the Flight of Time and the Chinese Torture Chamber. Of course, I had the equipment for these with me on tour. And the knowledge is here." He tapped his temple with a finger-tip. "Not on paper. That would be too dangerous. Only I know the secrets, plus my most trusted assistants, who are solemnly pledged to reveal nothing while I live, and at the time of my death to await the reading of my will to see what instructions have been left for them."

He paused to munch further at his unusual sandwich.

Sonia looked at Theo with curiosity. "Then you think it was other magicians looking for your secrets?"

"In that case," Howard commented, "it doesn't tie in with *our* burglary at all. That seems to require a stretching of the long arm of coincidence rather beyond acceptable limits."

Hardeen made a gesture with his left hand while he picked up a coffee cup with his right and washed down his food. "I told the police nothing untrue, you understand, and the burglars might indeed have been rivals of mine—or simple thugs in the employ of my rivals—but there is something else that I had with me, that I did not tell the police."

He paused dramatically; Howard and Sonia restrained themselves from demanding what the mystery was.

Hardeen placed his coffee cup carefully on its saucer, folded the fingers of his two hands and placed them under his chin. "You first made me aware of a fellow named John L. Baird, Howard. Do you remember who he is?"

"Of course. The Scotsman. He was experimenting with long-range transmission of television images."

"Indeed," Hardeen nodded. "And he was also working on a device called a *noctovisor*, you recall? The object was to facilitate television transmissions under difficult atmospheric conditions, at night, and perhaps beneath the sea."

"Yes, I recall."

"What I did not mention to the burglary squad was that I now possess a noctovisor. I suspect that the raiders were after it, not the Flight of Time or the Chinese Chamber."

Sonia was astonished. "How did you get the noctovisor?"

"I spoke with Mr. Baird. Identified myself. He knew who I was. In fact, we discovered that we had almost met twenty-five years ago. You're familiar with my brother's famous—or infamous—encounter with a Mr. Hodgson in Blackburn, Lanes. John Baird was in the audience, cheering for Houdini for all he was worth, and at the end of the performance, Baird was one of the mob that chased poor Hodgson down the street!" He ended the sentence in laughter.

"I didn't know you had been in Scotland recently, Dash." Sonia placed one hand lightly on Theo's immaculate cuff.

"I haven't been. As soon as I got home from that last little tour of New England, I telephoned Mr. Baird. The transatlantic service has been running for a few months now, and it works very well. I arranged to purchase an experimental model of Baird's device, and for the right price he carted it down to the wharf personally and put it aboard a Cunarder for me."

Howard Lovecraft leaned forward. "Does it really work? Have you had the chance to test it out as yet?"

"Well, my own intention is to use it under water. Think of the circusing I can do, if I could combine Mr. Baird's noctovisor with a big television screen. I could perform some spectacular underwater escape under the watchful eye of the noctovisor, run the picture of myself by telephone wire to the theatre, and project the image onto the silver screen."

"It would certainly make a more inspiring sight than the pudgy countenance of Secretary Hoover," Howard commented.

"I've a good deal more work to do before I'm ready to incorporate the noctovisor in my act." Hardeen paused to reach for a bread-stick, break it in half and butter one end. Then he used it as a pointer before he ate it. "It will require some planning and coordination. Maybe a double act would work well."

Sonia frowned. "A double act?"

Hardeen smiled. "Some of the greatest transfers and illusions in my trade involve two people. The audience believes that a subject—or the magician himself—is transported miraculously from one side of the stage to another. Actually there are two people all along. I've done doubles with Ehrich. So has Bess. Some of the leading magicians in the world—I can't tell you who—have been twins. One twin will take all the publicity, the other remain in the background. Then you get—oh, 'Can a man be in two places at once?' that kind of thing. They have to be very careful that both twins are never visible to the audience simultaneously. That would be a clear tip-off. But *almost* at the same time. But where was I? Oh yes—"

He stopped and bit off the end of the bread-stick, buttered the newly-exposed end while he chewed and swallowed the first. Then he said, "As I see it, I should perform my underwater escape, say in a river or large lake near the theatre. My feat can be seen on the great theatre screen, via noctovisor and television. As soon as that is completed I announce that I am going to fly through the air to the theatre. The house-lights flash on and off and I appear on the stage, fully dressed and soaking wet. I take my applause and my bows, ask to be excused while I change to dry clothing. The orchestra plays, I step through the curtains for thirty seconds and re-emerge, dry and immaculate!" He looked at Howard and Sonia. "What do you think?"

Sonia clapped her hands in imitation of the audience at Hardeen's hypothetical noctovisor show. "That's lovely, Dash, lovely. The only thing is. . ." A wistful look passed across her features.

The magician halted his fork halfway from his plate to his mouth, conveying a mixture of ground lamb and steamed rice. "Only—what, Sonia?"

"Oh, somehow I wish you hadn't explained that to me. About the doubles, the twins. I like having the mystery in magic. Of course I know it isn't *real* magic. Not supernatural. But I'm afraid that stage magic will lose half of its charm if I know how the tricks all work."

Hardeen's hand finished its interrupted task, and he chewed the rice and lamb meditatively for a few seconds. "You're right. I really shouldn't have revealed that. But I think we're getting into more serious business than stage illusions."

"The burglaries," Howard Lovecraft inserted.

Dash Weiss shook his head as if to clear it of some vision of the stage. "Yes, the burglaries. I don't know who the raiders were, of course, nor do I know why they were after the noctovisor. But it's somewhat far-fetched to attribute their deed only to stage rivals trying to steal the

Flight of Time. It isn't impossible, mind. But I am uncon-
vinced. Add the noctovisor to the equation, and it makes
more sense."

He stopped speaking and halved a stuffed grape leaf
with his knife.

"Well, *did* you test the device?" Howard asked. "We
somehow drifted away from that question."

Hardeen nodded affirmatively as he chewed and swallowed the stuffed grape leaf. He washed it down with a
sip of water. "There wasn't time to test the device before
my tour, but there was an ideal opportunity while I was
away. I had a booking in a lovely big theatre in Oakland,
California. I've always had a warm feeling for that little
city near San Francisco. Ehrich and I used to cross paths
there on tour. We got into the habit of meeting for dinner
at the best restaurant in town, then going to our respective theatres afterwards. Somehow the advertising and
publicity we obtained seemed to become combined, and
we always played to packed houses.

"This was my first time back there since Ehrich's
death." He pulled a handkerchief from his pocket and
wiped his nose, then bit off another section of bread-stick.
"There's a little body of water there that connects with
San Francisco Bay, but it's relatively shallow and calm.
The Oakland Estuary. I arranged an underwater escape
stunt the afternoon of my show, and had my assistants
set up the noctovisor beforehand. There was a scanning
tube concealed beneath a pier for the test—I don't want
any press notices before I'm ready to use the noctovisor
in my act.

"It worked perfectly. My assistants were able to see the
trunk lowered into the water, they saw the lid open and
saw me emerge and rise to the surface. This was despite
the poor lighting conditions under the water." He took another bite of bread-stick.

"And you think the burglars were looking for the noctovisor?" Sonia asked.

"I do."

Howard Lovecraft rubbed the bridge of his nose with
thumb and forefinger, even though he had not been
wearing his spectacles. "If there was a connection between the raids, which there surely is strong reason to

infer, the question then arises, what were the burglars seeking today?"

Hardeen pointed with his bread-stick. "There was nothing taken?"

"Nothing."

"Hmph. Sounds like a case for Dr. Doyle's celebrated detective."

"But if Dash is right," Sonia suggested, "if *his* raid was aimed at the noctovisor and nothing was taken away because he had the machine with him. . ."

Howard and Hardeen both looked expectantly at Sonia.

". . . then maybe they were after something in our home that wasn't there either."

"That makes them sound like a singularly inept gang of burglars," Howard said.

"Nonetheless," Hardeen prompted.

"Eh?"

"Nonetheless, it's an intriguing idea. Did you have anything with you when you left the apartment this morning? Either of you, Howard? Sonia?."

Sonia shook her head. "I carried my purse, as always. But I can't think of anything that was in it that would interest burglars. I never carry much money with me, or jewelry."

Howard Lovecraft stroked his long chin. "I had my manuscript with me. On the impulse of the moment. I almost left the house without it, but I'd just completed the book and I felt—I recall my feelings very clearly—like a mother with a new-born child. I didn't want to let the manuscript out of my sight, out of my grasp."

Hardeen slapped the table resoundingly with one open hand. "There's your answer!" A frown creased his brow. "I think it's your answer. There ought to be some link between your book and John Baird's invention. Can you think of one?"

For a few seconds the only sound was that of Theo Weiss biting off the end of a bread-stick and munching on the hard, dry dough. Then Howard Lovecraft said, "You remember our visit to Marblehead? The mysterious construction on the sea-bottom outside the harbor? I think that is the link. The people who are responsible for the construction include my publisher."

"And the noctovisor would be very useful in learning more about what is being built in the ocean," Hardeen added. "There's the link, all right."

"I don't see, though," Sonia Lovecraft said, "who the burglars are. It can't be your publisher, Howard. Why would he try to steal your manuscript? All he has to do is wait for you to turn it in."

Howard clenched his hands beneath the edge of the table. "And if it's some enemy of the group, why would they want to protect the Marblehead project from observation by stealing the noctovisor? It doesn't make sense."

Theo said,. "Yes it does. If it's someone who wants to block this political movement, they would very likely want to see your book, Howard, and if possible block it. And they would want the noctovisor not to protect the—what is it called? The *grundstruckvorhaben*—not to protect it, but to spy on it themselves!"

"But who could that be?" Sonia asked. "Bolshevist spies? German republicans? Our own government? Military intelligence?"

Howard shook his head. "I don't think it would be any of those. From what I've seen of the people in this odd alliance, there might be an open falling-out or some hidden treachery among them at any time. There are a lot of diverse and uncomfortably-allied groups there. How can the Ku Klux Klan make a permanent alliance with the International Catholic Truth Society?"

"But, Howard, I thought you were an admirer of this movement." Sonia looked concerned.

Howard rubbed the bridge of his nose, thought for a moment. "The experiment in mob rule called 'democracy' is nearing its end. The question is only whether society will move from this idiocy to an even more vicious and senseless *Bolshevist* plan, where all social orders are turned upside down and the crude and untutored lord it over their natural betters, or toward the restoration of an order based on the concept of aristocracy, in which intelligence, breeding, refinement and taste are restored to their proper place and a degree of lawfully-established tranquility achieved.

"The forces associated in the present social movement are not all of equal refinement or even of similar ethical legitimacy. The revived Ku Klux Klan is revealed, upon close examination, to be a travesty of its noble namesake of the last century. General Forrest would spin in his grave could he see the antics and overhear the uncouth quarrels of Dr. Hiram Evans and Colonel William Simmons. Had even the decadent Romanoffs survived the slaughter of Ekaterinburg, they would recoil in disdain of the adventurer Count Vonsiatsky and his social-climbing Countess.

"On the other hand, Father Curran has proven a most impressive individual, leading to the notion that critics of his associate Father Coughlin may exaggerate. Of the Germanic contingent, while the likes of Spanknoebel, Stahrenberg and Fritz Kuhn are obvious ruffians, Mr. George Sylvester Viereck has shown himself to be a man of surprising breadth and culture. His continuing allegiance to the Hohenzollerns is understandable if not entirely justified, while his admiration for the German-Austrian author of *Mein Kampf* is thoroughly commendable. The volume shows some disorganization of thought and certain crudities of expression, to be sure, but its virtues far outweigh its shortcomings.

"What is thus perceived is a movement founded upon valid premises, directed toward admirable goals, but partially tainted by its alliance with certain unworthy elements."

Howard stopped speaking and looked at Sonia and Theo for a response.

Hardeen waved a hand expressively. "I've got the noctovisor safely warehoused along with my other equipment. It's padlocked and guarded and I have no concern over it. But what are you going to do with your manuscript, Howard? Are you just going to give it to Sylvester Viereck? Where is it now?"

Howard felt a chill of apprehension pass through his body. "The manuscript is at the apartment."

Theo reached for his wallet and extracted a wad of the new small-size currency Secretary Mellon had introduced. He tossed several bills on the table as he rose to his feet. "Come along, then. I doubt that they'll come back, but we have to be certain."

Outside the *taverna* they climbed into the sleek Rickenbacker and Theo sped across Brooklyn to Parkside Avenue. He pulled the car to the curb with a screech and raced to the apartment building accompanied by Sonia and Howard. They hurried to the apartment and raced to Howard's files, where the manuscript lay, unmolested. A sigh of relief seemed to pass from person to person.

"Well, all right then. What *are* you going to do?" Hardeen asked. Howard Lovecraft slumped in a leather chair, his manuscript in its manila envelope lying across his lap, his head in his hands. "Let me think about this," he said. "Hmm—I suppose I ought to turn this over to Sylvester Viereck, but I am not entirely comfortable with the Marblehead project or with Viereck's connection thereto. He may be an honorable man under the influence of sinister forces. In fact, I am supposed to return his telephone call of this morning, but I think I shall put this" (he indicated the envelope) "in the mail before doing so."

"You could send it to your aunts," Sonia suggested.

"I would not wish to expose them to such a raid as we experienced today," Howard said.

"What about someone from amateur journalism like Reinhart Kleiner or Belknap Long, then? Or someone from the *Weird Tales* circle? Starrett or Robert Howard? They're all trustworthy."

"And all exposed. But—I think Clark Ashton Smith would be safe. Out there in the Sierras of California, no one would think to raid his house!" He leaped to his feet and began searching until he found a pasteboard box large enough to accommodate his manuscript in its manila envelope. He sealed the box with sticking papers and addressed it carefully to Klarkash-ton in Auburn, California, then turned to the others, holding the parcel before him.

"Farewell, *New America and the Coming World-Empire*. To the Wizard of Auburn I entrust thee. When the mystery is solved, may thou be retrieved and sent in quick order to the type-setters!"

~ ~ ~ ~ ~

After the parcel was mailed, Hardeen dropped Howard and Sonia at their door and drove off. Sonia set about domestic affairs while Howard reached for the telephone to call George Sylvester Viereck, but as he was about to lift the ear-piece from its hook the electrical bell rang signaling an incoming call.

It was from young Belknap Long, and he was so excited with his message that Howard was unable to prevent his blurting it out.

"Brother Pharnabus is up to his absent-minded tricks again, Howard. He sent me a copy of the November *Weird Tales*—I trust you have not seen it as yet? No?—with an advertisement for what he calls a *feast of stories*. He announces the forthcoming appearance of your 'Call of Cthulhu.' He calls it 'A superb masterpiece of outré literature.'

Howard managed to interrupt. "That's all very pleasant news, Belknapius," was as far as he got before the younger man's excitement boiled over once again.

"No, Howard, that isn't why I telephoned you. You see, Wright enclosed a letter saying that he wasn't sure where to reach you, at Barnes Street or Parkside, but knowing that we are usually in communication he sent something for you, to my address. A typical Pharnabusian vagary!

"It's a proof copy of the December Eyrie, readers' letters and a comment from the editor. It seems to be a virtual Lovecraftian *festschrift*, Howard, you must be patient and hear this out, and then I shall hand it to you at the earliest opportunity."

Howard decided that Viereck could wait another ten minutes and said, "Proceed, Belknapius."

"Yes. First, Howard, from your admirer in Dayton, Mrs. Snow. 'Lovecraft's story in the October issue, "Pickman's Model," breathes the eeriest, most paralyzing and yet most realistic atmosphere of horror I have encountered anywhere, fiction or fact. Most weird tales are fantasies, pure and simple, told in a manner that is momentarily convincing. But Lovecraft's tales make you halt in the middle of a downtown business street and say to yourself: Why, that might happen! Lovecraft is the realist of weird fiction.'

"And that one is just the first, Howard. Listen to this one, from a Max Myers in Pennsylvania. 'Mr. Lovecraft deserves paeans of praise for his latest, "Pickman's Model." It is my estimation of a weird tale in every sense of the world. I believe that his technique is unparalleled by any of the authors who contribute to your magazine. My apologies to Mr. Quinn."

"Ho!" Howard burst in. "Three cheers for Mr. Max Myers! My mundane woes flee at his words. Proceed, Belknapius!"

" 'Absence makes the heart grow fonder. Perhaps that is why I went into ecstasies of joy and whooped with delight when I found Lovecraft's name on a story in the October issue.'

"But that isn't the half of it," Long went on. "Listen to what Pharnabus himself says in reply to Snow and Myers. 'Such enthusiastic letters encourage us to give you the heartening news that Lovecraft's greatest story, "The Call of Cthulhu," will shortly be published in *Weird Tales*. We are fully aware that in calling this story Lovecraft's finest we are setting a high mark for the tale to live up to, for he has written such masterpieces as "The Outsider," "The Festival," and "The Rats in the Walls;" but we feel that the vaulting imagination the author displays in this story, his supreme artistry, and the uncanny hold that the tale takes on the reader make "The Call of Cthulhu" one of the greatest and most powerful works of weird fiction ever written.'

"What do you think of that, Howard?" Without waiting for any answer Long supplied his own. "I think it means that Wright is preparing his audience for a book of Lovecraft! I think that he kept you out of that *Moon Terror* collection to make the readers all the more eager for Howard Lovecraft! I think you can put aside Paul Cook's little *Shunned House* as a souvenir, and this political tome of yours as a piece of commercial jobbing. You are about to be recognized in your own right, Howard!"

CHAPTER THIRTY-ONE:

LOVECRAFT QUOTES ECCLESIATES

SONIA LOVECRAFT crossed the room to answer the polite knock at the door. Howard, chatting amiably now with Belknap Long, had slid into his favorite chair and only vaguely and gradually became aware of the conversation behind him. When he had placed the earpiece of the telephone back on its hook he rose from his chair and walked toward the front door.

"Ah, Howard," Sylvester Viereck called, "Mrs. Lovecraft has been telling me of the terrible incident of this morning. I'm sorry that I telephoned you when I did. I could sense that there was something the matter, and then when you did not call me back, I took the unusual liberty of driving here unannounced. I hope you do not mind."

Even as Viereck spoke, Sonia was ushering him and her husband back into the room. They were seated on sofa and easy chair, facing each other across a low table. Sonia offered to make a pot of tea and disappeared into the kitchen as the men exchanged information.

"How much did Mrs. Lovecraft tell you?" Howard asked. Then, feeling that he had phrased the question poorly, he added, "I shall fill you in on any details that Sonia omitted."

Viereck reached into a jacket pocket and extracted his elaborate cigar case. He extended it toward Howard, Lovecraft shook his head and Viereck asked with a facial expression if he might smoke. Between brief pauses to clip and light his *perfecto Colorado* he said, only that burglars had struck the apartment.

Howard looked up to see Sonia returning from the kitchen; he shot her a significant glance, then said, "Yes. It was very distressing. Aside from the actual loss, one feels somehow *violated*. The old notion that a man's home is his castle—but the moat has been crossed and the portcullis battered through, so to speak."

"I understand." Viereck nodded sympathetically. "I hope it is not an imposition to ask just now, but I was wondering how your work is proceeding. On *New America*, I mean."

Again, Howard caught Sonia's eye and transmitted to her an unspoken message. To Viereck, he said, "That is the worst part of the matter, Sylvester. When the police were here we conducted a rough inventory of the apartment and found nothing missing. One assumes that burglars are after silver, china, jewels or the like. One even thinks that a radio installation may be carried off." He gestured toward the chassis and power unit near one window, the loudspeaker that had been restored to its stand in the corner.

"Only later did I discover that my manuscript was taken. *New America and the Coming World-Empire* was completed this morning before dawn. I had gone to the park for a constitutional stroll and Sonia had left Brooklyn for her place of employment when the raiders struck. It was an incredible piece of timing—clearly a matter of fortune, for there was no way they could have known that the book was newly completed.

"And it is gone! The labor of half a year—no, longer. The product of nearly ten months' effort. If I could lay hands on the culprit I would rend him limb from limb!"

Viereck started in his seat. "The manuscript is taken? There is no carbon copy? No rough draft?"

Lovecraft shook his head. "It had been my plan to deliver the work in its present form, then make final revisions following discussion with you. The work was written by hand, hence there was no carbon copy made." He stood up and walked around the coffee table, hands clasped behind his back. "It was a grand effort. You would unquestionably have been impressed by it, Sylvester. I was looking forward to your reaction. The section on the illegitimacy of the rebellion against George III. The study of mob-rule and *Bolshevist* tyranny—have you followed the developments in Russia? Stalin and Rykoff and Bukharin have fallen out with Trotzky and Zinonieff and the final ouster of the latter is impending daily!

"The profiles of domestic movements—Evans, Coughlin and Curran, Maude de Land, Count Revel, Count Vonsiatsky, Heinz Spanknoebel. And the foreigners—Sylvester, if you could only have seen my critique of *Mein Kampf!*

"Gone. All gone. Gone."

He threw himself back onto the couch and sat with his head clutched in his hands.

There was a silence in the room that stretched into an audible tension that was broken, finally, neither by Viereck nor by Howard nor Sonia, but by the eerie wailing of the pipes of their never-seen Syrian neighbor. The piper sounded a particularly distressing run of minor notes that sent Howard into a stream of violent oaths.

As soon as he had completed the outburst, Sylvester Viereck spoke. "My mind is made up. I had intended to change my activities anyway, but this tragedy forces my hand and I shall prepare an announcement for the press at once."

He picked his half-smoked cigar from the ash tray before him and carefully re-lit it. He blew a large cloud of heavy smoke toward the ceiling, the electric light glinting off his horn-rimmed spectacles as he turned back his head to do so. "Howard," he intoned, "I am, as of today, resigning the editorship of the *American Monthly*. I have already selected a man named David Maier, a member of my staff, as my successor.

"As you know, I have just returned from a very extensive tour of Europe. I am convinced that the situation there is reaching a critical state. You yourself have cited the crisis among the *Bolshevist* leaders in Russia. The succession crisis in Rumania is continuing with the prospect of a Bonapartist regime arising from the Bratiano ministry. You know of the uprising in Vienna, you know that once Hindenberg goes, Germany will be fought over by Monarchists and Nationalists on one side and Reds on the other. Fascism is a huge success in Italy and will probably come to France before long. The Eurasian World Island is in ferment from Gibraltar to Peking.

"Of all your work in *New America and the Coming World-Empire*, I was most eager to see the critique of *Mein Kampf*. I have met with Hitler again, and I am increasingly convinced that his way is Europe's way. I still have hopes for a Hohenzollern restoration in Germany, but whether under a formal *Kaiserheit* or not, the NSDAP alone can save Germany from the Reds.

"Will you attend a conference with *Herren* Luedecke, Spanknoebel, Kiep and myself, Howard? Perhaps we can discover a means of regaining your purloined manuscript. Else I will bend every resource to aid you in reconstructing the work."

Howard agreed to attend the conference, and Viereck said that he would notify Howard of the time and place. He drank the tea which Sonia had brought, shook hands, and left.

Sonia asked Howard at once, why he had fabricated the story of the missing manuscript.

"As you know," Howard said, "I am not what you would normally consider a man of impulse. It is my usual practice to ponder facts and relationships in a scientifically rational manner before making decisions of import. However, in this case I have made an exception. The dispatch of my manuscript to Klarkash-ton was for the purpose of protecting the work against a hypothetical second burglarious entry—but it was also for the purpose of getting the manuscript out of the potential clutches of Viereck and his allies.

"My first impression of the man, a dozen years ago, was a negative one, and for all that I have come to hold him in higher esteem than formerly was the case, I find something unsettling in his behaviour and his associations. I trust him less with the passage of time, rather than more. Consequently, for the time being I propose to play a waiting game, my dear. Let Mr. Viereck call his meeting, and me hear the pleas of Herr Luedecke and the others. I will, in the meanwhile, hold my cards close to my vest."

The conversation was broken again by the sounding of the electric telephone bell. Sonia lifted the instrument and spoke into it while Howard grumbled at the unceasing series of interruptions to the day.

"Howard," Sonia turned, smiling, "it's Dash Weiss. He has made a most generous offer to us. Will you take the telephone?"

Howard identified himself over the telephone wire.

"Sorry to be a pest," Hardeen said in reply. "But, you know, there's a constant stream of free passes in the trade, and I've just come on two invitations for next week that you and Sonia might like to join in. They're for

Wednesday and Thursday evening, and I'll be going to both, myself."

Howard asked what the invitations were for.

"Here. Wednesday evening is opening night at the Fulton. That play from England that's been trying out, out of town. *Dracula* from the novel by the late Abraham Stoker. I know you are a follower of the stage. And the following night there is a motion picture opening at the Warner, supposedly a new advance, Vitaphone sound applied to speech and even to singing. It's called *The Jazz Singer*, with a fellow named Jolson in the role George Jessel performed in the stage version.

"If you and Sonia would be my guests for either the drama Wednesday or the film on Thursday, I would be pleased."

Howard Lovecraft snorted in disdain. "I don't see the cause for excitement over a Vitaphone film. Signor Mussolini used Vitaphone months ago for the dissemination of his speeches—in English as well as Italian. But I will be most gratified to attend the premiere of *Dracula*."

Theo Weiss laughed. "Jack Spratt. Very well. Sonia expressed a desire to see *The Jazz Singer* but declined to attend *Dracula*. You will join me, then, to attend the drama, and Sonia, for the motion picture. Is that correct?"

Howard checked with Sonia, told Hardeen that all was agreed upon and thanked him for the invitations.

"Not at all, Howard. Something bright to offset the raids."

~ ~ ~ ~ ~

Sitting at his rickety desk, staring melancholically at the keyboard of his tall Corona typewriter, Clark struggled desperately to think of a suitable topic for a column for the *Auburn Journal*. The drafty office of the little newspaper was bitterly cold this November night, and Clark's discomfort only added to his low mood.

Today of all days, he could have used some cheer. It was the first anniversary of the death of George Sterling, Clark's closest friend, his entrée to the bright literary circles of San Francisco and Carmel, his poetic mentor. But a year ago, Sterling had taken a fatal dose of poison in the plush surroundings of the Bohemian Club, and that was that. No suicide note, and Clark was loath to think that his friend had ended his own life, but the self-poisoning was hard to explain away.

And here, a year later, instead of attending a memorial observance of any sort, Clark had followed his usual routine. Rise early, see to the needs of his aged parents—Tim was 72 and dying of cancer, Fanny was 76 and feeble—clean out the chicken house on their little spread above the town (of all his life's tasks, Clark most hated the stench and mess of the chicken house!), spend the rest of the day at chores and somehow steal a few hours of sleep in the afternoon. That was vital, because later in the evening he had to make his way down the steep hillside into town and perform his duties as night editor of the *Journal*.

At least those duties were few—there wasn't much hot news in the town of Auburn, California. Occasionally some vacationer would drown in the American River; even more occasionally some die-hard prospector would claim he'd discovered a new vein of gold in the old, worked-out mining country; other than that, Auburn news was weddings and babies, school graduations and occasional fights.

The most interesting aspect of Clark's life was the day's mail, thrown off the passing Southern Pacific train passing from Truckee to Roseville. There was a lengthy manuscript from Clark's eastern friend, a puzzling book about politics, aristocracy, culture and race. A letter had followed, asking Clark to safeguard the manuscript, and signed Ec'h-Pi-El; Howard Lovecraft *a.k.a.* Grandpa Theobald, Humphrey Littlewit and a few other amusing pseudonyms, at least always wrote interesting letters.

Lovecraft was an admirer of Smith's works, too. He was one of the few people who remembered Clark as a short-story writer, sending friendly comments on Clark's old stories like "The Mahout" and "The Raja and the Tiger," that had run, Lord, back even before the Great War in *The Black Cat* in Boston.

Then, ironically, Houtain had paid Clark a few pennies to illustrate a Herbert West story by Lovecraft, for *Home Brew*, and when Clark started sending poems to *Weird Tales* a couple of years after that, Lovecraft had popped up again, urging him to produce fiction for the magazine. If you could do it for Umbstaetter's *Black Cat* you can do it again for Henneberger's *Weird Tales*, Howard insisted. And Clark supposed he was right, of course. He just wasn't very interested in writing fiction.

He envied his friends their exciting, cosmopolitan existences. Poor, dead Sterling, running back and forth between Carmel and San Francisco, lionized by Ambrose Bierce (disappeared in Mexico), Jack London (dead a decade at his own hand). Howard Lovecraft, bouncing from Providence to Boston to New York and back again.

And here was Clark Smith, night editor, nursemaid, chicken-coop scrubber extraordinaire, marooned with his sick old parents in tiny, frigid Auburn, California.

He opened Howard's letter and read it once again. At least Lovecraft had let off, for the moment, urging him to write stories. Poetry was what Smith cared about, and he had three published volumes and a nice scrapbook of reviews to show for his efforts, although he had no money.

Howard's letter was addressed from Brooklyn, explained that he had written a book on world affairs, and had to get the manuscript out of New York and into safekeeping. Would Klarkash-ton be so kind as to protect the book. He could read it if he wished but need not do so if the theme failed to interest him. Howard closed in haste—something unusual for Howard—with one of his "gag" signatures.

Well, safeguarding the manuscript would be no problem. Clark Smith crossed the *Auburn Journal* office, worked the combination on the old iron safe (smiling faintly at the implicit play on words), and put Howard's bundle inside.

He returned to his Corona. He *had* to get that column written, and all he could think of was poor Sterling. Well, the citizens of Auburn might not care much about dead poets (someday they'd have another in their midst, and not care about *him* either), but they were going to get a thoughtful piece on the subject anyway.

" 'A Wine of Wizardry' was the first work of George Sterling's that I ever experienced the pleasure of consuming," Clark Smith pecked out on the Corona. "The poem, spreading its necromantic music, its splendors as of sunset on jewels and cathedral windows, across the pages of the old *Cosmopolitan* magazine, glowed like a titanic fireopal cast somehow accidentally into a potato-bin."

Smith reread his words, sighed, continued pecking away.

~ ~ ~ ~ ~

Theo Weiss, Hardeen the Mysterious, was booked into the Academy of Music once again, and sat to dinner beforehand with his friends Howard and Sonia Lovecraft. They were a strangely matched couple; he'd sensed that from his first encounter with the gaunt, saturnine man and his plump, vivacious, attractive wife. The introduction had been casual—Howard Lovecraft was doing some ghostwriting for Theo's brother Ehrich—but through the casual acquaintanceship Theo had developed a great warmth toward Sonia, and a kind of affection, too, for her husband. Howard, Theo felt, had within him a warmth and even a spontaneity that were deeply buried and repressed by what, Theo could only guess. But that the characteristics were there, he knew.

The three companions held sway at a table at Tony Pastor's club that shared the building-front on Fourteenth Street with the Academy and Tammany Hall. Sonia Lovecraft had ordered breaded veal cutlet for herself; Howard, pot roast; and Theo, an extra-thick slice of prime rib *au jus*.

"I must again express my gratitude," Howard Lovecraft said, "for the invitation to the premier of *Dracula*. It was an excellent production. I can understand the reservations of the critics—especially Atkinson's complaint that the Hungarian Lugosi was too deliberate in his delivery—but Stoker's novel is a difficult one to mount for the stage, and I thought that Mr. Balderston's script captured as much of the original as might have been hoped for."

"You thought Bernard Jukes good?" Theo asked. "His heroics were not overdone for you? And you had no difficulty understanding Lugosi's delivery, despite his accent?"

Howard sipped at a glass of ice water. "The play is not the book, of course. One could hardly expect a full representation of a 500-page novel in an evening of theater. But Jukes seemed quite adequate to me, while I found the Hungarian's accent an asset to his portrayal rather than the opposite. The vampire was supposed to be a nobleman from the heart of Carpathia; it would hardly have done to portray him as speaking English as would a native of Albion. On the other hand, to give him a broken and stumbling delivery would have detracted from the nobility of the portrayal. Hence, the delivery of his lines in flawless prose, and yet with a deliberate and accented manner, was the sole correct choice."

Hardeen grinned at Howard's peroration, exchanging glances with Sonia. "You're quite an authority on the theater," he said. "I didn't know you were such a devotee of the stage."

"In fact, my dear Hardeen, I do not attend as often as might be my wish. But I was raised with an appreciation of the theater. Among my earliest cherished memories are recollections of the D'Oyly Carte company of Savoyards performing at the Providence Opera House. It was my mother's habit to bring me to matinees when I was yet too small to attend evening performances. I can see before me the sets and the costumes, hear the patter songs and the dialogue of *Mikado*, *Pinafore*, *Yeomen of the Guard*. But I believe that my favorite of them all was and still is *Iolanthe*. The fantasy, the spirit of the production are delightful. And yet again, *Ruddigore* has much to recommend it.

"But in more recent years, I must confess that my attendance upon the followers of Thespis has fallen away quite drastically. Until *Dracula*, I had last attended the theater some three years ago, to witness the travesty *Outward Bound*."

"Ehrich was very fond of that play," Hardeen countered.

"Indeed, sir. You recall that I sat beside him during the performance. *De gustibus*." He lifted knife and fork and set to work on his dinner.

"And I must thank you for escorting me to see *The Jazz Singer*," Sonia filled in. "I loved it, didn't you, Dash? I thought Al Jolson was absolutely the cat's whiskers. He brought such feeling to his role! I could believe every bit of the story. And the singing! Why, when the cantor sang the *Kol Nidre*, I wept! I actually wept as I sat there."

"It was a fine photoplay," Theo agreed. "I would also predict a great future for Vitaphone. We'll not see very many more silent flickers, I'd think! I shall have to make certain that we have a sound link when I incorporate the noctovisor into my act."

"I wish you had come along, Howard, to see *The Jazz Singer*. It wasn't just a film for women. Dash enjoyed it as much as I did."

"My dear, it was not merely the sentimentality which I knew would mark the film, which caused me to avoid it. It was the gross glorification of a cultural tradition which I find alien and obnoxious. We see at every hand the Old American society, so painstakingly built upon these shores by the Anglo-Saxon pioneers of past centuries, being swamped in the mill rush of Oriental hordes, swarthy immigrants who neither know nor care for the culture which is infused into the architecture, the literature, the language, and the very blood of this nation. Had I made the error of going to see *The Jazz Singer* I might have found myself unable to restrain an overpowering urge to attack the very screen upon which the images of the Slavic mongrels was thrown!"

As if to exemplify his statement, Howard attacked the slab of meat on his dish; Sonia and Theo exchanged glances across the table. There was an awkward silence. Theo examined his watch. Sonia lifted her glass and drank water. Theo reached for the bread-basket in the center of the table and buttered a hot, hard-crusted roll, dipping it in the gravy on his dish before consuming it in a few great mouthfuls.

He washed it down with steaming coffee, then attempted to get conversation started again. "Do you know if your manuscript reached California safely, Howard?"

Lovecraft swallowed the food in his mouth and wiped his lips carefully with his linen napkin. "Indeed, I received a note from Klarkash-ton in this afternoon's delivery. The book is locked away securely in a steel safe that no man but Smith or his fellow editor may open."

Hardeen grinned wryly. "Rather than count on the efficacy of any lock, I think your greatest protection is distance—distance, and the fact that no one knows where the manuscript is."

"Did Clark mention Fanny and Tim in his letter?" Sonia asked. "His parents are old and ill—I worry about them."

"Even though you've never met them, or their son," Hardeen put in.

Howard frowned. "Old and ill, precisely. I fear that they are more a burden to themselves and their son than anything else. May I never reach an age or condition in which I cannot pull my own weight in the world!" He transported a forkful of string beans to his mouth and chewed meditatively for a few seconds.

"Maybe Clark should send them to Dr. Brinkley in Kansas, for some gland treatments. Of course he could never afford to send them to Paris, to Dr. Voronoff. But there are miracles being worked today. Why, I was recently reading the most marvelous volume by Gertrude Atherton, called *Black Oxen*. It's a novel, of course, not a medical volume. Still—"

"Perhaps Klarkash-ton's enforced semi-hermitude will not prove an unmixed affliction," Howard resumed, totally ignoring Sonia's words. "He has been selling verse quite regularly to Pharnabus, and it is to be hoped that he will come around, in response to the pleadings of his admirers and the realities of economic necessity, to the writing of some fiction for the magazine. *Weird Tales* could well utilize more of Klarkash-ton's shimmering imagery of Oriental splendour, in place of the derivative and crudely narrated tales of gore that infect its pages."

Sonia shook her head helplessly. "Darling Howard, I think I love you all the more because you're so charmingly inconsistent. And because you have such a wonderful sense of values."

Suspiciously, Howard asked what Sonia meant.

"Why, I think you place the Viereck matter—your book, his remarkable circle of associates, and—from your description—the future of much of the world—in the scales. And on the other pan you set that silly little red-covered magazine—"

"You did not refer to *Weird Tales* in such terms when you pled with me to revise 'Four O'clock' and 'The Invisible Monster' for you, Mrs. Lovecraft, that they might meet the poor standards of that silly little magazine!" He was growing red in the face.

Hardeen the Mysterious cleared his throat loudly and announced that he had to leave for the theatre and prepare to go on-stage. "Now, now, just sit back, Dash." Sonia pressed down on his sleeve with one hand. With the other she soothed Howard Lovecraft's reddened forehead.

"Don't be angry with me, Howard dear. You know I love to tease you."

Howard subsided slightly, waiting for Sonia's further explanation. "What I mean is that you do place these two things in the scales, Howard. . .on the one side, from your own statements, the future of whole governments, nations, races, and on the other the matter of whether or not Clark Ashton Smith will write prose as well as poetry for *Weird Tales* magazine, and they seem to balance evenly. Don't you consider that a rather odd set of values?"

Howard quietly drew his hand away and placed it in his lap. "Your point is not wholly without merit," he conceded. Sonia smiled.

Theo Weiss looked at his watch again, lifted fork and knife and returned to his plate. "I should really have enough confidence in my assistants to let them set up for once. As long as I reach the theater in time to check all the equipment before the curtain rises."

"If one considers human affairs against the cosmic scale of an infinite and uncaring universe," Howard announced, "and if one but measures the duration not merely of a human lifetime but indeed that of all life upon this pitiful planet, one is led inevitably to a sense of cosmic despair and futility."

He looked from Sonia to Theo and back, making certain that they were attending fully to what he said.

"Therefore, let us eat and drink, for tomorrow we die," Hardeen quoted.

Howard raised his eyebrows. "Such scholarship impresses me."

"You forget that my father and grandfather were rabbis."

"But Corinthians!"

"One need not be narrow," Sonia volunteered. "Besides, Howard, you are an avowed atheist, aren't you, dear?"

"The Bible is a fount of language and philosophy, a virtual library of poetic and historical lore, and a not unworthy compilation of myth, as well as a religious document." He glared in mock antagonism at Hardeen. "A man hath no better thing under the sun than to eat, and to drink, and to be merry. I learned that in the Baptist Infant School, Providence."

Hardeen said, "Ecclesiastes." He signaled to the waiter to clear away their dishes, and after a course of dessert they strolled from Tony Pastor's to the theatre, arm in arm, Sonia Lovecraft in the center of the group.

CHAPTER THIRTY-TWO:

A SINGLE SNOWFLAKE

"IMAGINE," Frank Belknap Long, Sr., chuckled, 'some archaeologist of the year 5000 AD. That's the idea of this English fellow Huxley, Aldous Huxley."

He brandished the glistening, serrated knife in one hand, the long-tined fork in the other, standing at the head of the table in the Long apartment on West End Avenue, the cut-glass chandelier casting cheerful illumination over the group, the white linen table-cloth reflecting the electric light to add to the brightness of the room.

"I read it in the *Times*, this fellow Huxley was visiting New York and the reporter asked him his opinion of contemporary culture. And Huxley replied, Imagine some archaeologist of the year 5000 AD, studying our era, viewing flickering silver images of a row of Mack Sennett bathing beauties, and listening to an old panatrope disk of 'Yes Sir, That's My Baby.' What do you think he would conclude?"

The elder Long burst into tears of hilarity at the thought of the future scholar's likely reaction; only when he had regained his composure did he actually set to work, carving the Thanksgiving turkey that lay steaming on the maple carving board before him.

Howard Lovecraft smiled briefly at Dr. Long's notion, then said, "Well, what do *you* think that hypothetical archaeologist would have to say about this year of enlightenment, 1927, Belknapius?" He spoke directly to Long *fils*.

The younger man pondered briefly, then replied, "I should hope that the year 5000 will have better artifacts by which to remember the twentieth century, than bathing beauties and the outpourings of Tin-pan Alley!"

"Very good, very good indeed! Although one might entertain precious little expectation of such a fortunate sequel to our disordered era, one may at least hope!" He watched Dr. Long carefully dismember the bird: drumsticks, thighs, wings, then the fine white meat beneath the crisp brown-yellow skin. "One must concede that humankind is a strange product of the evolutionary process. We react with squeamishness to the very mention of certain topics, yet dismember the carcass of this sacrificial offering and devour its sad remains with ceremonial gusto!"

A uniformed maid appeared carrying a tray laden with silver bowls of freshly cooked green vegetables, sweet potatoes mashed and baked beneath a crust of whipped sugar marshmallow, giblet gravy, stuffing of croutons and chestnuts and celery roasted inside the turkey and removed before the carving, and a large bowl of jellied cranberries. She set the tray on a polished sideboard and proceeded to pass the serving dishes among the celebrants. A tray of freshly heated butter-rolls followed.

As the cranberries reached May Doty Long, the wife of the surgeon said, "These set me in mind of your native region, Howard. Have you heard from your aunts recently? I trust they are both well."

Howard said that he had frequent letters from his aunts as well as occasional telephone conversations with them. "I must confess that, with due admiration and appreciation of my hosts and present surroundings, I miss the tall spires and ancient hills of Providence Plantations." He gestured toward a westward-facing window where drapes only partially drawn showed a late afternoon sky, gray over the Palisades. White flakes drifted past the tall windows; in the distance the early evidences of construction work for the future bridge connecting Manhattan with Fort Lee at 187th Street, were dimly visible. A few freighters and coal barges were standing to in the Hudson. Ferries crept carefully among them, carrying passengers and motor vehicles between New York and New Jersey. The yachts of summer that turned the river into a body of deceptive picturesqueness had long fled down the inland waterway to warmer regions, or had been lifted on davits to spend the winter months in dry-dock.

In the Long apartment, casual conversation alternated with the sounds of crystal and silver as the diners reenacted the feast of the Pilgrims. Dr. Long volunteered to search for appropriate musical accompaniment on the family's recently-acquired Fada radio set. "Dr. Andrea is a genius comparable to Thomas Alva Edison, I believe. His sets are magnificent."

Long *pere* slid back his chair and walked to the radio set. He switched on the power and turned dials. A warm, assertive voice marked with a vaguely southern accent filled the room. The voice was speaking of the importance of Thanksgiving, the gratitude owed by modern America to the good Christian God for the blessings He had showered on the world's greatest nation, including the blessing of good health and life-long vigor. If you do not share fully in this blessing, the voice continued, you are being cheated of your share of God's bounty. Think of the bird you are carving today, the voice urged. In all likelihood, it is a capon, for the true tom turkey is too tough, too vigorous, too virile to come to the sad fate of the Thanksgiving feast. Nobody wants to be a capon, and if the price extracted from you by the passing years is your own vigor and virility, you belonged in the Brinkley Medical Center at Milford, Kansas.

With a snort of offended professionalism, Dr. Long swung the dial away from the assertive voice. He found a program of soft, semi-classical music. "Criminal poppycock! Man ought to be jailed!" He strode back to his seat and tucked his napkin between the buttons of his vest.

May Doty Long raised her eyes to her husband's. "I thought he sounded like a very kindly, generous man."

"Hardly," Dr. Long commented.

Sonia Lovecraft came to May's defense. "I agree with you. Dr. Long, do you know who that was? What is your objection to him?"

The senior Long looked surprised. "You mean you've never heard of that quack? That was John TROTZKY. Brinkley, speaking over his personal radio station. KFKB, Milford, Kansas. You know what KFKB stands for? Kansas Folks Know Best! Brinkley's a gland doctor. You know, for older men with younger ideas. Come to Milford and have the glands of a frisky young goat—pardon the indelicacy, but you did ask—have the glands of a frisky young goat grafted into your own, and the next thing you know seventy is performing like twenty. Not likely!

"The man. is a dangerous fraud. Fishbein has done a couple of journal articles on him that would curl your hair." He turned toward the uniformed maid standing at the sideboard. "Could we have some cider, please?" She disappeared into the kitchen to fetch it.

"I've heard Brinkley a few times myself," Long *fils* volunteered. "Some of the fellows at Columbia sent for his literature, filled out his questionnaires, it was quite a jape. But curl your hair indeed, the man is a charlatan of the first order. Mixes up a bunch of fundamentalist theology and a dash of anti-Semitism with his quackery, too. Has a couple of cronies named Pelley and Winrod who are both fundamentalist preachers—they mix their religion with politics, Dr. Brinkley mixes his with goat glands, it makes quite a stew."

Sonia Lovecraft sadly conceded that goat glands might not be the salvation of all aged parents after all. "My daughter Florence sent me some information about Dr. Serge Voronoff. He's a Russian surgeon who had to flee the revolution. He's been experimenting in France with transplantation of gorilla glands into humans. I suppose because gorillas are more like men than goats are. But you don't think there's anything to it, Frank?"

Dr. Long shook his head decisively. "Just a racket." He raised a crystal goblet of pale apple cider. "To Thanksgiving. To all of us, and may we have many more Thanksgivings to share."

The meal ended with servings of pumpkin pie and strong coffee. They sat around the table continuing their conversation as the uniformed maid cleared the *debris* of the meal and retired to the kitchen with the soiled china and silver. Dr. Long asked Howard how his grand project was coming along and Howard, trying to determine his own state of mind, gave a slightly edited version of the details.

"I suppose that what I finally do, will depend on what Sylvester and the others have to say at that meeting— when it takes place. He has left the *American Monthly* now. I suppose that things will have to be resolved soon.

"In any case, once this matter is cleared up I shall return to Providence where I can be surrounded by the beloved hills and streets and structures of my childhood. I thank you, Sonia," (turning to address this part of his statement to her) "for your generous hospitality these past months. But the white spires and green hills, the granite mountains and sparkling waterways of New England summon me! If I could, I would gladly trade a year in New York for a day in Providence, in Salem, in Athol. Each of us must find his own proper milieu, and mine own is that of New England."

For a while afterward, Howard Lovecraft and Belkna-pius retired to the latter's study for a good literary bull-session, while Sonia and the senior Longs remained in the living room over a second cup of coffee, chatting over trivialities.

Belknap Long said that he'd had a bit of trouble follow-ing Howard's explanation of the *New America* book. Was it, in fact, completed? And if so, what had Viereck's reaction been, to the manuscript?

Howard Lovecraft chose his words very carefully. "The book *is* complete, Belknapius. But I have declined to turn over my manuscript to the Jackson Press quite yet. To be utterly honest with you, I have sent the manuscript away for safekeeping. But I have not told this to Viereck, and he believes that burglars have made off with the work.

"I expect to let him think that, at least until I have re-ceived a better justification of the activities of this league of organizations which he co-ordinates. There are too many odd characters in the cast, I am just uncomfortable about the whole thing. That goat-gland man—"

"Brinkley."

"Yes. I'd not come across *him* before today, but his two friends, Pelley and Winrod, seem to circulate at the edges of some of the groups Mr. Viereck associates with. The Evans and Dilling and DeLand segments of the. circle; of course they would have nothing to do with the Russian or Italian or German elements, no less people like the Inter-national Catholic Truth Society.

"And there's still too strong a taint of anti-Briticism there, for me to swallow. Viereck has managed to smooth over it in his personal statements and conduct. But some of these others are still rallying behind Mayor Thompson in Chicago, wanting to burn all the books in the library and the schoolroom that have anything to say in favor of England. *Brrr!*

"Consequently, I shall just hold my fire until I have heard what new statement Viereck and others have to make, and then I shall decide what I'm to do."

Belknap smoothed his moustache with his forefinger. "You must have very strong feelings, Howard, to imperil your book in this manner. But then, if Pharnabus Wright and Henneberger come through with their implied promise to get out a collection of your stories, I suppose that might make *New America* less important to you.'

Howard conceded that was so. "And I do wish to get back to writing fiction anyway," he added. "This year—most of a year, anyway, since I completed *Charles Dexter Ward*—has been useful and educative for me, but I find myself already thumbing through my commonplace book, toying with images and scenes, actually chomping at the bit, as it were, to get back to my desk in my own Providence home and commence some new creative work. Perhaps some stories will even come out of this year's experiences."

With a discreet knock at the door, May Doty Long entered the room. "We have a little treat, Howard, Frank. Would you boys like a dish of ice cream, or is your dinner still too heavy on your stomachs?"

Howard grinned. "Only if it's vanilla," he said. Then, after the briefest noticeable pause, "Or any other flavor."

"Count me in as well," Belknap said. They left their discussion and rejoined the others for their second dessert, then Howard and Sonia, the former reluctant to depart from his friend's home, left the Longs and returned to Brooklyn.

~ ~ ~ ~ ~

Throughout the early weeks of December, Howard found himself drifting slowly into a mood of despair and lethargy. His life for nearly a year, he realized, had been devoted to *New America and the Coming World-Empire*. Not only to the book itself, but, through his research work for it, to the entire movement, the entire world image, upon which it was founded.

His contacts with the people he had met through George Sylvester Viereck had opened a new dimension to him. Some he had liked and admired. George Pagnanelli was an enigmatic individual, Howard had not got to know him as well as he would have liked to, and thought that it might prove rewarding to seek the journalist out and try to reestablish their acquaintanceship. Others he had found himself scorning—Evans for one, the Detroit rough-neck Kuhn for another. Still others seemed in a way sinister, yet fascinating—Count Revel, Dr. Otto Kiep, Kurt Luedecke. And still others—he thought of the Count and Countess Vonsiatskoy-Vonsiatsky—had a tragicomic dimension to their posing, for all the while that they played at the roles of exiled nobleman and revanchist, Russia was being racked with persecutions, killings, tyranny. Howard wished that he had learned more of the situation in China, also. Again and again war threatened between that nation, racked as it already was with internal fighting, and its neighbor the Soviet Union. When a communist force seized the city of Canton and threatened foreigners, marines were landed by the United States, Britain, and Japan. Chiang Kai-shek's troops re-took the city and executed hundreds of dissidents including the Soviet vice-consul and most of his staff. Russia threatened invasion. The widow of Sun Yat-sen fled to Russia and condemned the actions of her brother-in-law Chiang.

In the wake of the British raid on the Soviet trading mission and its unmasking as a headquarters for propaganda and agitation, the Soviet mission in Turkey was revealed to be a similar front for political intrigue. The previously warm relations between the new Turkish republic and the Soviet Union became chilled and hostile.

In Moscow the Communist Party Congress convened and the long anticipated *coup de gras* was administered to the critics of the Stalin-Rykoff-Bukharin triumvirate. The entire oppositionist group were ousted from the party: Trotzky, Zinonieff, Preobrajenski, Kameneff, Radek.

In Atlanta, Hiram Evans issued a statement blasting Al Smith for his Catholicism and his Wetness, and threatening that if the Democratic Party nominated Smith for President, the Klan might bolt and throw its support to the Republicans or to a third party. Back in Jamaica, New York, the Klan was still disgruntled over its maltreatment by the police. The Klan's organizer for the region, Paul M. Winter, sent a letter of protest to Governor Smith; Smith's reply was a polite suggestion that Winter and the Klan seek redress through the courts.

Each day Sonia Lovecraft would leave Parkside Avenue for her job at Russek's while Howard still slept. When he rose, later in the day, he would walk to the lobby and check the morning's mail delivery for items of interest; his days were spent in a state of suspension, orbiting between the telephone, awaiting a call from Viereck to the delayed meeting, and the mailbox, hoping for a letter from Farnsworth Wright or Joseph Henneberger (or even Vincent Starrett in the role of intermediary) regarding the book of Howard's short stories with which Henneberger's Popular Fiction Publishing Company would follow *The Moon Terror*.

None arrived.

Occasionally Howard would bundle himself with sweater, muffler, overcoat and gloves, and brave the winter cold to travel to Manhattan for a visit or an outing with some friend. Most often he would meet Belknap Long and they would browse the book shops of Fourth Avenue and Greenwich Village. There would be late-night explorations of the odd alleys and blind streets of lower Manhattan, bowls of spaghetti and loaves of Italian bread across the checkered tablecloths of inexpensive restaurants.

Once in a great while they would go out of their way to see a motion picture. Howard waxed enthusiastic over *London After Midnight*, playing at the Capitol in midtown. He even invited Sonia to join himself and Long *fils* but Sonia, intuiting Howard's real preference, excused herself on grounds of fatigue.

The film was a huge success. Howard found himself praising not only Chaney in his portrayal of Burke of Scotland Yard, but Todd Browning's direction and story, the brooding, atmospheric sets of Cedric Gibbons and Arnold Gillespie, the performances of Conrad Nagel, Polly Moran, Marceline Day. It was an altogether magnificent photoplay. To add to the gala aspect of the occasion, Howard Lovecraft and his friend Frank Long had attended the opening night performance of the film, and the souvenir program booklets were fine additions to their respective collected memorabilia.

The next day—Monday, December 12—Howard's telephone message arrived from the Jackson Publishing Company. Sylvester Viereck himself took the telephone line, and told Howard that the meeting might extend as long as a few days. He had therefore reserved a block of rooms for the conferees at the Flagler Resort Hotel in Woodbridge, New York. If Howard would present himself at the Jackson Press office on East 42nd Street at ten o'clock Friday morning, Viereck would be pleased to provide transportation to Woodbridge.

Howard accepted the offer gladly.

When Sonia arrived home that evening, he told her of the call, and of his expected absence over the following weekend.

Sonia put down her fox-collared gray coat. "I had hoped that you would be here this weekend, Howard. I was hoping you would accompany me to Hanukkah services Sunday night. You might find that my religion isn't quite as obnoxious as you've always thought it was.

"And this is our last chance to attend services at Temple Emanu-El. Even if you have no sympathy for my faith, I know that the building itself would be of interest to you. It's beautiful. The style is Moorish and Saracenic, almost unique in the Western Hemisphere. Leopold Eidlitz designed the building seventy years ago, and people have come from all over the world to see it.

"But it's going to be torn down and the congregation is building a new home farther uptown."

Howard frowned. "There is nothing admirable in the Jewish pseudo-culture, as far as I am concerned. If the synagogue is an interesting edifice, I suppose that the culture embodied in it was indeed stolen from the Saracens and the Moors, But in any case, I will not be in New York by Sunday. Why don't you find some coreligionist of yours to take you."

Flushing, Sonia said, "I will. I am sure that there are many gentlemen who would be pleased to accompany me to services." She crossed the room and lifted the earpiece of the telephone. Howard heard her give Central a number which he recognized as that of Theo Weiss.

Thursday afternoon Howard packed a bag for himself, bundled into his warmest clothing and ventured out of 259 Parkside. He arrived at the Long apartment on West End Avenue by dinner time. Rather than join the senior Longs, Belknap and Howard took an informal meal for themselves and left the apartment once more.

They toured the avenues of the city, gazing into the windows of department stores and specialty shops decked for the Christmas season. At the Davega store near Stern's on 42nd Street they stood listening to Christmas carols broadcast through loudspeakers while men dressed in the red wool and white imitation fur of Santa Claus rang bells and urged passers-by the drop their coins into little irons pots for the poor.

Belknap asked Howard his plans for the Christmas holiday, and Howard announced that his aunts had written, inviting him and Sonia to join them for Christmas in Providence. "I hope that my obligation to Viereck will be cleared up by the meeting which begins tomorrow at Woodbridge," Howard explained. "I have made an informal pledge to Mrs. Lovecraft that I will remain in residence at 259 Parkside through the end of 1927, but if she is invited to join me upon the Ancient Hill, I would hope in exchange to extract from her a release from the final week of my commitment. Ah, Belknapius, could you but know the beauties of the Christmases of my childhood. The tall tree standing in the parlor of our house on Angell, its lights glowing and reflecting from the tinsel. To the small child it appeared infinitely great as I stood before it, gazing upward into its forest-green depths. The tiny flames were as remote suns, the silvery threads and wreaths were glorious pathways leading one from the mundane and ordinary away into an infinity of beauty and splendor, a fairyland where daily cares were nonexistent and the magical powers of druid and elf rivaled those of the Grecian hamadryad and faun!"

Frank Long turned his eyes skyward. The night sky above the island of Manhattan was invisible against the glare of electric lights from the buildings that towered over the two men. Long fumbled in the pocket of his topcoat and extracted from it his favorite pipe. He struck a match and drew the pipe into life, then watched fascinated as a single large snowflake drifted down and landed on the dancing spot of blue and yellow flame.

There was a hiss, barely audible, as the snowflake and the flame annihilated each other. He tossed the damp match into the gutter. "I thought that our own tree was rather attractive," he finally said. He sucked a small mouthful of smoke from the pipe, held it in his mouth for a few seconds, then yielded it up to the cold, damp city air.

"Of course." Howard Lovecraft stamped his feet, clapped his hands a few times to encourage circulation. "I've got to reach a place of warmth or I shall be in serious difficulty, Belknapius. Suppose we make our way into a subway kiosk and see what we are going to do with the remainder of the evening."

They walked together down the metal-shod stairway of the Interborough Rapid Transit Company station. A newsboy had stepped inside the kiosk to escape the chill of 42nd Street and waved a copy of the *Evening Sun* at Lovecraft and Long. Howard let his eyes roam briefly over the headlines; an astronomical diagram accompanying a story looked interesting and Howard found two pennies in his pocket, handed them to the boy and accepted a copy of the newspaper.

He and Belknap stopped in the warm corridor leading to the subway platform and looked at the news item. Dr. Leland Cunningham of the Harvard College Observatory had plotted the path which the comet Skjellerup, due to appear next Sunday, would follow. It would appear at first to the southeast of the star Altair, passing alongside the star by December 21, passing to the west of Vega by Christmas night and continuing on a northerly path across the heavens, to the vicinity of Deneb before disappearing early in January, 1928.

The only other items of note—Howard's attention was drawn by the Chicago dateline, which set him in mind both of his friend Starrett and of the entire *Weird Tales*-Popular Fiction enterprise—dealt with politics and crime. In the latter regard, Al Capone had been arrested on a gun charge. Everyone knew that nothing would come of the matter: he had City Hall, police headquarters, and the *Unione Siciliana* in his hip pocket; only a rare, courageous holdout like the newsman Jake Lingle dared stand up to Mr. Brown. Still, some policeman had had the courage to walk up to Capone and place him under arrest. That was news.

The political story had more bearing on Howard's activities. The mayor of Chicago, Big Bill Thompson (himself a Capone man), had ordered the entire 6,500-man city police force, to enroll in a right-wing political movement called "America First." There was a $10 initiation fee. "America First" had therefore netted $65,000 in Thompson's single move, as well as securing an entire city police department for its membership. Howard examined the news report to see if the name Elizabeth Dilling or the Patriotic Research Bureau appeared in it. They did not, but the Bureau was tied in with "America First," and that meant that Mrs. Dilling, and through her the Viereck circle, were indirectly involved.

Howard almost automatically clipped the three items and slipped them into his notebook for later transfer to his research files. Then he remembered that the book was completed and had been shipped to Klarkash-ton, 3,000 miles away, for safe-keeping.

Howard and Belknap stopped at a cafeteria in the subway arcade; Long smoked his pipe and sipped a cup of coffee while Howard devoured half a dozen doughnuts. Then they took their nickel ride uptown and returned to 823 West End Avenue. In the Long apartment they listened to Dr. Long's Fada set, discussed matters of literature and amateur journalism, Howard's anticipated resumption of his career as a *fantaisiste*.

Belknap Long, handing down copies of his carefully ordered and preserved collection of amateur journals including Howard Lovecraft's own *The Conservative* dating back to 1915, urged his friend to pursue his calling as a literary artist. "And look at this, Howard," the younger man said, "Do you remember this copy of *The United Amateur*?"

Howard Lovecraft took the small, neatly-printed magazine and ran his eye over its contents. "Belknapius, the Theobaldian hat is off to thy true squirrelhood. I wish I could keep things in order the way you do." He stopped and read the opening lines of a short story, then closed the magazine and laid it aside. "How could even the old gaffer himself forget 'The Eye Above the Mantle,' grandchild? I remember your Poesque evocations very well; 'twas this very tale that caused me to write in admiration, and that led to our lengthy and rewarding acquaintanceship."

"Yes, and it was your kind introduction to Joe Henneberger that brought about the launching of my own professional career. I have much to be grateful for, Howard." Long mulled over his feelings, made several false starts at something that he wanted to say, finally managed to speak his mind. "One is sometimes accused of being too firmly wedded to the past in this modern era. I know that you have faced the very charge, Howard. And yet—it seems to me that much change is *not* for the better. Please stop me if I am intruding into a personal area where comments are unwelcome, Howard, but it seems to me that all of this running around you've been doing, to political demonstrations and semi-clandestine meetings; your turning from fantasy and true creativity to realms of sociological comment. . . do not really represent your, ah, your working to your strength."

He waved one hand in a vague gesture, grasped the carven arm of his chair with the other. "I seem to detect the strain which is beginning to tell on you, and for all that it is a pleasure to have you in residence in New York, I speak as a friend in saying that I thought you were better off in Providence, writing your arcane fantasies for Baird or for Wright."

He stopped again, reddening. "I fear my comments are an intrusion."

Howard shook his head negatively. "On the contrary. I believe you are entirely in the right. Once this meeting is over—tomorrow morning's meeting with Viereck and his associates—I hope to resolve the matter of the political book, and then return to the ancient hill, to my two aunts, to my fanlighted town houses and white-steepled chapels. Then it will be a farewell to the mongrel hordes of the metropolis, a return to my contemplative life. And I shall, of course, resume the production of stories."

"Certainly when Henneberger publishes your collection, Howard, it will launch you on your career as a literary artist, not a mere writer for hire."

Howard grinned broadly. "I can't wait until exchange copies arrive at the offices of Alfred A. Knopf and G. P. Putnam's Sons! Their rejections were so complimentary, and they would be pleased to read a novel by the author, but you must realize, Mr. Lovecraft, that short story collections are not in as great demand today as once they were. Today's reader prefers the novel, and we must obey the dictates of commerce.

"Commerce! I wish I'd never heard of the damned thing! What's commerce anyway, but the crass trading of materialistic, greed-inspired men in the product of the labors of others! The stock-marketeers, the Jews and the Marxists—one and the same, ultimately! There's no such thing as art for that kind of mind, only products to be bought and sold, squeezing the creator at one end of the transaction and the consumer at the other end, and all for the profit of the Semitic merchant who stands in the middle, taking his slice as they come, his slice as they go!"

He jumped to his feet and paced the room angrily.

"I wish that the second volume of *Mein Kampf* were available!"

Frank Long blinked up at his friend, at the non-sequitur.

Howard paused before a window, gazing out over the Hudson. In the darkness it was impossible to see very far, but directly below the apartment building vehicles crawled north and south, their headlamps casting cones of illumination in the night. Howard turned back, his fury gone as suddenly as it had arisen. "It's very late, child. Your family have all retired. There's no need to keep you up. Get thee to thy bed and I shall read or write until the morning. It will be easier for me to do that than to retire now and try to rise early."

CHAPTER THIRTY-THREE:

A WEIRD AND INCOMPREHENSIBLE SPECIES

HOWARD WAS listlessly perusing the *Morning Telegram* over toast and fried eggs when the Longs' telephone bell sounded. The uniformed maïd who had brought him his breakfast answered the call in the parlor, then returned to summon Howard.

"I explained that you were having your breakfast, sir, but the caller insisted that it was a matter of urgent business."

Howard laid the paper aside, swallowed a mouthful of black coffee, and rose from his chair. He went to the parlor and lifted the instrument to his ear, identifying himself to the caller.

The voice he heard was that of a woman, only faintly familiar in intonation. "I'm so glad that I was able to reach you, Mr. Lovecraft. This is the Jackson Press calling. You had an appointment with Mr. Viereck for this morning, to join him at a meeting in Woodbridge?"

Howard grunted agreement.

"Mr. Viereck was called out of town last night, Mr. Lovecraft. It was very sudden, very urgent. We tried to reach you last night but could not, but we reached Mrs. Lovecraft at your Brooklyn location, Mr. Lovecraft, and she suggested this number, in care of Dr. Long. I hope you aren't ill, sir?"

"No, no. Purely social. What about Mr. Viereck?"

"He asked me to tell you that the meeting would have to be put off. He'll contact you as soon as he returns to New York."

Howard rubbed his forehead with the back of his hand. "Did Mr. Viereck say where he had to go now?"

"I think it was somewhere in New England," the caller said. "I'm sorry I don't have the details, sir."

"All right," Howard said. He tried to think of something else to say, some other question to ask, but there was nothing. "All right," he said again, "thank you." He dropped the earpiece onto its hook and replaced the telephone on the table.

Frank Belknap Long, Jr., wearing pajamas and dressing gown, entered the room. "Everything all right, Howard?" he asked.

Howard explained the postponement of the meeting. "I wonder where Viereck went?" he added. "His office said merely New England. Could be anywhere. Hmph." He thanked Belknap Long for his customary hospitality, retrieved his suitcase and returned to Brooklyn through crowds of office workers and Christmas shoppers. He spent the day studying his commonplace book, trying to work out some ideas for new stories. After a while that activity palled, and he wrote letters for the rest of the afternoon—to Starrett in Chicago, to Henry Whitehead in St. Croix, to Two-gun Bob Howard in Cross Plains, to Clark Ashton Smith in Auburn.

Finally he composed a lengthy letter to Farnsworth Wright at the offices of the Popular Fiction Publishing Company on North Michigan Avenue in Chicago. He thanked Wright for the Eyrie proof sent in care of Frank Long, mentioned that Parkside Avenue was still his own residence for a short while but that he was returning to Providence for Christmas and that future correspondence would best reach him at Barnes Street.

Then he got down to the serious part of the letter. He was pleased to hear, from Vincent Starrett, of progress on the collection featuring *The Moon Terror*, and understood by inference that his own exclusion from the collection—coupled with the publicity buildup taking place in the Eyrie—could well be used to whet the appetites of readers for a collection of Howard Lovecraft's stories.

He was flattered by the notion of the book just as he had been flattered by Wright's praise of him in the November and December numbers. Phrases like "superb masterpiece of *outré* literature," "masterpieces," "vaulting imagination," "supreme artistry," and (applied to Howard's forthcoming story "The Call of Cthulhu," which Wright had previously rejected) "one of the greatest and most powerful works of weird fiction ever written," could turn the head of a younger man, but were accepted with due humility by himself.

Loath as he was to raise the subject, it would of course prove needful at some early date to discuss the terms under which the book was to appear. The title of the volume, the selection of the stories, and the procurement of appropriate accompanying material must all be taken under consideration. Belknap Long had done a fine introduction for the Cook volume of *The Shunned House*, presently in production. Presumably a comparable foreword or essay of appreciation would be a valuable adjunct to the stories in Howard's own collection, but who should be the author of the foreword? Vincent Starrett was a possible candidate; Bob Howard was another; Clark Ashton Smith, a third.

There were still other contract terms to be settled upon, one of them being the *bête noir* of the dedicated but impecunious artist, money. Howard imagined that a standard arrangement must exist, providing for a down payment by the publisher at the beginning of the project and a royalty on each copy sold once the book was issued. Howard's contract with the Jackson Press contained such provisions.

In any case, Messrs. Henneberger and Wright were to understand, please, that Howard was not really interested in such matters as contract terms and down payments, but the reality of functioning in a crassly materialistic society when one was not a person of independent means rendered it incumbent upon one to take note, however reluctantly, of these matters.

Howard commented upon a number of recent stories in closing, giving particular praise to "The Shadows" by the Reverend Whitehead in the November issue—a fine story, with a real brain and fancy behind it—and anticipating a reply from Henneberger or Wright.

He searched until he found a sheet of two-cent stamps in a lower drawer, affixed them to the letters he'd written and made his way, muffled and sweatered and mittened, to the mailbox. When he returned to the apartment he found Sonia in the hallway removing slushy galoshes and they entered together. Sonia expressed a little surprise at seeing Howard still in Brooklyn; he explained the telephone message from the Jackson Press ("I'm happy they found you at Frank's," Sonia commented, "so you didn't have to ramble all through the cold city for nothing").

Sonia asked if Howard had substitute plans for the weekend; he had none, but expected that he would stay close to home, with the radiators turned on, and watch the cold world of Prospect Park through tightly-shut windows.

"Please come with Theo and me," Sonia urged. "I know you don't like Jewish culture, but you'll love the Temple and this is the last chance you'll have to see it. It's lovely architecture. You speak of loving the Arabian Nights, Howard, you write of that strange Arabian mystic, Abdul Al-hazred—"

"I am Abdul Al-hazred," Howard said. "Or at least, I was as a child. Ed Price says that my Arabic derivation of the name is faulty, but it has a flow to it, I still like the name."

"I'm sure Mr. Price is a very learned and well-traveled man."

"He is."

"Well, Howard, the point is that you will love Temple Emanu-El. It will be like a real visit to the Arabian Nights for you. And Dash is coming by in his car for me, you know he admires you for the help you gave his brother, he'll be happy if you come along too. But mainly I will."

To Sonia's surprise, Howard agreed. He spent the rest of the weekend in the apartment, not budging into the December streets of Brooklyn, reading and writing, commenting to Sonia on newspaper stories (a *Times* feature on the Piltdown Man excited his interest hugely; he clipped the photograph of a dioramic reconstruction to send to Two-gun Bob with suitable commentary on the true nature of barbarian splendor).

Sunday's headlines in every paper featured the same story: a marine tragedy just west of Provincetown at the tip of Cape Cod. The navy's new submarine *S-4* and a Coast Guard destroyer, the *Paulding*, were involved. The *S-4* had been undergoing tests; in addition to the submersible's captain, Lieutenant Commander Jones, and the 40-man crew, there were inspectors from the Navy Department in Washington.

The *Paulding* had been on routine patrol duty, guarding the stormy New England waters against rum-runners.

The *S-4* had been undergoing deep-submersion exercises in twenty fathoms of water, and was rising to the surface of Cape Cod Bay. The *Paulding* had been steaming through mist and wind-driven rain on a course at right angles to that of the submarine. Just before the submarine reached the Bay's surface, the destroyer had sliced across the bridge of the *S-4*, crushing her deck, wrecking her conning tower, springing her plates, flooding most of her compartments and sending the hapless *S-4* plummeting back to the floor of Cape Cod Bay, almost 120 feet below.

The *Paulding* had limped back to port.

Rescue craft had been sent at once to the *S-4*, including the Navy's greatest divers, Thomas Eady, Edward Ellsberg, William Carr. Hope was held out for some if not all of the crewmen of the *S-4*. Later newspapers would carry word of further developments, and bulletins would be furnished to radio stations.

Theo Weiss, resplendent in chesterfield topcoat and homburg, doeskin gloves and silver-headed ebony walking-stick, arrived to drive Sonia and Howard into Manhattan. The Rickenbacker purred across the Williamsburg Bridge, the chill waters of the East River black beneath, the lights of the city less frenetic on this Sunday evening than most other nights.

Howard managed to endure the Hanukkah service, enchanted as Sonia had promised by the Oriental splendors of the Temple. It filled half a block on Fifth Avenue, sharing the frontage between 43rd and 44th Streets with the Harriman National Bank, with only a tiny old house squeezed between the two edifices. The Moorish and Saracenic features of the synagogue, the almost Islamic spires and minarets of the edifice's exterior, the arches and columns inside, were like a dream of exotic architecture.

The service itself, with its chanting and singing in Hebrew, was strange enough that Howard was able to enter a fantastic realm of ancient and alien species, imagining the chants as survivals of a weird and incomprehensible race that had otherwise long vanished from the earth.

The congregation bore little resemblance to the noisome and disgusting Asiatics of the subways and the alleys of New York. Instead they were well-dressed men and dignified women of refinement, more nearly resembling Theo Weiss, Sonia Greene Lovecraft, or Howard's friend Samuel Loveman.

Dash Weiss suggested that they stop off for refreshments before returning to Brooklyn, but Sonia said that she needed an early night's rest. "Tomorrow starts the last week before Christmas," she explained. "Every day will be longer and harder than the one before." Hardeen laughed understandingly.

On the way back to Parkside Avenue in the Rickenbacker, Howard said that he had enjoyed his visit to the synagogue. "It gives one pause," he stated. "When one reads a passionate and persuasive volume like *Mein Kampf*, and then has an experience such as mine this evening—perhaps Herr Hitler has been observing the wrong class of Jews."

Theo Weiss said, "That is a dangerous man, Hitler. I've looked at his book, and I know some of the territory to which he refers. Ehrich and I both visited Berlin, Vienna, other cities he makes mention of. There is a terrible violence and hatred in that man. I fear for Germany if he comes to power, and if he comes to power in Germany I fear for all of Europe."

Howard grunted deprecatingly. "Hitler does have a tendency toward hysterics, but I think he's really interested in cleansing Germany of what he regards as alien cultural strains, nothing more than that."

Hardeen gestured with one hand, holding the wheel of the Rickenbacker with the other. "But Howard, what does he mean by cleansing? What would he do with the Jews of Germany? There are millions of them. Would he obliterate Hebrew culture and religion? Ban the speaking of Hebrew and of Yiddish? Expel all the Jews? And if so, where will he send them?"

"Details to be worked out," Howard replied. "We should have his second volume shortly, and that will tell us."

Weiss shook his head. "I cannot share your sanguine outlook, Howard. I sense a darker intent on the part of that man. I've heard you speak of Bill the Butcher in the past. I believe that if Herr Hitler comes to power in Germany, the world will look back at the days of the *Kaiserheit* as warm and flowery times. I know you have been associating with some of Hitler's people, and I beseech you to examine their intentions before you grant them any assistance."

After the briefest of pauses he added, "Europe is not as far distant from America as it used to be. Not in this age of Captain Lindbergh."

Somehow the mention of Lindbergh brought the subject to transatlantic travel, to ships and submarines and the *S-4* disaster. "I intend to contact the Navy Department early in the morning," Theo said. "I don't know if Mr. Baird's noctovisor will be of any help to them, but I will offer it. Both the noctovisor and the undersea escape knowledge that Ehrich and I devised. I am afraid it will little help those poor souls at the bottom of Cape Cod Bay. The problem is, you need to have the Ryan Special knowledge and equipment with you, inside the trap, before you submerge. But I'll do as much as the Navy Department permits."

The Rickenbacker drew up alongside the curb opposite Prospect Park. The park had been transformed; from its summer green and autumnal gold it had entered a period of drab brown and gray at the onset of winter, but now, powdered with snow, it looked like a midnight painting of moon-illumined sand dunes.

Hardeen wished Howard a merry Christmas and Sonia a happy Hanukkah, then drove off through the night.

Upstairs in their apartment, Sonia went to bed. Howard sat up, mulling over his unusual experience. Finally he drew pen and paper and wrote a long, thoughtful letter on the subject to Henry Whitehead. Whitehead was a most unusual character: Howard had come across him solely in the role of a fellow contributor of *outré* fiction. A warm correspondence followed. Howard learned that Whitehead was a onetime newspaperman, professional athlete, and had finally been ordained an Episcopal priest. He had risen in the hierarchy of his church, and now divided his time equally between a prestigious pulpit in Connecticut and an Episcopal See in the American Virgin Islands, with residence on the island of St. Croix.

Howard expressed his mixed feelings about Jews and Judaism, about the influence of what he regarded as "foreign" cultures in the United States and in other nations, about Hitler and the latter's theory of "folkish," a curious blend of the racial theories of Huston Stewart Chamberlain with ultra-nationalism and anti-Bolshevism. Howard had been overwhelmingly attracted to Hitler's notions (following his initial dismay at the garbled prose in which the German-Austrian expressed them); certainly these views had been in close concert with Howard Lovecraft's own, even with the latter as they had been expressed in his essays and letters of the past decade and longer.

Even Sonia Lovecraft's and Samuel Loveman's arguments that Howard could not bring his anti-Semitic sentiments into consonance with his marriage to a Jewess, his close friendship with the Jewish poet, and his longtime admiration for and association with the Ehrich and Theo Weiss family, had not shaken Howard from his basic antipathy toward their race. Individuals were individuals and peoples were peoples; from the finest stock there might occasionally spring a weakling, a defect, a black sheep; and from even the most depraved of races there might rise occasionally a Sonia Greene, a Samuel Loveman, a Houdini or a Hardeen.

As a priest, Whitehead was educated in the religions and cultures of man, and must have a good understanding of this forebear of Christianity, and while Howard was strongly anti-Christian, recognizing only the aesthetic, not the theological, values of the Catholic and Anglican denominations, he would respect Whitehead's insights. Further, through his dealings with the jumbee-worshipping natives of Christiansted and the countryside around it, Whitehead had had unusual opportunities to observes the relationship of race to race and culture to culture in a manner that might help Howard come to grips with his own present ambivalence.

Howard finished the letter with a line of praise for Whitehead's recent story "The Shadows" and sealed it in an envelope. He was tempted to splurge and spend the 10 cents needed to send a letter by air, but such service was not yet available to the Virgin Islands, so he made do with a regular 2 cent stamp and set the missive aside.

Christmas week was brightened by visits to the Long apartment and another invitation to a performance by Hardeen the Mysterious. Howard managed to cope with the frigid streets by bundling into his warmest clothes and hurrying from doorway to doorway whenever he had to pass between buildings. At the Hardeen performance he

chatted with the magician backstage about the progress
(or rather, the tragic lack of progress) in the *S-4* rescue
efforts.

Courageous divers—particularly Ellsberg, Edie and
Carr—had risked their lives to be lowered from the storm-
swept surface of Cape Cod Bay to the submarine lying in
120 feet of near-freezing brine. They had found the wreck
with relative ease and tapped messages in code on the
hull.

Replies were received.

There were six survivors inside the *S-4*. All the rest had
been killed in the collision with the *Paulding*, either
crushed in the crash itself, or swept away to die at sea, or
drowned in the compartments of the submersible. But
these six had survived in one watertight compartment.
They had enough air to last three to four days. If the *S-4*
could be raised in that time, or if they could somehow be
got out of the sunken craft, they would survive. Otherwise, death by suffocation was inevitable.

The divers tapped back messages of encouragement.

The six trapped men tapped out messages to their
families.

Cables were slung under the submarine but attempts
to raise it failed. There were suggestions for welding an
escape chamber onto the hull of the *S-4*, then cutting
through the submarine's plates to get the survivors into
the escape chamber. Storms on the surface hampered
rescue efforts. More efforts were made. Time might be
bought by inserting air hoses into the sub; work began on
this. More messages were passed from the survivors to
their families and back.

The Continental Laboratories in New York dispatched
experimental resuscitators to Provincetown, to be used if
needed. The devices had been developed by a German
experimenter and were the only ones of their type in the
western hemisphere.

In Washington, House Speaker Nicholas Longworth
launched an official investigation of the incident. How
could the *Paulding* and the *S-4* not have known of each
other's presence before the fatal moment of their collision? The investigation was temporarily hampered by the
absence of the Secretary of the Navy, Mr. Wilbur, the
Chief of Naval Operations, Admiral Hughes, and the fleet

commander, Rear Admiral Brumby. All had traveled to Massachusetts to superintend rescue efforts.

"I don't understand it either," Howard Lovecraft said to Theo Weiss. They were seated in Hardeen's dressing room at the onetime Pike's Opera House, now known as the Grand Opera House at Eighth Avenue and 23rd Street. No opera had been performed in the hall for decades, but it was a fine theater with excellent stage facilities and a good auditorium.

"Understand what?" Hardeen asked Howard.

"How the *Paulding* and *S-4* could collide that way, neither of them aware of the other's presence. I suppose a surface craft doesn't ordinarily expect a submarine to rise beneath it at any moment, but I should think that the captain of the submersible would consider such dangers as a matter of course."

Hardeen nodded agreement. "I'm sure that Mr. Longworth would like to ask Captain Jones a few questions about that point. But have you seen the survivors list? Captain Jones was not among the six. Nor were Commander Calloway or Mr. Ford of the Navy Department. If the six men do get out, they may have some information to give, but unfortunately not the key facts, I fear."

Howard gestured stiffly. "Then it will be a mystery for all time."

"Mm." Hardeen appeared deep in thought.

"One would think that a man as familiar with undersea rescues as yourself might have a theory," Howard suggested.

"I don't wish to make sensational charges without evidence, but I have a terrible suspicion, Howard. This tragedy seems so very unlikely to have arisen spontaneously. Yet if there is any suggestion of foul play. . ." He began to pace around the tiny room, picking things up, looking under them, pulling drawers from the little dressing table and shoving them back once more.

"Is something missing, Theo?"

He stood still. "Not missing. I was just looking for a map. How near is Provincetown to Marblehead, I wonder."

"That is my part of the country. Here." Howard Lovecraft had extracted his Waterman and notepad from his suit pocket, and without hesitation sketched in a map of the Massachusetts coastal region, Cape Cod with its easterly jut and crooked extension, like a finger crooked in summons, Provincetown at its tip. Quincy and Boston lay on the mainland, slightly north of due west of Provincetown; Lynn, Salem, and Marblehead to their north, northwest of the *S-4*'s position.

"From Marblehead to Provincetown is less than forty miles, bee-line," Howard stated, "although it would be triple that to travel by automobile."

"I didn't mean by land anyway. Less than forty miles. And from, say, Satan Rock or Cat Island off Marblehead, to the site of the collision—what would you say? More like thirty?" Howard agreed.

Hardeen resumed his pacing, more calmly now, grinding a beefy fist into a calloused palm before him. "Call this a wild fantasy if you will, Howard, but I can't separate them in my mind. I can't separate that mysterious activity we saw last summer, off Marblehead, from the sinking of the *S-4*. I don't see what the connection is, but I feel that there is one."

~ ~ ~ ~ ~

The telephone rang at 259 Parkside after Sonia had left for the day but before Howard had fully awakened. It seemed to shriek into his dream, setting off wild flights of rubbery, gibbering ghouls that carried him through midnight skies over moonlit landscapes dotted with tumbled, deserted ruins of some ancient cyclopean civilization. All around Abdul there was a shrieking, screaming, ululating cry. He struggled to—

Howard sat up, turned and lowered his bare feet to the carpeted floor. In striped nightshirt he made his way to the table where the telephone stood and lifted it, receiver in his right hand, ear-piece in left.

Central was on the line, and after Howard had identified himself Central announced that a long-lines call was awaiting him.

The voice was weak with distance and distorted with the pops and crackles of the telephone system, almost like that of Randolph Carter in one of Howard's early tales, yet the words were understandable and the intonation distinctively the rich delivery of George Sylvester Viereck with its bare suggestion of an accent.

He was calling from Massachusetts. The postponed meeting had been rescheduled, he told Howard. Viereck spoke with excitement, with a taut wire of tension in his voice, but he easily controlled himself. If Howard could travel to Marblehead once more. . .the meeting would take place the following week. . .Friday morning. . .yes, if Howard would arrive by railroad. . .yes, a car would be dispatched to meet his train at the old Boston & Maine station. Yes, and Howard would bring clothing and toilet articles for a stay of some days, should the meeting become protracted. Yes. All was agreed.

Howard heard Viereck click off. He hung his own earpiece back on the hook, placed the instrument on the table and raised his hand to rub the bridge of his nose between forefinger and thumb.

He spent the day writing, making outlines and notes for new stories. He felt pleased, energized as he had not for many months.

When Sonia arrived from Russek's, Howard inquired as to her obligations for the remainder of the week. Sonia said that she would be working every day, lengthy hours, until Christmas Eve. That day the store would close early, and of course the next day would be closed. In fact, since Christmas would fall on Sunday, the following day would also be celebrated as a holiday.

Howard suggested that Sonia join him, in that case, leaving directly from her work on Saturday, and traveling to Providence to spend Christmas on the ancient hill. He told her that he would have to spend the following Friday at Marblehead—perhaps several days after that. If Sonia wished, she could remain in Providence with him during the week, and either travel on to Marblehead with him or return to New York from Providence.

Sonia thought it a wonderful plan, and said that she would remain with her husband for as long as she could stay away from work. The days between December 27 and 30 might be hard to get off, but she would ask for them.

CHAPTER THIRTY-FOUR:

CHRISTMAS AT THE CATHEDRAL

THE EASTERN Steam Ship Lines' *Boston* left its Manhattan pier in a gray and misty afternoon. The sun was already gone behind the New Jersey palisades; the winter solstice was only three days past and the day had been short, dim, and clammy. Still, the crowds of shoppers had filled the stores and bustled along the sidewalks. The tinsel and holly that decorated the city's buildings had struggled bravely to overcome the gloom of the December day, and hard largely succeeded. Howard Lovecraft had traveled uptown to his friend Belknapius' apartment to spend the afternoon of Christmas Eve, and with the early closing of Dr. Long's practice, a family gathering had followed.

Howard conceded that the tall, imported Piñon pine was fully as handsome—if not quite as large—as the trees that had brought their splendid color and fragrance to his grandfather's house on Angell Street thirty-odd years before. "I know it isn't as tall," Howard claimed, "because when I stood before the tree in Angell Street, it was easily three times my height. While this specimen, for all its grace, is barely a third taller than I am.

"Everything seems to have shrunk since I was a child," he concluded mournfully.

"But—just a minute," Long *fils* countered. A frown creased his usually smooth brow. "Thirty years ago you couldn't have been much taller than—" He bent and held his hand out flat, palm down, two or three feet above the carpet-nap. "And now. . ."

Howard was nodding and laughing, at first quietly, then working his way gradually into a series of guffaws that were shared by Frank Long, Sr., then May Long, and finally, embarrassedly, Belknap.

A bowl of creamy eggnog, its yellow-white surface marked with swirls like windswept dunes and dotted with ground nutmeg, stood invitingly on a sideboard. May Long offered cups all around—"The help have the afternoon off," she explained—and Dr. Long held up his hand to delay the proceeding.

"I've brought something from the hospital. Purely medicinal, you understand, hence altogether legal." He produced a bottle of ancient brandy, broke the pre-war seal around its cap and held the bottle above the frosted silver punch bowl. "I trust no one will object?"

Howard said, "I normally regard myself as a teetotaler, but in the spirit of the occasion, I shall make an exception today."

Dr. Long tilted the bottle, stirred the eggnog with a long silver ladle, then personally served his wife and son and their guest. They all toasted the season, then Howard, sipping his eggnog, commented, "I always wondered what oral surgery was like. This is hardly as unpleasant as one would expect."

Dr. Long laughed. "I wish I could make things as pleasant for all my patients, Howard. So you and Sonia are off to Providence Plantations this evening, are you? Going to take a late Christmas Eve supper with your aunts at Barnes Street?"

Howard shook his head. "That was my initial thought, sir. But Mrs. Lovecraft suggested that we take the steamer instead of the train or bus. They run to Providence as well as Boston, although not as often. We're to sail to Providence on the steamship *Boston*," he grinned. "We'll spend our Christmas Eve on the high seas of Long Island Sound, and make Narragansett Bay around dawn. Then we'll ride a car up the ancient hill and join Aunt Annie and Aunt Lillian for a noonday dinner. Afterwards there should be an exchange of gifts—Sonia has picked out some little baubles for the aunts—and a quiet evening."

After a moment's contemplation, Howard added, "Perhaps we might leave the apartment to participate in an evening Nativity service at some nearby church."

Frank Long *fils* had been holding a cold briar pipe in one hand, his silver cup of eggnog in the other; he dropped the pipe in astonishment and barely saved the eggnog from joining it on the light-colored carpet. "Nativity service! You, Howard? The grand champion of atheism and materialism of the entire United? Do mine ears deceive me?"

Howard's small grin betrayed a sheepish quality. "I remain as dedicated an opponent of the supernatural as ever. But you are aware that I have always acknowledged the beauty of certain religious expressions—the architecture of old New England chapels as well as of grander Sees, the effects of skillfully wrought stained glass, as well as some of the more impressive liturgical costumes and music. You know my story 'The Festival.' "

Long had retrieved his pipe and slipped it into the side pocket of his casual tweed. "Ah, well, I should have known better than to suspect you of infidelity to your convictions, Howard. Well, I join my father in wishing you a most felicitous holiday. And should we not see one another during the remainder of 1927, may I propose an early toast to joy and success in the coming year."

~ ~ ~ ~ ~

The steamer *Boston* pulled away from her slip with a full complement of passengers. Howard and Sonia Lovecraft had settled into their little cabin on the starboard side of the steamer. ("We shall see less of the land and more of the sea that way," Howard commented.) They arranged their belongings, made their way to the lounge and enjoyed a quiet dinner while the ship's orchestra played Christmas carols. A number of passengers had brought children with them, and a burly sailor, decked out as St. Nick, distributed small gifts among them.

The evening passed calmly on the *Boston* while outside a steady fall of snow hissed on the surface of the Sound.

Christmas morning dawned with a high, tiny sun shining on the hills and roofs of Providence splashed white with fresh snow. Despite the uncomfortable cold, Howard was unable to contain his joy at the sight of the city and the knowledge that, whatever the outcome of the impending conference at Marblehead, his latest (and, he swore inwardly, his last) New York sojourn was at an end.

Streetcars were running normally even though the snow made the hills of the city difficult for automobiles. Howard and Sonia took a streetcar from the pier to the center of the city, then transferred for their ride up College Hill. Howard drank in every house, every commercial structure, and finally every building of the Brown University complex with the eyes of a lover reunited after long-enforced parting.

At 10 Barnes he ran from sidewalk to the front door of the house and took the steps two at a time, his long legs devouring the distance. He embraced his two aunts once inside, first dropping his suitcases, then lifting each of the older women into the air and whirling around like a dancer, exclaiming "Annie, Annie," and "Lillian, Lillian," while the middle-aged women giggled and twittered over him like plump country mothers over a soft-cheeked baby.

At last, breathless from laughter and exertion, Howard and Annie and Lillian stood still. The two aunts exchanged handshakes with Howard's wife.

They passed the day as planned. The meal was most pleasant, and Lillian and Annie expressed gratitude for the gifts Sonia had chosen for them. Each aunt presented Howard with gifts in exchange: a bulky knitted sweater from one, a warm scarf and a pair of warmly lined gloved from the other.

Most of the day passed, for Howard, in reacquainting himself with his belongings and the furnishing of the apartment. Most of the furniture and utensils of the place had been in the family for generations, coming not from the Lovecrafts but from the Phillipses. Some had been brought by Captain Whipple Phillips, Howard's grandfather, from far ports where his ship had called in the previous century. There were others that had originated in England still earlier.

At mid-afternoon Howard pulled on his new warm clothing and a pair of old galoshes rescued from the depths of a cluttered clothes closet and set out, alone, for a brief stroll. The temperature was far below his preference, and he felt some discomfort of the face and extremities, but he kept his fedora pulled down on his head and managed to enjoy his outing. The happiest moment came when he heard a feline outcry on Angell Street and saw that both Nigger-man II and Yaller Gal were prospering despite the snow and chill weather.

He had gifts for them, having prepared himself at the family ice box before leaving Barnes Street, and squatted on the white-covered sidewalk to distribute the scraps to his friends. He was rewarded with buttings and purrs, and rose happily to return to Barnes. He would have liked to continue his walk to the banks of the Seekonk. It would probably be frozen now, and would present an aspect of austere beauty, a chiaroscuro image of gray banks, white ice and dark silhouetted hills and houses on its easterly edge. But Howard knew that he was near the limit of his stay; to remain outdoors longer would invite discomfort at least, real danger at most.

He returned to the apartment and found his aunts seated in the parlor before the small Christmas tree they had trimmed in Howard's absence these past weeks. Sonia had retired to the room that the aunts had kept for Howard during his time away from Providence.

They made a cold supper, largely of the remnants of their earlier meal, and when Howard suggested that they attend evening services at a church all were astonished. Howard explained his reasons (making no mention of the Hanukkah service he had attended on Fifth Avenue in New York, however) and the aunts readily assented.

They agreed that Howard should choose the church, and he named the Cathedral on Broad Street. One aunt expressed surprise. "Why travel so far on a cold evening, Howard? Besides, isn't that a popish church? What's wrong with the good Protestant Cathedral of St. John, right here on College Hill?"

But Howard was adamant, and they made their way down the hill, across the Providence River by streetcar, and to the Cathedral. Inside, Howard pointed out the beauty of the pictorial vaulted windows, the flickering votary candles, the rising incense. "Of course it's all fraudulent nonsense," he whispered to the aunts, "but most rewarding to the aesthetic senses." His eyes flickered about the nave and the transept as the service proceeded. At its completion he lingered with his wife and aunts until a family group, elderly parents dressed as somberly as was Howard, daughter more brightly garbed, passed them in the aisle.

The elderly man's eyes flickered keenly across the faces of the persons standing between the pews. When he saw Howard he halted, grunted a few words (not in English) to a broad-shouldered, dark-suited younger man striding beside him, then extended his hand to Howard.

"Mr. Lovecraft," he said. "I did not know you were a Catholic."

Howard flushed slightly. "I'm not. But I brought my family here to partake of the beauty of the edifice and the ceremonies." He introduced Annie, Lillian and Sonia to the Morellis. Again they shook hands all around, then continued out of the church. On the steps they halted and gazed at the sky where the comet Skjellerup blazed spectacularly midway between Altair and Vega.

"Beautiful, beautiful," murmured Morelli. "Mr. Lovecraft, you have an automobile here? No? Permit me to offer you a ride in one of my cars." He turned and spoke over his shoulder. Another beefy young man in dark clothing answered briefly. Morelli took Howard's elbow and the two family groups proceeded down the church steps. "Ah, when the holiday comes on Sunday as well," Morelli said contemplatively, "Mass three times in the day. It does good for the soul, but the body is not as resilient as it used to be." He laughed self-deprecatingly. "Good to see you again, Mr. Lovecraft. Maybe you and Mrs. Lovecraft could come to dinner again some time. I know my daughter enjoys discussing literature with an intellectual like you.

"Ah, too bad about those fellows in Massachusetts, eh? Those two foolish radicals and that fellow Madeiros. Two brothers in one family, eh, in the same year. What a pity, what a pity!"

Two cars had pulled up to the curb, and Morelli handed the Lovecraft party into one before escorting his wife and daughter to the other. The driver of the Lovecraft car turned to speak. "College Hill, that where you live?"

Howard told the man the address.

The driver didn't speak until the car had pulled to the curb at 10 Barnes. Then he hopped from the car, stood holding the door for Sonia and Howard and his aunts. "Mr. Morelli wishes you a happy and prosperous 1928, Mr. Lovecraft." He climbed back into the car and pulled away, up the street.

Two days later Howard sat near a radiator, bundled even in the apartment of his aunts against the 18° weather. He held the morning's *Providence Journal*, reading the latest reports on the *S-4* tragedy. All efforts to save the six survivors had failed; divers had succeeded in piping in a fresh air supply when it became clear that quick rescue efforts would not succeed, but even that device had come too late. The forlorn tapping from inside the hull had ceased days earlier, and was not resumed.

Admirals Hughes and Brumby had said that the cold and rough seas would prevent further attempts to raise the *S-4* until spring, but Navy Secretary Wilbur had overruled them and ordered efforts to raise the submarine at once. The mine-layer *Falcon* steamed to Provincetown, then to the disaster site, to provide support for the divers. The aircraft carrier *Saratoga* with a complement of 83 Vought Corsair observation planes and advanced Boeing F24 fighters stood off Quincy to offer assistance if needed.

As Howard leafed casually through the *Journal* he heard the doorbell and found that the afternoon mail delivery had arrived. He laid aside the description of the snarled cables that divers had found the *S-4* trapped in and examined his letters. The most interesting bore the imprinted return address of the Auburn, California, *Journal*.

Howard returned with the letter to his tall leather chair beside the hissing radiator. He laid the letter on the seat and went to the kitchen for a moment, returning with a cup of hot coffee to open the white envelope.

Clark Ashton Smith had written; as usual his epistolary style, while formal and elegant, showed little of the crystalline effulgence of his few short stories or the weighty (and suggestively decadent) emanations of his poetry.

"The surprising arrival of *New America and the Coming World-Empire* prompts me to comment not only on the impressive manuscript itself, but on your recently published fiction, which I have been remiss in responding to. 'Pickman's Model' in *Weird Tales* is a highly effective evocation of horror through mystery; its *suggestion* of the gruesome, the terrifying elementals that await us in realms just beyond the ordinary, makes for a most satisfying performance.

"To turn then to the almost naturalistic tale 'The Colour Out of Space' in *Amazing Stories* is a surprise; a shock; yet a most pleasant one. You have seldom used the *materia* of scientifiction before, Ec'h-Pi-El, and seldom has anyone used these *materia* with the skill that you have. One might raise the question, Why did the doomed Gardner family remain on their farm to the end? Why did not Ammi Pierce *force* his neighbors to flee the deteriorative influence of the stone from the sky? Why, in the end, did Nahum himself remain?

"But to me this seems the very point of the story: that in the face of horror beyond human comprehension and beyond the ability of puny mortals to cope, man becomes a helpless, passive object rather than an active subject in passing events. A depressing theme to assay, Theobaldus, and I hope a false one, but no less a powerful statement. My congratulations!

"Now as for *New America and the Coming World-Empire*. I read the manuscript with greatest involvement. I hope you do not mind my having done so. You asked me to safeguard it for you, and I have done so; you did not specify whether I was to read it or not, so (as I always am rewarded by reading your works, of whatever sort) I have availed myself of the opportunity.

"The literary and intellectual aspects of the book are incontrovertible, as expected, Howard, and I cannot praise your manuscript too highly on those, purely aesthetic, grounds. However, as regards the political aspect, I fear that I must sound a warning tocsin. Perhaps it is because I have had greater experience than you with the somewhat bohemian elements of San Francisco and Carmel, and, as a consequence, their adversaries, that I perceive certain potentials in the movements you praise that are not apparent to you.

"I fear, my dear friend, that you treat these Tsarist revanchists, Kaiserian restorationists, the Klansmen and Blackshirts, and most of all this Austrian fellow Hitler, as if they were fellow participants with you in amateur journalism. As such one might theorize, expostulate, propound, rebut, etc., to one's full satisfaction, while still living in the relative comfort and freedom of today's world— especially today's America.

"But these men are serious, friend Howard. I took the trouble, on a recent visit to San Francisco, to visit the local offices of the *Freunde des Neuen Deutschlands* of which you speak in your manuscript. It is located in the cellar of the Thor Hotel, a dingy establishment located in a narrow alley halfway between the Embarcadero and

Chinatown. The kind of place where you could well set an atmospheric tale, Howard.

"The place is dark, smoky, mildly alcoholic (I don't suppose that Prohibition is taken any more seriously in San Francisco than it is in any other cosmopolis in the land). The establishment is run by a bruiser who intimidates any unfamiliar visitor into a quick withdrawal unless he produces a credential of one sort or another. Fortunately I am still regarded as some sort of petty celebrity in San Francisco (although not in Auburn! A prophet, etc.), and was admitted into the cellar, although not without many a fish-eyed glance.

"The *habitués* are chiefly German emigrants and German merchant seamen on leave from ships tied up in the Bay; the sailors stop off at the Thor for a social hour *en route* to the more innocently unsavoury establishments of the Barbary Coast and the Tenderloin. There are many veterans of the World War, including some of the survivors of the scuttling of the fleet at Scapa Flow—but not the Red revolutionaries, let me hasten to add. The contrary!

"These men visualize a new order for the world, all right—but it is a brutal one! They will make the world into a huge, disciplined, brutalized camp if they have their ways. The theories of race and culture that you admire so in *Mein Kampf* are not golden ideals to these men. To them, these ideas mean one thing: the terrorization, beating, persecution, and ultimately the annihilation of those people they regard as 'inferior'. I have seen squads of sailors setting out from the Thor to waylay and beat Jews—their favorite target—and return laughing and gloating, totting up their score of bloodied faces, broken teeth, smashed eyes!

"This is not a game, Howard, and you must understand the type of men with whom you are becoming involved. Intellectuals and *litterateurs* like your associate G. S. Viereck may serve as a screen for these men, but behind the screen stands the Hun, the brute, grasping the same knout that ever he held.

"Beware!

"Paul Cook sent me a copy of his magazine containing your lengthy essay 'Supernatural Horror in Literature.' A most admirable and informative work. I commend you upon it. Please do remain in communication with me."

~ ~ ~ ~ ~

Two days later—Thursday afternoon—a large envelope arrived from Belknap Long. Howard opened it to find an ordinary business-size envelope and a note from his friend saying that it had arrived at West End Avenue, and was being forwarded (unopened of course) with best wishes for 1928, and in the hopes that the letter contained pleasant news.

Howard handled the second envelope, becoming aware of strains of music from the next room. Sonia had brought some panatrope disks of seasonal music, and was playing a brainless but peculiarly catchy tune called "Christmas Morning at Clancy's," a really funny dialect song performed by an amusing comic Irishman.

Grinning at a joke in the music, Howard opened the envelope. The return address was that of the Popular Fiction Publishing Company at 840 North Michigan Avenue in Chicago. The inner letterhead, then, was as expected: *Weird Tales, A Magazine of the Bizarre and Unusual.* Howard ran his eye down the page, expecting to see the usual typewritten signature of Farnsworth Wright. Instead, he found an elaborate autograph: that of the publisher Joseph Henneberger, the same Henneberger who had repeatedly tried to hire Howard as an editor.

Perhaps this was another business proposition from Henneberger: a welcome event if Howard's Jackson Press connection was to be severed! From the other room, Howard could hear the end of "Christmas Morning at Clancy's." Sonia lifted the needle, turned the disk and restarted the panatrope. The new tune featured a comic lyric also, "Santa Claus Hides in the Phonograph."

Henneberger's letter began, "Dear Lovecraft:

"I write to extend to you greetings for the holiday season, and to proffer my best wishes for the new year and all the years to come. As you know, our association has extended for several years now, almost from the beginning of *Weird Tales*, back in our Indianapolis period under the old Rural Publishing aegis. It is my hope—and Wright's as well, of course—that it continue for many years of fruitful effort.

"Wright informs me that he has scheduled your new effort, 'The Call of Cthulhu,' for the February number, and I look forward to enthusiastic reader response to it and to all your other works for us. Wright also tells me that he has several examples of your verse in his inventory. While, as you know, we continue to rely primarily on prose to fill our pages, an occasional bit of rhyme is not unwelcome. In all candor, however, I must tell you that I'd rather see your stories in our manuscript file than your verse—the name of the magazine remains *Weird Tales* after all, not *Weird Verse*.

"We received a most pleasant visit the other day from our mutual acquaintance Vincent Starrett the newspaperman, who has now resumed his residence and his journalistic career in Chicago.

Starrett had only the highest compliments for you, but he brought to our attention an apparent unfortunate misapprehension on your part which I hasten to clear up at this time.

"Apparently the absence of your stories from our *Moon Terror* collection coupled with the effusive responses to your writings that have appeared in the Eyrie have led to your anticipating the appearance of a collection of your own tales under the Popular Fiction imprint.

"Such a volume would be of undeniable merit, and I will not try to hide from you the fact that Wright and I have discussed that possibility several times. However, we have been monitoring the preliminary responses to *The Moon Terror*, and I must tell you that they have been far from encouraging. In fact, I'm afraid that the volume is going to be somewhat of a disaster for us, and it is only the hope of recouping part of the expense we have already poured into it that prevents me from canceling the book outright. There is apparently sufficient demand to justify the existence of a magazine like *Weird Tales*, which we can sell for 25 cents per copy. But the book will have to cost $1, I'm afraid, and our readers just are not willing to pay that price. So much for the nation's vaunted prosperity!

"At any rate, what this means is that any plans we might have had for *The Selected Tales of H. P. Lovecraft* (or whatever the title might have been), are quite emphatically shelved, for the time being at least, if not permanently. Please do not interpret this as an expression of any lack of esteem for you or your works on the part of Farnsworth Wright or myself. It is purely and undisguisedly a business consideration, and must be handled with utter ruthlessness lest we put the corporation (and *Weird Tales* with it!) out of action!

"However, your submissions will continued to be read with the greatest of interest—as will those of Mrs. Lovecraft, should she care ever to resume her own literary endeavors. (Are there any more Sonia Greene stories in the works, by the way?)

"With all fondest regards,

"Joseph C. Henneberger"

CHAPTER THIRTY-FIVE:

"MARBLEHEAD. END OF THE LINE"

THE BOSTON & MAINE local pulled out of Lynn headed north toward the last stop of the Marblehead spur line. Howard and Sonia sat side-by-side on the dark green velvet-plush seat, Howard, on the aisle, gazing abstractedly past Sonia into the dim December noon. The year 1927 was drawing to a dismal close. It had started with high hopes for Howard: at the age of 37 he was at last to have his books published, and not one book only but three—*The Shunned House* from Paul Cook, *New America* from Jackson Press, and (most treasured of all) *Selected Tales* from Henneberger's Popular Fiction Publishing Company.

Cook was still going to do his volume, or insisted to Howard that he was, but there was no indication of when (if ever) it would actually appear. And it was an amateur production at best. *New America* was in suspension; Howard was not really certain, himself, why he had sent it away to California and told Viereck that the manuscript had been stolen, but he had become very uncomfortable regarding the political forces that swirled around Viereck, and the comments of Dash Weiss and Clark Ashton Smith made him more so. His hopes were then pinned to the Henneberger project, and that, after all, was the kind of book that he really wanted to do anyway. That had looked like a certainty until the "Dear Lovecraft" letter's arrival— and now Howard's hopes lay shattered and scattered about his feet.

A smartly-uniformed conductor rolled back the door at the end of the car and strode into the aisle. "Marblehead. Marblehead. End of the line. End of the line."

Sonia smiled at Howard and touched him warmly on the back of the hand. "It looks awful out. I've never been here in this time of year. You'd better bundle up, Howard dear."

The train shuddered to a stop beside the old concrete platform and Howard and Sonia rose to their feet, fastened their warm clothing and gathered their light luggage from the rack overhead. They made their way to the end of the car amidst the few shuffling passengers who had made the run from Boston. Marblehead had few visitors in wintertime; most of the traffic in and out comprised natives traveling to and from Boston for shopping or business.

A black car waited at the end of the platform; its hood ornament was a three-pointed silver star. Howard recognized the license plates as those of the consular service. The uniformed driver surreptitiously examined a photograph palmed in one hand and stepped forward to relieve Howard of his suitcase. "Herr Lovecraft?"

Howard said that he was indeed that person.

The chauffeur spoke to him in German, indicating Sonia with his gestures. Howard did not understand the man's words and the chauffeur apparently spoke no English.

Sonia said, "Howard, I think I can speak to him. I don't really know German, but it resembles Yiddish. I'll try, anyway." She turned toward the chauffeur and said, *"Ich bin Frau Lovecraft."*

Howard could tell that the language was the same, or at least very similar, and also that Sonia's intonation was very different from that of the chauffeur.

The chauffeur looked as if he had bitten into a lemon but he gestured to Howard and Sonia and said, *"Kommen Sie mit mier, bitte."*

He stood at attention and held the car door open, slammed it behind Howard and Sonia, stowed their light luggage and climbed into the driver's seat.

Howard turned toward Sonia. "Viereck said he'd have a car meet us, but this is all very mysterious. I don't suppose there's any point in trying to talk to the driver."

"I don't think he likes my German," Sonia commented. The car proceeded slowly, through narrow, slush-clogged streets. The chauffeur pulled to a stop at a wharf overlooking Marblehead Harbor and carried Howard and Sonia's luggage to a small boat waiting at the pilings. He returned, opened the passenger door of the car and said, simply, *"Bitte."*

Howard and Sonia followed the man. He gestured them into the boat, climbed in behind them and started the engine. Sonia asked Howard if he would be all right. The bleak gray sky showed almost no trace of sun—there was a pale, watery bright spot that must be the sun filtered through thick winter clouds.

Howard said, "For a while, anyway. I have on my warmest clothes. He turned up the collar of his overcoat, pulled down the brim of his dark fedora. Sonia reached for his hands and held them between her own. The warmth of her hands plus the protection of Howard's gloves should suffice.

The small boat made its way to a trawler standing to in the harbor, and they transferred from the small boat to the larger one. On the trawler there seemed to be only a minimal crew, all of them speaking German. Howard and Sonia were ushered below decks. A pot of coffee stood steaming on a small stove. Howard asked if he might have a cup, and even in English his question was understood. A beefy man in well-cut sailor's garb—Howard took him for a petty officer of some sort, despite lack of markings on his outfit—reached into one pocket, pulled out a ring of keys and unlocked a wooden cabinet beside the stove. He extracted a half-filled bottle and added a dollop of *schnapps* to each of three cups. He poured coffee into two of them, handed them to Howard and Sonia, raised the third (containing only *schnapps*) and said, "*Prosit!*"

He drained his cup; Howard and Sonia sipped theirs.

The trawler's engines send a throbbing through the craft. Howard peered through a porthole and saw the harbor slowly falling behind them, through the gray December day. He and Sonia sat on a padded bench at one side of the cabin for a while, then the petty officer gestured them to follow him and led them to another cabin.

They were outfitted with diving suits; to Howard, the experience was now familiar. He assisted Sonia into her canvas-and-rubber outfit, the heavy boots. The petty officer donned similar garb.

The trawler drew to a stop; the throbbing of her engines ceased. Howard could hear the sounds of the sea-anchor being lowered. The petty officer led Howard and Sonia onto the deck of the trawler. Howard had been provided a knitted sailor's hat and he pulled its edges over his ears to protect them from the sting of the winter air.

They stepped onto a diving platform; crewmen approached and lifted copper diving helmets from the deck, dogged then onto the collar rings of the three canvas suits. Howard could see Sonia's lips moving through the glassed window of her helmet. He bent his head so their helmets were in contact, murmured a reassurance to her and straightened.

A winch was connected to the platform; crewmen started the donkey-engine and the platform was lifted over the side of the trawler, lowered into the choppy water outside Marblehead Harbor. Just before the water closed over Howard's helmet he looked left and right, saw Cat Island and Satan Rock.

~ ~ ~ ~ ~

George Pagnanelli sat at the metal table bolted to the deck-plates of the main wardroom of the *grundstruckvorhaben*, firmly anchored to the ocean floor between Satan Rock and Cat Island. Six of the seven men who were to attend the meeting were there already: Pagnanelli himself, his printer Peter Stahrenberg, the propagandist G. S. Viereck, Heinz Spanknoebel of the *Freunde* organization, Dr. Kiep from the German consulate and the chairman of the meeting, Kurt Luedecke of the NSDAP. Even though Luedecke was chairman and consequently in authority, he had delegated to Viereck the primary responsibility for dealing with the problem.

All were in the United States legally, and all were able to leave and re-enter the country through legal channels, although it was sometimes more convenient (and more discreet) to travel surreptitiously. The submarine *Traum* that rode deep-anchored to the *grundstruckvorhaben* was their means of travel between the United States and Europe when they did not wish it known that they had been out of the country.

With the rasp of protesting hinges the doorway swung open and a petty officer ushered two people into the wardroom. Pagnanelli was surprised: he had expected to see only the lanky, cadaverous-appearing author, Howard Lovecraft. Instead, in addition to Lovecraft, the petty officer ushered in a woman, a few years older than Lovecraft, mildly on the fleshy side but with a vitality to her that was immensely powerful and attractive, even in the stuffy and unpleasant confines of the metal room.

There was a quick exchange in German between Luedecke and Kiep, then between Luedecke and Viereck. Viereck rose and strode around the metal table, shook hands with Lovecraft and exchanged a few sentences with the author. There was some nodding and gesturing, then Viereck turned back toward the group.

"Mrs. Lovecraft," he said, "may I introduce my colleagues." He named all of them. "I believe you all have met Herr Lovecraft before today." Pagnanelli saw Lovecraft nod toward the group at the table; Pagnanelli returned the gesture.

"Mrs. Lovecraft's presence is—" Viereck hesitated, "—ah, a most unexpected pleasure. What we have to discuss is purely a business matter. I'm sure that Mrs. Lovecraft will find it very uninteresting." Pagnanelli wasn't sure whether Viereck was speaking to the men at the table, to Howard Lovecraft, or to the latter's wife.

"Why, I—" the woman began, but Luedecke cut her off with a quick statement to Viereck.

Viereck smiled behind his horn-rimmed spectacles. "I'm sure that you will be much more comfortable in another room, Mrs. Lovecraft." He snapped a few words in German to the petty officer who had brought the man and woman into the wardroom. The sailor took Mrs. Lovecraft firmly by one elbow and ushered her toward the door. The woman looked back questioningly at her husband; he nodded emphatically and she submitted to the petty officer's guidance.

"Please, Howard," Viereck resumed after the door was dogged shut. He indicated a chair. Lovecraft sat in it.

"I will take responsibility for the unfortunate misunderstanding," Viereck said. "It was not my intention to invite Mrs. Lovecraft."

The cadaverous author shook his head. "What's done can't be undone. But what is the agenda? I thought this was to be a meeting of Jackson Press staff, to discuss New *America and the Coming World-Empire*. I will say that I was very surprised at the selection of this place for the meeting, but it must be assumed that there were reasons for the choice."

Viereck exchanged a look with Luedecke. "Howard, you told me that your had completed your writing, but that your manuscript had been taken from your home."

"From Parkside Avenue. Yes."

"The police never solved that burglary. Or the one at the home of your friend Mr. Weiss." Howard shook his head.

Viereck let out a deeply drawn breath. "In fact, the burglary has been solved, Howard. Our good friend George Pagnanelli here has very widespread contacts, very carefully cultivated connections throughout the patriotic movement."

Howard said, "I know Mr. Pagnanelli. He has a very impressive collection of membership documents and publications in his home."

"It might have been better if George and I had written the book ourselves," Viereck said. "We could have done it. The problem was, we are both foreign-born. So I asked you to do the job, Howard, with your impeccable Old American credentials. I had read many of your works. Mr. Merritt and Herr Kleiner both vouched for you. I was certain that you would participate reliably. Your manuscript was not taken by the burglars."

The swarthy Pagnanelli took over in his accented speech. "The burglaries at your home and the home of Mr. Weiss were committed by members of Count Vonsiatsky's All-Russian National Socialist Labor Party, Mr. Lovecraft. The Count did not trust Mr. Viereck. That was most unfortunate. If fellow patriots cannot count on one another, their effectiveness is terribly limited. The Count was afraid that Mr. Viereck would put his own pan-Germanism above his general restorationist sentiments. Count Vonsiatsky also knew that you were far from a faithful admirer of Slavic peoples generally. And he was aware of this odd television machine that your friend Weiss had imported from Scotland."

Kurt Luedecke interrupted Pagnanelli with an angry statement snarled in German. Viereck leaned over and whispered a translation to Pagnanelli, who nodded in agreement. "None of us know quite what Count Vonsiatsky had in mind to do with the television device." He shrugged his shoulders to indicate his puzzlement.

"But the Count had both Mr. Weiss's apartment and your own, entered. And—I'm afraid that Vonsiatsky is somewhat less than competent—his people did not find what they were after. In either place. The television device was not at 21st Street, and the manuscript, which Count Vonsiatsky wanted to examine, was not at Parkside Avenue."

Viereck signaled Pagnanelli to silence. He exchanged a few sentences in German with Luedecke and Dr. Otto Kiep. Then he turned and said, "Mr. Lovecraft, did you write the book at all? *Is* there any manuscript?"

Howard stared straight ahead.

"You must tell us, Howard. You have seen and learned a great deal this past year. We need to know what is in your book. If it exists at all. George and I can still take over the project, but we don't want your manuscript reaching the wrong people. We need to see it first."

Howard stared straight ahead.

Luedecke snarled at Viereck, who blanched visibly. "Howard," Viereck said more gently, "I'm afraid that I've got myself into rather hot water over this. But we can all come out of it all right, if you will cooperate. Did you write the book? Where is it?" There was another brief colloquy in German. Viereck reddened. "I didn't know that Parkside had been entered again, Howard, this past week, while you and Mrs. Lovecraft were visiting in Providence. This time some more efficient people were sent to do the work. There is still no manuscript. Plenty of notes and files, but no book."

Howard still refused to answer.

Luedecke issued an order. The bulky Spanknoebel and the heavy-set printer Peter Stahrenberg stood on either side of Howard's chair. Luedecke barked some further words in German.

Viereck looked very serious, very sympathetic, and very troubled. "Howard, I want you to think about this. You are dealing with people who are dedicated to their ideals. You've doubtless heard of the tragedy nearby, involving the *Paulding* and the submarine *S-4*. What you haven't heard—because the Navy Department doesn't know it either—is that the *S-4* had come dangerously close to this *grundstruckvorhaben*. Our own U-boat, the *Traum,* was involved. If we had not taken steps, there would have been visitors here that we didn't want. It is a pity that the men on the *S-4* died, but you must understand the seriousness of your own situation, from the tragedy of theirs."

Still Howard refused to speak.

Luedecke barked commands to Stahrenberg and Spanknoebel. "You and Mrs. Lovecraft will be detained then," Viereck sighed. "You will have until tomorrow to reconsider your attitude, Howard. I suppose really it is for the best that Mrs. Lovecraft did accompany you. We will want her also."

For the first time at the meeting, Dr. Otto Kiep spoke to Howard. "The *Traum* will depart for Europe late tomorrow, Herr Lovecraft. If you do not cooperate we will try to convince you to do so. If we fail, you will not return to the United States. Not living, at any rate. You will simply disappear, along with Frau Lovecraft. Perhaps bodies will be found floating in the—" he turned to Viereck "—*frostig, eisig*? *Ja, danke*—" and back to Howard Lovecraft "—in the frigid water. *Hein*?"

"Think on this seriously," Viereck reiterated. "This is no game, Mr. Lovecraft."

Spanknoebel and Stahrenberg grabbed Howard by the elbows and lifted him bodily from his chair. He was hustled across the wardroom, the door was undogged and he was shoved through, manhandled into another, smaller room and shoved inside. Spanknoebel and Stahrenberg followed closely.

Howard saw his wife seated on a small metal chair. There were bruises on her face and her hair was disordered. She said, "Howard! What have we got into?"

He shook his head said nothing. Stahrenberg and Spanknoebel shoved him into a chair like Sonia's. While the chemist from Detroit stood threateningly over Howard, the printer fetched a chain and padlock and fastened Howard's ankle to the metal leg of the chair. The chair was fastened to the floor of the room. He could see, now, that Sonia had been similarly treated.

The two bruisers left the room without a word. Howard could hear the door being dogged shut behind them. Then the room was plunged into darkness. Howard felt Sonia's hand groping for him, then clinging to his arm. Through sobs, she said his name over end over.

~ ~ ~ ~ ~

The face loomed over Howard, pale and huge, framed with dark, curly hair. The face leaned back and Howard, tiny, could see the dark coat, twin rows of brass buttons shining, as the full-grown man leaned forward, drew back, leaned forward. Little Howard watched, fascinated, as the face grinned and ran; sores appeared, pustulant and dripping. The mouth opened slackly, the eyes glazed, a senseless titter shook the man.

Little Howard gazed up. The face returned to normal, the buttons gleamed. The man held a hand to his mouth, the dark cavern of his gullet opened wide, he shoveled something into his mouth, slack jaws working up and down, a frightening, hissing sound escaping from his lips. Little Howard reached forward and slapped the giant, grinning, slobbering madman on the knee.

"Why, father," little Howard exclaimed, "you look just like a young man!"

The white face writhed in insane laughter. The pustulence reappeared, syphilitic sores stinking and dripping their disgusting ooze onto little Howard, onto his little hands, onto his upraised face, onto his carefully pressed short trousers.

"Why, father," little Howard exclaimed, "you look just like a young man!"

A hand was clamped over his mouth, silencing him. His eyes bulged open. The white face still circled and wove, hovering above his own. He squeezed his eyes shut. He was covered with a clammy sweat. He struck out with both his hands; they were batted aside, one by a waving beam of light that returned in seconds to the white face.

From beside him Howard heard Sonia's whispered exclamation, "Dash!"

This time Howard recognized the hissing response even as he saw Sonia rise from her chair and throw herself into the arms of Theo Weiss. Weiss held a miniature electric torch trained on his own face. Now Howard was fully awake, recognized the white countenance not as his father's, distorted by madness and the sores of shameful infection as it had been when Howard had last seen the man thirty years before, but as that of Theo Weiss.

Howard looked around the tiny metal-walled room, could see almost nothing except for Theo's face. He reached for the hand holding the flashlight, directed it to the leg of his chair where his ankle was shackled to the metal. Theo knelt and examined the chain and padlock, then moved his light carefully until he saw that Sonia was similarly shackled. Howard started to ask how Weiss had known where they were and how he had got into the undersea construction but Weiss hushed him with another hiss.

The famous handcuff king chuckled under his breath at the padlocks that held Sonia and Howard to their chairs. He reached inside his dark sweater to some inner pocket and extracted a tiny jimmy. In seconds both locks lay open on the floor and Howard and Sonia were free.

Hardeen led them to the door of the chamber. It was undogged. Hardeen opened it silently a crack, peered into the dimly lighted companionway, then stepped through and motioned Howard and Sonia behind him. Howard saw a man in sailor's garb lying apparently asleep beside the door. Theo motioned Howard to help with the man, and they hefted his body into the abandoned prison-room. Howard saw blood on the companionway floor where the sailor's head had lain.

In the airlock Howard started to ask Hardeen how he had known where he and Sonia were, how he got into the *grundstruckvorhaben*, what would now happen; Hardeen said there was no time to talk, explanations would follow. There was a diving platform awaiting them.

They sealed themselves in diving gear. The airlock was built to be operated by a sailor inside the structure, but Hardeen's escapes had taught him to operate it from within. Quickly they made their way to the platform; Hardeen signaled the surface and shortly they were aboard a navy minesweeper, the *Falcon*, wearing fresh, borrowed clothes and conferring with the ship's officers.

They could see that it was now afternoon—Howard and Sonia had lost track of the passage of time while imprisoned, but clearly they had been kept in isolation, dozing and waking fitfully in the dark, for more than eighteen hours. It was now a gray, damp December 31 and wet snowflakes were falling onto the surface of the ocean.

"If only *Falcon* were a destroyer or even a mine-layer," a khaki-clad officer complained, "we could stop those pirates from escaping."

"It's no use," another replied. "That submarine of theirs, *Traum*, is gone by now. God knows where we could catch it—if anywhere!"

Howard Lovecraft, warming his long-fingered hands by wrapping them around a heavy mug of soup, shook his head as if to shuffle into order all of the questions that buzzed through it. "How did you get here?" he asked. "Theo, how did you get to us? What will happen now to Viereck? To the whole structure down there? What will happen to *us*?"

A naval officer wearing the silver maple leaf insignia of a full commander answered. "I can't speak for the government, Mr. Lovecraft, but I would guess that you'll be all right. It might be possible to bring a charge of sedition against you; in wartime you might even have been charged with treason. But from all that I can learn—Mr. Weiss has told us everything he knows—you were more a dupe of these plotters than anything else."

"But how did you—?" Howard asked only half the question.

Let anyone answer who would.

"I was suspicious from that first incident with the trawlers, Howard." Theo Weiss looked to the naval personnel, asked if they might have some rolls or sandwiches to go with their soup. An officer dispatched a sailor to the galley for food. Theo resumed, "After the two burglaries—especially the one at Parkside—I went back to the police. You know, Ehrich and I were always on good terms with them. They sent me to the federal people and I wound up with the navy.

"I turned over the noctovisor to them and—"

"We had that device duplicated," the commander took over. "I suppose the State Department will have to make some arrangement to buy off the inventor, what's his name, Barnes, Baird. For a patent infringement. But there wasn't time to settle that first.

"We've had noctovisor-equipped ships and aircraft patrolling the coast for weeks. Did you think this undersea construction was unique, sir?"

Howard ran a hand over his face, rubbing it over the stubble of unshaven beard that had appeared since he left Providence. "I—I—had not thought of that. I assumed there was only one. Sylvester told me that it was for future commercial development. Are there more than the one?"

"Commerce indeed!" The commander leaned across the table, pointing a finger for emphasis. "We've found similar constructions all up and down the Atlantic seaboard. There's one at the Narrows at New York, there's one in Chesapeake Bay, one at Sea Islands in Georgia. At least six. We're still searching. We're going to blow those things out of the water. They're nothing less than staging bases for future warfare. Submarine pens. They may even have intended them as assembly points for marine landing forces."

Theo Weiss looked up gratefully as a steward entered the room with a tray of sandwiches. He reached for one, bit a corner off it happily, then more solemnly said, "It sounds as if we are very close to a war, Commander."

The officer shook his head slowly. "I doubt that, sir. Again, it's up to Washington, of course, but—war against whom? From what we know, these structures don't belong to any government, to any state. There's some sort of international conspiracy. Mr. Lovecraft will certainly be called upon to give some testimony on that."

"I have it ready for you, sir," Howard announced. "I have my files in Brooklyn, if they haven't been taken. Even if they have, my conclusions are thoroughly documented. I wrote a book on the subject. It is in California, where I sent it for safekeeping."

The officer nodded. "We'll have to get that document, sir. I'm sure that your cooperation will undo any charges that might have been brought against you." He spread his hands wide. "As for the immediate response, naval ships and army bombers will be moving against these secret bases almost at once." He stopped and examined his watch. "In fact, they are probably on their way by now. Captain Yarnell is steaming here from Quincy with the *Saratoga*. And army planes will be moving against the Narrows structure as soon as commercial shipping can be cleared from the area."

He stopped talking for a moment and looked away. "We have to pay whatever price is needed to clean this up. I have a son—had a son, Mr. Lovecraft. We're an old navy family. My boy was aboard the *S-4*."

Howard said only, "I'm sorry."

The officer nodded. "As for the domestic aspects of this. . .that's up to civil authorities. The President, Attorney General Sargent. And the A.G. has that bright youngster working for him, running that new investigative group. Hoover, something. Not the Secretary of Commerce, another Hoover. Seems to be very efficient. We'll have to see what they decide to do about some of these people like the Klan and Christian Front. It will be hard to prove anything on them, I'm afraid. But some of the foreigners—that Russian duke or whatever he says he is, and that Italian fascist fellow. Let's wait and see if Justice starts deportation actions, at least."

He looked deeply into Howard's face. "You'll make yourself available for whatever action follows, Mr. Lovecraft?"

"Of course." Howard stared earnestly into his cup. With one hand he reached for that of Sonia, who had sat quietly through the conversation. He felt her twine her fingers through his own and a surge of gratitude ran through him.

~ ~ ~ ~ ~

They arranged to stay another night in Marblehead. There would be long involvements with the government over the matter. Howard would have to retrieve *New America and the Coming World-Empire* from Clark Ashton Smith. Howard wondered if the cellar of the Thor Hotel would be raided as a secondary result of the whole affair. Of course his book would never be published. What would happen to Sylvester Viereck, George Pagnanelli and the rest, was another puzzle. They had escaped with the *Traum*; would they try to sneak back into the United States and deny their involvement in the whole matter, or would they stay in Europe for good? There was no way of knowing.

The future looked complicated, difficult, rocky, but not entirely bleak.

For the present, it was still December 31, 1927, and Howard and Sonia stood side-by-side by the window of their room in the Spite House, looking through the darkness toward the waters of Marblehead Harbor. Wet snow still fell, striking the tall windows of the house, melting, running slowly down the panes like tears.

There was a flash from the harbor; a few seconds later the Spite House shook with the shock-wave of the distant explosion even though the damp air and hissing wet snow damped out the sound almost entirely. There was another flash, another shudder. The Vought Corsairs and Boeing fighters of the *Saratoga* were dropping their explosive charges on the *grundstruckvorhaben* beside Satan Rock.

Sonia turned toward Howard and slid her arms about his waist, laid her head softly on his shoulder. She asked some question that Howard only half-heard. He pressed his still unshaven cheek against her thick, luxuriant hair. Over the top of her head he was still watching the snow-flakes strike and run, the darkness beyond, the periodic flash and shudder of explosives dropped from noctovisor-equipped military aircraft.

Sonia was asking something, something about Howard's giving up his planned return to Providence, something about returning with her to New York to resume their marriage fully, something about going elsewhere if he disliked New York. She earned good money, she had saved her salary. They could sail for Europe, visit Florence, her daughter, meet the members of the Paris literary circle if Howard wanted to do that.

Howard half-listened, grunted noncommittally. Inside his mind he was working with the images of the undersea construction, the military action, the explosions, the search for plotters. It seemed as if it should make a pattern. Something that he could turn to artistic effect. Something that would overcome even the resistance of the difficult and eccentric Brother Pharnabus of North Michigan Avenue. He would use a sober, documentary style. He would avoid purple prose and lengthy strings of adjectives. He could keep the setting of the actual events, keep his story as close to the truth as the government would let him. Marblehead would be transformed as it was in his other stories, as Salem had so often become Arkham. "During the winter of 1927-28 officials of the Federal government made a strange and secret investigation of certain conditions in the ancient Massachusetts seaport of Innsmouth," Howard thought. "The public first learned of it. . ."

His hands, which had been holding Sonia close, began to move almost of their own volition, the left reaching toward a desk drawer in search of a pad of foolscap; the right, toward Howard's jacket pocket, feeling for his familiar black Waterman.

THE END

RAMBLE HOUSE's

HARRY STEPHEN KEELER WEBWORK MYSTERIES

(RH) indicates the title is available ONLY through RAMBLE HOUSE.

The Ace of Spades Murder
The Affair of the Bottled Deuce (RH)
The Amazing Web
The Barking Clock
The Book with the Orange Leaves
The Bottle with the Green Wax Seal
The Box from Japan
The Case of the Canny Killer
The Case of the Crazy Corpse (RH)
The Case of the Flying Hands (RH)
The Case of the Ivory Arrow
The Case of the Jeweled Ragpicker
The Case of the Lavender Gripsack
The Case of the Mysterious Moll
The Case of the 16 Beans
The Case of the Transparent Nude (RH)
The Case of the Transposed Legs
The Case of the Two-Headed Idiot (RH)
The Case of the Two Strange Ladies
The Circus Stealers (RH)
Cleopatra's Tears
A Copy of Beowulf (RH)
The Crimson Cube (RH)
The Face of the Man From Saturn
Find the Clock
The Five Silver Buddhas
The 4th King
The Gallows Waits, My Lord! (RH)
The Green Jade Hand
Finger, Finger
Behind That Mask
Hangman's Nights (RH)
I, Chameleon (RH)
I Killed Lincoln at 10:13! (RH)
The Iron Ring
The Man Who Changed His Skin (RH)
The Man with the Crimson Box
The Man with the Magic Eardrums
The Man with the Wooden Spectacles

The Marceau Case
The Matilda Hunter Murder
The Monocled Monster
The Murder of London Lew
The Murdered Mathematician
The Mysterious Card (RH)
The Mysterious Ivory Ball of Wong Shing Li (RH)
The Mystery of the Fiddling Cracksman
The Peacock Fan
The Photo of Lady X (RH)
The Portrait of Jirjohn Cobb
Report on Vanessa Hewstone (RH)
Riddle of the Travelling Skull
Riddle of the Wooden Parrakeet (RH)
The Scarlet Mummy (RH)
The Search for X-Y-Z
The Sharkskin Book
Sing Sing Nights
The Six From Nowhere (RH)
The Skull of the Waltzing Clown
The Spectacles of Mr. Cagliostro
Stand By—London Calling!
The Steeltown Strangler
The Stolen Gravestone (RH)
Strange Journey (RH)
The Strange Will
The Straw Hat Murders (RH)
The Street of 1000 Eyes (RH)
Thieves' Nights
Three Novellos (RH)
The Tiger Snake
The Trap (RH)
Vagabond Nights (Defrauded Yeggman)
Vagabond Nights 2 (10 Hours)
The Vanishing Gold Truck
The Voice of the Seven Sparrows
The Washington Square Enigma
When Thief Meets Thief
The White Circle (RH)
The Wonderful Scheme of Mr. Christopher Thorne
X. Jones—of Scotland Yard
Y. Cheung, Business Detective

RAMBLE HOUSE's Other Loons